CHILD
OF A
MAD GOD

TOR BOOKS BY R. A. SALVATORE

R. A. SALVATORE

CHILD
OF A
MAD GOD

TOR

A TOM DOHERTY ASSOCIATES BOOK

NEW YORK

This is a work of fiction. All of the characters, organizations, and events portrayed in this novel are either products of the author's imagination or are used fictitiously.

CHILD OF A MAD GOD

Map by Rhys Davies

A Tor Book
Published by Tom Doherty Associates
175 Fifth Avenue
New York, NY 10010

www.tor-forge.com

Tor® is a registered trademark of Macmillan Publishing Group, LLC.

Library of Congress Cataloging-in-Publication Data

Names: Salvatore, R. A., 1959– author.
Title: Child of a mad god / R. A. Salvatore.
Description: First edition. | New York : Tom Doherty Associates, 2018. | Identifiers: LCCN 2017039662 (print) | LCCN 2017044102 (ebook) | ISBN 9780765395283 (ebook) | ISBN 9780765395276 (hardcover) | ISBN 9781250190772 (signed edition) Subjects: | GSAFD: Fantasy fiction. | Occult fiction.
Classification: LCC PS3569.A462345 (ebook) | LCC PS3569.A462345 C49 2018 (print) | DDC 813/.54—dc23
LC record available at https://lccn.loc.gov/2017039662

Our books may be purchased in bulk for promotional, educational, or business use. Please contact your local bookseller or the Macmillan Corporate and Premium Sales Department at 1-800-221-7945, extension 5442, or by email at MacmillanSpecialMarkets@macmillan.com.

First Edition: February 2018

Printed in the United States of America

0 9 8 7 6 5 4 3 2 1

Writing is my journey,
It is how I make sense of the world.
These people I come to know in the books show me.
They speak to me. They lead me to my truth.
They give to me my sight.
So this is to Aoleyn,
Who made me look at the world from a different angle
And in a different light.

THE LAKEMAN'S LAMENT

On the fíreach deamhain sit
Curses muttered, fire spits;
Hunting people, their delight
Spilling blood and making fright.
Better fear than praise of men
The deamhain strike with spear not pen;
For the bounty they will take
Food and furs and bones to break.
Deamhan footfalls leave no mark
Coming silent, can'no hark;
Come in fury and in shade
Come with magic in the blade.
Glit'ring spear alit with fire
Lightning speaks with deamhan ire;
Throwing stones without a sling
Fly away without a wing!
Oftentimes a lakeman strays
Into fíreach deamhan's way;
Oftentimes the deamhan's smile
Bleeds the kill for all the while.
Usgar deamhan, why such joy
To break the smile of a boy;
Usgar deamhan, why delight
In spilling blood and making fright?

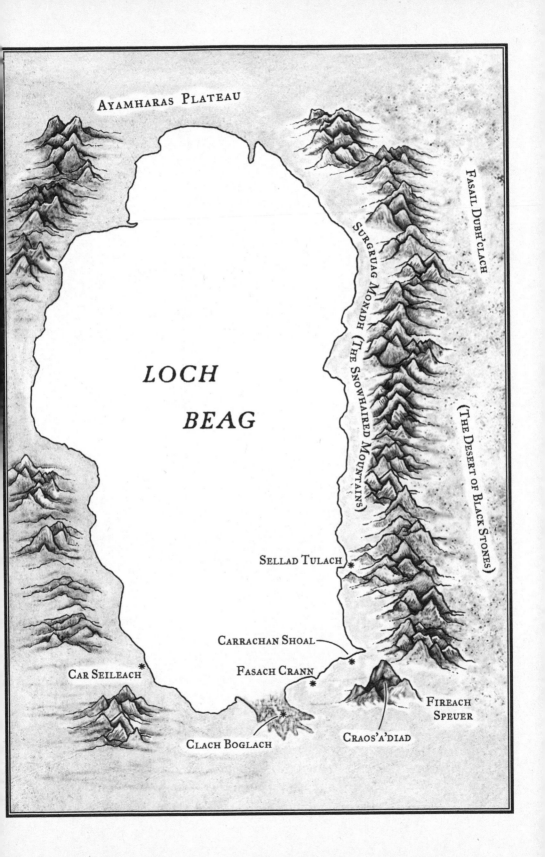

CHILD

OF A

MAD GOD

PROLOGUE

The moon called it forth, the summons of blood. Long and sleek and low to the ground, the fossa crept across the underground crawl space, some areas with no more than a foot of clearance. The demon creature felt every jag and bump in the stones, for it had little fur left on its six-foot-long body, with only occasional tufts across its reddish, angry skin of welts and boils. Its tail extended back three feet, perfectly straight, and was flattened and hardened, with its edges scraped keen like a scythe.

It walked on four padded paws, moving catlike, killing claws retracted, and perfectly silent, save the occasional scrape of that hard tail on stone.

The demon creature came through the narrow and rolling crawl space into a taller corridor, and there it paused and inhaled, smelling the scent of life on the mountain, and hearing the song of the mountain's magic, a sensation that drove the beast mad with hatred.

So many months, it was trapped in its lair of murder, in the darkness, that maddening song echoing about the stones. But it could not go out and kill the singers. It could not release its rage upon an animal, or a man, or a sidhe. For under the light of the sun, or the stars, or the normal moon, the song was too strong, and would drive the fossa back into the cave.

But not tonight. Tonight, the moon was red, the Blood Moon, and so the fossa could come forth.

And taste blood.

And devour magic.

And silence the singers.

Faster it loped, through the corridor and into the small cave, then to the mouth, and there the fossa paused and looked up to the night sky, to the huge full moon, hanging red.

Promising food.

What would it kill this night? What creature's bones would add to the litter of the deep den beyond the long crawl? What singer's throat would crush beneath the press of its maw?

It came out into the open air, under the red moon. Hunger called it to the hunt.

Perhaps a deer. Perhaps a bear, or a warthog, or a great roc, or a giant mountain ram, or one of the ugly sidhe humanoids. None of them gave the demon fossa pause. None could stand against its savagery. None, though, were savory, and gave the demon the pleasure it truly desired.

A sensation froze the creature just outside its bone-littered cave. At first, the vibration drifted on the night breeze as just a tingling, teasing and tickling, but then those sparks became something more, something that stung, something unpleasant. The creature let forth a feral growl that reverberated about the mountain stones, a warning, a protest, against the painful intrusion, the maddening resonance of magic.

And that was the rub—not the pain, for the fossa was ever in pain, but the vibration of magic, an incessant burr the creature could not scratch away.

How the demon fossa hated magic! The song of it played as an endless voice, a pervasive and incessant ringing, just a single, maddening note in its ears and vibrating throughout the creature's body with a singular message: murder.

But the growling stopped very quickly.

The fossa sensed the pulse of magic.

A human was out on the mountain this night, under the Blood Moon. And that human carried magic, and that magic had been called and so it was singing now.

The demon fossa set off, silent as the shadows. The animals of Fireach Speuer could rest easy this Blood Moon night.

Aye, for the fossa's favorite meal was served.

Ravines did not slow it, nor high slabs of stone, for the creature traversed ledges with sure-footed ease and could leap straight up a score of feet, two score, and with claws that could catch hold in the stone as readily as a cat might climb a tree.

Down the mountainside it went, down and around to the west, where the plateau rolled out wide before it and the red moon reflected in the waters of the great lake, far below. There was no pause to take in the grand vista, though, for the song grew louder and more focused as the fossa neared.

So much louder, then, and the fossa slowed.

Over one rise went the fossa, through a tangle of trees and into the brush at the edge of a field of chokeberry bushes. There the creature hunched and watched and waited.

The man came over an angled stone across the way. He carried a long spear, its tip glowing with magical energies, singing brilliantly. He moved down slowly into the low brush and stepped his way to the middle of the patch.

He was hunting, the fossa understood. He was hunting the demon fossa.

He was a fool.

The man stood amidst the chokeberry bushes and whispered something the creature could not understand, but the sounds gave the fossa pause. It hunched further and from the concealment of the taller brush scanned all around, ensuring that this one was alone.

The human spoke again, as if not alone, but the fossa saw no others.

There were no others.

The fossa issued a low growl, then silently circled as the man turned toward the sound.

The man sniffed. He could smell the demon and the demon fossa could smell his fear.

The man set himself, that horrid, magical spear tip forward, toward the place where the fossa had growled, as if expecting a charge.

But the fossa wasn't there anymore, there upwind from the human so that he could still smell its lingering scent. No, the fossa was already across the way, watching the human from behind.

The breeze gusted, the chokeberries shivered, and the human shifted left and right, but with his focus still to the spot where the fossa had been.

Belly to the ground, the fossa moved, gaining speed, readying a killing leap.

But somehow the human knew! And he spun about, that spear flashing across!

The fossa burst from the chokeberries and cut fast to the right, then back across to the left, too swiftly for the man to keep up with his lumbering sweeps. The spear tip chased, but could not catch up, and right by the man rushed the fossa, and out the other way.

But as the creature passed, its tail, a sword of bone, slashed across to take the man's legs out from under him, and to take the man's feet from his legs.

A short distance away, the fossa skidded to a stop and spun about, to see the man struggling to his knees, bringing his spear around defensively. He seemed excited, elated even, ready for battle, and he moved as if to stand.

The fool didn't even know.

Only when he extended his leg as if to stand did he scream out in pain and then—and oh, it sounded as the sweetest music of all to the fossa!—in fear. Only then, the fossa understood, did the human even realize that he had no feet, that both of his legs had been severed at the ankles!

The human looked all about frantically, even reached for a severed foot, sitting atop a nearby chokeberry bush.

Amused now, the demon fossa watched the human regain some measure of courage, stubbornly using his spear for balance as he forced himself to his knees. Then he took up his spear in both hands and shouted a challenge.

The fossa calmly stalked a perimeter about him. Time was not on the human's side, not with his lifeblood pouring from his severed ankles.

The man spoke again, as if in conversation with some unseen other human. "My daughter will not be shamed!" he yelled.

The fossa stalked before him and stood staring.

"Come on!" the human yelled, waving his spear.

The fossa sat down and let him bleed.

But then he hugged his spear, that crystalline tip glowing with magic, and whispered again, as if to the spear, and the magic intensified suddenly, the song assailing the demon creature, particularly so, for it was a song of warmth and healing! The human closed his eyes and seemed to bask in that healing.

The fossa ran to the side. It could smell the lessening of the blood flow; it could hear the song of healing magic.

"Where are you?" the human cried, seeming stronger again, invigorated, healed somewhat.

"Coward!" he taunted, or tried to, for the word came out with a giant exhale as the demon fossa slammed into his back, its fangs closing fast onto the back of his neck. The fossa knew that he wanted to turn and strike, but knew, too, that its fangs had cracked through the neckbone, that the human's body would no longer answer commands.

Down they went together, the fossa smashing him down face-first through the chokeberries.

The fossa didn't finish him. Not then. It would drag the human to its lair and eat him slowly, while he was alive.

But first . . . that spear! The magical crystal!

The fossa released the human's shattered neck and sprang for the spear, its powerful maw clamping on the spear tip, cracking it, shattering it.

And the demon knew that it was not alone, that the human had indeed not been alone. For through this magical spear tip, there loomed a spiritual connection to another human, the true singer of the magic!

And she was there, in the spirit realm, joined to the man in his hunt.

And the fossa heard her song and felt her trying to strengthen the flow of magic into the doomed man who lay in the chokeberries.

But the fossa was more than a physical being. So much more. And the spirit world was its truest domain.

Into the darkness it went, and it found her.

And it knew her then: Elara.

She tried to flee, to send her spirit flying back to her own corporeal form far away. But the spirit of the fossa saw her and followed her.

She could not escape.

The fossa couldn't bite her neck or her mortal coil at all, of course, but it didn't have to. It could eat her soul. It could shatter her mind!

This kill was less substantial, perhaps, but to the fossa proved far more satisfying.

To its surprise, the magic singer spun back and returned to the man, and found him there, and he, her.

And the fossa found them both, their spirits huddled, embracing as the demon closed.

And it knew him then, too: Fionlagh.

The human spirits drew comfort from each other, but the fossa was amused, knowing such comfort a fleeting thing. The demon creature mocked them as it dragged its victim to the dark hole in the dark cave. It watched them as it consumed the man's corporeal body, watched his spirit flitter away.

The woman's spirit flew away, but it could not escape, the fossa knew.

It sat in its hole, atop a pile of bones, the torn carcass before it. But part of the demon creature went with the woman, too, back to her tent, where she lay on her back, staring blankly, seeing only darkness, her magic consumed, her life force diminished, her mind shattered by the horror.

The horror.

PART 1

CURIOUS

CHILD

Do I believe in redemption?

I suppose I must. For how can I forgive myself my own sins if not in the belief that I can, and must, atone? Are my crimes so monstrous that I can never return the balance of justice? So heinous that no matter what I do with the rest of my life, I will never lie in peace on my deathbed confident that in the end I left this world a better place than I found it?

I can only shrug, for that is not for me to judge, nor is it why I believe in redemption, nor is it, in the end, the measure of redemption. For such reparation is first and foremost an internal truth, a realization toward the proper and just course.

You told me of Brother Francis, so long a thrall to the evil Father Abbot Markwart, who was responsible for the death of your own brother, Grady. You spoke of how Francis, in the end, found repentance in tending to the suffering peasants who had been caught by the rosie plague. Francis, this man, your enemy, gave his life in service to them, willingly, joyously, because he found the light of goodness and it swelled his heart.

And in the end, in the moment of his death, you stood with him and felt generosity in your heart, and felt sadness at his passing. And against your own anger in his last revelations of his part in the death of Grady, you threw aside your pain and anger and forgave him, and even wanted to save him.

How can I know the tale of Jilseponie and Brother Francis and not believe in redemption?

So many times since my defeat and exile have I been told that I was tainted in the womb, that the demon dactyl, in battling my mother, had found a way to paint my heart with its darkness. I do not doubt that there is some truth to this, for those who have made the claim, from Lady Dasslerond of the Touel'alfar to my mother herself, who lies forever still beneath this freshly tilled ground, knew well the evils of her great foe.

But the demon I harbored from my past, the stain of Bestesbulzibar that infected my soul when I was a babe in the womb, is no excuse. The dark influences that weighed upon me, whether by Marcalo De'Unnero or the dactyl demon itself, do not exempt me from blame, do not diminish the truth that it was I, Aydrian, who ultimately made the choices. It was I who exacted suffering upon others for the sake of personal gain and glory.

We are not trapped by heritage or by childhood. When we come of age and discover the ability to see the world as it is around us, the choices we make, whatever our demons, are our own.

The love my mother held for me was lasting and generous, and so many times those who love us will offer such excuses, blaming friends and peers for taking us down a dangerous and dark path.

No, I say.

Simply no.

I reject your excuses, beloved mother, even as I weep for losing you. Whether or not the demon dactyl did as you believed, and so cursed me with blackness in my heart, I long ago accepted the responsibility for my actions.

That acceptance has not broken me—far from it! And that darkness, whatever its root, does not remain within the heart of Aydrian Wyndon. I have passed my third decade of life now, my heart is clear, my mind uncluttered, my course vivid in my mind.

I believe in redemption, but only because I believe that I must redeem myself. Not for any personal gain, not even for some ephemeral concept of honor—except as doing so would honor you, and Elbryan my father, and the work you both undertook and the good you both accomplished.

I have forgiven myself and dismissed my shame at my failures, and the dark reflection I cast upon Elbryan and Jilseponie, the heroes of Honce.

But only because I know that that darkness is now no more.

We cannot change our past, and denying it serves no good end. For changing how we speak about it might deceive others, but not ourselves. Those chapters are written, the words are clear, the ink dried. But the book is not complete so long as we draw breath.

This, then, is my vow to you, Jilseponie, my mother. I will write better chapters.

Aydrian Wyndon, Jilseponie's graveside eulogy

1

THE WORLD BEYOND
THE WORLD

(The last day of the ninth month,
Parvespers, God's Year 839)

The long arms of the strong and lanky boatman reached far ahead,
slowly and silently dipping the paddle through the glassy surface of the
giant mountain lake. He had never been formally trained, but still, the
clever frontiersman moved the paddle so gracefully and smoothly, barely
disturbing the water, and thus, not disturbing the huge and ferocious
monsters that lived in the deep waters of Loch Beag.

Talmadge wore his hair long and beard thick and both showed a
deep mix of red and dark brown. He kept his hair pulled back, sometimes tied and sometimes loose, but always with a thin braid pulled
aside and hanging from beside his left ear and over his left shoulder.
"Something to chew on," he often said, and often did, using the braid
as a constant reminder to pay attention to every detail, to watch for
every sign and potential threat. Talmadge had lost track of his own age,
but he knew that he had passed his twentieth year. That simple fact
proved to any who knew this dangerous land that he still had much to
learn, for though he had spent the entirety of his adult life and even
much of his midteen years on his own out here in the western wilds,
beyond even the Wilderlands, and far, far from the borders of the

civilized kingdom known as Honce-the-Bear, Talmadge was still green compared with the other trappers and traders, still of the age where it was expected that he would meet a terrific and horrific ending. The gatherings of the frontiersmen were full of such stories.

"Low branches," complained his companion, a wily and grizzled old wood-cat named Seconk, but known more commonly as Badger, because of his fondness for brawling and his penchant for leaving the other guy broken and bleeding in the dirt. Short, barrel-chested, and spindly-armed, it was often whispered, and teased, that Badger had a bit of the powrie dwarf blood running through him. Badger took those taunts as a compliment, though, for the bloody-capped powries were legendary for their toughness.

"Then duck," Talmadge replied. "Need I really tell you that?"

"I paid yourself well for the passage," the indignant Badger answered.

"If you'd not, I wouldn't have taken you."

"Bah, young idiot, but your mouth'll get you killed soon enough."

Talmadge glanced over his shoulder to note Badger staring out at the wide lake, then aimed the canoe in closer and leaned way back as they glided under a very low strand of hanging moss.

The distracted man behind him got a mouthful, and spat a mouthful back out. "Bah, too close, longlegs!"

"Then duck," Talmadge repeated, and he didn't keep a chuckle out of his voice.

"You're too damned close to shore."

"I'm not close enough," Talmadge retorted. "You want us out there on the open water, in the morning fog?"

"We know the direction," Badger argued.

"Getting lost isn't my concern," Talmadge assured the man.

Badger snorted. "That again?"

"Oh, there be monsters."

"Bah! No fish's eating Badger, but Badger's eating fish!"

"Might that we should have cut you your own canoe, that you could run farther out," Talmadge said slyly.

"I been on lakes more days than yourself's been alive!"

"Not this lake," Talmadge replied without hesitation, and in a more reverential and somber tone. "Not a lake as deep and as cold, and as filled with dark shadows. Don't doubt that one of Beag's hungry beasts would find us were we floating deeper."

"Badger eats the fish!"

"Who said anything about fish?" Talmadge asked, turning about so the old grump could see the gravity in his expression. Indeed, that honest expression seemed to steal the bluster from Badger.

"We are staying near to shore, so keep low and keep alert and try not to let a branch catch you and flip you off the back," Talmadge went on. "I'm not turning around for you, and your furs would catch me a finer price at Fasach Crann than you'll be getting at Car Seileach."

"Strange words, eh?" Badger remarked. "Car Seileach!"

"Short Willows, then, if it makes you feel more at home," Talmadge replied sourly. This gruff older man was not going to do well among the tribes of Loch Beag, he knew. Here, the names of places were more tied to the land, more descriptive and informative. Simple and pragmatic, like the people, with habits and routines designed to accommodate the ways of the lake, the mountains, the valleys, and the creatures that inhabited them.

There was a beauty in that simplicity, Talmadge had come to appreciate, a kind of commonsense harmony and simplicity to their existence. Unlike in Honce-the-Bear, out here in the wilds, the land itself was more honored, more respected, and more dangerous than the castles of the barons and the kings, and so the tribes existed on the edge of utter ruin, where a winter storm could make seven tribes into six, or fewer. Or the lake monsters, or a bear, or a mountain cat, or a goblin (which they called the sidhe, and which were quite a bit bigger here than back in the civilized world) could take the most vulnerable child, or the most skilled warrior, and so quickly. And, of course, there were the warrior men of the mountain, the Usgar deamhain, always there, above them, looking down.

The villagers along the shores of Loch Beag did not have the luxury of complicating life. Death always hovered nearby, an ill, but constant, companion.

With gentle ease and practiced movements, Talmadge navigated around a tumble of rocks. At one point the long canoe, hollowed from a giant cactus, glided in water so shallow that Talmadge could scrape the end of his short paddle on the rocks glimmering below in the morning sun.

"A better price, you're saying?" Badger asked slyly. "Why're you stopping short, then? Another ten pieces of silver for yourself to take me all the way to this Crann place."

"They would kill you," Talmadge said matter-of-factly.

"They don't kill Talmadge, do they?"

"It took me many visits and introductions from Seileach tribesmen," Talmadge explained. "A stranger does not simply walk into one of the villages unknown and unannounced. Car Seileach is the entry point for all of the seven tribes about the lake, the village most amenable to folk from beyond the mountain plateau. This is where you will make your acquaintances, and if you prove as lovable as Talmadge, you might work your way about the shoreline to the other settlements, in time."

"Seven tribes? Been told there were eight? What's yourself hiding from old Badger?"

Talmadge settled the paddle across his lap and turned to regard his companion. He put on a grin for Badger, a mocking grin.

"Keeping all the good markets for Talmadge, eh?" Badger asked.

Talmadge laughed and directed the other man's gaze up to the huge mountain anchoring the southeastern corner of the lake. "Oh, there's an eighth tribe," Talmadge explained. "More nomads than villagers, wandering the great mountain's high ways. I can point you to them, but you'll go alone. And you'll not come back. No one comes back."

The ominous ring of his warning hung in the air for a bit, until Badger harrumphed and spat back, "Bah, but they're all savages, aren't they? And ugly, too!"

With a chuckle, Talmadge went back to his rowing, not interested in correcting the stubborn old fur trader. Talmadge thought that he was quite the clever young man those years ago when he somehow managed to escape the rosie plague and discovered that he could survive in the Wilderlands and even west of that remote region with his wits and intelligence and the few skills his father had taught to him. Now, still a young man, but so very much more worldly than his years, the greatest truths Talmadge had come to know involved his own limitations. Talmadge had survived and often thrived because he accepted that many of the things he believed he already knew he didn't really know at all.

Savages? From someone who had grown up in a kingdom torn by war, with dueling kings and fighting abbots, with fields of dead men piled atop each other, "savages" was not the word Talmadge would use to describe the folk of Loch Beag.

He couldn't deny Badger's other claim, however, for the people of Loch Beag were indeed quite ugly by the standards of the eastern men. They wrapped the heads of their infants tightly to reshape their skulls, and to truly shocking effect. Some skulls were simply elongated, some shorter but with a thicker, almost mushroomlike hump, and some bizarrely formed into a double-hump appearance that was indeed quite off-putting. The few folk back in the Wilderlands who had come this way wouldn't even call the lakemen human, often explaining their weird appearance as the result of mating with goblins, or powrie dwarves, or that they were, instead, some demonic perversion of humankind.

But Talmadge knew better. These were indeed humans, quite civilized and quite sophisticated, and he loved this time of the year, autumn, because in the autumn each year, he could come to Loch Beag and be among the tribes.

He snickered again as he considered Badger's reactions, for the eighth tribe the man had spoken of were not ugly at all, and did not reshape their skulls with wraps or anything else. To the lakemen the eighth tribe were deamhain—demon gods—and from all that Talmadge had heard and seen, it was a description, a reputation, well earned in spilled blood.

Talmadge sincerely hoped he never saw one of those deamhain ever again, nor ever again witnessed the aftermath of one of their devastating raids on the more gentle folk of the lakeshore.

"Getting close?" Badger asked sometime later, the western corner of the southern shore of the lake in view, although with many miles yet to go.

"Tonight or on the morn," Talmadge replied. He eased his paddle up again and glanced out to the lake, spotting the distant sails of the small fishing boats, far to the west of his position.

Probably from Fasach Crann, he thought, for they were coming out right under the shadow of the great mountain, Fireach Speuer.

Talmadge smiled. Fasach Crann was his favorite settlement, and to his surprise, his initial revulsion at the elongated skulls of the villagers there had worn away to the point where he often found, with a proper tease of the hair, the look striking and quite appealing.

He thought back to five years before, to when he was more boy than man, innocent to the world and safe in his family bed. He recalled his mother and father, and his six siblings—of late, he found that he could hardly even remember their unblemished faces anymore.

Still, Fasach Crann reminded him of that town on the western edge of Honce-the-Bear. This one village on the mountain lake felt a little bit like home to Talmadge—home before the plague had swept through the land. Home before he had watched his parents and siblings bloat and die horribly, covered in red sores, something he wished he could hardly remember.

He asked himself for the thousandth time, "Why me?"

He winced with the weight, the guilt of surviving. He dipped his paddle in the water, pushing the canoe ahead, suddenly eager to be rid of Badger and any other reminders of that faraway world and its complications.

The sun was sinking low behind them when Talmadge guided the canoe about the hanging moss and drooping branches of short and wide willow trees that leaned over the water thirstily.

The young trader knew then that he wouldn't make Car Seileach that day, unless he traveled long after sunset, and far too many dangerous creatures lived in or about Loch Beag for him to like that proposition. So, he began to scan the bank for a good place to set camp.

On one clear stretch of still water, he put up his paddle and began to turn to tell Badger of his decision, but he stopped halfway around, caught by a most curious sight. A line of orange needles wove its way toward him from the deeper water, and if that was not strange enough, several other such lines were moving all about, and even as he stared at them, many more appeared.

It only took Talmadge a few heartbeats to sort it out, recalling the clo'dearche, the huge orange lizards common about the lake.

Huge and aggressive.

And now they were coming in from the depths in a swarm. He saw a dozen, two dozen!

Talmadge splashed his paddle into the water left of the canoe and gave a tremendous pull, slightly turning the boat for the shore.

"Put in your paddle on the right and hold it flat there!" he cried to Badger.

"Eh, what?"

"Turn! Turn!" Talmadge yelled.

"What in the name o' King Danube?"

"Just turn, you fool!" Talmadge retorted, though in truth, he had the craft almost facing the shoreline then, so he corrected, "Just row! To the trees—they don't climb!"

"They?"

"The lizards!"

Badger gasped and Talmadge knew he had finally caught on.

"Are we to outrun 'em?" the old veteran asked.

"Just row!"

The canoe bounced as Talmadge pulled and he grimaced and moved his hand near his short sword, thinking that one of the lizards had bumped up against the craft. But no, he realized, it was Badger, up and running the length of the boat, then leaping ahead to the shallows. If it wasn't bad enough that the man had deserted the boat and their supplies, Badger landed in the water, spun about and shoved back against the moving canoe, nearly capsizing it, and knocking Talmadge off-balance.

"I can outrun yourself!" Badger said, splashing to the shore and laughing wildly.

Talmadge grabbed both edges of the craft, trying to steady it. He had to get up and out, he realized, but even as he started to rise, the boat lurched again, mightily, and rushed in for the shallows, propelled by a powerful lizard. The canoe leaned heavily to the right and turned sideways. It scraped the bottom, hit a stone, and lurched, and Talmadge tumbled out sidelong.

He was smart enough to roll with the throw, and savvy enough to grab a rather large stone as he came around, splashing to his knees and hopping to his feet just as the lizard got its feet onto the sand and stones of the shallows, tossing the canoe about like a child's toy with a simple shake of its large head, and pressing forward at Talmadge.

The man pegged it, right on the skull, with the stone.

The clo'dearche hissed and opened wide its maw to display lines of needlelike teeth. Twice as long tip to tail as Talmadge was tall, and four hundred pounds of claws and scales and murderous jaws, it reared up onto its hind legs, fiery orange in the slanting late-afternoon sun rays.

Talmadge fell back and drew the short sword from his belt, certain that he was doomed. He glanced at the trees to see Badger already in the lowest branches, and knew that he could not get there, and understood, too, that the man wasn't coming back to help.

The clo'dearche hissed savagely, and a fan of skin, like small and furious wings, opened wide about its neck, and vibrated fiercely, the slapping of skin against scale adding to the sound.

And warning Talmadge.

He dived aside as the beast spat, a giant wad of ugly, sticky, dangerous goo. He knew more than one Seileach tribesman whose eye had been burned out by the acidic spittle.

Splashing and stumbling, Talmadge got to dry ground, but there his heart sank as more of the giant lizards exited the water left and right, with the hungry beast's snapping maw so near behind him!

His mind whirled—these were not pack hunters, but solitary beasts except in the spring during their mating frenzies. Why were so many about? And how?

Talmadge took two steps before he had to swing about and slash across with his short sword to keep the lizard at bay. He nicked one foreleg, but got hit himself, by the other, scratching in at his sword arm as it passed.

How easily the lizard's claw sliced through his thick leather sleeve and gashed his flesh! He knew that he was lucky that his arm hadn't been sheared off at the elbow. Instead of countering with a backhanded slash, Talmadge flipped the blade into his left hand and tucked his wounded right elbow in close as he retreated.

He glanced left and right, seeing huge orange lizards rushing by. With a flick of his head, he sent his thin braid up to his mouth, where he clamped onto it, chewing, trying to sort this all out. For a moment, he feared that he was being flanked, but no, these other beasts were fleeing, scrambling, scrabbling, heads and tails whipping side to side.

But not the one before him. Up on two legs still, that one came on with murderous intent, claws twitching, tongue flicking. Talmadge jabbed his sword repeatedly, but had to give ground.

"Be a good lad, then," Badger called from up in the nearby willow tree. "Might that yourself'll be dead soon enough, so offer some words on how I'm best to speak with them Seileach folk, eh?"

"Help me, you fool!"

"Oh, I'm not thinking that'd be in my plans," Badger replied with a snort.

The clo'dearche lurched forward, maw snapping, then fell forward, nearly overwhelming Talmadge as it went to all fours once more, sending the man rolling away.

"Badger!" he called.

"Aye," came the answer. "Right here, watching, and thinking that my own self'll do fine since I'll have twice the haul of furs and skins."

Talmadge growled and fended the charging lizard with a series of slashes and stabs. Back up on its hind legs went the beast, and those collar wings began to chatter, the creature gathering spittle.

Talmadge set his legs wide, taking a count of his heartbeats by chomping on his braid, measuring the lizard's delay. Right as the orange lizard spat, the man whirled about to the side, again only narrowly avoiding the putrid goo.

"I knew a lass who could spit like that!" Badger called. "Or swallow it, too, ha ha!"

Old Badger actually felt bad for the younger man down there, and it occurred to him that watching this ugly critter eating his guide wouldn't be much fun.

So be it.

This was the truth of the frontier, the wilds beyond even the Wilderlands—beyond in both senses of the word: farther from the civilized kingdoms and wilder still! Death was a common companion to the folk of these parts, particularly the traders, who lived as hermits for most of the year. Every spring, Badger would go to the gathering known as the Matinee to discover that men and women he had known over the years were not to be seen again, ever.

With a resigned sigh, Badger rested back against the thick trunk of the tree and watched the spectacle play out below him, the lizard trying to eat Talmadge, and the poor, doomed man trying just to stay away, and with no apparent hope of actually beating the thing.

But none of the orange ugly things were coming for Badger, after all, or seemed interested in climbing any trees, and that was all that truly mattered.

The old frontiersman looked about at the trees, at the short willows, and figured he could find his way to Car Seileach easily enough. And now, of course, he'd have far more goods to barter. Even if he had to give all of Talmadge's bounty to the ugly-headed tribe, at least he'd be the lead contact thereafter, and any of the other traders hoping to deal with the lake tribes would have to look to him for expensive guidance!

Of course, he had to stay alive.

"My own self'll be taking your haunt as my own, I expect," he called down.

He winced as Talmadge dived aside, whacking the lizard with his sword, to no apparent effect. Talmadge almost got away, but the creature bit him on the boot and held fast as he sprawled, and Badger grimaced again and looked to the lake, not wanting to watch the ugly lizard feast.

And he looked, too, to the cactus canoe, nodding with relief to see that it remained secure on the sand and rocks in the shallows. Some of the goods had fallen out when the lizard had tossed the boat aside, but they were still right there, up against the craft.

He thought that perhaps he should slip out to the boat and float away while the lizard ate.

His pondering fell aside, however, as another commotion stirred just off the shore. At first Badger thought it the crest of a wave, but no, these were fish, small fish in tight schools, breaking the surface with a series of leaps in a silvery display. And they were throwing themselves right from the lake, onto the beach.

Badger crinkled his face, not understanding, and stroked his long and scraggly gray beard, casting his gaze out farther onto the lake.

And his eyes widened and his jaw drooped open.

A huge shadow passed beneath the surface, not far out. The water rippled and Badger noted a series of sinewy, snakelike humps gliding through the clear lake. He couldn't make out the exact shape of the thing, except that it was enormous, and dark—black like death. He never even saw the monster's head, just that giant, serpentine body, but that was enough for him to understand that the thing could swallow him whole.

Badger understood then why the creatures of this small bay were rushing from the water, even formidable creatures, like dozens of these huge clo'dearche lizards, fleeing for their lives.

The shadow passed, gliding away under the deep waters of Loch Beag, and it took Badger a long time to remember to breathe.

Suddenly, he wasn't so sure that he wanted to claim dead Talmadge's items.

He looked down to see the man fighting bravely, and futilely. Talmadge limped as he moved about, his foot torn and bleeding. He had his sword back in his right hand, but he grimaced every time he waved it to block or to drive the stalking lizard back.

"Hurry up and be done with it," the grizzled old fighter in the tree whispered.

"I'll spit on your rot," he heard the battling Talmadge grumble, and Badger could only shrug and reply, "As you wish," under his breath.

The standing lizard swayed, snakelike, as if trying to mesmerize him.

Talmadge wasn't falling for that! He didn't let his short sword dip at all, keeping its fine blade ready to stab against any advance.

"Come on, come on," he whispered under his breath. He glanced to the side, to the tree with Badger, and growled, for the man clearly wasn't coming down to his aid.

And there was no way he was getting up a tree, for the clo'dearche was devastatingly quick. He still couldn't understand why the other lizards had run past, and were, he hoped, still running, for they were nowhere Talmadge could see.

A sparkle down at the lake caught his attention briefly, and he knew it to be a wave of silver fish, leaping from the water, as they would to avoid larger predator fish. But he heard the splashing by the bank and realized that many had thrown themselves there and now flopped helplessly in the shallow water!

Before he could make sense of the suicidal flight, though, the lizard before him reared higher, and out came the winglike neck flaps, hissing, gathering another blast of spittle.

Talmadge didn't angle himself to dive aside, and he didn't roll away. He chewed his braid, watching the lizard's yellow eyes—eyes that would roll to white right before the creature spat.

Talmadge counted again, silently, ready to spring.

Even as the lizard's eyes rolled back, Talmadge leaped ahead. He ignored the pain in his arm, and stabbed with all his strength, with all his weight behind the blow, right into the middle of the clo'dearche's chest, right between its waving forelegs.

He didn't even know if the thing had a heart, or if his stab had a chance of felling the monstrous lizard. But he struck, with all his strength, a last, desperate try. Good fortune was with him, for he knew that had the beast not snapped forward at the same instant to launch its spittle, he never would have been able to pierce its hide as wounded as he was. The sputum flew over Talmadge's ducking head.

Once the tip of the short sword got through the outer armor, Talmadge drove it home, plunging the fine blade in deeply, pressing it, pushing it, right to the hilt as he crashed into the standing lizard, driving it over.

Talmadge pitched ahead, the lizard falling over backward—not straight back, for the long and powerful tail countervailed, but off to the right, the two coming down heavily, the lizard's forelegs snapping in tight, claws cutting into the man's clothes and flesh.

Talmadge threw his left arm under the thrashing beast's jaw, fighting to keep that terrible maw up too high to bite his face off!

And they thrashed and they rolled, and the heavy thing crushed down upon him. And Talmadge screamed out for Badger, certain that he was about to die, trying to cover, unable to defend.

It took him a long while to realize that the clo'dearche was dead as it lay atop him, and took him longer still to roll the thing aside and climb out from under it.

He came up to his knees, only half hearing Badger's calls of "huzzah!" as the man at last slid down from the tree.

Talmadge was too busy inventorying his many scratches and punctures to take note.

"Ah, but you killed it good!" Badger said with a wheezing laugh.

Talmadge struggled to his feet, shaking, trying not to look at the man so that he wouldn't reveal his outrage, and his continuing wariness.

"Something big swum by," Badger informed him, walking over. "Big and dark, and chased them uglies from the water."

Talmadge nodded, still trying to sort it out. Was it possible that the fabled beast of Loch Beag had come so near? The mere thought of it had Talmadge rocking and unsteady, and explained the clo'dearche exodus and the suicidal flights of the silver fish.

"The blood's leaving your face, ha!" Badger taunted. "You killed the damned lizard to death and now you're blanching?"

"The beast of Loch Beag," Talmadge explained, his voice low, speaking slowly. "The lakemen sail hard to shore, any shore, to be away from it. It eats them. It eats their boats. It is a demon monster as sure as is the dactyl. How many lizards ran by us? Scores?"

"Seen plenty," Badger admitted.

"And if all of them had turned to fight the monster instead of fleeing, they'd all be dead now. And if their flight hadn't warned us, we'd be in the belly of the monster by now, bitten to pieces."

The older man shifted uncomfortably.

"I knew you'd be beating it," Badger said with a snicker, clearly nervous and trying to change the subject.

"You wanted my skins," Talmadge casually replied.

"Wasn't about to fight that thing!"

"You could have thrown me a rope."

"Well," Badger said with a shrug, still a few strides away. "We're all to die, eh? And profit's profit!"

"People do not survive out here alone," Talmadge said, again with a level of complete composure. "There are too many things wanting to eat you, or rob you for their wares. Or sacrifice you to some god you've never even heard of. That you would care more for my wares than for my life marks the end of our arrangement and any pretense of friendship."

"Friendship?" Badger replied with that wheezing laugh. "I paid yourself to take me, nothing more!"

"Well, that arrangement, too, is at its end," Talmadge said, and he turned and started for the lake. "Take your wares and find your own way."

When he faced away, Talmadge brought his left arm in front of him and jerked his elbow slightly, dropping a wide cuff of treated, reinforced leather down over his hand. He sheathed his sword on his left hip, too, pointedly so, that Badger would take note. "I'll spit on your rot," Talmadge whispered again, under his breath.

Predictably, Badger closed the gap fast, deftly drawing his long sword, and he stabbed it for Talmadge's back.

But the younger man had anticipated just that, and he swung about, left arm leading, the heavy leather covering his hand catching the side of the blade and slapping the strike aside. And his right hand moved with speed and practice, a single, simple attack routine he had practiced every day since he had first learned the art of fighting.

To draw and to stab. One movement, fluid and fast.

He saw old Badger's surprised expression, shocked even, that he had been so easily goaded by this young man.

Badger wore that disbelieving look even as Talmadge stepped into the opening and slid the short sword into his chest, slicing his lung, cutting his heart in half.

"We're all to die, eh?" Talmadge said, his lips only an inch from Badger's face.

The man could only wheeze in reply, and Talmadge shoved him backward, let him slide off the blade, dead before he hit the ground.

The battered Talmadge rolled his head about and flexed his shoulders, stretching away the pain. He glanced around, figuring that the monster, or whatever it had been, was gone by then, and so the other clo'dearche would likely soon return.

Talmadge wanted no part of that.

He looked to the canoe, to the dead lizard and the dead trader, and noted that Badger did indeed have a length of rope looped at the side of his pack.

Talmadge shook his head, disgusted, and muttered, "So be it."

He took what he could from the man, and now had a finer sword hanging on his left hip, his short sword on his right.

And he put Badger's rope to use, as well, tying the man by the ankles and hoisting him up over a low branch. He struggled to get him fully off the ground, low enough for the voracious clo'dearche to reach him, but high enough to keep them busy for a while.

He thought to do the same with the dead lizard, but he knew he hadn't the time, or likely even the strength to hoist the thing.

He gave a last look at the dead man, and took a moment to fulfill his vow and spit on the corpse. Talmadge went to the lake, loaded the canoe—and took a few flopping fish as well as they floundered about the lakeshore, including one that was as long as his forearm—then dragged the boat from the shallows and started away, his eyes always to the deeper waters in search of dark things that swam below.

He had barely moved from the spot when he heard the first returning lizard, its neck flaps slapping. It probably thought Badger was still alive as he swayed on lake winds. He heard the spit, then more gruesome sounds, the chewing and the tearing.

Talmadge could only sigh and shrug.

2

DEAMHAIN OF THE MOUNTAIN

"They'll be returning, not to fear," the old crone assured the child.

"But what if they don't?" the girl asked in an even and clear-minded tone that belied her tender age, for she was only then a few months past her third birthday. She looked up at the older woman and locked her eyes, and gave a shrug as if to simply accept the possibility.

The crone smiled down at her, which elicited a grin in response. It was hard to tell with this little one. She had a slightly crooked jaw, the right side of her mouth a bit lower than the left, and the asymmetry became particularly apparent whenever she smiled, and so every smile seemed a smirk, and made it seem as if the child had a lot more going on behind the grin than simple merriment.

The crone nodded, thinking that aspect quite appropriate for young Aoleyn, if she could even be rightly called "young Aoleyn." This one was wise and perceptive beyond her years, possessed of an old soul and a calculating mind. Her large eyes were beyond brown, were black, like the thick wavy hair bouncing about her shoulders, and anyone who took the moment to look deeply into those inky orbs would glimpse their own reflection through a turned prism.

Some of the Usgar tribe didn't much like the feeling of those reflecting eyes, for the child's smirking glance sometimes provoked a feeling that the little one was judging them—or perhaps it was simply because they did not like what they saw. The crone, on the other hand, secure in the way she lived her life, had come to truly appreciate this different child.

"They will, child. They're always to return."

The black smoke from the bonfire curled into the air more thinly now, as the once-great flames settled into a hive of angry eyes. The tribe's witches, who had been dancing fervently as the sacrifices burned, slowed their movements in graceful and coordinated fashion, and now stood in place, swaying gently, each whispering prayers for the success of the war party.

Outside the circle of witches, the warrior men milled about, no longer entranced by the magical dance. Some sat and shared drinks, relating stories of previous battles, while others preferred a solemn and solitary preparation, winding sap-soaked cloths about the shafts of their war spears or wrapping their hands and fingers with treated strips that would offer limited protection from the cut of a blade or the punch of a club. They performed their acts methodically, using the movements to bring them to meditation and a place of quiet readiness.

One warrior in particular paid very close attention. Barely twenty, Tay Aillig had been granted the honor of leading this war party on this most important raid, a position usually reserved for men ten years his elder or even twice his age. But he had earned it, he knew. He had been down the mountain on such raids and all about the mountain on hunts since his fifteenth summer, and had distinguished himself with his ferocity and fearlessness each and every time.

Now, finally, it was his turn to lead; he would finally garner the glories of all those successes he had helped the tribe achieve for five years.

On a sudden and sharp call from their leader, the dancing witches stopped their swaying and held perfectly still. All movement outside their ring halted as well, all eyes focusing on the women in their almost-sheer plain white shifts, and conversations became whispered prayers.

As one, so practiced that it seemed as if on command, the witches bowed low to the smoldering embers of the dying fire, then turned away, standing perfectly straight, arms at their sides, eyes closed.

The whispers ceased and the warrior men rose, dropping their weapons, their drinks, anything else they held. They waited, silently, until all were in place.

Tay Aillig glanced from man to man, studying, scrutinizing, trying to determine the weakest of those he would lead this day, trying to determine those most likely to let him down and cost him his proper due.

The strong men wore fear on their faces, little Aoleyn recognized, and was surprised by that even though she had seen this before. She had heard the cries of pain and seen the grimaces as the warriors completed the ritual. The child remembered what was coming and so did the strong men, and for all their outward bluster, for all their grim determination, for all their courage in even participating in this ritual, there was within each a measure of fear.

She heard a sharp whistle and turned toward the tribe's greatest woman, Mairen, who was Usgar-righinn. The witches of the Coven stepped farther out from the hub of their circle, opening the way for the warriors, who, as one, approached the dying bonfire.

Aoleyn could see the slightest of hesitance in their steps, near universal among the group, indeed in all but one of the men, a tall and long-haired giant with fierce eyes and thick, sinewy muscles. They didn't want to do this, but neither did they shy, and whenever one seemed to falter, he looked to that bravest man, the tall man, young and strong.

The men formed a ring around the fire. Each lifted his right arm out to the side and placed it on the left shoulder of the warrior beside him, and when the circle was complete, the men bent forward and sent their left hands into the embers, reaching for the glowing crystals, red and blue and violet and shining with an angry inner light.

Out came the hands, trembling under the burn of the crystals, the men standing and trying to hold perfectly still, and trying not to cry out, and trying, most of all, not to drop the hot treasures.

Aoleyn got a slight whiff of an awful smell, though she didn't yet recognize it as the smell of burning flesh.

One man groaned, another cried out. A crystal fell to the ground. Another man went to one knee, driven down by the agony.

Now it was more than a slight whiff, and all about the fire, people crinkled their faces, covered their noses, even turned away.

It was a mark of honor to take up the blessed crystals without cries of pain, but many of the men could not contain themselves, and several short outbursts sounded, followed by a longer tirade of cursing from a young raider.

Tay Aillig grimaced and gritted his teeth, but would allow no sound to escape his lips. In defiance, he tightened all his muscles, his chest rippling, his arms locking. Nor did he bounce the crystal he had taken from the pyre in his hand to try to lessen the burn. He sent his thoughts out from his body, to another place, another focus, that he could ignore the fiery pain.

He thought of his first kill, from his first raid, an ugly lakeman whose head was shaped into two huge lumps. Tay Aillig remembered the look in the lakeman's eyes when he, barely a man, had twisted the spear in his enemy's chest.

Tay Aillig had watched the life spirit flee the man's body, so vividly, so clearly, the light of life winking out in the ugly man's blue eyes.

What a fight it had been! For some reason he could not then understand, the magic in Tay Aillig's blessed spear tip had failed him, and so unexpectedly that he had been caught off his guard and nearly killed by the lakeman's long knife.

But he had recovered and riposted, and scored a mortal blow. With his free hand, Tay Aillig held fast the man's weapon arm, by the wrist, and as he let the dead man fall away, he pulled from that wrist a copper cuff, set with a pale orange stone, spangled in purple. Almost immediately upon taking the item, Tay Aillig had sensed its power, a power so similar to the blessings the witches placed upon their crystalline spear tips.

He had broke that small amethyst-studded sunstone from the larger bracelet and hidden it away, and still kept it secret these five years later.

Without thinking, his free hand moved toward the little pocket he had stitched into his breeches, just in front of his right hip.

He wished that strange stone could ease his pain now, but no, these were the fires of burned wood, not the magical flames of a crystal-created fireball.

Mairen whistled a second time, and the witches turned about and began to sing. The warriors of the raiding party looked to Tay Aillig, and he met their desperate stares with a wicked smile.

He closed his hand tighter on the crystal he held, and refused to so much as grimace at the pain, so much was he enjoying the pleading stares, the begging, from the other warriors.

Finally, he nodded, and the men ran to the buckets of water on the outer perimeter and plunged in their burned hands and the hot crystals. Tay Aillig, though, took his time, walking calmly to his pail and dropping in the crystal from on high. Then he paused and looked around, smiling against the burning pain and letting everyone see him before finally plunging in his hand.

He was the first to leave the comfort of the cool water, too, moving to his spear to set the blessed crystalline tip. He fixed his judgmental stare on any lagging warrior; the witches would not heal the burns of any warrior until every spear was completed.

Finally, it was done, and so the raid was considered blessed. The warriors moved to their assigned witch for healing, Tay Aillig alone to the Usgar-righinn. He pointedly did not look her in the eye when she cast her healing magic upon his burned hand. He refused to acknowledge her at all, and moved off into the shadows with his war party.

They could have set off right then, but Tay Aillig held them to watch the ending of the ceremony. A whistle from the darkness brought forth the tribe's dozen slaves, the uamhas, the monsters with misshapen heads.

Aoleyn wrapped her arm around the crone's leg and pulled herself closer. She didn't want to look at these ugly creatures, but she couldn't turn her eyes away. They were mostly human in appearance, entirely so, actually, except for their strangely bent or stretched skulls. Several had grossly elongated heads, huge and conical. Three others were even worse, with skulls that protruded upward both left and right, like blunted, hairy horns—this trio of young uamhas had been captured the previous year, from one of the most celebrated raids in Usgar memory. Another, the youngest, wasn't older than Aoleyn, and was cursed with a forehead that rose up far too high and bent sharply to the right.

The uamhas collected armloads of kindling comprised of mostly thin, long branches, and rushed to drop them just outside the perimeter of the dying bonfire. Then they scrambled away into the darkness, toward the pine grove that housed them in the summer months, chased by the hateful glares of the tribe.

The witches stepped forward, encircling the low-burning fire once more, and collected the kindling as the Usgar-righinn produced her mighty scepter, a crystalline cylinder that appeared to be made of starlight, with a line of red shot through it within. Mairen closed her eyes and hugged the scepter close, and began to glow, her body encased in a divine shroud of white light. She stepped onto the bonfire, ignoring the flares of flame caused by her bare feet. Unbothered, she curled down into a ball.

The witches lay their kindling atop her and all about her and stepped back, and began again their swaying, hypnotic dance and quiet song.

Aoleyn heard the Usgar-righinn's chant from under the pile, and so she shouldn't have been surprised. But she still jumped when the bonfire exploded, flames engulfing the new kindling immediately and lifting mightily into the night sky with a sudden roar and a wave of heat that washed over everyone in the encampment.

The witches danced wildly again, chanting with full throat. This time, they were singing their goodbyes to the warriors. Little Aoleyn had been promised that she would learn this song soon, and many other songs, and that perhaps she would be strong enough to join this part of the ritual in a few years' time, as many outside the ring of witches were also singing. The girl jumped again when Mairen stood up suddenly amidst the flames, her arms lifted to the heavens, her scepter glowing with fiery reflection. She floated up into the air above the fire!

How glorious she seemed! How powerful! Above the fires and above them all!

Mairen held that pose, floating in the air above the fire, for a long while, until the song drifted away and melted into the night like the Usgar warriors.

"Will they bring things back?" asked the entranced girl, turning to the crone.

"Oh yes, child, they will bring back many things," answered the crone. "Darker days close in, and we'll be needing to last through the cold blow."

The girl nodded silently. She was young, but she already knew to fear winter up here on the great mountain. She looked around at the village, a few dozen structures of conical tents that had been fashioned of a thin, angled pine skeleton overlaid with elk hide, sticking up from the already snow-covered ground. She understood what was coming next, though she didn't really remember it from the previous year and only knew because the old crone had reminded her many times over. The Usgar tribe would not sit idly while the raiding party left the mountain in the hunt for supplies to last through the brutal cold. Before the raiders returned, the village would be moved from the summer camp to the sacred winter plateau.

A shiver ran down the girl's back just thinking about that place. Not a shiver of fear, nor of cold, but of excitement. Despite its location high on the side of the mountain, the sacred plateau was always warm, even in the midst of the fiercest of blizzards. Two open pits tunneled into the depths of the mountain, and the heat radiating from them made fires unnecessary, other than for light or cooking. A stream burbled past, unfrozen, clean and fresh, to the edge of the plateau. The girl had peeked over that edge the previous winter, expecting to see a waterfall; instead, she saw the water turn to cold white ice as soon as it crossed the edge of the plateau, frozen almost instantly in a spray of snowy crystal flakes.

She had found that thoroughly enchanting.

But even anticipation of these magical trappings did not fully explain the child's giddiness. Something about that winter home simply resonated with her, made her hair stand on end in the best possible way.

"Why can't we live on the winter plateau all year long?" she asked.

The crone laughed her grating, wheezing snicker, one that mocked all questioners with its surety. "'Tis a sacred place," she explained, and not for the first time with the precocious Aoleyn. "One mustn't stay there too long, or sure you'll be driven mad."

"But the Usgar-forfach lives there," the never-satisfied child protested.

"Aye, and so the Elder's quite mad, he is!" the crone said. She burst out snickering and chortling again, but the laugh quickly faded into a cough.

Her demeanor changed instantly, and the crone cast a stern look at Aoleyn. "Do'no repeat that," she warned harshly. She extended a gnarled finger at the girl menacingly. "Do'no e'er repeat that!"

Aoleyn nodded her assent, but found herself more curious than afraid of the woman's sudden demeanor change.

The crone looked as if she was about to speak again, probably to repeat her warning, but a low chanting filled the air, and the old woman fell silent.

Aoleyn looked back to the roaring bonfire, where the gathered witches had stopped dancing. Then, as Mairen floated from above the blazing fire and slowly lowered to the ground, the witches began singing the last of the sacred chants, this one in the old tongue. Aoleyn knew these sounds well, but not the words, for the old tongue was the sole province of the Coven and was not typically spoken except in these few public rituals.

"*Nach's e agam am fialach oir geamrah a'buan a'm nhitheas fuaraich easb-hui annad.*"

The crone, who knew the old tongue well, although she had never been in the Coven, translated. "'Return to me with bounty, for the winter's long and sure I'll grow cold without you.'"

Two dozen warriors of the tribe set off down the mountain, the final and most important raid before the deep snows closed the high passes. The chanting of the thirteen witches continued long after the men were out of sight, but the other men and women witnessing the event scurried about as soon as their warriors were lost to the darkness, breaking down the pine and hide tents, preparing them for the litters that would be dragged up the mountainside and off to the north a bit, to the sacred winter home of the Usgar.

The Usgar-righinn called out above the song, and from the shadows came the primary litter bearers, the uamhas with their oddly shaped heads.

"Will the warriors bring any more slaves?" Aoleyn asked the crone.

"If the blessing's pure enough, aye," she answered. "We're always needing more slaves!"

The icy-cold, crystal clear water of Loch Beag swirled around Huana'kal's feet, numbing him to midcalf. Northwest, across the great lake, the morning sun caught the top of the mountains, shining brilliantly off the snow-covered peaks, but Kal remained in shade, for the sun hadn't risen enough yet to get past the wall of the great mountain looming dark behind him.

The shadows of Fireach Speuer often darkened the lake town of Fasach Crann, the Wilderpine, both literally and figuratively.

Kal dipped his ceramic jug into the water, sending silver streaks of minnows darting. Were it leaner times, these minnows would be an important food source, and Kal was quite practiced at catching them, but for now he let them be.

Kal savored the feel of the frigid waters against his legs. Autumn was on in full, and here on the high plateau, that season often meant storms and snow. Today promised to be bright and glorious, though, and it was already quite warm. And Kal had been walking since before the dawn, back and forth from his home to the food shed, to the market, to the lake. To wherever his wife, Innevah, had asked. Her belly swelled with their first child, due at the onset of winter, and that child, boy or girl, would be tall and strong, Kal knew. His anticipation gnawed at him—he couldn't wait to tightly swaddle his child's head, to stretch its skull to the heavens.

He poured a bit of the cold water over his own head to rinse off the sweat. He poured a bit down his throat as well. He started to turn for home, but paused simply to enjoy the peaceful moment, the village waking up around him. Innevah wouldn't notice he'd delayed. He took a deep gulp of the water, savoring the soft morning air.

Loch Beag's mood this fine day was glassy and bright. A gentle breeze pushed ripples across the surface, but not enough to cloud the water—and not just here in the shallows, Kal knew. Like every other adult in the village, he had spent many hours out on the deep waters, sometimes a mile from shore or more. Loch Beag was a mountain lake, wholly surrounded by the towering peaks of the Surgruag Monadh, the Snowhaired Mountains, and nearly a mile above the flat sands of Fasail Dubh'clach, the Desert of Black Stones, to the east. The waters were very deep, deeper than any lines the fishermen dared fashion to drop into them. For in the depths of Loch Beag lurked dangerous hunters, and one monster in particular that the people of the tribes living all about the lakeshore knew all too well.

Visibility down into the water often meant the difference between life and death out on the ways of Loch Beag, for when the shadow of the beast passed far below, the fishermen knew to take up their oars and unfurl their small square sails and get fast to the shallows. Even boats of the other tribes, often rivals, would raise their flags of warning to the other villages, and calls of "row!" would echo about the waters.

And when the lake's mood shifted, when the streams that fed Loch Beag ran fast with the spring melt or with heavy rains and so stirred the lake bed into clouds, or when the warm southern winds excited a fog, the lakemen knew to be fast off the deep waters.

For the monster knew those days, too, and too often hunted well the slowest boat.

There had been a lot of fog this season, and so the supplies of Fasach Crann were running lower than desired with winter coming on fast.

Kal looked down at the pretty dace again and nodded.

The young man took another deep drink from his jug, dipped it into the shallow water to refill it, and splashed back to shore, heading for home and his very pregnant wife. He noted a pair of elderly men sitting on low chairs woven of treated white birch bark tied about a pine frame, a very common sight down here by the lake this time of morning.

"Over in the cove, they've not been hit in years," one was saying as Kal walked by. "Might be their turn." Though he was anxious to get home, Kal paused, intrigued. The winter neared, after all, and that meant the demon gods who lived on the mountain would almost certainly be out hunting soon.

"Nor the village in the cleft," said another.

"Plenty o' easy pickings there, if I'm to be asked," said the first.

"The Usgar aren't asking," the other said, and both nodded resignedly. "The demon gods take as the demon gods see."

Kal grunted an acknowledgement as he walked by. These two old fisherfolk, one bald, the other with gray wisps of hair scattered about his head, were too infirm to work on the boats, and so had become mainstays near the lake bank, sitting back in their chairs, sometimes picking at the dace bones and always full of chatter, mostly complaining, predicting the weather, the fishing fortunes, offering dire warnings of Usgar raiders, or of the lake monster. Still, despite their often growly demeanor, they had become something of friends to Kal in these last months, as he had remained ashore, as custom demanded, to help Innevah. The men and women of the lake villages both worked equally, and Innevah was herself a fisherwoman of no small repute. Indeed, she and Kal had begun their relationship on a fishing boat, or rather on two fishing boats, when they had collided while jostling for position over a school of sunfish.

Surely Innevah wanted to be back out there on the waters as much as Kal did, but in the village, as in most of the settlements about the lake, when a woman became pregnant, both she and her chosen mate were compelled to stay off the boats until the child was born. Life here on the Ayamharas Plateau was dangerous, life on the lake even more so, and children were the most precious gifts that could be given to the tribe.

All that, however, didn't stop these two particular old-timers from giving Kal a lot of grief during his somewhat idle days wandering about the village. "Ack, but we're old and brittle," they usually greeted him, "and we've not the balance to stand in a boat. And our fingers are no more for pointing straight. What's your own excuse, boy?"

They began that very litany as Kal walked away, but they paused, as did he, when a third man strode in from the other direction, heading with purpose for the elders. Kal turned about as the man passed him by with a gruff nod, one returned by Kal for he hardly knew this man, a trader with a skull that had not been shaped by wrapping, who had come from across the lake, and from lands far away. The tall and lanky man's appearance unsettled Kal; with his unshaped head he was masquerading as a god—and not a god of blessing, like those that gave the fruits and the fish, but a demon god, an Usgar.

The lakemen of Loch Beag would never think to allow themselves to resemble those awful demons of Fireach Speuer!

"What tidings, then, Talmadge of the East?" the old gray-hair asked.

"Same grumbles as this morn?" the bald-headed elder added.

"I am telling you plainly," Talmadge replied. "I have looked through my fortune glass and I have seen them. The mountain men are soon coming down from their high perch."

"You're needing magic to tell you that?" the gray-hair answered with a snort. "Could've put my finger up in the winterly wind and told you the same."

Talmadge winced—it seemed to Kal as if he was in pain—as he brought his right arm up to hold aloft a strange item, a brass ring with a clear crystal set in the middle, like some kind of lens—except that it was not concave like a lens, and it did not focus the sunlight shining upon it, but rather threw the light about into a thousand sparkles.

"I thought you should know," he said. "My fear is that they'll come straight down the mountain to Fasach Crann," he said, which alarmed Kal until the two old men scoffed at the notion.

"We're always the closest to the deamhain," said the bald-headed man. "But we're the hardest to strike!"

"I've looked through your 'fortune glass,' too, and do you know what I seen?" the gray-hair added. "I seen whatever's on the other side, and that's all, but a bit stretched and blurry!"

He and his friend sniggered at that. "Seven villages on the lake and we're the strongest," he went on. "The deamhain are mean, I'll be giving you that much, but they're a bit mortal, at least, and they try to stay alive, aye? They got easier pickings north and south. You're sure to see it, too, aye, Water-stilt?"

It took Kal a moment to realize that the old man was addressing him, and to further realize that he wasn't even trying to hide his eavesdropping. He flushed red, a bit embarrassed to be caught so off guard, then nodded sharply.

"He's just trying to sell you that magic fortune glass," Kal said, dripping the word "magic" with sarcasm.

But Talmadge was shaking his head before Kal even finished. "Nay, it is not for sale," he said flatly.

"'Course it's not," said the gray-haired old-timer. "Not for sale unless we're to make the right thick offer."

His partner cackled at that, and the pair of them turned back to gaze at the lake and away from the trader.

Kal started to turn away as well, but the man caught his gaze. "A fair warning is all I can offer you," he said quietly. "Pray you be wise and take it. I'm packing my canoe and paddling away from here long before nightfall."

Kal gave him a curt nod, turned, and walked off.

Something about the man's demeanor continued to play on Kal's sensibilities—perhaps it was the surety with which Talmadge had made his claim. It took Kal a half-dozen steps to remember that the man was just a trader, not a prophet. In another dozen, he had come within earshot of his house, and he could hear Innevah, complaining loudly to the midwife about her lazy husband who probably went for a swim when he was supposed to be getting her water, and by the gods of the tallest pines, was she parched!

By the time he crossed the threshold, to be greeted as both a savior, with a relieved sigh, and as *late,* with an accompanying scowl, Kal had already forgotten the trader and his warning.

True to his word, Talmadge was out of Fasach Crann in short order, paddling his canoe to the northwest along the shore, where lay the remaining three villages with which he hoped to trade. As soon as he was beyond the small harbor that sheltered Fasach Crann, and with the village's fleet still in sight far out on the lake, Talmadge took out his seeing scope again.

He rolled the item over in his hands reverently, and wistfully, for this was the first thing he had secured when he had left his home those years before, and he had traded most of his worldly possessions at that time for it. It was indeed possessed of magic, the gemstone magic of Honce-the-Bear, with a lens held within a brass ring. Upon that metal ring, opposite each other, were set a pair of quartz gems, the source of the item's magic power. For those who could bring forth that magic, the clear lens would not distort the image on the other side, as the old Fasach Crann villager had remarked, but would instead fill with a vision— an honest look—at a faraway place.

Talmadge had looked up the mountain the previous day, and had happened upon an Usgar war party. He couldn't be sure of where they were, but the thickness of the trees about them made Talmadge certain that they weren't up at their high perch near the mountaintop.

The trader brought the item up before his eyes once more and called upon the magic. The distorted image in the lens clouded over and was soon replaced with a mountain scene, a high outcropping of towering stone.

He willed the magic about and found slopes filled with trees, even a wolf at one point, lumbering about the forest.

But no Usgar deamhain.

Talmadge continued a bit longer, but was already growing weary. Finally, he brought the item to his lap and looked up at the wide and huge Fireach Speuer with his naked eye. Far up the slopes he could see the individual trees, but nothing moving about them would be visible to him, of course, for he was too far.

He glanced back to Fasach Crann and thought of turning about. Perhaps he should go back and impress upon the villagers the need to be alert. Perhaps he could entice those on the shore into their boats, or even call the fishing fleet back in to shore.

But what had he really seen the previous day? Where were the Usgar warriors he had so briefly glimpsed? Were they even on this side of the mountain? For Fireach Speuer was huge and round.

And were they really coming down to attack a village?

"You fool, you're still on edge because of that idiot Badger," he scolded himself, and with a last glance at the fleet on the lake, and one in the direction of his favorite village of all, Talmadge turned about and slid his paddle into the water, pressing on.

Silence preceded them, silence followed them. Their practiced footfalls skimmed the stones, barely setting down, making little sound, little impact. Their smooth run was aided by the green flecks in their crystal-line weapons, the magical blessing lifting them, lightening them. These particular green flecks were most common in all the crystals chosen for hunting and war parties because of this very enchantment.

> Deamhan footfalls leave no mark
> Coming silent, can'no hark

Their figures remained blurred and indistinct, stone-gray clothing invisible against the mountainside, which was still deep in gloom with the early sun not yet climbing above the peaks. In this camouflage, too, the warriors were aided by the magical energy contained within their weapon tips, the crystals having also been selected for a propensity of sparkling diamond chips, which the witches understood to bring forth a wispy darkness, shrouding and blurring the forms of those carrying the blessed item. Indeed, the crystals chosen to tip the spears had been carefully selected, then blessed by the singing of the witches so that the weapons hummed with the song of Usgar. The rituals had made those magical properties of the crystals accessible to the warriors, ready to unleash devastating powers against any who felt the bite of an Usgar spear.

Untiring, the Usgar raiders flowed down the mountain, guided by the first rays of dawn tickling the far side of the long lake.

Usgar was not a large tribe—the seven villages scattered about the banks of Loch Beag were each more populous, some with more than five times the number of Usgar. But the folk down here lived an easier life. They preferred bargain to battle and floating on the water to running over stony jags up and down and along the mountainside, where one misstep could cost a man his life. To the Usgar, then, the lakemen were soft.

And the folk along the shore of Loch Beag did not have the crystals. They did not have the blessing of the Usgar-righinn, who spoke for Usgar, the Crystal God, whose voice filled Usgar weapons with power and deadly magic. The mere sight of a single Usgar warrior would often send a full hunting party of lakemen running.

To the lakemen, the Usgar were gods, or demons.

Even more than the crystal magic, that perception, one rooted in terror, was the greatest advantage of the war parties, Tay Aillig understood.

Tirelessly, the powerful young man led the warriors down the steep slopes of Fireach Speuer, leaping to lower stones, legs bending expertly to absorb the shock of a ten-foot, even twenty-foot, fall—drops that would have shattered his bones if not for the magic in his spear.

The magic had to flow fluidly, and could only do so with the wielder's full trust in the blessings that had been placed upon the crystal tip of his spear. A veteran of several raids and many hunts, Tay Aillig had that confidence, without the slightest hesitation. Nor did he need to concentrate on the crystalline tip of his spear as so many others, particularly the younger warriors, would. He felt the magic and simply let it flow through him. So his pace continued, even quickened.

He thought of the last image in his mind of Mairen, the woman upon the pyre, being buried under the kindling she would set ablaze. He had noted the telltale white glow about the Usgar-righinn, her magical shield against the fiery bite.

Even as he thought about it, Tay Aillig's hand went to his belt, to feel the stone tucked in the pocket inside the waistline. He had thought of grabbing it back then, at the ceremony. With its magical power, or rather, its ability to defeat magic, he might have stripped that shield from Mairen.

She would have cooked in her own conjured flames!

A smile came to his face. Yes, that would have been enjoyable.

He heard the grunts behind him as the two dozen raiders tried to keep pace, but that only widened Tay Aillig's smile. He had just passed his twentieth year. He basked in the glory of the Coven's song. He had a special understanding of Usgar, of magic. He was invincible.

If the others were not, that was their failing, not his.

He charged ahead to a rounded boulder that he knew to be the top of a rocky outcropping. Hardly slowing, Tay Aillig went over, dropping fifteen feet to the steeply sloped looser dirt in an acrobatic roll.

And he thought of the ceremony, of Mairen who had so often tormented him, and he grabbed at the secret amethyst-crusted sunstone he had tucked away and called upon its power before he even realized his action.

That nearly cost him dearly, he understood, for he was suddenly heavier, bouncing more roughly. He let go of the pocket and he kept rolling, absorbing the shock as he went, hugging close his spear so that the magical green flecks of a stone called malachite would again make him lighter and lessen each impact. He had left the outcropping far behind by the time he was able to stop and regain his footing, that he might properly glance back.

He saw the others coming in a tumbling line, some more gracefully than others, none as smoothly as his own descent. There would be many minor wounds here, he knew, but nothing that should slow his war party while the battle lust coursed through their blood.

Even as Tay Aillig nodded at that thought, though, he heard a cry from the darkness up above, a broken note. Surely it was one of the new warriors, he understood, for the high-pitched shriek sounded like a boy who was barely a man. This was the first war party for four of the raiders, an unusually high number. They were the most likely to die, of course. In the harsh heritage of Usgar, experience had to be earned through the highest of stakes or it was worth nothing at all.

The war party leader blew an angry growl and started back up the slope, following the whispers of several voices, including more than one telling the broken young warrior to be brave and stifle his cries.

When he got to the scene, Tay Aillig waded through the gathered circle of men.

There squirmed the young warrior, Aghmor by name, one leg broken so badly that the bone was sticking out through the skin, one shoulder so far back that it was almost certainly out of its proper joint.

"He was drifting down and he just fell," one man said.

"Hard," said another.

"He forgot the blessing!" the first replied.

Tay Aillig wasn't so certain, but he didn't speak his concern, surely. For that concern was regarding his own action. With his call to the stone, had he left behind a small residual area of countering magic to defeat any blessing?

Perhaps this young man lying before him, bone sticking through the skin of his leg, had been felled by Tay Aillig's action.

The twinge of guilt didn't last, however. The others had come through. Tay Aillig had pressed through the interruption of the magic in his own spear.

This failure was still Aghmor's failure.

Tay Aillig knelt beside Aghmor and tucked a strip of hide deep into Aghmor's mouth, muffling his cries. In the predawn light, the veteran could see lots of blood upon the young one's face, and it seemed like much of it had come from inside of him, and not from superficial cuts.

"Whose spear is strong with warmth?" Tay Aillig asked the others. Though most held the green flecks and the sparkling diamond chips, none of the weapons were identical, with varying hues hidden within each crystal tip, offering magical accents to the blessing of the Coven. Off to the side, a pair of men compared their javelins, nodding, then decided upon the weapon strongest with the warm healing offered by the gray flecks within the crystal, the wedstone. The warrior hustled forward and presented the weapon to Tay Aillig.

The war party leader hugged it close and felt its power, then nodded and gave the gift giver the spear of the broken young Aghmor. He placed the spear strong with the warmth of healing across Aghmor's chest and pulled the young man's arms up to hug it.

"You are very hurt," Tay Aillig said matter-of-factly. "Without this, you will die. With it you may die anyway, if you are not strong enough." He looked up and around a bit and gave a little laugh. "Even if you are strong enough to gather the healing warmth," he added with a wicked smile, "out here, bathed in blood in the morning hours . . . there are hungry wolves and bears, and great cats that will eat you while you still live."

That brought many nods from the men about the broken young warrior.

"Unless you remain strong enough to fight them off," Tay Aillig warned.

Poor Aghmor's eyes opened wide and he shook his head in a desperate plea and began issuing a series of pitiful wails.

Tay Aillig just pressed the spear in tighter, and put his face very close to that of the wounded warrior.

"Are you a boy or a man?" he asked coldly.

Aghmor seemed to relax a bit, his pride forcing him to battle back against the terror.

"The lake is not far," Tay Aillig explained. "We will pass by this place before the sun has dived into the far waters of the west. If you are strong enough to pull the warmth of healing from the blessed spear, you may live, and we will carry you back to the Coven for care. You will know no shame for your fall. If you are strong enough to live and kill a wolf that comes to feast, then perhaps Aghmor will find glory yet this day."

"We cannot leave him," another voice sounded, and the warriors all gasped and Tay Aillig was up to his feet in an instant. He noted the speaker, another of the first-year raiders, and he offered the dark-haired lad a comforting nod as he approached.

"We should bring him back now," the youngster was saying meekly. "Come back another day—"

He ended flat on his back with the wind blasted out of his lungs, compliments of a sudden and powerful kick from Tay Aillig. Before he had even recovered his wits, the impetuous and foolish young man found the tip of a spear hovering a finger's breadth from his eye.

That silenced him, certainly, and when he eased into a more submissive pose, Tay Aillig moved the spear aside, reached down, and yanked the young man to his feet with frightening strength.

Over to the side, Aghmor groaned, and looking that way, Tay Aillig began to appreciate the extent of the unfortunate young warrior's injuries. For Aghmor could hardly hold the spear, let alone find the power to draw any magic from it. Tay Aillig hated the thought of losing a young warrior—the tribe was not large and every able body mattered. But he could see then, particularly when Aghmor began coughing up more blood, that this one would very likely not be alive when they returned.

But perhaps he could find some gain here in this loss, Tay Aillig thought. He turned to the impetuous young man. "What is your name?"

"Brayth."

"The boy of Imrich," someone said.

"Imrich?" Tay Aillig asked, sounding somewhat impressed, for that man had gained a fierce reputation.

Brayth straightened his shoulders and seemed to garner some strength from that recognition of his bloodline.

Aghmor groaned and vomited blood once more.

"The wound is mortal," Tay Aillig told Brayth, and he grabbed the young man's spear and pulled it and Brayth's arm out in front, pointing the weapon and the wielder toward Aghmor. "You do it."

Even in the dim light in the deep shadow of the huddled mountain, Tay Aillig could see the blood drain from the young man's face. All about, warriors gasped, and one began to argue, but was quickly hushed by the others.

"He will lie in pain throughout the day," Tay Aillig said when Brayth hesitated. "Would you let your cowardice cause him that terrible death?"

"Imrich," someone in the back reminded.

Brayth straightened his shoulders again and took up his spear more forcefully as Tay Aillig let go of the shaft. Brayth strode over and flipped the spear, and with only the slightest of hesitation, stabbed it down at poor Aghmor.

Or tried to, for Tay Aillig kicked him again just as he began the killing blow, sending him tumbling aside. Brayth came back to his feet angrily and in clear confusion, and only calmed when others cheered him and called out the name of his father and moved to pat him on the shoulder.

"You would have done it," Tay Aillig said.

"You lead the war party," a confused Brayth replied. "You told me to."

"But Aghmor is your friend, and you would have killed him. What are we without loyalty?"

"I would not see him suffer," the young man stuttered, and Tay Aillig offered again that wicked smile, seeming very pleased at Brayth's obvious discomfort. "You . . . you said he would die," Brayth meekly argued.

Tay Aillig laughed at him, pushed him away, then fell over Aghmor, pressing the healing spear tight against the fallen youth's chest. "Ignore your pain," he whispered harshly into Aghmor's ear. "Defeat your fear. Nothing matters but this blessed weapon. It alone can save you, but only if nothing matters but this blessed weapon."

The war party leader stood back up and spun on his heel. "We go," he told the others, and led them away.

Tay Aillig's dark eyes gleamed as he turned back toward the lake, toward the smoke of the cooking fires of the village directly below. The smoke would be darker soon, and thicker. So much thicker.

And all the villages of Loch Beag would see it and know that the Usgar had come, and they would be afraid. They thought the Usgar godlike.

Tay Aillig felt godlike.

3

THE DARKNESS OF USGAR

"Back for more water?" the old gray-haired man chided Kal when, bucket in hand, he walked past the pair at their usual spot down by the bank.

"Innevah is plump with my child," Kal said in his own defense. "Her feet are swollen. The cold water—"

"Hire one of the young ones!" the old gray-hair said, waving his arm up to the north along the coast, where a group of children splashed by the lakeshore.

"Aye, just give 'em a wiggly minnow to play with and they'll haul your buckets all the day," the other agreed.

But Kal could only smile and shrug. Innevah wanted him to do it, and he understood that this was her way of making him prove to be a worthy partner in this endeavor they had chosen. The water wasn't actually the point of it all; having him go and get it, without complaint, was.

And Kal didn't mind, because he was glad to prove his worth to his wonderful partner. Besides, it was a warm day, the sun high overhead, and he didn't want to stay inside the hut. The cold lake water would be invigorating. He looked to the fishing boats far out on the water and wished he could be there, with Innevah, then reminded himself that the sacrifice this season was worth the prize. They were both young and strong and clever, and their child would be wonderful.

"Catch them a wiggly silver fish now," the gray-haired man said. "Come and throw some bones with us while they take your water to your swollen wife, eh? We've got us a few shells to bet."

"Aye, and we've got some black pearls, and pink," the other teased, holding up a small pouch and shaking it about. "To be sure, you can outplay a couple o' old men."

Kal smiled and shook his head.

"Well, get me some water, too, then!" the old gray-hair grumbled, and he tossed a pail to Kal, who caught it and nodded, glad to oblige.

He started for the water, but had only gone a couple of steps before a scream sounded from the southern end of the village, away from the water. And such a scream it was, different in pitch than anything Kal had ever heard, more primal, more filled with terror, the absolute terror, as if in the moment of death realized.

Kal swung about, noting the youngsters doing likewise, his first thoughts revolving around a snake perhaps—some big ones had been seen recently—or perhaps a bear had wandered too near.

It wasn't until the rumbling intonation of a conch horn sounded that Kal remembered the warning of Talmadge the trader that very morning, and when other horns began to blow, those words seemed suddenly to be a dire reality. He shook his head, trying to deny the obvious. Fasach Crann had sentries out far from the huts, out near the mountain's foothills and along every likely approach to the village. Those guards should have given a more advanced warning! But the scream had come from inside the village perimeter, and the horns blowing now were among the houses.

"To the boats!" the old gray-hair said, stiffly rolling out of his seat and walking stiff-legged toward the shore. "Away all!" he yelled up the beach to the youngsters, who indeed were already sprinting for the small boats tucked up on the sands. They had been taught well, as had all in Fasach Crann, that the conch horns meant one thing and one thing only: Usgar raiders. And when the deamhan gods descended from Fireach Speuer, those who could not fight were taught to simply drop everything and get out onto the water.

Kal spun about, confused, his thoughts climbing all over each other and swirling in a dozen directions, but every one ultimately leading back to Innevah. He glanced at the lake, to see the fishing boats already putting up their square sails, oars already in the water. Too distant, he knew, for it would take a long while for the fleet to get back to shore and the men to coordinate a defense.

The old gray-hair grabbed Kal by the arm. "To the boats!" he yelled in Kal's face, but Kal yanked his arm free and stumbled away from him, shaking his head, at a loss.

He scrambled through the sand, tossing aside the buckets, stumbling and trying to get his feet under him as he charged for his home. On the far side of the village, ahead and to Kal's left, there came a crash as a hut collapsed, and a belch of black smoke and a swirl of sparks lifted into the air.

"Innevah," the man said repeatedly, running with abandon. She could hardly walk on those swollen feet! How could she possibly escape?

By the time he got to his modest hut, which was halfway across the village, more screams filled the air, and smoke rose from a dozen fires. Kal even caught sight of some of the deamhan raiders at one point, though thankfully they didn't seem to notice him!

He threw open the door to his hut, to find the place empty.

Nodding, trying to clear his thoughts, he scrambled back outside and rushed toward a nearby copse of trees, a place he and Innevah had long ago spied out as a refuge in case of an emergency. His focus entirely on that spot, a tangle of brush hiding a hollow under a tree, Kal did not notice the growing commotion to the side or behind. He threw himself headlong to the tangle and pulled aside the blocking branches.

He gasped with relief and nodded when Innevah's face looked back at him.

"You should be on the boats!" she whispered harshly.

"I could not leave you," he said, belly-crawling in. But Innevah stopped him, and when he looked at her with puzzlement, he found her face ashen as she stared past him.

"Oh, *faoin*," Innevah cursed, calling him a fool. "The boats . . ." She shook her head, crestfallen, a woman who knew she was doomed.

Kal glanced back and rolled to the side, seeing a raider rushing his way, a young man, perhaps still a teenager, clutching one of the distinctive crystal-tipped spears of the Usgar, and with a look on his face that surely unnerved the lakeman.

A look of wildness, feral even, beyond fear.

Demonic.

Kal spun and scrambled to his feet, taking up a branch. He shook away his fears, remembering Innevah, remembering his child. He had to find some way to defeat this demon, and quickly, and be on his way if he and his wife were to have any chance of getting to the lake!

Or perhaps he could chase this one off, he thought, and he charged with all the ferocity he could muster, growling even, and waving the branch with abandon.

But the demon calmly held his ground and slapped at the branch with his spear, and after the first exchange, wisps of smoke rose from Kal's weapon, and the crystal-tipped spear, tinged red within, showed licks of flames.

The god-power, Kal silently cursed!

Ahead Kal charged, and the youth would not run, and so Kal understood that he had to get a quick kill. "To the lake!" he called to Innevah. "Go!"

He heard her crawling out of the hollow behind him, and he pressed on with ferocious abandon, driving back the young Usgar raider.

He glanced left as Innevah started to stumble away, and he gasped as she reversed course, yelped, and dived back into the hollow.

Kal should have looked right instead.

For then he would have seen the spear flying for him, and might have fully dodged aside. Still, Kal was a warrior, and a fine one, and as soon as he felt the scrape of the tip just under his ribs, he pivoted gracefully on the heel of his right foot, turning fast. He got gashed badly, but he breathed a tiny sigh of relief, thinking he had avoided complete disaster.

A very short-lived moment of relief, for that spear's demon magic was a bit different than the one the youth before him held, its crystal tip showing a dark gray beneath its sparkling surface. As it sliced through Kal's skin, that magic ignited, a sudden and jolting burst of lightning that had Kal crying out in surprise, replete with a fiery pain that sent him lurching and stumbling to the side.

His teeth chattered and his hair stood on end, and he went many heartbeats without a heartbeat. Still, he might have recovered, and even regained his balance, but the young demon raider before him, with cold and dead eyes, didn't hesitate at all, and used Kal's moments of imbalance to find an opening.

With a growl the Usgar drove his spear past the frantically waving branch and into Kal's chest. This weapon, too, released its magic upon impact, and Kal felt the sudden burst of a fireball within his ribs, beneath his skin, sizzling and searing and dropping him to the dirt with a level of agony he had never before imagined possible.

And the young Usgar followed the thrust and stood over him, holding the spear shaft, its tip still buried into Kal's chest. The demon locked eyes with Kal, and Kal saw clearly the young man's tears.

His tears?

Tears in the eyes of a deamhan god?

But they proved to be merciless tears, cold and full of some anger Kal could not begin to decipher.

The young warrior pressed the crystal spear tip in deeper and ground it about.

Kal fast went beyond pain. His head lolled to the side and he saw Innevah, his dear Innevah, being dragged out of the hollow by another Usgar, then punched hard in the face as she tried to resist.

Kal was beyond comprehension by then, however, his thoughts locked on the reality of the moment of his death. He stared into the yawning darkness.

And it stared back.

Tay Aillig nodded with satisfaction as he watched his raiders leaving Fasach Crann, their backs bent under packs heavily laden with winter supplies.

The war-party leader glanced back as another hut collapsed in flames, and lifted his gaze to the lake, where the boats full of able-bodied villagers still hadn't come ashore to mount a defense, so swift and efficient had the Usgar swarmed the town. Tay Aillig smiled widely at the success, at the pain and humiliation his troupe had inflicted here, at the smoke spreading the warning to all the villages of Loch Beag, the certain reminder of the martial superiority of the mountain tribe. At least five villagers lay dead, another dozen had been wounded and left to writhe in pain—and in humiliation, for their elongated skulls had been etched with the markings of Usgar—the angled crystal of the sacred grove known as Usgar's Horn—as a permanent reminder to them and to their village fellows of their defeat this day.

Another dozen villagers were dragged away with the departing warriors, including a handful of women who would be used to satisfy the excitement of the raiders, then sent back down the mountain in shame, and perhaps impregnated with Usgar seed; an elderly pair who would be sacrificed to Usgar; four children still young enough to be broken of all spirit that they might serve for a time as slaves; and the pregnant woman Tay Aillig had personally dragged out from the hollow under the tree after helping Brayth kill her mate.

Normally the captured children would be viewed as the greatest plunder, for the value of proper, broken slaves could not be underestimated. But even that prize would be overshadowed here by the rarest and most coveted catch of all: the pregnant woman. This one was afforded special treatment in the long march back home. She could not be violated by the warriors as the other women would be, nor abused or injured in any way. Indeed, the strongest men bore her on a stretcher, and gently.

She carried within her the perfect slave, and one that wouldn't be so repulsive to look at, like its long-headed kin.

Tay Aillig led the group at a strong pace right to the foothills of Fireach Speuer, and up to a defensible position atop a high rocky jag, which offered a clear view of the lakeside village below. There they watched for a long while, ensuring no pursuit (though they really didn't expect the weak and cowering lakemen to mount any kind of counterattack), and there the raiders feasted on their booty, the meals of fish and crabs and oysters, and the pleasure of the women captives.

Tay Aillig found Brayth upon one high stone, where the young man had volunteered as a sentry.

"That one is young," the war-party leader said to his novice warrior, indicating one of the captive women, who was really more a girl, barely into her teens.

"She will make a fine slave then."

"No, she is too old," Tay Aillig explained. "She will never stop looking for her home and so will cost too many eyes to keep her from mischief. And she has too much strength to hold her until the next sacrifices." He guided Brayth's eyes to the doomed elderly couple, who would suffice to quiet the Crystal God through the difficult winter season.

"You will enjoy that strength and fire now," Tay Aillig promised, and Brayth stared at him curiously.

"You would have me kill her?"

"We've no reason to kill her. We are warriors, not cowards."

"Then what?"

Tay Aillig directed his attention to the side, where a group of raiders huddled above another captive, four men holding her down, while others took their turn upon her.

"Take her. Enjoy her," Tay Aillig told him. "You have earned your pleasure by spilling the blood of your enemy."

Brayth hesitated and appeared quite scared, which made Tay Aillig smile all the wider. He remembered his first time, returning from a raid much like this one, with all eyes upon him. This offer was not so unlike his order for Brayth to kill Aghmor on their way down the mountain, for it too was a demand to put aside fears and doubts and do as expected.

Brayth licked his lips nervously and glanced about as if cornered, seeming as if he meant to turn and leap from the high rock to his death. It took him many heartbeats to steady himself enough to go, and even then, he walked with steps slow and hesitating. Tay Aillig motioned to some others, and to the frightened young captive girl, and they rushed over, pulled her down, and tore off her clothes.

Tay Aillig nodded as he watched Brayth perform as was expected of the promising young Usgar. The raid leader nodded with satisfaction, thinking that he had shaped a competent young warrior here.

Yet another victory for his successful raid.

Later that same afternoon, with the sun low in the west beyond the lake, they found Aghmor, still alive, surprisingly, and clutching the enchanted spear in desperation.

Tay Aillig bent over him. "So are you brave and powerful to survive your trials?" he asked, soft enough so that only Brayth and a few others nearby could hear.

The gravely wounded man, shivering and sweating, managed a weak nod.

"Or are you so much the coward that you fear death?" Tay Aillig taunted, and he spat on the ground to the side as he rose up and turned away from Aghmor.

A few steps away, Tay Aillig looked back at the weakling, and had to remind himself repeatedly that the numbers of Usgar were simply too few to discard any, no matter how worthless. He also reminded himself that returning with the full war party would only heighten his own glory. On his command, his minions built a second stretcher to carry Aghmor home, while others were dispatched to find a proper place to camp for the night.

The next morning, after a night of indulgent revelry, the Usgar set free the captive women and sent them running down the mountainside. Tay Aillig pulled Brayth to his side and together they followed the departing prisoners to make sure that they would not stop running all the way back to their village. Tay Aillig wasn't about to let any turnabout to follow the war party's ascent, thus revealing the secret trails that allowed easier access to the high passes of the Usgar.

"They are so ugly," Brayth said when Tay Aillig at last informed him that they could turn back to catch up to their fellow raiders.

"But she was pleasurable," Tay Aillig replied. "First time, yes?"

Brayth nodded, a bit embarrassed.

"This is why we live," Tay Aillig told him. "To hunt, to fight, to swive. To be the strongest is to please Usgar."

"To be a man," said Brayth, and Tay Aillig nodded.

"The lakemen are weak. Weak and ugly. They are horned women, nothing more." He pulled Brayth close and looked him straight in the eye, then grabbed him tightly in the crotch to accentuate his point. "And they do not understand the power of that horn. Now, you do."

Brayth winced a bit from the uncomfortable squeeze, but he managed to paint on a determined expression.

4

THE SECRET AND THE SACRED

Talmadge knelt over the body of the man called Huana'kal, studying the corpse's curious wounds. He noted the blackened skin under the right side of Kal's ribs, at the end of a long and jagged scar.

"I've seen a wound akin to this," he told the few villagers beside him.

"Tell us, then, trader," one man replied.

"Poor Kal was struck down by the god of thunder on a clear day!" another asserted.

"A deamhan, not a god!" a third argued, and so a commotion ensued as Fasach Crann villagers argued back and forth.

Talmadge closed his eyes and ignored the bickering, sending his thoughts back to the days of his own village, when he was a boy. A trio of Abellican monks, maddened by the carnage of the rosie plague upon the lands of Honce-the-Bear, had come all the way out to his village and other settlements nearby, crying for repentance from the people, blaming the men and women, one and all, for the plague, which they insisted was a curse from an angry god.

Talmadge let just enough of the conversation about him into his consciousness to note the eerie similarities.

"Gods and demons," he spat, to himself more than any of the others, for he understood that they wouldn't listen to his reasoning anyway. "Such a fine excuse."

No god and no demon had done this, he knew. He thought back to the crazed monks, Abellican brothers with magical gemstones who inflicted great pain upon themselves, telling the flock that they would take unto their own flesh the suffering of the world, to spare all others.

"Idiots," he whispered under his breath.

He looked to the blood and burn on Kal's chest, and pulled the tattered remains of Kal's shirt aside to study the wound. Obviously, a spear had been driven into the man, a wound that surely looked mortal, and when Talmadge inspected more closely, he realized just how undeniably fatal that blow had been. For under the surface, he saw melted flesh and charred bone—it was as if a monk had shoved his hand inside of the man and in there had released the fiery power of a ruby.

How could this be?

Talmadge settled back on his heel, his eyes lifting to the great and tall mountain, lit now with the rays of the late afternoon sun, the red maples and yellow-leafed autumn oaks shining brilliantly. A display worthy of a god, Talmadge thought, but no, these Usgar were not gods.

But they had gemstone magic.

He looked around at the villagers.

"They took Innevah from here!" one man cried from the side, from near a large tree. Talmadge didn't understand the significance. He locked gazes with another man and wanted to explain about the gemstones, and thus, the Usgar.

But he didn't, for what would be the point? Given the obvious advantage of this mountain tribe, perhaps it was better for the folk of Loch Beag to think of them as deamhan gods, and to flee whenever the Usgar drew near.

"They took Innevah, thick with child!" the man cried.

"They took several women," said another.

"And young ones are missing!" another wailed, and indeed, Talmadge could hear the calls of men and women, yelling out for their missing children.

"Will you give chase?" Talmadge asked, secretly, and ashamedly, hoping the answer would be no. The Usgar had gemstone magic and would obliterate any rescue party, he believed, but still, he understood the call of duty here, and so added, sincerely, "I will go and fight beside you."

The Fasach Crann men and women shifted uncomfortably, looking to each other, and none replying, which in and of itself was all the answer Talmadge needed.

He looked back up at the mountain, the darkness creeping up its side now as the sun began to dip behind the western horizon, the beautiful images of shining autumn leaves replaced by a brooding shadow.

They couldn't go in pursuit, Talmadge understood. They would be slaughtered to a man, to a woman.

"It is not so unlike the world I left behind," he quietly mouthed.

"Gather him," said a villager, the old gray-haired man from the beach. "Give the dead to Loch Beag. And now we can rest easy, for there will be no more raids this season."

Talmadge turned on the man at those words, staring at him hard, wanting to remind him that he had come through that very morning with a warning—one this very same gray-hair had ignored. And indeed, a warning the man lying dead before him had ignored.

But again, to what end?

Talmadge merely nodded and rose from the body of the man named Huana'kal.

Long before the warriors returned from the raid, the remaining members of the Usgar tribe had moved the entire village to the sacred winter plateau. This was the secret of Usgar—the secret and the sacred—a private place of warmth and comfort in the midst of winter blizzards and freezing winds atop the towering peak known as Fireach Speuer.

In the summer months, on the lower slopes, the tents were arranged haphazardly, following the whims of each warrior's desire for his morning view, his shelter from the rain, or whatever else he might choose. Up here, though, the Coven organized the layouts. Each of the women made sure that the tents sat in a tight, organized circle, all door flaps facing inward, sheltering each other from the relentless wind.

The day had been bright but was turning gray, a distinctly chill breeze blowing down from the north and carrying heavy clouds. With a potential storm brewing, the efforts to finish the camp increased to a frantic pace, and the child found herself more often underfoot than of any use. She tried to help, but the adults wouldn't even slow down enough to give her instructions, and so the crone either did not notice or did not care when Aoleyn skipped away from the bustle of activity.

Just a few dozen strides from the tent ring grew the only real trees this high on the towering mountain, a brooding, densely packed stand of pines that stood only three times the height of the tallest men, but still created a wall of green.

Aoleyn glanced back before she slipped into the grove; because she was a girl, the place was not forbidden to her. Men were not allowed in here—ever! As far as Aoleyn could tell, this was the only thing for which or from which men were forbidden, whereas the women of Usgar were ordered about without recourse all the time.

Aoleyn had been in this place before, with the crone as her guide. She had never gone deep into the thick copse, just wandered about the boughs of the outermost trees. Now, though, she dared push through the branch tangles, often looking back, expecting that the crone would find her and slap her hard.

It was worth the risk, she decided, for she suddenly realized that she wanted to see the Crystal God. It lived in here. It gave power to the Crystal Maven and the dozen other witches of the Coven. Those who heard the god could make fire and lightning, and float off the ground— little Aoleyn wished that she could float, fly even!

Aoleyn had wondered about this excursion many times during the few days the warriors had been gone, and particularly when the encampment had been reset on the plateau beyond the grove. She wanted to meet the god, and planned to secretly visit Usgar often this winter, even against the wind and snows of a blizzard.

The grove was not large, no more than a couple of acres in all, but it was thick and the trees were not in neat rows, and often overlapped. One could easily get lost in here.

She plowed inward, but then stopped abruptly, in both movement and rebellious mirth, when she realized that she had come to the last line of trees. She bent and twisted, trying to peer through the thick boughs. She could tell that there was a small lea beyond, but couldn't make out more than that, nothing distinct at least. The too-curious child chewed her lip, wondering how to proceed. Women were allowed into the grove, but only the Coven could pass through to Dail Usgar, the meadow of the Crystal God, and even they didn't come often.

But Aoleyn wanted to meet this god and had come too far to simply turn about. She scanned the nearby trees for a proper perch, pushed past the pliable branches, and began to climb.

She realized almost immediately her mistake, though, and knew that the crone would know and that she would get into trouble, for the sap of the sticky trunk got on her hands and in her hair and on her clothes.

Her panic passed quickly, though, for what did it matter? She had barely begun her climb and the sap was already upon her. There was no escaping a whipping at this point, so there was nothing left to lose by continuing.

Up she went, her lithe form barely swaying the supple pine. She pulled herself through tight wedges. She cut her hand at one point, but just pressed it against the trunk, letting the thick sap stem the bleeding. She paid that hand so much heed in the next few climbs that it took her a long time to even realize that she was fully in view of the circular meadow.

And of Usgar, the Crystal God.

It protruded from the ground, an eight-sided obelisk, as tall and thick as the biggest warrior in the tribe, but angled to the side so that its end was no higher than Aoleyn's head, had she been standing before it. Looking upon it, Aoleyn found that comparison—to a man—easy to come by, for the sacred crystal reminded her of a boy, of how a boy was different from a girl.

She hugged the trunk of the pine to secure herself, to protect herself from her own distraction, for the sight of the Crystal God did not disappoint. Nay, it overwhelmed her, filling her with a sense of magic and warmth that made her shiver.

There was life here, and power. Aoleyn thought of the blessed weapons—the magical crystalline tips of the spears—and how they must be children of this god.

The light reflecting off the leaning obelisk teased her with subtle hues. She didn't know the difference between a reflection and an inner glow, of course, but somehow she understood the light to be coming from inside the crystal. When the sun peeked out from behind the heavy clouds, the light at the crystal did not much change. It was the god! She was seeing god! And she saw god then, too, in the glowing crystal tips of the warrior spears.

The breeze blew. Aoleyn closed her eyes and felt the warmth of Usgar, and in that moment, she fully understood why no snows could ever take hold in this meadow, and the sanctuary just beyond. No one could survive out on the high mountain in the winter, except for this blessing.

She could have spent the whole day up there, just basking in the warmth and marveling at the beauteous sight, but the blare of a distant horn alerted her.

The warriors were returning!

Aoleyn scrambled down from her perch and forgot all about the sap that covered the front of her clothing. She moved through the trees with purpose, exiting the copse at exactly the same spot where she had entered, a feat of navigation that would have impressed the crone had she known about it.

She glanced all around, spotting a high rocky outcropping not far to the side, and ran for it, nimbly scrambling across the stones. From her high vantage, the girl could see the entire landscape around her. The winter camp lay below and not far from her perch. Beyond it, the rocky slopes of the mountain rose and dived in a mesmerizing pattern, all the more so because they were partially covered in snow. Directly behind her, sheer cliffs led to the tip of the mountain, and there clouds gathered, warning of an approaching storm—though, by the feel of the air, not a particularly bad one. To Aoleyn's right, a trail wound up steeply to the higher ground, weaving between rows of broken stones and tum-

bled boulders. This led to another important place, Aoleyn remembered, to a hole in the mountain called Craos'a'diad, the Mouth of
God, and she could see that up there, a light snow was already falling.

Aoleyn had seen that hole, so she was told, but her memories of the
place were more based on words the crone kept telling her than anything
direct. There, the tribe fed god so that god would be kind to them.

Yes, the child remembered that part. Remembered the screams.

She dismissed that part of her memory with a shudder, then, as only a
child could, she turned her emotions completely around, and watched
the dance of the snow for a bit, enjoying the whimsical flight of the light
flakes as they made their way from cloud to land. Then she shook off that
distraction as well, and focused on the events below. She wanted to be
the first to actually see the returning war party—she thought she would
be important if she became the herald to announce the return.

Even at her tender age, Aoleyn liked being important.

Almost as soon as she had turned back, the girl noted Tay Aillig
leading his war party through a tumble of boulders not far below.

"Here! Here!" she cried out, loud as she could, and she stood straight
on the high rocks and waved her arms frantically to gain attention,
then pointed to the boulder tumble.

Yes, young Aoleyn felt very important in that moment, with so many
eyes looking up to her for direction, and her crooked little smile nearly
took in her ears. She basked in that pose for a long while, until Tay Aillig and his group came in full view of the camp itself and all attention
turned from her. Then she scrambled back off the high perch and skipped
her way back down to the tents, to watch the procession.

Most of the Usgar talked excitedly, greeting returning friends, taking the heavy packs of bounty that would need to be quickly sorted.
Aoleyn saw the Crystal Maven and her witches rushing about near two
stretchers that had been placed upon the ground, though there were
too many legs moving all about and more than one witch kneeling at
each stretcher for her to see anything important or exciting. She did
understand that someone was badly hurt, though, given Mairen's call
for crystals thick with the gray wedstones, and also from the sheer
volume of the frantic prayers of other witches.

The girl's attention was stolen almost immediately, though, when she saw the slaves, an elderly couple and a group of children no older than her. She glanced around desperately, finally spotted the old crone, and rushed to the woman's side, hugging her leg.

"They're so ugly," she whispered, and the crone laughed.

But even as she heard her words—that same litany of lakemen ugliness so often jeered about the Usgar encampments—Aoleyn had trouble reconciling those words, her words, with her thoughts.

She didn't think the captured children handsome by any means, with their garish elongated skulls, but in her heart, that reality seemed far less important.

For she saw the eyes of the children.

She saw their fear, their very human fear.

She would feel the same, she knew.

The realization of that common bond, some shared sense of humanity that she was too young to understand, shook Aoleyn profoundly.

Finally she looked away, turning her gaze back to the stretchers. She noted the wounded Usgar man and knew him as Aghmor. He wasn't a bad fellow, and she hoped that the witches would be able to help him.

But even that thought proved fleeting when Aoleyn noted the other person lying on a stretcher, a woman from the lake tribe.

"What is wrong with her?" she asked, not expecting an answer.

"She is fat with a lakeman's piglet," the old crone answered, and her tone, despite the derision, made Aoleyn recognize that the crone thought that a good thing.

But Aoleyn hugged the old woman's leg tighter. On that one occasion when Aoleyn had seen Craos'a'diad was because of a pregnant woman whose baby had been born dead. All that woman did after was wail and throw herself about the ground. She wouldn't eat and wouldn't talk. The men decided she was cursed, and so they took her to the chasm and cast her in.

The girl hoped this woman's child would not be born dead. Even though the woman was ugly and scary, Aoleyn did not want to see her cast into the chasm, too.

5

YOU ARE STUPID

The callousness of the Usgar women as they tended the slave jarred Aoleyn's young sensibilities. The ugly long-headed lakewoman was obviously in agony—her screams echoed off the rocks all across the mountainside, but the Usgar attending her seemed more amused than concerned, even mimicking her cries in a mocking way.

"If your foul spawn's ready and you're not, then know we'll be glad to let you die," one witch told her repeatedly.

"We'll cut it out!" another promised, and seemed happy to do so.

Aoleyn almost cried out aloud at that, but wisely bit back her sound. She wasn't supposed to be here up in the pines overlooking a small clearing to the side of the circular meadow that held the crystalline manifestation of Usgar. She knew that she'd get whipped hard if she was caught, but she couldn't resist. The cries had pulled her to this place. She had to see.

And from her vantage point, she did see, indeed, all of it, and heard all of it, and she didn't want to anymore, but she simply could not tear herself away from the spectacle. Her black eyes rimmed with tears and she felt a sense of helplessness and sorrow that overwhelmed her. She had lost her own mother soon after her birth, she had been told, though the circumstances had never been explicitly explained to her. Looking at the long-headed lakewoman, at the obvious agony and the blood—so much blood!—Aoleyn figured the death of her mother must have had something to do with this painful process!

Often had the growing young girl wondered about her lost mother. She had never known her father, either, and no one would speak of him. She didn't even know their names!

And now she saw, and heard the screams, and feared that her mother had died in agony.

She held there, clutching the tree trunk, staring at the bloody gash, then up to the slave woman's face, which was flushed red, so red, as she gritted and groaned and cried out that she could not do this.

Aoleyn winced when a witch slapped the slave hard across the face, then grabbed her by the hair and yanked her elongated skull back so they could lock stares.

"Push, you fool. For all your worthless life," the witch demanded. "Push, or I will cut it out of you!"

The level of cruelty in this most private of moments surely startled Aoleyn. She was but a child, but she could sense the sheer wrongness of it! Aoleyn knew that the women could be cruel—the crone's bony hand had stung her enough times!—but this was different. This was a level of contempt and disgust, woman to woman, that Aoleyn had never considered before.

She tried to block out the uncomfortable reality and focus on the event at hand, and just in time, for she witnessed then the birth of a baby, a young boy, a new slave, and then saw, too, all the blood and gore that came with it.

One of the women cleaned the baby off and held him aloft for the others to see, and from her perch, Aoleyn got a good view. The child's head had a bit of a cone, perhaps, but nothing like the ugly mother.

Perhaps the skull would grow, the girl mused, and she shook her head in denial of the notion that this little baby was cute, reminding herself that he would grow into one of the ugly lakemen, with a long and sloping forehead that allowed his hair to hang loosely far behind his ears and shoulders. Like his mother. Of all the strange head shapes that came from the various tribes, Aoleyn thought this version, the single long lump stretching the head back and up, to be the worst.

The women began cleaning up the area then, and roughly tossed the baby down upon the exhausted mother.

Aoleyn slipped down from the tree, thinking it wise to be long gone from the scene.

Many weeks later, the winter snows had lessened and the wind carried less bite. The Usgar began talking of returning to the summer encampment with great excitement evident in every syllable. The raid had brought enough food to get them through the difficult winter, but they were anxious to hunt again, and to enjoy the taste of fresh meat and juicy berries and pears. Down below on the lower slopes, the snow was letting go its wintry grip.

And the Usgar were anxious to have a little room apart from each other, Aoleyn realized. Never before had she felt their winter encampment to be so cramped, but now, a year older and a year less dependent upon the others, she had begun to truly appreciate the boundaries between herself and those around her. Truly, the almost-four-year-old was coming to enjoy her time alone, and such moments were very rare up here, shockingly so! To venture away from the camp, a place warmed by the Crystal God, was to walk into the winter wind of the towering Fireach Speuer, and it took no time at all to recognize that the wind up here hurt! Even the trees could not grow up here, except around the magical lea. And beyond the camp, the snow lay as deep as those trees of the sacred grove were tall!

It wouldn't take the wind long to freeze the blood solid in a wanderer's limbs, or for the stinging snow carried on it to harden and kill the skin so that it cracked apart and felt as if it were on fire. And so the whole of the tribe, more than two hundred strong, had to exist in the small area about the grove, and the narrow pathways of magical warmth up to the Mouth of God—and half of those areas were denied to all but the witches or, in some instances, the warriors and older and venerated men.

The trail, called th'Way, up from the encampment to the Mouth of God, contained a long channel of towering, broken stones that groaned and moaned loudly and continually in the ceaseless wind. The angles of the obelisks as they had rooted in the ground had created a series of shallow, natural caves. They weren't comfortable shelters, weren't very protective from the wind or the blowing snow, and the stones sometimes grew so cold that they burned to the touch. Still, and perhaps because of this, these many natural alcoves served the tribe well as winter cells for the uamhas.

And so Aoleyn had to go to this area often, for many of her menial tasks involved bringing food and water to the ugly slaves. Every morning, the crone would indicate a cave by which side of the channel it was on and the number along the line, and Aoleyn would gather a sack of food, usually scraps from the previous night's meal, and a small jug of water, and would run to her appointed delivery.

She had always before been directed to the small caves along the right-hand stone wall of the channel, barely alcoves, where the older girls and women were kept—they each had their own chamber, and there were chained.

Often, though, when Aoleyn found them in the morning, the slaves were not alone. Often an Usgar man was there, disheveled and sometimes even still asleep.

But never did she find the slave girls asleep. Usually she found them sitting and folded tightly, huddled and rocking, sometimes crying, often bruised. Whenever one looked up to see her, Aoleyn was struck by the look in her eyes. Hollow, vacant, absent, even, as if there was no one really there anymore behind the glazed and hopeless façade.

A look that scared the child, who wasn't old enough to understand the reason.

"Will I see the old man with the giant wrinkled head?" Aoleyn asked one morning when the crone had unexpectedly instructed her to take the largest basket of food, and told her that this day, she would go to the central cave on the left-hand wall. That was the largest cave in the channel, Aoleyn knew, where all the child slaves were kept.

"No, child, he is gone," the crone said.

Aoleyn looked at her curiously.

"His woman, too," the old woman said with a look that Aoleyn couldn't quite place, though it seemed rather gleeful.

"The Crystal God needs to eat, child," the old crone said with a cackle, seeming very pleased with herself. "Go, go," she added, shooing Aoleyn away, then lifting her hand as if she meant to swat the little girl, which sent Aoleyn running.

Despite the unsettling words of the crone, Aoleyn rushed up the trail toward the rocky channel with a spring in her step, anxious to see the children her own age, perhaps even the baby whose birth she had witnessed. It wasn't a conscious thought, but she was also glad that she would not have to go to the women slaves this morning.

Up the channel, she turned through a boulder tumble and moved around a very large slab of stone to the tall triangular entrance to the main uamhas cave. She noted immediately that she wasn't the only Usgar there, for a pair of guards, strong warriors, stood watch just inside the large cave's entrance.

They smiled at Aoleyn as she entered.

"Be quick, little one," a warrior told her.

As soon as she got fully through the entrance, Aoleyn knew that she hadn't needed the prompt, for the place smelled awful, with piles of poop lying all about. The slave children ran from her, even the boys who were twice her age and size, and none dared look her in the eye for more than a moment before shying and whimpering and scrambling aside.

Even in the dim light, Aoleyn could see their open sores. Somewhere in the back darkness of the place, she heard another young slave vomiting and crying.

She felt as if the walls were closing in on her, as if the stones themselves were alive, and hungry. She rushed for the central stone and dumped her basket upon it, as she had been instructed, and turned to flee as fast as her little legs would carry her.

But amidst the cries and the retching sounds, the many coughs and the whistling of the mountain wind through the cracks in the stones, Aoleyn heard a different sound: a voice, comforting and steady, and in the cadence of a litany or one of the witches' spells.

She veered to the side as she made her way back to the exit, avoiding the rush of half-starved slaves as they tried to get to the feeding stone.

Aoleyn glanced at the Usgar guards, who were chatting and paying her no heed. She considered the earlier warning, but still moved to the side, to the darkness, inching her way around an outcropping of stone in the cave wall.

She saw the new mother, sitting with her back to Aoleyn and rocking slowly. The woman was chanting, Aoleyn heard—and to her baby, Aoleyn saw as she shifted.

"You are stupid. Too stupid to talk."

The words shocked Aoleyn and left her with a foul taste in her mouth. How horrible! No wonder the lakemen were such pitiful creatures, she thought, if their mothers talked to them so from the time of their birth!

The woman seemed not to notice her and continued her chant, or lecture, or admonishment, or whatever it might be, but Aoleyn's attention was fully stolen then as the mother shifted again, this time bringing the baby's head under a single shaft of light that sliced in from a hole in the natural ceiling.

Little Aoleyn opened wide her eyes and wide her mouth and fell back in surprise. The baby's head wasn't stretched, not even the little bit she had seen when she had witnessed his birth. He looked perfectly normal, and perfectly pretty, with his soft light hair and, when the light hit him just right, a pair of sparkling eyes the color of the waters of Loch Beag on a bright summer's day.

The little girl fell back around the outcropping and leaned heavily on the wall, trying to make sense of it. Was this the same child? Was it an Usgar child, substituted in for the slave to wet-nurse?

But no, none of the tribe's women had given birth in the last year.

She started back around for another look, but stopped short when a guard called out to her.

"Out!" he demanded. "When the uamhas are done eating the food, know that they'll start eating your own flesh, silly girl!"

Aoleyn left the cave in a dead run, scrambling back to the main channel and down to the village.

The seasons passed quickly for the growing Aoleyn, because even in the boring routines of the day, the spirited young girl found new adventures and new paths to wander, both physically and mentally. Her chores regarding the slaves had lessened these last few years, and she had been given much more freedom to roam, to move about the camp and out of the camp, to learn some of the ways of Fireach Speuer on her own. In many of those wandering moments, Aoleyn would find herself watching the uamhas. Not so much over the winters, where she preferred to sneak into the grove near the physical incarnation of Usgar, and because the slave caves were quite horrible through those months, but in the warmer months and the summer encampment, the uamhas inhabited a thick pine grove, with branches bending low to form protective natural chambers. Here, the uamhas could go out instead of simply filling their freezing lair with urine and feces.

Watching the uamhas women fascinated Aoleyn. They were the only adults among the slaves and their communal mothering of the younger uamhas touched Aoleyn deeply. Never once did she see one strike a child, and most of the contact came in the form of hugs. Still, most fascinating of all to the girl was the slave boy three years her junior, one whose head was not misshapen. The Usgar guards called him Thump—even the uamhas called him that—and none of it was in an affectionate way. His movements were always simple, his behavior dull, and in all the times Aoleyn watched him from afar, she never saw him speaking.

His mother had kept him, though, even though very early on, she had known he was quite stupid. Even thinking of that moment in the slave caves high up on the mountain made Aoleyn wince. That and his birth were her earliest memories, the only two from that year that she really remembered at all.

For all her curiosity, though, Aoleyn could only give the uamhas a passing thought. Much of her time out of the encampment was spent exploring the mountainside and gathering food or herbs, and she thought it would not be a good thing to steal the berries near to the slave quarters, for those were likely the best food the poor folk would get.

During these years, too, Aoleyn took great care to never fail at the tasks the old crone gave to her, even when her curious eye took her far afield. Her successes became a source of pride and also a source of mutual endearment between her and the old woman.

Indeed, as the years passed, Aoleyn came to suspect that the crone even appreciated her daydreaming side adventures—on one winter's day in her eighth year, Aoleyn became convinced that the crone had seen her in the grove, up in the tree overlooking the Crystal God. That was against Coven rules and should have brought a stern punishment to Aoleyn, but the crone had said nothing, had merely smiled when next they were together. In fact, only a few days after that incident, the crone brought to Aoleyn a crystalline spear tip and held it out for her to take it.

She did, with trembling fingers, wondering if this was some punishment. Her trepidation couldn't last, however, for in that magical moment, trembling fingers closing tight over the blessed weapon barb, Aoleyn had come to understand why the Crystal God was so revered, even beyond the wintry warmth it offered. She could feel the power within the spear tip, manifesting itself in varying ways. She felt warmth, and a deeper hint of stinging heat, like she could thrust it within a pile of branches and set it ablaze. Similarly, she felt like she could float off the ground, and suddenly she wanted to do that, and oh, wouldn't it be wondrous?

She only held the spear tip for a few glorious and inspiring heartbeats before the old woman yanked it away. "Someday you will know," the crone promised.

"When?" the eager girl asked then, and day after day from then on. Even at her tender age, Aoleyn knew that there was something special to be found here with the magic of Usgar, something otherworldly and profound, something beyond her mortal experience. She didn't know how to express it, didn't understand the significance of it, and certainly knew no way to comprehend the deep passions for which the Coven led the tribe in service to Usgar.

But she knew that there was something . . . something powerful and profound.

"Someday" became her litany as the seasons changed and the Usgar continued their traditions, moving their camp every spring and autumn, chasing the rhythms of the great mountain. Aoleyn found that many of her chores once again involved the slaves as she passed her tenth birthday, mostly running food to their caves or the grove of pines near the summer encampment, and never involving any lengthy stays or interactions. Indeed, she had been warned in no uncertain terms not to interact with them any more than necessary.

But, as with everything about her, Aoleyn did observe the uamhas at length, and as closely as she could. It seemed to her that the faces changed as the years went on, mostly with the few boys. Aoleyn couldn't be sure, though, because these ugly people of the lake all looked alike to her (other than the varying grotesque skull shapes). Still, she seemed to recall that there had once been boys bigger and older than she, and now the oldest of them seemed about her age now, and only one was bigger.

Two things had remained constant with the slaves, though: the mother and her son, the one Aoleyn had watched being born those years before. The one whose head was not elongated—was still not elongated!—which confused Aoleyn more than a little. She had asked the crone about it, had even put forth her theory that because he was born on the mountain, the Crystal God had prevented him from being ugly.

The crone had laughed and told her she was right, but Aoleyn knew that the old woman was lying to her, or at least, that she was not divulging the whole truth of the matter.

Still, the mystery remained, and Aoleyn took special notice of the young slave boy whenever she spotted him at his chores. He never talked to the others, she noted, and rarely lifted his gaze from the ground unless his task at hand forced him to look up.

Aoleyn remembered vividly the mother's words to this boy.

She felt bad for him, because he was stupid.

But at least he wasn't ugly.

Things began to change again for Aoleyn as the summer of 847 began to wane. She had just passed her fourteenth birthday, and was no longer a child.

"My time with you is short," the crone explained one hot morning, completely without warning. "You will soon become a woman. You may even one day find a place in the Coven—such a journey has been whispered about you."

Aoleyn held her breath, her sadness at thinking that this old woman would no longer be overseeing her washed away at the mere thought that she might get to handle those magical crystals on a daily basis.

"When?" she asked.

"When, what?"

"When will I join—?"

"Silly girl, that has not yet been determined," the crone replied. "Not the time, nor even that you will. You do not join the Coven, you are brought into the Coven, but only if there is room and only if you are the worthiest. There can only be thirteen dancing in the magical circle. There are thirteen now, and most are still young and quite powerful, even Mairen."

"How, then? You must tell me."

"I must do no such thing. There is no answer, nor would it be my place to tell you even if there was an answer!"

Aoleyn huffed a sigh of frustration.

"Child, the sun is warm before you," the crone said, and offered a common blessing in the old tongue, a hope that the sun would be bright and warm. "*Grian dearsach's'blath.* There are only three other Usgar girls around your age, and none have your wit or the heart you found for the blessed weapon crystal you once held."

Then it was a test, Aoleyn thought, but did not say. She remembered when the crone had given her that spear tip, and now suspected that all the girls were handed one to touch and feel in their hands and in their heart as they neared the change to becoming young women.

"Perhaps you will be called to the Coven young—some are," the crone went on. "Perhaps you will be thrice your present age and will have birthed several children before you are called. Perhaps you will die before the opportunity is given. We cannot know." She reached up and gently stroked Aoleyn's thick raven-black hair. "But the sun is warm before you. I have seen the eyes of the warriors upon you." Now it was the crone's turn to sigh, and it seemed to Aoleyn to be an exhibition of sympathy.

"You are not tall," she explained, "nor will you be. Such a small thing! Your hair and eyes too dark, your body too thick with muscles and curves, perhaps."

Aoleyn crinkled her face in surprise. She knew that she didn't much look like most of the other women of Usgar, who stood tall and very lean, with brighter hair and eyes, but she hadn't really given it much thought to that point. What did it matter, after all?

"Most warriors want larger wives, that their children will be big and strong," the crone explained.

"I am strong!" Aoleyn protested. It wasn't that she wanted a warrior to marry her, but she wasn't much enjoying these demeaning words!

"I know you are, child," the crone replied, quite condescendingly. "And you might be strong in the crystal—I sense that in you—and so you will perhaps find a place in the Coven. If that happens, a great warrior will desire you as a wife, and so your place in the tribe will be one of rank in any case."

Aoleyn resisted the urge to shout at the crone for even saying such a ridiculous thing. Her place in the tribe would be determined by the man who decided that she was worthy to mother his children?

She started to question, trying hard to be polite. "But—"

The crone held up her hand. "Enough."

"But—"

"You have work to do," the crone interrupted in a tone of finality.

"I have not yet given you over to your next teacher. Do not end our time together wickedly."

Aoleyn wisely nodded and went back to her chores.

"That is Egard, Tay Aillig's nephew," Mairen said to the crone and another woman, middle-aged, standing beside her, the three watching some children, including Aoleyn, fighting from a ridge not far away. It had only been a few days since the crone's serious discussion with the fourteen-year-old Aoleyn, and here the girl was, off her duties and focus.

"I warned you," said the crone, and the third woman snickered and shook her head.

"She's her mother's spirit," Mairen remarked.

The third woman, Seonagh by name, nodded her head and looked on with a mixture of emotions. It pleased her to see Aoleyn standing up to Egard and two other boys—she had knocked one down hard and had Egard up on his toes by taking a handful of his balls with a mighty twist. She hadn't backed down at all from the three, and would send them running!

But she had done so for a reason that could not sit well with Seonagh. Egard and his friends were bullying a slave boy, the simpleton. Aoleyn had come to his rescue.

Soon to retire from the Coven, Seonagh had a special interest in this one.

"That spirit got Elara killed," Usgar-righinn Mairen warned, and walked away. "Aoleyn will be yours to teach from morning of the spring equinox. Break that spirit."

"As you command."

"And teach the idiot girl the difference between human and uamhas!" Mairen insisted. "She'll get herself thrown into Craos'a'diad with such foolishness! For the sake of a slave!"

Seonagh didn't watch Mairen go, but kept staring at Aoleyn, who was still facing the nephew of mighty Tay Aillig. The girl was possessed of a tender heart, clearly, but for a slave? Seonagh sighed, remembering another so much like that. And not just emotionally. The black eyes, the black hair, small of stature but packing a mighty wallop, like there was simply too much fight within her tiny frame. Aye, another so much like Aoleyn, full of fire and fight and so willing to bend the rules.

So full of spirit.

Until that spirit had gotten her shattered by the demon fossa.

Aoleyn was so much like her.

So much like Seonagh's dead sister.

6

MATINEE

"A full month?" the huge, shaggy man said, shaking his head and grinning his near-toothless smile.

"Two if I tarry," Talmadge replied.

"All the way to the mountains? Mountains in the west?"

"Mountains you cannot see from here," said Talmadge. "I'll leave about midsummer's day, but I'll be in good fortune to get to the lower mountain trails before the end of Octenbrough."

That brought a snort and a head shake. "A month and a half if you're lucky?"

Talmadge shrugged.

"Mountains as tall as those splitting Vanguard from Alpinador?" the large man asked.

Again, Talmadge shrugged. "I've never been to those, nor to Vanguard, nor even over the mountains that mark the rim of the Wilderlands. But those mountains are as far to the east from here as I am walking west."

The big man chuckled and looked about the gigantic tent of the Matinee, the yearly spring gathering of the women and men who roamed the western wilds, hunting and trading, and here trading stories of the long winter, speaking rumors of those who weren't there, or of those who had gone back to the east to more civilized lands, or of those who had passed on from this life. He pointed to one handsome and sturdy young woman, nodded his head, and pointed to Talmadge.

"You should be taking that one along for company," he said.

"I take no one for company." Talmadge's face turned stern as he said that. In the eight years since the Badger incident, he had steadfastly refused any requests to accompany him on his now-fabled annual and arduous footslog.

"Better 'n curlin' up with a bear!" the shaggy man wheezed.

Talmadge lifted his cup of foamy ale and gave a nod, even though he had no intention of making any exceptions, man or woman. He'd have enough of the company of his peers over the next couple of months, roaming the trails, hunting, trading and bartering, collecting trinkets he thought might be of interest to the lakemen of Loch Beag, a market that was exclusively his own to exploit. The other nomadic traders of the frontier couldn't get enough of the pearls Talmadge brought back from the tribes. Many would pocket the pearls they had traded for this very week at Matinee and rush to the east, to the outskirts of Honce-the-Bear, and there profit handsomely.

The shaggy trader downed his ale and stumbled toward the kegs for some more, and Talmadge was glad to be rid of him, and of the stench of his breath. He glanced again at the woman the big man had indicated, and lifted his mug in toast as she met his gaze. He wouldn't take her with him—and she probably wouldn't want to go, for few would and most thought Talmadge crazy for making the dangerous trek year after year.

But he wasn't leaving before midsummer, and perhaps a bit of womanly company would do him good. She certainly didn't seem put off by his apparent interest, so perhaps it was time to make that interest more obvious.

"Khotai Tsentsen," Talmadge echoed. "That is an interesting name."

"Perhaps I am an interesting woman," Khotai replied with a grin.

Talmadge nodded, not about to disagree. Khotai Tsentsen was taller than most of the men at Matinee, and there was nothing scrawny about her arms and shoulders, her muscles solid and imposing beyond the limits of her sleeveless, and quite revealing, vest. Her long hair was dark, her small eyes dark, her face round and flat, and strangely inviting. Talmadge had never seen anyone who looked quite like her, and he was sure she had never before been at Matinee in those weeks he had attended the festival.

This woman, he would not have forgotten.

"How long have you been hunting the frontier?" he asked.

"I'm not, really," she replied, placing her forearms on the back of a chair and leaning forward toward Talmadge. "I only come to Matinee, to see what I can bring back to my village."

Talmadge cocked his head, intrigued.

"Beyond the southern mountains, in the foothills on the south face," she explained.

"The steppes?"

"To-gai, yes."

"You are To-gai-ru?" Talmadge asked, trying unsuccessfully to hide his surprise. There were some To-gai-ru, the famed and ferocious horsemen of the steppes, at Matinee year after year, but Talmadge hadn't considered that. Now that Khotai had mentioned it, though, he could see the similarities, particularly in the woman's ruddy coloring and the shape of her face.

"A bit," she answered. "My father is. My mother is half of Behren and half of Alpinador."

"What?" Talmadge blurted before he could find the sense to hold his tongue, and he silently cursed those last two mugs of ale as perhaps two too many.

But Khotai laughed happily, obviously taking no offense. "A strange mix, aye," she said. "My grandfather was a pirate—he probably still is!"

"So you hail from the frozen north, the eastern deserts, and the southern steppes, yet speak the language of the central kingdom of Honce-the-Bear as well as I?"

"All points blended into the middle?" she asked, and Talmadge laughed and lifted his mug, but only took a sip. He didn't want to be especially drunk right now.

"I speak To-gai-ru," she said, and translated it to, "*Hind hoc* Vinyar. And Behrenese, *shon-ton hais* Seeah." She narrowed her eyes, painted on a wicked little grin, and lowered her voice to add, "*Brid bol dah*, Alpinadoran.

"*Jaggar til'din sang*," she said in a husky voice, and though Talmadge spoke not a word of the barbarian language, and so did not understand, with her inflection and suggestive body language, he surely understood her meaning!

Before he could reconsider, he brought his ale to his lips and swallowed the whole of it in one great gulp.

He was fumbling in his thoughts for how he might accept the invitation, if that's what it was, and he was pretty certain that it was, when a cry erupted over at the far side of the gigantic tent.

"Redshanks!" more than one, more than ten, voices raised.

Both Talmadge and Khotai turned about to see the man, and both couldn't help but smile. Redshanks was known, by name at least, to everyone on the frontier, with tall tales of his godlike exploits growing taller at every Matinee. He had lived with bears, danced with wolves, worn living leopards as scarves, sucked the poison out of a mountain viper's fangs, dulled the hats of powries, castrated giants with his teeth, caught lightning and thrown it back and yelled louder than the thunder for good measure!

He could outspit, outfight, outlaugh, outsing, outdance, outrun, out-climb, outswim, outhunt, outfish, and outswive any man or woman alive, and those were his least achievements.

He came into the big tent dancing a quick-legged jig, wearing his trademark kilt and bright red knee-stockings, to match his red beret—a powrie's own bloody cap, no less! All the people nearest rushed to share their flagons with him, wanting the honor of having Redshanks himself drinking from their cups.

Talmadge watched it all with a widening grin as Redshanks the legend took control of the festivities in the great tent.

"You know him?" Khotai asked, jarring the lanky frontiersman from the spectacle.

"Redshanks? No. I've seen him a couple of times, years ago, but never more than from afar."

"He's not been to Matinee in several years," said Khotai. "But he's been about the mountains in the south." She turned a sly eye to Talmadge. "Would you like to meet him?"

"You know him?"

"Very well," she replied, and in a way that brought a twinge of jealousy to Talmadge, surprising him.

As if to prove her point, Redshanks came bounding over then. He took Khotai by the arm and swung her about, the two launching into a spinning and dipping dance as smoothly as if they'd been practicing together for years.

The crowd cheered and took up a song, and by the time the couple had finished, Khotai's forehead was wet with perspiration. The much older Redshanks, though, seemed barely winded.

After the bows and final cheers, Khotai wouldn't let go of the man's hand, and dragged him over to Talmadge.

"My old friend, this is . . ." She paused and looked at the lanky frontiersman curiously.

"Talmadge," Talmadge blurted, realizing that he hadn't yet gotten around to telling Khotai his name.

"He's to blame for the—" Khotai started.

"The pearls," Redshanks said. "Aye, the pearls!"

Talmadge could hardly catch his breath, overwhelmed that this legend knew anything at all about him.

"I'm off for a drink," said Khotai.

"Make it three, then," Redshanks bade her. "Tell 'em one's for me and get yourself a better price!"

He turned right back to Talmadge. "Your pearls have found their way along the roads to Honce," he said.

"Forgive my confusion, sir, but I don't remember ever trading them with you, or anything with you."

"They find their way to my purse anyway," Redshanks explained, "from them who're not going far enough to the east to make good use of the things. Too few folk in the Wilderlands to put so many of the gems in there. So I get 'em, and cheap, but hey, I'm not selling them cheap in Palmaris and Ursal!"

Talmadge's eyes sparkled. Palmaris and Ursal, the two largest cities in the kingdom of Honce-the-Bear, with more people in either than he had ever seen in his life, likely!

"Where're you from, Mister Talmadge?"

"You wouldn't know it."

"Try me."

Talmadge had to spend a moment composing himself. His former home was not a name he often spoke, nor even recalled, for with it always came the pain of watching his family wither and die.

"It was called Westhaven," he said somberly.

Redshanks seemed to deflate a bit, and issued an audible sigh. "The rosie plague," he said quietly.

Talmadge stared at him, caught by surprise. Westhaven was little more than a tiny hamlet on the western edge of the westernmost forest of the Wilderlands. In his childhood and early teenage years living there, Talmadge had seen no more than a handful of visitors, if that.

He gave a slight nod.

"You're one o' the few from that doomed place still living, would be my guess," said Redshanks.

Talmadge nodded again, and was glad when Khotai returned with the three flagons. She handed them out and led a toast.

"You must have been but a boy," Redshanks remarked.

"A very young man," Talmadge answered to the old frontiersman's nod.

"What?" asked Khotai.

"You've been out here ever since?"

"Just a few months longer than my time in Westhaven," Talmadge replied.

"What?" Khotai asked again.

"Wasn't a choice, then, but just the way you walked," said Redshanks.

Talmadge nodded and Khotai shied back a bit and quieted—no doubt from the somber look on his face, Talmadge thought.

"Do you miss it?"

He kept nodding.

"I'll be going back that way when this damned party's over," Redshanks said. "Road's wide enough for two." He paused and offered a wide smile at Khotai. "For three, even."

Talmadge shook his head.

"You can, you know," said Redshanks. "The plague's long gone now—gone a decade and more. And there's so much fightin' and dyin' over in Honce that none're bothering to look to the western lands. Things're troubled in Ursal in God's Year 847, aye, and troubled times are profitable times for a young man with good wits."

"How would you know my wits?"

"Still alive, ain't you? Aye, alive and finding your way to Fireach Speuer, and not many can do that and come back, eh?"

Talmadge's jaw drooped open in surprise. How could he know that detail?

"You think old Redshanks hadn't got himself a few of those pearls on his own?" Redshanks answered before Talmadge could ask. The older man—and he had to be at least sixty, Talmadge thought, and maybe closer to eighty—laughed. "I knew the eight tribes before you knew how to open your eyes! Of course, there were eleven tribes then, but we both know the dangers there, eh?"

Talmadge nodded.

Across the room, someone called out for a Redshanks dance.

"Think about it," Redshanks offered, and he gave a slight bow to Talmadge and moved off to greet some other old acquaintances.

The unexpected honor he had just been paid, along with the startling information, had Talmadge feeling as if a slight breeze would knock him to the floor. He closed his eyes and tried to replay that surreal conversation. He didn't have to think about Redshanks's offer, though, for returning to the east wasn't a new proposition to him. In the year after the death of Badger, Talmadge had learned that Honce-the-Bear had become peaceful and prosperous and by all accounts civilized under the guidance of good King Danube and good Queen Jilseponie. Certainly that would have been the perfect time for Talmadge to go home, or to find a new home in the easier lands to the east.

But Talmadge wasn't out here in the dangerous wilds because of any crime that had gotten him chased out, like many of those around him, but because he felt pressed in by large gatherings of people. Even here in Matinee, he was pushing his emotional limits, and so couldn't wait to be back on the trail.

"So where are you going, then?" Khotai asked, drawing him from his contemplations.

"What?" he replied, but then added, "To the west, as soon as I've done some trading, that I can gather supplies and goods."

"Alone?"

Talmadge started to respond, but the tone of her voice stopped him, sounding very much as if she was offering to go along. Or maybe not quite that, but surely there was a hint in there, as in her eyes as she stared into his, as in her inviting smile.

"What about him?" Talmadge asked, regretting the jealous question as soon as the words slipped past his lips.

"Who? Redshanks?" Khotai said with a lighthearted laugh, and she turned to regard the man.

"You two seemed quite friendly."

"He's a bit old, but I'd be a liar if I told you I wasn't ever interested."

"Then why not?"

Khotai laughed again. "Redshanks isn't interested in ladies beyond dancing," she answered.

Talmadge's face twisted with confusion and surprise. "But his reputation . . ."

"Mostly earned and mostly true," Khotai said. "Mostly."

Talmadge drank his ale in one great gulp. He simply couldn't help it.

"I wouldn't mind a few more dances," Khotai offered.

"I . . . I don't . . ."

"Oh by the truth of the winter wind you do!" she said, and grabbed his hand and dragged him out for a twirl, and before Talmadge could pull away, the room erupted in song once more, led, loudest of all (of course), by Redshanks, who did indeed have a marvelous singing voice, to no one's surprise.

Truly, it was the best Matinee Talmadge had ever enjoyed, and over the next few weeks, he got to know Khotai very well, and realized that the initial promise of, and attraction to, the woman was nothing compared to the truth of her.

Still, when he set out for the west on midsummer's day, he walked alone.

Bits of the thick rope he had used to hang Badger from the tree were still there, he knew, and he'd see that grim reminder when he passed— and could probably even find the bones of the man below if he decided to look.

Even though he had come to yearn for this unusual and formidable woman who lived in To-gai, Talmadge wanted more to keep the winds of Loch Beag separate and solitary, his personal refuge from all the ugliness of the "civilized" world.

7

HUNT

"I know what you plan," Innevah said, sweeping through some tangled branches to find a young couple huddled in a pine tree-cave in the slave barracks. The two stared at her wide-eyed. These two, a young woman of fifteen years and a boy nearing manhood, had been slaves to the Usgar longer than the eight years of Innevah's indenture. They were not from Innevah's village, evidenced by the double-humped shape of their heads, the wrapping practice more common in the westernmost village of Car Seileach and in the easternmost settlement of Sellad Tulach.

The boy held up his hands helplessly, his expression quite panicked, but the young woman merely smiled disarmingly. "What we plan?" she asked.

"You are running," Innevah flatly stated.

"That would be foolish," said the young woman, as the boy issued a small whimper. "Where would we go?"

Innevah sighed and looked behind her, even poked her head up and out from the overlapping branches to ensure that no one else was about.

"I do not blame you. I'll not dissuade you," she said when she came fully into the natural chamber once more. She looked at the young woman with deep sympathy and said, "You were visited."

The woman's face twitched—truly she seemed just a frightened girl at that moment—and she seemed to be holding back tears.

"We are not running," the boy blurted. "We're not that stupid! Only your own son is that—"

"Shh!" the young woman chided, slugging him on the back of his shoulder.

"I do not blame you," Innevah said again, calmly and evenly. She wasn't upset that the boy thought Thump stupid, of course. She could only hope the Usgar believed it as well, for that ruse was her dear child's only chance to survive!

"And I will help," Innevah promised.

"You wish to come?" the boy said, his tone somewhere between terrified and hopeful.

Innevah laughed sadly and shook her head. "I am visited every day and every night," she explained. "You'd not get much of a lead on our captors were I to go." She looked at the young woman, the girl, with deepest sympathy at the reminder that this one, too, would soon enough suffer such a fate as Innevah. Only one warrior had taken this young woman, a mere girl, thus far, but word would soon enough spread among the savage, insatiable Usgar demons.

"What is your name?" Innevah asked the woman. "Sandashae, I have heard."

The woman nodded. "He is Dunen Bloch. We are from Sellad Tulach, above the low desert."

Innevah nodded. "You should not try to get there, not straightaway. Go straight down the mountain, to Fasach Crann, my village. If you can get among the huts, use my name. Remind them that I was the wife of Huana'kal. Tell them you have come with my blessing. My people will protect you."

The youngsters looked to each other uncertainly, then back at Innevah, and she saw more than a little skepticism painted on their faces.

"Just get off Fireach Speuer," Innevah told the boy pointedly. "And soon. We both know why," she added to the young woman, drawing her attention to her young companion. Dunen Bloch would soon be a man, and thus a threat (and perhaps even a temptation to the Usgar women), and so his time grew short. He would surely be killed later that same year when the tribe returned to the winter plateau, and most horribly.

Dunen Bloch looked back and forth between the nodding women, his expression growing desperate.

"I d'not want to go alone!" he said, suddenly gasping for breath.

"It is not just for him," Sandashae said, and put a comforting hand on Dunen Bloch's shoulder.

"No," Innevah agreed. "And even if he weren't here, my counsel would be for you to run. I know what your life among the Usgar will be."

"You wish to come with us!" the boy accused.

"I already told you that I cannot," Innevah calmly replied. "But yes, I wish I could. So many times have I thought of running, even of casting myself from a high rock. Every day for eight years. But I cannot."

"Because of your son," Sandashae said quietly.

"The stupid one," Dunen Bloch said, and Sandashae slugged him in the shoulder again.

"Because of Thump, yes," Innevah said. She looked Sandashae right in the eye, forcing her to lock stares, and added, "And that is why I have come to you."

Dunen Bloch seemed at a loss, but the young woman's expression of surprise only lasted a moment.

"You wish us to take your son," she stated.

"He will not be missed before you are missed," Innevah said. "He is of Fasach Crann, his mother, Innevah, his father, Huana'kal. He will ensure your safety there until my people—his people—can take you home across the waters to Sellad Tulach."

"We can'no—" Dunen Bloch started to argue, but Sandashae hit him again to silence him.

"Thump is swift and sure-footed, and he knows the ways of the mountain," Innevah assured them. "I must get him away, before . . ." She looked at Dunen Bloch and winced, then closed her eyes to compose herself and find her courage. This boy who was almost a man sitting before her had waited too long, she feared. He knew his fate, and surely the Usgar knew that he knew his fate. They wouldn't be surprised to discover that he had run off.

It was a desperate plan, to be sure, and one riddled with traps, and so Innevah almost reconsidered asking them to take Thump along.

But there weren't many uamhas in between the ages of Thump and this boy, Dunen Bloch, and so Innevah feared that this might be her last chance to save her child, desperate as it seemed.

"Take my boy with you," she said determinedly. "I will lie for you when they come looking. I will say that one of the women came for you, all three, and sent you out on an errand to collect pinecones."

Sandashae didn't blink, and Innevah couldn't tell if she was getting through to the young woman or not.

"Dunen Bloch and I will speak of it," Sandashae finally said.

"We can't be slowed!" the boy interjected.

Innevah started to plead, to argue, but Sandashae cut her short with an upraised hand. "There is much to consider. And we have time. We'll not be leaving for many days still."

Dunen Bloch started to respond again, but Sandashae cut him off forcefully, with a look, a punch, and a growl.

Innevah tried to decipher that, but she understood that there was little more she could do at that time. She nodded respectfully to the young woman and backed away, pausing only briefly to try to hear any residual comments.

And indeed, Dunen Bloch started to speak, but again was cut short by his coconspirator.

Worry followed Innevah all the way back to her tree-cave.

"She said she would lie to them to help us," Dunen Bloch said when Sandashae scouted about and confirmed that they were alone once more. The boy was shaking his head as he spoke, though, clearly struggling with this new dilemma.

"If we are being pursued, we should go to Fasach Crann," Sandashae said. "Innevah helped us by telling us."

"So we should bring her stupid boy?"

Sandashae cast a pensive glance in the direction Innevah had gone, and chewed her lip, hating her answer even as she shook her head.

"He'll slow us down!" Dunen Bloch went on, unaware that she was agreeing with him. "And he's ugly. He looks like them. Like the ugly Usgar demons!"

Sandashae turned and cast a glare of consternation at the boy.

"Every time I see him, I want to kick him," Dunen Bloch admitted.

"He is not Usgar," Sandashae quietly reminded. "He's just uamhas, like us, and if we could take him, I would."

Dunen Bloch started to reply, but paused and looked at the young woman curiously. "But you agree we will not?"

"I do," she said. "And we go this very night."

"But you told the long-head woman—"

"Exactly," Sandashae said, and she sighed. She had lied to Innevah to give her and Dunen Bloch space to get away.

She looked back in the direction of Innevah's tree-cave, and toward the adjoining one of Innevah's poor little boy, as well. Truly she wished she could get all the slaves out of the Usgar village and to the safety of the lake, even those who were of tribes that often battled with the folk of Sellad Tulach out on Loch Beag. No one deserved this fate, not the boys who would be worked to near-death and then tortured the rest of the way when they became men, and not the women, like Innevah, and now like Sandashae, who had to accept the violations of the ugly demon warriors.

She wanted to take all the lakemen from this awful place.

But she could not.

She moved to the side and pushed a bed of needles out of her way, then dug in the soil to retrieve a bag of food she had cleverly stashed. Then, her expression grim and determined, Sandashae reached out for Dunen Bloch's hand.

It was time to go.

Quite a commotion greeted Aoleyn when she went out into the camp that morning. People hustled all about, whispering excitedly. To the side of the encampment stood the uamhas, in a line, and with a long rope binding them all together ankle to ankle. Aoleyn couldn't miss the nervousness on their faces, all of them, including Thump, who seemed absolutely mortified.

"A runner," she heard the crone mutter, the woman coming out right after Aoleyn.

"A pair of them," came an answer from the side.

It took Aoleyn a few moments to sort that out. "A runner?" she whispered under her breath.

She saw the warriors gathering, lifting weapons, saw the witches of the Coven hastily blessing those long and terrible spears, and then she understood.

Now she looked at the line of uamhas more carefully, and indeed, two were missing: a young woman only a few years older than she, and a boy of about her age.

One of the men stepped before her, and it took her a moment to sort him out and recall his name, Brayth, a friend of the warrior named Aghmor who had been kind to Aoleyn through the years. This one was very different, she thought, with his bulging muscles and stern face— he never seemed to smile. There was strength behind his scowl, she recognized, and fire behind his gray eyes, and Aoleyn found an unexpected tightness in her throat as she looked at him then in the morning light.

He glanced over at her and offered a grin she thought perfectly wicked, then nodded and hoisted his spear.

He was eager to be on his way, she understood.

He was eager for the hunt.

He rushed off, sweeping up his friend Aghmor in his wake, the two of them moving fast to join the great warrior, Tay Aillig, at the western end of the camp, at the mouth of the trail that led down Fireach Speuer.

It surprised Aoleyn when Tay Aillig looked over Brayth's shoulder to her, his stare locking her gaze. She felt as if he was studying her too intently, as if he was looking into her heart and soul in his mind. She did not like that feeling at all, particularly now after the strange and unknown reaction she had felt in staring at the other strong warrior.

She closed up a bit, moving her arms across her chest, and Tay Aillig gave a little laugh, nodded to his charges, and ran off.

Aoleyn stood there watching them go, still postured defensively, unblinking.

"Don't worry," said the crone, coming up beside her. "They will catch the fleeing uamhas."

Aoleyn nodded, but for her teacher's sake only, because in her heart, she was afraid of that very thing, that the warriors would catch the runners.

Buoyed by the magic in their crystalline weapon tips, the small hunting party led by Tay Aillig streamed along the mountain trails, weaving through copses of trees and scrambling over boulder tumbles.

Whenever they slowed in an area rife with hidey-holes, Aghmor brought his spear tip up before his eyes, looking through the green-tinged crystal, its magic transforming his vision into something that could see and identify the sensations of nearby life instead of simple physical forms.

"There!" he announced at one flat area filled with towering stones, many of which leaned together to form small alcoves. He pointed to an apparent cave.

"No, wait!" he corrected even as his friend Brayth eagerly started for the spot. "It is a bear."

Brayth backed away immediately.

Tay Aillig looked to Aghmor, but the younger man could only shrug. He wasn't detecting any human life beyond the members of the party.

On they went with all speed, Tay Aillig leaping down rocky slopes and relying upon the witch's levitation blessing upon his weapon to keep himself upright. Invariably, Aghmor found himself at the end of the line through such difficult and dangerous passages, his caution the result of a hard lesson he had learned on his first raid eight years previous.

Another reason kept him near the back, as well, he knew, but wouldn't admit, even to himself. Fireach Speuer was an enormous mountain, wide and uneven, with hundreds of valleys and miles of hidden ways. But with their crystals that could allow them to move so swiftly, that could sense life, that could grant distance sight, the size and complexity of Fireach Speuer benefitted not the runners, but the hunters.

Surely the fleeing uamhas had deceived themselves upon leaving the camp the previous night by looking at the lights of the villages far below on Loch Beag. Those lights appeared closer than they were, and it seemed an easy run to them, no doubt. The height of the Usgar camp made it all look so tantalizingly straightforward, so obviously within reach.

Aghmor and the others who lived up here and ran the ways of Fireach Speuer understood that deception.

The runners thought they could sprint and slide, tumble and skip their way to the lake towns.

They could not. Not in time.

And that was why Aghmor secretly carried a great weight with every step.

Sandashae, dirty, exhausted, and bruised, stumbled into the small camp, one arm before her held high in surrender, one behind her dragging Dunen Bloch along, supporting him, for he had torn one of his legs badly on a slide down a stony slope.

"Please, we need help," she said, her voice choked and raspy. "Please."

Three men stood facing the two youngsters, their spears ready. A fourth hunter, a woman flanked about the side of the camp, just beyond the firelight, looking for more unexpected visitors. They all had the elongated skulls common for the village of Fasach Crann, and so were not kin to these surprising visitors—and they wore that fact clearly with their grim expressions.

"Sellad Tulach," Sandashae pleaded. "Sellad Tulach!"

The nearest man looked at her curiously. "Sellad Tulach?" he echoed.

"You're a long way from home, girl," said another man to the side.

"I've not been home since I was . . ." Sandashae replied, fighting to hold her mounting emotions in check. She held her hand out at about waist height, to indicate that she had been just a child when last she had seen her home.

"Where you coming from, then?" asked the third man in the camp, his voice growing weak with fear.

Sandashae looked back over her shoulder, up the steep mountainside.

"Deamhan Usgar!" Dunen Bloch blurted.

The words hit the hunters of Fasach Crann like a punch in the gut. Even in the light of the low-burning fire, Sandashae could see the blood draining from their faces.

"We've got to run," the man before her whispered, as much to himself as to anyone else.

A few hundred yards above and behind the camp of the Fasach Crann hunters, Tay Aillig walked out onto a high, exposed rock.

Looking down and to the right, as Aghmor had directed, the warrior drew out a crystal-bladed dagger and peered through its translucent, magical blade. His vision became removed from his physical eyes then, left his body, offering him a glimpse of a scene far below, a scene unfolding before the orange embers of a low-burning fire. He saw four hunters leaping up from their bedrolls, gathering their weapons, one rushing out into the darkness, the other three coming forward cautiously to meet the unexpected guests.

Tay Aillig grinned wickedly, replaced his dagger, and lifted his spear. Now he looked through the magic of that weapon, envisioning the sight he had been offered by his dagger, and focusing on the man who centered the trio.

He concentrated on a sense of attraction from the spear to a medallion the man was wearing, and though he couldn't see that medallion without the far sight of his magical dagger, couldn't even see the man or the camp, Tay Aillig surely could sense it!

His free hand motioned, sending Brayth and Aghmor streaming down the left side of the outcropping on which he stood, the other two warriors skipping and rushing down the right-hand side.

Tay Aillig steadied his breathing, and kept his focus on the spear tip, on the gray stone within it that was showing him the way. He brought the spear up high over his shoulder and cocked his arm, then paused, letting his warriors cover the ground toward the camp.

He felt the pull of the distant medallion.

He sent his spear soaring high and far into the dark night.

He kept his mind connected to its magic, mentally drawing a line from himself to the flying spear and to the hunter wearing the metal medallion. He could feel the enchanted missile changing directions as it battled the wind to hold true to that line, for the gray stone within its tip had attuned to the metal of the man's necklace, and sought that medallion.

Tay Aillig nodded, satisfied with the throw, and drew his dagger and a crystal-bladed axe. He leaped from the rock, gathering the magic of the axe to lighten his weight as he swooped down, lessening the jolt as he touched the ground below into a swift, bounding run, each stride propelling him long and far down the mountainside, the trees flashing by him to either side.

"They'll be coming, the demons," the hunter said, glancing left and right at his fellows. "We've got to run!"

The last word came out with a rush of air as a missile swerved to the magnetic call of the medallion around the hunter's neck, the spear charging the last expanse to plunge into that medallion, through that medallion and into the hunter's chest, through his backbone and out, driving him backward and down. He didn't immediately fall over, though, for the spear buried its tip into the ground behind him, and held him there, briefly, right before the horrified Sandashae.

The dying man craned his neck to look at the tail of the spear shaft, still protruding from his chest, and he looked past it, to the wide-eyed young woman, and with an accusation clear in his eyes.

She had brought this doom to him.

The dying man tried to grab at the spear shaft and the movement of his arm overbalanced him.

He rolled slowly to the left, then fell hard to the ground, blood quickly pooling about him.

A cry of surprise farther to the left caught the attention of the four people still standing in the camp, and before the two remaining hunters could call out to their flanking companion, two forms broke through the perimeter.

Usgar warriors.

The nearest hunter drew a long knife and charged at them. The other turned around and ran out the back of the camp. Or tried to, for two more Usgar appeared from the right, charging in pursuit, one leading with a flying spear that impaled the fleeing hunter in the lower back, slowing him until the two Usgar caught him and leaped upon him, bearing him to the ground beneath them.

Sandashae could only think of flight, could only hope the remaining hunter in the camp could hold back the fierce warriors—although she noted that he had already been stabbed once, and was again even as she watched! Still he fought on, and waved his knife menacingly, and got stabbed again by a long spear.

"Run!" Sandashae told Dunen Bloch, and she tugged his hand.

But he pulled free of her, it seemed, and she spun in surprise.

And saw Dunen Bloch lifting into the air, a dagger in his belly, angled up for his lungs. With one powerful arm Tay Aillig hoisted the boy higher, and how poor Dunen Bloch cried and screamed then as the vicious dagger tore at his guts.

Up higher he went, the powerful Usgar so easily lifting him, high enough so that the blood spurting from around the wound splashed over the mighty Usgar.

Sandashae fell back step by step.

The man to her side went down to the ground, the two Usgar stalking over him, stabbing down with their spears repeatedly, so clearly savoring every blood-splattering plunge.

Dunen Bloch continued to squirm and cry. He even managed to plea to Sandashae by name, so pitifully.

And she could only look at him, could offer no solace.

Tay Aillig's powerful forearm twitched, jarring the dagger, and it sent a jolt of agony through the boy, whose arms shot out to the side and stiffened, then fell limp.

Laughing, his face spattered with the boy's blood, Tay Aillig turned to stare at her.

"Not going with you," Sandashae said with as much resolve and defiance as she could muster, and she inched away a step to feel a spear tip against her back, for one of the Usgar who had chased down the fleeing hunter had returned.

"Oh dear, ugly, stupid girl," Tay Aillig replied, and he flicked his arm and sent the dead Dunen Bloch flying away, then lifted his crystal-bladed axe and turned fully upon the girl, eyes wild, teeth shining, "we know that."

As dawn broke over the dark heights of Fireach Speuer, Aghmor glanced back in the direction of the destroyed camp, marking its location by the handful of buzzards circling, waiting patiently for their turn.

The Usgar war party had left the runaway girl alive, tied down, naked and spread-eagled, her belly cut open from ribs to crotch, with the skin peeled back to invite the carrion eaters.

The last thing Tay Aillig had promised the doomed uamhas was that she'd be alive still when the first bird pecked out her eyes.

Aghmor thought of her.

He blocked out the whoops of joy and savage glee from the four warriors moving up the mountainside just before him, and he thought of the girl in her last pose, certain that it would haunt him forevermore.

PART 2

THE ILLS AROUND HER

As I wander the ways of the western Wilderlands, far beyond the Barbican Mountains, I have found cultures and creatures far more varied than those I knew in my days within Honce-the-Bear. Perhaps this was how the land I viewed as home had once been, before Bannagran the Bear united the feudal lords into a singular kingdom, before the followers of St. Abelle had created a church that would become dominant and far-reaching, although I suspect one would have to look further back in time to find a level of distinct tribal identity as I've encountered in the wider and more wild lands.

The people I have found here are separated into smaller communities, remote from each other, suspicious of each other, often warring with each other. The only common perspectives come from the traders, mostly frontiersmen who have left Honce behind, who pass from village to village, whose wares grant them passage where others dare not tread.

I believe that many of these tribes follow some form, some varied path, of the Samhaist religion, though I have never heard any identify it as such. To them, the world around them is replete with gods, and they revere death and life equally, and will often incite violence over others for the satisfaction of proving their power over death. To me much of it seems both simple and pragmatic. It makes sense, though, as I consider it, for the lands are too wild still for any to sit back and ponder deeper meanings and deeper causes for that around them. While Abellican monks peer at the night sky and try to unlock the pattern of the heavens and so find deeper truths about the seasons and the length of days, the tribes of the wilderness look at the sky only to discern the weather they'll soon face.

This might be the similarity I see to the older Samhaist religion. Perhaps these folk merely adhere to older cultural rituals and superstitions, similar enough to what I have found in my readings of the Samhaists to make me suspect a connection.

That would be an interesting question to explore, but I expect that the answers have been lost to the turning centuries. The men of the wilderness tribes to whom I have spoken claim no knowledge of the Samhaists, and the few remaining Samhaist enclaves would not take credit for them, I am sure.

The harshness of these traditions—torture, sacrifice, self-flagellation—harken to more primitive and desperate times, with death ever-present, looming and leering. Torture and sacrifice give to these people some measure of power over suffering and death itself, perhaps, as they are all intimately touched by death on a regular basis.

Even among those tribesmen I have encountered who smile more than they frown, there is an edge of danger and a measure of severity I ignore to my deepest peril.

My armor, my weapons, and my magic are all superior to anything I have encountered, but I remain vigilant, always, or surely I will be buried— nay, not even buried, but simply left for the vultures!—hundreds of miles from any place I ever called home.

I wonder, am I to judge these peoples of these wild lands? Or am I to excuse their traditions as just that, once necessary and perhaps still valuable to their survival? I can understand the brutality somewhat in the face of the leering specter of death, but understanding is not excusing. For surely these brutal rituals are not acceptable in the modern mores of Corona. Not in Honce-the-Bear, where Midalis is King and Father Abbot Braumin Herde leads the Abellican Church. Under their civilized conduct and laws, it would be easy for one to look upon these wild tribes with judgment and disdain.

But what if Marcalo De'Unnero had won the day in Honce-the-Bear? What if I, his errant puppet, had remained upon the throne? I am sure that I could have justified acts no less brutal than those that now give me pause—nay, that now cause me to recoil!

Does that not make morality itself a sliding scale, dependent upon tradition and level of enlightenment?

Or is it just a very human thing, even among the races that are not human, to justify our own actions and condemn those of others?

Aye, for I have witnessed brutality no less wicked in those lands I called home, in the land I once claimed as my kingdom.

And woe to any who venture near Andur'Blough Inninness, the valley of the elves, for they will be caught in the deceptive web of Lady Dasslerond and led to danger, perhaps even death.

Woe to any who cross onto the steppes of To-gai, for the untrusting and severe horsemen will run them down and fill them with arrows.

Woe to any who cross into Alpinador carrying the ways of a culture contrary to the teachings of the savage barbarians, for those travelers will surely find the blade applied slowly and repeatedly.

Woe to any who traverse the deserts of Behren, with its merciless nomads and trained murderers.

Woe to any who venture too near to Tymwyvene, for they will be cast into the bog and raised as servile zombies by the brutal Doc'alfar.

These are the truths I carry, and so any feelings of superiority I might hold over the peoples of these unnamed lands are tempered with humility. I look at their rituals, their parochial (and often brutally patriarchal) and insulated views, their prejudiced intolerance, and feel as if I can offer them better paths in resolving their distrust, and many truths about their commonalities to their neighbors. In my heart, I know that I can show many better ways, many better roads, the generosity of mercy, the oneness of humankind.

But, I was once a tyrant king, mentored by a man so full of anger that he could physically transform into a tiger, and in that form tear apart any who crossed him.

All that I do now must be tempered with the truth of who I was, with the judgment I must put upon myself, and with the constant reminder that my entire life now is one of atonement, freely offered, and that I am greater for it.

I have known the demon, without and within. We are all possessed of it, and in that knowledge, so too must we be possessed of humility and generosity.

Yet still, I cannot easily excuse the brutality of the rituals and traditions I encounter here in these wild lands, and their being based on ancient fears and superstitions does not make them acceptable in the face of continuing barbarity, even depravity.

But my judgment must remain internal. I am a visitor here, come to find myself, to find my truth, but uninvited.

And so I am not the arbiter of redemption.

Aydrian Wyndon, "In My Travels"

8

THE YOUNG WOMAN

(The last day of the fourth month, Toumanay, God's Year 852)

Aoleyn fidgeted, as usual. The sixteen-year-old could not sit still on the best of days, and today was worse than normal. Though four decades removed from that age, Seonagh understood the girl's impatience.

Great turmoil roiled within Aoleyn, both physical and emotional. Her breasts were evident now, and that hadn't sat well with the energetic young woman, who was more at home running about in rough play with the boys than in being ogled by them. And though she had begun to bleed more than a year earlier, only now had it become a predictable occurrence. Her days considered as a child in the tribe neared their end now. Soon enough, the Usgar-righinn would formally declare her a woman.

It was clear to Seonagh that Aoleyn wanted to savor her remaining time as a child, and this day was proving especially trying. For spring had come to Fireach Speuer, and the wind had shifted, bringing the warm from the desert far below. Truly the weather had blossomed gloriously this particular day, with the sun shining brightly, the breeze full of springtime aromas as the eager scent of the mountain flowers washed across the camp. This was the kind of day where the chores proved especially difficult for all the children of Usgar.

Seonagh watched Aoleyn carefully at her work. She was the oldest girl-child in the tribe, and so the oldest of any still considered as a child. For the boys were declared as men after their fifteenth winter, even if some still sounded more like chattering songbirds than Usgar warriors when they spoke.

Now time was short, and so Aoleyn had much to accomplish. She had to learn all the chores of an Usgar woman, and master them. Only then could the Usgar-righinn decide if this one was worthy to be considered for the next opening in the limited ranks of the Coven. The old crone who had long taught Aoleyn had insisted that the daughter of Elara, like her mother, was quite powerful with the magic of the Usgar and would prove a worthy witch.

Aoleyn blew a frustrated sigh and uncrossed her legs to stretch them. "I cannot feel my foot!" she complained.

"Because you can never sit still," Seonagh scolded.

"Why would I want to? I want to feel the wind. The streams are running fast."

"Their water will freeze your blood," said Seonagh.

"It is wonderful!" Aoleyn replied. "It makes you feel . . . everything. It makes your skin happy and alive!"

"It numbs your legs."

"Not as much as sitting here cross-legged, weaving this stupid basket."

Seonagh shook her head. "You will never be a proper woman."

"I'm not even knowing what that means."

"Aye, you do'no. And to think that you've the Coven's eyes upon you!"

That got her attention. Aoleyn put down the basket and hopped up, shaking out her sleeping legs. As she had been all along, Aoleyn remained quite small by Usgar standards, barely above five feet. Nor was she lithe, like so many of the tribe's willowy women. Even at her still-tender age, Aoleyn's body was shapely, and muscular. From all that running and tree-climbing, Seonagh knew, and even Aoleyn's penchant for wrestling with the boys—and beating them. A couple of the women had remarked favorably upon seeing the girl tackle a boy and pin him to submission, but only a couple.

She even preferred to still wear shirt and pants instead of the simple long dress more typical for the women.

"Always thinking to be what you're not," Seonagh whispered, and with obvious disdain and disappointment. For Aoleyn's antics drew more frowns than nods among the women, and almost universal scorn among the men. She would be tamed, Seonagh had heard more than once, and by warriors who would happily do it.

Aoleyn shook her head, her thick hair flying all about, her black eyes sparkling with the promise of the spring wind.

"Back to your work," Seonagh told her.

"Let me go and feel the wind," she pleaded. "Then I will finish."

Seonagh's switch came down hard against Aoleyn's hip, drawing a grimace.

"You could have just said no," Aoleyn said, rubbing the sting, then shifting to the other side as Seonagh snapped off a backhand on Aoleyn's other hip.

"You're to stay until you've finished," the older woman explained, her tone level and final. "And when you are done with your basket, then and only then will you begin your other tasks this day. And if you give me another word, I'll add a second basket-weaving to your chores, and you will be working until late into the night."

Aoleyn plopped down and crossed her legs, assuming proper form for her task. She lifted her unfinished product—it was beginning to look like a basket, at least—and scooped up a strip of birch, then dropped it back and took up some silver-pine bark instead, nodding as she brought it up before her eyes. Her hands moved rapidly, deftly, weaving the strands of bark together tightly. She nodded and smiled. As much as she hated these mundane tasks, she knew that in the end, she would make a fine and pretty basket. All of her baskets were good enough, if not superior, and had been since the very first one she'd woven.

Despite the whipping, Seonagh couldn't help but smile (even as she shook her head) as she watched her niece at her work. Even in the tasks

Aoleyn most hated, she performed with pride and skill. This precocious child—nay, young woman!—didn't like failure, and seemed to take it as a personal insult. Seonagh surely understood, given her own tumultuous history, but she also surely remembered that such a headstrong attitude would land Aoleyn many beatings over the next few years.

The older woman thought of her sister, then, who had been very much like Aoleyn. Yes, Elara would be proud of her daughter, if also a bit concerned.

Seonagh rubbed her face and muffled a sigh. The girl could not sit still, even as she worked. She sat cross-legged, her basket in her lap, but her leg continually twitched, moving the basket up and down. How that motion didn't ruin the basket, Seonagh didn't know.

That constant expression of an abundance of energy bespoke power, Seonagh understood, but also threatened abject failure. Yes, Aoleyn's basket would, as always, be an acceptable one, even a good one, but the quality of the basket wasn't the point of this exercise. An uamhas could be trained to make a basket. This task was more a way for a proper Usgar woman to learn to temper her energy. The crystal magic required power and strength, yes, but also a level of pure meditation, an ability to sit still and fall into the power of the crystal, to give oneself over to the magical song and let it flow through one's body. Simply put, a woman worthy of the Coven needed to learn to sit still, and Seonagh feared that Aoleyn was fully incapable of that, even more so than Elara had been.

The switch came down hard, across Aoleyn's knuckles. She stopped weaving—and stopped fidgeting—and turned to glower at the older woman.

"Sit still," Seonagh commanded her.

"I was sitting still," Aoleyn countered.

Seonagh said nothing, just sighed helplessly, and Aoleyn went back to weaving. She kept her legs silent for barely a count of ten before the twitching began again.

This time Seonagh did not wait. As soon as Aoleyn's leg twitched, the switch came down again, with a sharp *thwack*, harder than before, this time striking at the bare skin showing just above Aoleyn's knee. Aoleyn let out a slight whimper of pain and looked up with surprise, for that strike had raised a welt.

Aoleyn shoved her half-finished basket off her lap and leaped to her feet, spinning to face her teacher and tormentor. Her black eyes flashed with rage, her little hands balled into fists at her side. She opened her mouth to speak, but only a snarl came out.

Seonagh returned an unimpressed stare as she readied the switch again.

"Sit down," Seonagh ordered.

Aoleyn took a half step toward her.

Sconagh brought the switch down again, stinging Aoleyn's shoulder. Aoleyn did not acknowledge the blow, even as another welt rose where she'd been struck. But she did stop her advance and stood there, glowering.

"A woman does not rise threateningly," Seonagh said calmly.

Aoleyn continued to glare.

"Be thankful that I am no man," said Seonagh. "For if I were and you behaved such, your pain would be coming from more than just the bite of a switch."

Aoleyn did not appear impressed or particularly afraid, but her hands remained at her side, clenched in fists though they were. After a long moment, she collected her basket, sat down, and resumed her work.

"More basket-weaving," she muttered under her breath, but loudly enough for Seonagh to hear—intentionally, Seonagh was sure. "When it's not basket-weaving, it's cooking. It is cleaning. So much foolish cleaning as if the dirt would burn like acid." Her voice rose with each word. At last she turned back to Seonagh. "When will I be free of this boredom? When will you teach me the secrets of the Coven? Of the crystal magic? When will these foolish chores be done?"

Seonagh was upon her in an instant. The switch came down again, hard. Startled, clearly not expecting such a harsh reaction, Aoleyn tried to pull away from the older woman, but Seonagh grabbed her by her thick black hair and yanked her to her feet.

"When will they be done?" the older woman echoed, the frustration in her voice only partly due to Aoleyn.

"They're never done," Seonagh shouted in Aoleyn's face. "You will always find boredom as your companion, as your place until the day you die. You'll do these tasks for me, then, if you are fortunate, for the Coven. And soon enough, for your husband. You'll do for him as he demands, and without your endless whining. Learn that lesson well." She tugged hard on Aoleyn's hair, pulling her head to the side, ripping out a clump as she did. She dropped the switch and slapped the stunned girl hard across the face.

Seonagh understood that she was striking as much from her own frustration as with any anger toward Aoleyn. She also understood that this one had to be broken, fully, if Aoleyn was ever to have a chance to find escape from her place as a woman in the tribe within the beauty of the Coven.

Aoleyn yelped in pain, and Seonagh released her and shoved her away. Aoleyn tripped and fell to the floor, but only for an instant, springing right back to her feet. Her fists once again clenched, but this time she did not hold them at her side.

Seonagh wasn't caught by surprise, recognizing that the too-proud girl would never take such a brutal lesson easily. Now, as Aoleyn came at her, Seonagh was not unprepared. As soon as she had shoved Aoleyn away, Seonagh had reached into a pocket of her loose-fitting tunic and grasped at the contents. Now as Aoleyn cocked her arm to swing, Seonagh brought her palm up, hand open, something small and glittering resting in her palm.

A bright flash filled the open tent with blinding, stunning light, and Aoleyn stumbled backward, dazed.

"You desire a lesson in the ways of the Coven, child?" Seonagh said, advancing. Another flash, more brilliant than the sun at midday, radiated with painful intensity from her upraised palm. "Very well, then. Here is your lesson. The witches are powerful. You are not." A third flash, more brilliant than the last, left Aoleyn reeling, staggering to her knees, covering her head with her arms to try and find some shelter from the blinding, burning light.

Seonagh brought her hand forward, and Aoleyn whimpered. But another flash did not come.

It took several long minutes for Aoleyn's eyesight to fully return, during which she stayed put, kneeling, covering her head. Once she had recovered her eyesight, many heartbeats later, she dared peek out at the older and much more powerful woman. She expected to see a crystal with diamond flecks in Seonagh's hand, but instead, Seonagh was holding a small pinecone.

Aoleyn looked at her curiously.

"This is the cone of a blue spruce," she said. "They are few about the higher spans of Fireach Speuer, but they are the first to go to seed. Even now, though spring is not old, the cones are falling. Go out into the woods and collect three large baskets full of them. Do not return without the cones, even if you must spend the night there."

"But . . . why?" Aoleyn started to ask.

"And if you fail, then hide well and hide high, for the moon is full, and the Usgar-righinn whispers that Iseabal might show her red face this night."

"But why?" Aoleyn asked again.

"If you ask why again, if you protest, if you do not do this task right now without question, I will blind you once more. And when you are helpless, you will know more pain than you have ever known. Might that you will live, might not. But that's my price, for you have used up all of my patience."

"The Crystal Maven—" Aoleyn started to reply, her voice wobbly.

"Will thank me for saving her the trouble of wasting her days on the likes of you," Seonagh assured the young woman.

The threat shut Aoleyn up, though Seonagh could see the simmering anger lurking behind those large dark eyes.

But Seonagh also knew Aoleyn well enough to know that she would not try anything foolish. Aoleyn had been beaten here and was no match for Seonagh, and they both knew it.

"Take a slave woman to carry the cone baskets," the old witch instructed. Aoleyn started to protest, but Seonagh had already turned away before a word left her mouth.

Aoleyn sniffed, turned up her nose, and spun on her heel, stomping off toward the slave grove with a very audible "harrumph."

"And take your care to be back in camp and about the fire ere twilight," the older woman said, contradicting her earlier demand. "Three full baskets or expect the switch, and before Iseabal looks on Fireach Speuer and wakes the deamhan fossa!"

"She is tamed?" Tay Aillig asked Seonagh, the two of them standing outside the man's tent. He was into his late thirties now, but still carried the strength, spring, and passion of someone ten years his younger. In a way, those fires seemed to burn more intensely now, even though Tay Aillig's days of leading raids had all but ended. He was too valuable to the tribe now, and had been named Usgar-laoch, the War Leader, the organizer and tactician for the tribe's raids, but commanding from behind while others did the fighting. Only in a time of great desperation would he be sent down Fireach Speuer to do battle. More than once had Tay Aillig tried to persuade the elders to let him personally guide war parties, and his words had gained strength of late since the raids of the last few years, without the inspirational and powerful presence of Tay Aillig, had proven mostly unsuccessful.

Tay Aillig's face bore several distinct scars now—he thought of them as tattoos of honor from that day three winters past when he had overthrown Feuerie, the tribe's previous Laoch, and had thus claimed the position for himself. In her last act as a witch of the Coven, Seonagh herself had treated those wounds, and she remembered still Tay Aillig's command to her to not heal the gashes too cleanly.

Tay Aillig welcomed the scars. He wanted all who looked upon him to be reminded of his conquest.

"She obeys," Seonagh replied. "But with complaint, always. She is as headstrong as ever, and does not like to be commanded."

"It is a woman's place to be given orders," the man said with casual and dismissive confidence, almost daring Seonagh to offer a snort of protest.

"Of course, Usgar-laoch," she said, lowering her gaze. "But Aoleyn does not yet see it."

Tay Aillig stood silently for a moment, looking out the tent flap to watch the young woman cross the village toward the pine grove that housed the uamhas. He noted a distinct bounce in Aoleyn's step. She was a small one, but seemed larger somehow, a powerful presence even as she so beautifully seemed a part of the majestic landscape all about, a will-of-the-wisp flitting about the trees, her long black hair bouncing all about her like shadowy extensions of a life force too great to be confined in so small a coil.

"Does she accept the beatings?" he asked at last.

"Yes. Well . . ."

"Does her spirit break in them and so she will do as commanded?"

Seonagh winced. "Yes," she replied, and she was surprised to hear that her voice was full of sadness.

"Then her husband will have to beat her," Tay Aillig said callously. He might as well have been speaking of training a dog. "She is almost of age to be claimed, and will be promised when she takes the ritual." There was no flexibility in Tay Aillig's tone, no room to protest or comment, so Seonagh stayed silent. It scared her to think that Aoleyn was already a woman and would be claimed by a man, almost surely. But she was small, and didn't look like most Usgar women and so that man would not be a warrior in great standing.

She thought of her sister, Elara, and Fionlagh. Fionlagh had a good heart and was kind to Elara, true, but he was no great warrior, and so he had failed, and his failure had dragged Elara to Ifrinn beside him.

Aoleyn wouldn't likely be as fortunate as Elara, and surely not if she couldn't tame herself enough to be called to the Coven. Then she would have a terrible mate, a man bullied and with no title or honor. Then the switches of Seonagh would very likely be replaced by a brutality born of frustration that young Aoleyn was not ready to withstand or accept.

Tay Aillig turned to face her. "Does she progress in the teachings of Usgar?" he asked. "I heard of magic in your tent this morning. Was that the girl?"

"That was me," Seonagh explained. "Aoleyn has not yet learned the truth of the crystals or the crystal caves. She is not ready."

"She must be ready," he answered. "She crosses now her sixteenth summer, and so is able to bear children."

"She is not ready," Seonagh dared reply, but Tay Aillig's icy glare cut her short.

"Then make her ready, witch," said Tay Aillig. "She will be promised before we return to the winter plateau. She must learn her tasks. All of them."

Seonagh swallowed hard, unable to hide her fears.

"You took her to the crystal caverns when she was very young," Tay Aillig reminded. "Your predecessor placed an enchanted crystal into her hands, that she could measure her."

"That was her task, yes."

"Does Aoleyn not hear the magic of the crystals?"

Seonagh started to answer, but held her tongue. Was it possible that Tay Aillig eyed Aoleyn for himself?

It made no sense to Seonagh. The man could have any woman in the tribe he desired—he was unchallenged as the Usgar-laoch, and everyone expected him to one day lead the Usgar wholly. But nearing the end of his third decade of life, he had never shown much interest in any woman to Seonagh's knowledge. Oh, he went to the uamhas women every now and then, but not very often, and he had spent time in Mairen's bed, so said the whispers, though he wouldn't take it further than that, of course, since she was too old to bear him any children.

But Aoleyn? Tiny Aoleyn, with her black hair and black eyes?

She was never going to be tall, nor were her eyes ever going to reflect the blue of the daytime sky, but there was no denying the exotic beauty of her niece even with, or perhaps particularly because of, the darkness of her eyes and hair, blacker than any other Usgar. Although young, she was shapely, her body strong and able. She could work long hours without tiring, could spend the whole of the morning running gracefully along the steep mountain slopes, and could move her hands brilliantly in weaving, her fingers following her keen and discerning eye. Her baskets were not the best Seonagh had ever seen, not hardly, but if

Aoleyn had actually cared about them, they likely would have been quite handsome and sturdy.

And the crystals! The affinity the girl had for the magic was strong and undeniable—too strong, perhaps one day a threat to the supremacy of Mairen herself!

Like her mother, Elara, Seonagh knew, and she had to increase the pressure on Aoleyn to perform. Elara had been claimed and wedded before her magical power had bloomed, and so she had become the wife of Fionlagh.

Fionlagh, who had failed.

And in that failure, Elara's considerable affinity for the song of Usgar had, indeed, doomed her.

Aoleyn, too, had that gift, and could hear well Usgar's song. But she had not found the place of calmness within herself to prove her worth. Not yet, perhaps not ever.

"She hears the magical song," Seonagh replied. "I studied her with the stone of spirit and she is possessed of the power, I am sure."

"Then teach her to be proper."

"She lacks patience and discipline," Seonagh protested, though she knew Tay Aillig would not hear it.

Indeed, he motioned toward the girl, now rounding a bend out of sight to the uamhas grove. She carried a short stack of pine-bark baskets, large and unwieldy.

"She obeys," he said somewhat wickedly.

"She obeys when the switch makes her obey," Seonagh corrected.

Tay Aillig cast her a knowing look. A shiver ran up Seonagh's spine, and she was not surprised when the brutal man added, "Perhaps I'll fashion a thicker switch."

Seonagh nodded—what else could she do? She didn't enjoy beating her fellow Usgar women, but reminded herself that sadder would it be if this one, Aoleyn, could not calm herself enough to find the beauty of the Crystal God's magic, the great gift that gave Usgar women purpose and gave all the Usgar this perch in the heavens, far above the lesser peoples of the lake.

She didn't much like the idea of Tay Aillig taking her as his own, even if his stature in the tribe could not be doubted. Seonagh remembered too keenly Tay Aillig's role in Fionlagh's shame, and the brutish man's spiteful glee when Elara had gone into Craos'a'diad. . . .

Seonagh's eyes opened wide and she looked to where Aoleyn had disappeared and painted an image of the young woman in her mind's eye. So much like Elara!

She glanced over at Tay Aillig, who walked past her and out of the tent.

It didn't matter, she reminded herself, that there were dire implications for Seonagh here as well, should she fail. She nodded. She would soon begin Aoleyn's lessons in magic in earnest.

In their earlier encounter, Aoleyn would have fought back against Seonagh if she could have—the image of the young woman's clenched fists flashed in Seonagh's mind. Certainly Aoleyn had known that she could not win such a fight against Seonagh alone. But how would the impetuous young woman respond when she opened the power of the crystals? When she was armed with the might of Usgar's song?

How would Seonagh maintain her superiority over this child, this young woman, who made the crystals sing with her mere presence?

9

BAHDLAHN

Aoleyn tentatively approached the thick and tangled pine grove that harbored the slaves throughout the warmer months. She hated the slave grove as much as she hated the slave caves up atop the mountain beside the winter encampment—not because of the occupants, though, for Aoleyn held no particular grievances with the uamhas, other than their ugliness. In fact, of late it had been quite the opposite. All the Usgar, she felt, looked down on her because they thought her an irresponsible child, and also simply because of her sex.

The uamhas, though, had to show Aoleyn respect regardless of their age or gender. The greatest among the uamhas was far below Aoleyn and had to obey anything any Usgar, even a young Usgar woman, might command.

Perhaps because of that very fact and the security it afforded her, and although she never ordered any of them around, Aoleyn discovered that, to her surprise, she had come to actually like some of the slaves, especially the slave women. No, the slaves were not the problem with the slave camps.

Rather, Aoleyn hated the pines and the caves beside the winter encampment because she would often run into the Usgar men there. In the village, around the tents and trees and the open air, she could avoid the men when she was not in the mood to talk to them. The pine grove, though, was a maze of overlapping boughs, tighter and smaller and full of blind turns. In this grove, Aoleyn often could not avoid them.

She approached the pines cautiously, trying to figure her best way to get in, grab a helper for her pinecone hunt, and get out.

Aoleyn slowed as she neared the thick grove. These were towering trees compared with those up at the Coven's meadow, and with thick branches, the lowest of which sagged down to the ground at their ends.

As she neared the grove this day, though, Aoleyn's fears eased into a wide smile. One of the slave boys sat out in front of the pines, his back to her, holding a stick and doodling absently in the dirt. He was almost thirteen years old, Aoleyn knew and knew well, knew even his exact birthday, because she had watched him being born.

Seeing him sitting outside the sheltered areas all alone made Aoleyn believe that his mother was likely busy with an Usgar warrior. They all liked that one, she knew.

Looking upon the woman's son, Aoleyn was reminded of why, for the woman, Innevah by name, did have a pretty face, despite her grotesquely elongated skull. She was the oldest of the slaves, but still young and strong. And this one, her son, resembled her and was quite the handsome boy, with pretty shining blue eyes and light brown hair, and a head that was perfectly shaped!

What a shock it had been to Aoleyn a few years earlier when she had asked the old crone about this child, about why his head was not long, or double-humped, or otherwise misshapen.

"Oh, she tried to wrap it," the old crone had replied. "But to be sure that we stopped her."

"Wrap it?" Aoleyn could hardly comprehend.

What a shock it had been, for Aoleyn had then learned that the people of the lake purposely shaped their skulls! And that their heads, without their intense meddling, would be perfectly normal.

Aoleyn remembered well that conversation. "They are not wise," the old crone had told her. "They believe that making their heads larger will allow them to become less the fool, but no, dear, they remain quite stupid, all of them."

Yes, Aoleyn remembered that conversation because she remembered, too, the words she had overheard this boy's mother emphatically telling him.

"Stupid and ugly," she whispered, and she shook her head, unable to come to terms with this craziness. Why would they make themselves so ugly?

But not this boy. He had escaped that half of the curse of the lake folk. He was pretty.

"Boy!" she called. "Ugly boy!"

The youngster didn't stir.

Aoleyn walked over and kicked him lightly to get his attention. He turned his bright blue eyes up at her, but immediately cast them back down again, to some picture he was drawing in the dirt.

"I am talking to you," she said more insistently. When the boy did not react, Aoleyn bent low, tucked her middle finger behind her thumb, and flicked him hard in the ear.

That got his attention! He jumped to his feet and spun to square himself to his assailant. Anger flashed in those blue eyes, but only for a moment. It seemed to Aoleyn that he only then had realized that she was not another slave, but a master from the tribe, for a look of utter terror replaced his anger. He dropped his stick, and dropped to his knees with a grunt.

"You remember me," Aoleyn protested, trying to calm him. She hadn't interacted with him in years, but on the last occasion, she had rescued him from a pair of bullies.

"Stand back up," she ordered. When he did not quickly react, she tucked her middle finger behind her thumb again, readying for another flick, but the boy hopped to his feet before she could deliver the stinging blow. He kept his gaze cast down, though.

"The others still call you Thump, you know?" Aoleyn teased.

The boy swirled his foot in the dirt.

"Do you know what that means?" she asked.

No response.

Aoleyn grabbed him by the chin and forced him to look up at her.

"Of course you know," she accused. "They make fun of you."

She thought she saw a flash of pain in the boy's blue eyes, but it passed quickly.

"Thump," she repeated. "They call you stupid."

He didn't respond.

"Stupid!" she said, and she shoved him backward. He caught himself and glanced up and she was certain that he was going to cry.

Suddenly Aoleyn felt ashamed. He might be stupid, but he certainly understood the mocking, and it had wounded him. And she had just done that, had just inflicted pain upon him for no reason at all. Perhaps she was no better than the two boys she had beat up on Thump's behalf.

She started to apologize, but she bit it back, for no Usgar could ever say that to an uamhas! But now she knew that every time she called him by his name, he would remember this moment, and it would bring him pain.

"Is that your only name?" she asked.

No response.

"Does your mother call you something other? Other than Thump."

"Thump," he grunted.

Aoleyn shook her head and heaved a sigh.

"Bahdlahn," she decided suddenly

The boy looked at her curiously, but said nothing.

"Thump," she explained. "It means 'thump.' They call you Thump because it seems to be the only sound you are smart enough to make, and so by calling you Thump, they are calling you stupid!"

He tried to look down again, but she stopped him.

"Are you Thump?" she asked.

He grunted and tried to pull away, even offering a slight nod. Aoleyn thought that progress—at least she had elicited some response other than a simple emotional reaction.

"Do you like that name?" she asked, letting him go. "Thump?"

He was looking down again, but she heard a little growl and noted a slight shake of his head. Yes, he understood her, somewhat at least.

"You don't like it, then," she said, and she giggled, and that brought his gaze back up, a slight flash of anger in his eyes. "Then I won't call you Thump," she said. "I will call you Bahdlahn."

He seemed to her to be confused.

"Bahdlahn means many things," she explained. "It is the noise of a drum, or a dancing foot. Or the sound of the hooves of a running elk."

The boy grunted and nodded his head very slightly. It seemed to her as if he wanted to say something, but he only licked his lips and lowered his gaze. Bahdlahn was tall for his age; despite the three-year difference between them, they stood about the same height. Although it was hard to tell since he kept hunched over, his gaze focused on Aoleyn's sandals. She ducked her head slightly, trying to look him in the face, but the boy turned his head.

"Look at me!" she commanded. The boy shook his head and continued to avert his gaze. Aoleyn held up her hand, finger cocked to flick him again.

Bahdlahn let out a groan and began whimpering.

Aoleyn heaved another great sigh. Perhaps the boy really was feeble. It did seem as if he could barely speak in anything other than grunts. Aoleyn started to address him again, but paused, remembering that long-ago day when she had happened to eavesdrop on Bahdlahn's mother. Between that ugly woman and the stern warriors of the tribe, Bahdlahn had been taught not to look at the faces of the Usgar for the sake of his very life. Yet here she was, commanding the poor boy to break that taboo, to look at her directly. And she was backing up that command with a threat.

She stood up straight, and held her hand in front of the boy's face so he could watch as she disengaged her finger and thumb.

"I'm not going to flick you again," she said. "I'm not here to hurt you . . . Bahdlahn. Do you understand?"

Bahdlahn didn't say anything, not even one of his customary grunts, but his shoulders, indeed his entire frame, seemed to relax a bit.

Aoleyn dropped the stack of baskets at his feet.

Bahdlahn looked at them, his face a mask of curiosity. He even glanced up to look into Aoleyn's black eyes for a split second. She caught the look of confusion on his face before he quickly averted his gaze.

"I have a task for you," she said. "Well, it's a task for both of us. Come, pick up the baskets."

Bahdlahn hesitated. He was much younger than his years in many ways, and had seen far too much for one of his age, but Aoleyn could judge that he was still just a child. His body would soon become that of a man, but his mind?

He was rarely used by other slavers for any task beyond the mundane, like distributing the meager dinner portions, or cleaning the feet of a warrior after the Usgar man had spent some time with a slave woman.

So of course, he was confused at this unexpected confrontation.

You really are stupid, Aoleyn thought. She felt the heat of shame rising again up her neck. Her impulse here to resist the spirit of Seonagh's orders—she had been told to take a slave woman, after all—felt like cruelty toward this undeserving boy. He might even get in trouble for accompanying Aoleyn.

With a harrumph, Aoleyn pushed that shame aside. So this boy, this *slave,* would have to suffer a bit. So what? She had to suffer, as well. She may as well pass some of that pain along.

In addition to that, Aoleyn truly couldn't stand the thought of being in the company of one of the uglier slaves throughout this beautiful day. Just thinking of those misshapen heads sent a shudder through her.

"Pick. Up. The. Baskets," she commanded coldly, all hint of sympathy gone from her voice. "Pick them up and follow me. I command you. Do it or I'll be hurting you again, don't doubt." She scowled at Bahdlahn and raised her hand once more, this time in a fist.

Bahdlahn offered a confused and sheepish grunt, one that made Aoleyn feel rather silly at that moment, standing as she was with her fist in the air. The boy glanced back at the dark entrance to the hollow beneath the pine boughs that served as his home, seeming unsure, but a chirp from Aoleyn had him moving faster.

Triumphantly, the conquering Aoleyn headed for the nearby woods, her captive dutifully stumbling along behind her, fumbling with the baskets.

The coveted pinecones were not very large and were quite difficult to see, as they were the same brown color as the thick bedding of soft needles covering the forest floor. They were not difficult to find for someone who knew how, though, and Aoleyn had been taught a simple method.

She took off her doeskin sandals and looked to Bahdlahn, who, of course, was barefoot, like all of the uamhas. She hoped his feet weren't so calloused and hard that he would prove all but useless in this task.

"We must fill these baskets with the cones. Keep your eyes to the ground and walk slowly," she instructed him. She started off, the boy right behind, but she stopped short and pointed to the side. "Go that way!" she scolded, and let out a sigh to let him know that she was displeased.

She thought he seemed wounded by her obvious disgust as he walked off, his gaze low—as instructed, and surely it wasn't a difficult command for this one to follow, since he always seemed to be staring at the ground.

But Aoleyn again felt bad about her actions and attitude. She could not determine why.

A few heartbeats later, Bahdlahn let out a pained yip, and Aoleyn spun about to regard him, and smiled as he bent low to pick up the little pinecone that had stabbed his bare foot.

He looked back at her, held up the cone, and nodded, then dropped it into a basket and started off again, but now more slowly.

Aoleyn started to laugh at him, but that giggle turned to a yelp of her own, as her bare foot, too, came down on one of the nasty and pointy little pinecones.

She sucked in her breath and hopped backward, trying to keep her weight off that foot. She glanced over at Bahdlahn as she did, scowling and ready to thrash him for laughing back at her.

And indeed, she caught a flicker of his smile, but it was short-lived, and replaced by a look of seemingly genuine concern. He was crouching, and fished about the needles to produce the cone that had stung him.

Aoleyn moved to do likewise, but discovered that she didn't have to, for the cone was still there, stuck into her foot! She plopped down onto the bedding and folded her leg in close to rub the wounded foot and extract the prize.

"Maybe that's what they want them for," Aoleyn said with a growl as she gingerly reached for the cone, but pulled back in pain as soon as she touched it. "They should toss them about the edges of the camp like caltrops and then no one will be able to raid us!"

She was startled, then, to hear Bahdlahn's giggle at her quip, and from right beside her. She snapped her head around to regard him.

The boy swallowed hard and shrugged, his gaze diving to the ground.

Aoleyn went for the daggerlike pinecone, sucking in her breath as her fingers brushed it. She wasn't going to cry here, she told herself. If she let this foolish slave see that, she'd have to beat him and make sure he never, ever told anyone!

Maybe she'd even have to kill him.

The preposterous thought helped ease the young woman's tensions, and she moved her hand back for the pinecone, grunting defiantly as she slowly closed her fingers about it.

Stunningly, Bahdlahn intercepted and blocked her hand. Aoleyn looked at him with pure incredulity.

He held up his dirty hands submissively, then slowly moved them toward the cone, eyeing her directly all the way as if asking her permission.

He brought his hand to her foot at the base of the pinecone, and rubbed and manipulated her skin quite soothingly. Then, fast as a white-furred snake, his other hand snapped in and yanked the pinecone free.

Aoleyn yelped again, but more in surprise than in pain.

Bahdlahn, meanwhile, kept his tight grip on her foot as he tossed the extracted cone into a basket and produced a small strip of cloth from his pocket. He gently but firmly placed that over the wound, stemming the trickle of blood, then carefully, and caringly, wrapped her foot and tied it off.

Aoleyn just watched, her jaw hanging open. The boy was quite good at this, she thought, particularly when he manipulated the fingers of his hand to give her foot a soothing rub.

Aoleyn rested back, closing her eyes and looking up at the sun to take in the warmth of the sunshine and the feel of the gentle wind. She wasn't really paying attention to Bahdlahn's movements, and so she was surprised again a moment later when she realized that he was placing her sandal back over her foot.

"What are you doing?" she asked, too harshly, she realized, and pulled her foot away. "It will take longer to find any cones if I am not—"

Bahdlahn repeatedly poked himself in the chest. "Uamhas," he said.

Aoleyn started in surprise, not sure what to make of that, for it was the first time she had ever heard this one, this Thump creature, speak a word with more than one syllable.

"What did you say?" she pressed slyly. The boy seemed panicked and he looked down and roughly shook his head. "You can speak?"

"Uamhas," he said and looked up, nodding stupidly, and insincerely, it seemed to Aoleyn.

"Uamhas get. Uamhas do," Bahdlahn went on. "Uamhas. Thump. Uamhas."

Aoleyn stared at him for a long while, trying to sort out his awkward movements and stilted language. Something seemed not quite right here, but she couldn't quite sort it out.

"We must fill the three baskets," she protested, but Bahdlahn nodded happily and wagged his head.

"Three!" she said more insistently, convinced that the simpleton had no idea of what she meant. She held up three fingers, then pointed to each of the baskets in turn.

Bahdlahn grabbed up all three and tossed one far to his left, one to the right, then began rushing up the middle, scraping his feet. Occasionally he hopped, as he stumbled across a pinecone, but the speed of his movements showed Aoleyn that he wasn't much concerned about hurting.

He swept back toward her just to the side of his trail, then reversed and rushed along again, and by the time he had turned back, Aoleyn could see that his basket was more than half full.

The young woman rested back, lifted her sore foot to rub it a bit, and let the boy finish scouring the area.

She removed her sandals when they moved off to another grove, determined to do her part, and walked gingerly while Bahdlahn plowed through the needles with abandon. Soon enough, his basket was full, while hers wasn't yet near the halfway mark.

They moved on again, Bahdlahn slinging the full basket on his back and carrying Aoleyn's basket in his arms, leaving only the still-empty basket for Aoleyn to bear.

Aoleyn watched his movements and could see that he was straining. Individually, the pinecones weren't heavy, but a basketfull could be quite a load, and Aoleyn felt bad for defying Seonagh and not bringing along a stronger adult woman. But Bahdlahn didn't complain.

The next grove of trees was deceptively far away, she realized when they came around a bluff to find a sheer drop before them. They'd have to go around that hidden ravine, back up the mountainside for quite a distance.

Aoleyn grabbed the half-filled basket, but Bahdlahn wouldn't let it go.

"I'll carry it to the next grove," she said, but the boy didn't budge.

"Uamhas," he said, not daring to look up at her.

"Don't be such a fool," she replied. "You'll be no use to me when you fall down from weariness." She tugged the basket harder, yanking it from his grasp, and thrust the empty basket into his arms when he reached for his previous bundle.

She started up the rocky slope determinedly, but was soon enough limping from the soreness in her foot. And Bahdlahn was right there, ready to take back the loaded basket.

"Uamhas," he said emphatically, poking himself in the chest. "Usgar," he added, pointing at her.

"So you must do all the work?"

Bahdlahn nodded, but Aoleyn quickly snatched the basket back from him.

"Woman," she said, poking herself in the chest when he looked up at her in surprise. "Usgar women work."

He grunted, seemingly in disagreement, and shook his head while staring at the ground.

Aoleyn dropped the basket at his feet, its contents spilling. When the shocked boy went to it, she grabbed him roughly by the chin and forced him to look up at her.

"It is all right," she said as comfortingly as she could. "You have been a great help."

He seemed confused. He seemed terrified.

But there was also a measure of gratitude in his sparkling eyes, she thought, so she reinforced her words with a genuine smile.

"Help me pick these up and then I'll carry the basket," she calmly instructed.

He dropped immediately for the task, but Aoleyn stood straight and looked all around. Her foot was starting to throb.

"I know a better way," she said, and she dropped to help Bahdlahn refill the basket, then grabbed it away from him and gave a warning glance that halted his forthcoming protest.

They locked gazes for a long heartbeat then, and Aoleyn nodded and said, "Come along."

With the load redistributed, they made better time, right back past the initial stops, and farther around the mountainside, over a lower peak to a point that looked out on the western sky. Though spring had come to Fireach Speuer, the days were still short, and even shorter on those stretches of the mountain shadowed from the afternoon sun.

On this bare stone outcrop, though, the sun beamed on the faces of the two, and the mountain stretched wide before them, the long waters of Loch Beag sparkling, down to their right, far in the distance.

They probably shouldn't have been out this far from camp, Aoleyn knew, for Seonagh's warning hadn't come without merit. The moon would be up soon in all her glory, and the fossa hunted when Iseabal showed her red face.

They still had time, Aoleyn decided, and despite her sore foot, she picked up her pace and led Bahdlahn down the mountainside, to where the trees were thicker, taller, and more varied.

Aoleyn yelped as a pinecone bit into her foot more than once, but she just laughed it away and worked as fast as she could to try to keep up with the plowing Bahdlahn. It became a competition, if only a lighthearted one, full of yips and yelps and triumphant raised hands whenever a pinecone was found.

Soon enough, the baskets were full and sitting in a line on the ground.

"Pick them up and follow," Aoleyn instructed Bahdlahn.

The boy swallowed hard, his fingers rolling nervously. He slung the first over his back as before, setting the rope straps about the front of his shoulders. He tried to pick up the second basket with one hand, to leave the third for his free hand, but he overbalanced and would have tumbled, but Aoleyn was there, grabbing his arm, propping him, and, with a nod and a smile, taking the basket from him to strap about her own shoulders.

As she did that, Bahdlahn hoisted the third, but Aoleyn shook her head.

He looked back at her, confused.

She took one edge of the basket he held and pulled it to her side, her holding one handle, him with the other, the weight balanced between them.

The sun was low then, almost touching the far-distant mountains beyond the lake, but Aoleyn had picked her course carefully and knew that the Usgar camp was not far. Still, she realized that they could not delay, so despite the throbbing of her foot, she set a swift pace.

It occurred to her as they walked side by side that she couldn't quite place the exact moment when this had ceased being her task alone, or the moment when Thump had actually become Bahdlahn.

Here they were, sharing the load, as though they were equals.

It wasn't until they neared the camp, the central bonfire in sight, that reality descended once more. Bahdlahn stopped suddenly and yanked the basket from Aoleyn's hand, placing it on the ground before him. He motioned for the one on her back.

"I can carry—" she started to protest, but the boy stomped his foot and motioned more forcefully, then seemed as if he was about to cry.

Aoleyn heard a stir in the trees not far away, a footstep.

She rolled the basket off her back and gave it to Bahdlahn, who plopped it atop the other and lifted them both even as the Usgar sentry bounded into view, crystal-tipped spear ready to throw.

He looked from Aoleyn to the slave boy.

"The fossa will eat you," he growled at Aoleyn, noting the late hour. Then he turned a sidelong glance at the slave boy and seemed about to strike him.

"It is my fault," Aoleyn said. "I hurt my foot and it slowed us greatly."

The sentry's glare at the boy turned wary, threatening.

"I tumbled from some stones," Aoleyn quickly added. "The boy ran down to help me. We could not go straight back up, because it was too steep, and the trail back wound far afield."

The sentry stared at her hard for a bit, then nodded his chin for the camp. "Be quick," he ordered, and nodded from the camp to the higher black silhouette of the mountain framing it, and on the topmost rim, where the pale sliver of moonlight glistened.

The fierce warrior smiled widely, grotesquely, even, at that, and moved his face very close to Aoleyn's. "The fossa will eat you," he said wickedly.

A shaken Aoleyn tried not to reveal her fear—fear of the man and not the beast called fossa.

She thought the fossa a fable. Though the tribe spoke of the beast often, it was never, so it seemed to her, actually seen.

When the warrior finally backed off from her, though leering still, Aoleyn set off quickly, Bahdlahn in tow and struggling to keep up. She did glance back, and grimaced as she noted that the poor boy was bowing under the weight of the three full baskets.

But he did not complain, and with the image of the leering warrior still chilling her bones, Aoleyn dared not slow, and certainly dared not help the slave.

With the gloom deepening and the moon not yet beyond the black barrier of the mountain's silhouette, the bonfire of the camp burned bright, and many milled about it. Not wanting any more confrontations, Aoleyn stayed in the shadows just outside the perimeter of the camp, leading Bahdlahn all the way around to the back of Seonagh's tent. She did not really feel like dealing with the teacher at that moment, even though she had completed her task efficiently and effectively and would probably receive some praise. For some reason, though, Aoleyn did not desire any interaction with any of the tribe's adults at that particular moment. But she knew it had something to do with the boy at her side.

On her nod, Bahdlahn set down the three baskets, then straightened and turned slowly left and right to shake out the tiredness; he seemed relieved to be rid of the heavy things. He didn't stop himself in time, apparently, for he looked Aoleyn in the eye and offered her a little smile.

He clearly understood her lie to the sentry about falling, and knew that the lie had saved him more than a little grief.

In a flash, though, Bahdlahn's expression turned to one of panic and he dropped his gaze to the ground again. Aoleyn understood. Out in the forest, the child could smile at her all he wanted; here, in the village, he had to be a slave, a disciplined uamhas, and nothing more. He had to keep his eyes down, to not look an Usgar in the face.

"Come on, Thump," she said, her voice full of sympathy, and even a hint of regret in using his more common moniker. "I'll bring you to your shelter." She reached for his hand, but he refused it, wisely, and Aoleyn let out a frustrated sigh, aimed not at Bahdlahn but at the rules that said she couldn't take this boy by the hand.

After all, the Usgar men took the uamhas women by a lot more than their hand.

She led him to the pine grove, and through the tangles of boughs. The many natural shelters used by the slaves opened up all about her, a veritable maze of paths, tree trunks, thick branches, and small shelters beneath the heavy canopy—a maze made all the more confusing by the many skins that had been hung to separate different chambers beneath the low ceiling of tree limbs.

There was little light in here—no fires, of course—just what little bonfire glow could sift through the pine needles and drips of starlight here and there.

"Which way to yours?" she asked Bahdlahn.

The boy brought his finger to his lips, making a slight "shush" sound, then pointed off to the left, through a break in the trees.

Aoleyn took him by the hand—it was unlikely that she'd run into any Usgar, so she decided she could ignore some rules here—and led him across the way, pushing aside an old ram-skin hung between two widespread branches. Bahdlahn followed her in, but only a step before he stopped cold.

"What's . . ." Aoleyn began to ask, confused by the scene in front of her. The light in the small natural chamber before her was brighter, a break in the branches allowing more glow from the campfire and the starlight. A pile of skins formed a makeshift bed on the far wall of branches, and atop the skins she saw an Usgar warrior, his naked back covered in tattoos, moving up and down, and beneath him a slave woman, one that he had punched in the face more than once, apparently.

Not just any slave woman, Aoleyn realized. It was the woman from the lake villages, who had been brought back from the prewinter raid.

Bahdlahn's mother.

The man seemed to take no note of the children entering the chamber, but the woman did. She looked over at Aoleyn from under the warrior's straightened arm. There was no fear in her eyes, no worry that she should not be meeting the gaze of a tribesperson.

No, Aoleyn saw something else, something she had seen before, a sadness so deep and profound that Aoleyn could hardly bear it.

Rage welled up in Aoleyn's chest. She wanted to scream out, she wanted to run over and shove the man off the poor woman. She wanted to break off a nearby branch and beat the warrior over the head with it until he was bloodied and bruised. She went so far as to take one deliberate stride into the room.

But she felt a tug on her hand, slight but insistent. Bahdlahn grunted, barely audibly, and pulled on her arm. It took all of Aoleyn's willpower to not simply shove the boy away and charge at the distracted warrior.

But she did not. She turned away, swept Bahdlahn up, and dragged him out of the room.

"Come on," she whispered. "We'll wait out here until the warrior—"

Bahdlahn looked surprised, and so small and helpless. But he shook his head and motioned for Aoleyn to go.

She was shaking her head right back at him before he finished. "No! I'll be waiting with you," she said, and sat down on the ground between the branches. A rare break in the canopy gave her a clear view of the starry sky above, and she motioned for Bahdlahn to sit beside her.

He paused, but did indeed take a seat.

They waited in silence. The moon came up above Fireach Speuer, and Iseabal's full red face did rise into the night sky above the mountain: a Blood Moon, brightening the area. They heard louder noises from beyond the ram-skin flap, but tried not to listen, and then the Usgar stalked out, casting a curious glance at Aoleyn as he passed, tossing her a chuckle, too, but saying not a word.

When he was gone, Aoleyn motioned for Bahdlahn to go back inside, to go to his mother. She considered joining him, but the look on the woman's face was too fresh in her mind, and she did not want to see it again, not right now. The rage she'd felt welled up in her chest again, impotent and directionless.

She watched Bahdlahn cross beneath the ram-skin door, watched the old thing flop back into place, and shoved her way back through the tangle, pushing past the branches as if they, as if the haunting emotions of this desperate place, were suffocating her.

10

TORMENT

The creature flung itself against the stone wall, all four paws raking and clawing. The demon beast's devastating hooked claws dug deep gashes into the stone and held the fossa aloft on the vertical surface for many heartbeats.

Catlike, the beast leaped away, clunking down and scuttling about on the bone pile that floored its smelly den. So many bones—human, bear, lion, deer. It didn't matter. If a creature lived free of torment and crossed the angry fossa's path, that creature would be destroyed.

It had to be destroyed.

But mostly the humans—yes, the humans! They were the ones who pulled the crystals from the mountain. They were the ones who gave maddening voice to the magical flecks of gem and mineral.

And that voice, that song, drove the fossa mad.

Particularly so on nights such as this. Those about the mountain would see the red moon lifting from the eastern horizon, but the fossa could feel it, could hear it.

The Blood Moon called out to the beast, summoning it to the hunt.

The old memories of the fossa, before it came to hear the discordant and maddening song of the crystals, tried to resist, tried to fight back against the call to murder.

The creature flung itself against the wall once more. Claws dug deep gashes, cutting the stone, sending flecks flying to rattle into the bone pile.

Against the wall, the creature could hear the song, humming from deep within Fireach Speuer, from the subterranean crystal garden near the mountain's summit. And that song drove it to heightened fury, the claws scratching furiously. The fossa hated the song, and yet that was what sustained it. Without that magic, the creature would have died long ago.

Somewhere deep inside its animal brain, the fossa understood that truth, and it only made the demon beast hate the magical song of Fireach Speuer even more!

Better to be nonexistent than this madness!

The beast fell to the bone pile, its scythe-like tail swiping through, throwing leg and arm bones about and crunching through the rib cage of a long-dead victim.

The fossa thrashed, launching bones all about, flinging them up the walls of the pit it called home and caring not at all when they crashed back down upon its own head. Not content with its tantrum, the fossa clawed and grasped the largest bone it could find, the thigh of a great brown bear, and gnawed at it with all its might, biting right through in short order.

It sensed the red glow of the moon, and it was a call the fossa could not ignore.

Hating its very existence, hating the magical song, hating everything alive, the fossa leaped straight up, clearing the twenty feet of the pit with ease and grasping at the sloping stone of the lone tunnel, the singular exit from the secret mountain cavern.

Claws dug in and the fossa pulled itself along, low to the ground and through an opening barely wide enough for it to squeeze through. Growling and snorting, the creature dug along, coming to a wider opening and a drop to a larger tunnel.

The aroma of the death pit filled the lightless air even out here, and the fossa breathed deeply, reveling in it, thinking it sweet.

A few moments later, the fossa leaped over a boulder and through a small opening to emerge into the open air, the nighttime air of Fireach Speuer, and with the red moon beginning its climb up the eastern sky.

On padded paws, claws retracted, the fossa stalked off, sniffing for the stench of life, human or animal, it didn't matter.

Just something to kill.

And with every stride, the fossa listened for the song of magic, and hoped in its black heart that it would find the human singing it.

That would be the sweetest kill of all.

The beast charged through some trees to a cliff face and leaped straight up, thirty feet, to the ledge above. Three more strides and the fossa sprang far and high over a ravine, landing silently, sprinting off, but then skidding to a sudden stop, its hairless, scarred face coming up and swinging about.

Ears twitched and the fossa curled the remaining half of its upper lips, showing gleaming fangs, its few whiskers, remnants of another existence, feeling the night wind, measuring the scent against the currents, honing in. Then it was off at a blistering pace, springing up the side of a tree, leaping far to land lightly upon a large boulder, where its supernatural claws dug in and froze it in place, to pivot and spring off to the side.

The fossa could outrun anything on the mountain, with ease, and it was so quick with its four legs that it could change angles over a berm or fallen log without the slightest of hops, keeping its back smooth and straight and fast across broken ground, even small ravines.

The scent grew stronger, driving the hungry creature on.

It noted the flicker of white, the tail of a deer, and veered, buzzing through the brush, singularly focused.

A short distance ahead, the deer leaped a ravine and turned down the descending mountain trail, around a high outcropping. The fossa went up instead, leaping godlike to the top of the outcropping, thinking to fly down from on high to bury into the deer on the other side.

And indeed it spotted the animal, and tamped down its rear legs for the killing spring.

But then the creature's snarl dissipated and its expression changed as its head came up, turning to the sky, to the southern sky. For there, splayed across the starry sky, lay the Halo, the planetary ring of the world of Corona, glowing softly across the spectrum of colors, a great rainbow encircling the whole of the world.

The fossa could not ignore its call, for this ring, full of gemstones and minerals, was the magical god of Corona, the antithesis, the mortal enemy, of the demonic magic that gave the fossa immortality.

The ring gave this world its name. The ring of Corona fed the magical gemstones to the world, the blessed items that had birthed a religion in the east, that bolstered the power of kings and given monks the ability to produce fireballs and lightning bolts, even to fly. In more ancient times, the ring of Corona had scattered across the world its seeds of magic, like those that had grown to become the crystal cave of Fireach Speuer.

The demon fossa knew all of this, and knew most of all that this ring taunted, that the magic of this ring threatened.

The demon fossa was death.

The ring of Corona was life.

Far below, the deer was long gone, leaping and springing along the slopes of the huge mountain.

The fossa did not try to spot it among the lower slopes, or to regain its scent.

No, the demon beast stood there and stared at its nemesis. It flexed its claws, digging them into the stone as easily as a man might clench his fist in the sand. The lip curled again and a long and low roar came forth, rolling through the mountain valleys, echoing off hard stone walls, carried on the night breezes all the way down the mountain, where the villagers of the seven tribes took note.

All about that high outcropping, deer fled, bears scrambled aside, leopards sped away, and small animals crouched deeper in their burrows.

They all knew. They all understood that the moon was red and death itself had ventured out onto the slopes of Fireach Speuer.

For a long while, the fossa sat there, growling at the glow of the planetary ring.

Finally it turned away and plodded off around the mountainside, but no longer looking for something to kill, its appetite stolen by the sight of the awful ring. Now the creature was more interested in defying the energy that gave life to the world of Corona.

It turned and stalked for a high crevice, a gorge from which flowed the magic of the mountain, a place the Usgar called Craos'a'diad, the Mouth of God.

11

STARING INTO HELL

Aoleyn sat in the tree in the sacred grove, the same tree, the same spot, where she had first viewed the crystal obelisk, the physical manifestation of Usgar, more than a dozen years previous. She remembered that long-ago day, when the warriors had returned from their lakeside raid. That was the first day she had seen Thump's mother.

"Bahdlahn," she corrected herself aloud. His name was Bahdlahn, not Thump. The helpful and friendly little boy deserved a better name than Thump.

Aoleyn had returned to this grove only a handful of times over the years, and not at all in the last couple. She was older now, and coming here was forbidden, and she knew that the consequences of being caught here could be dire. There were whispers that she would one day become a witch of the Coven, and though she didn't understand all that such a position entailed, if it brought her closer to magic, to the crystals and the Crystal God, it would, she thought, be a very good thing.

Better that than stepping on pinecones like a serving girl, or bending over to the demands of a warrior husband who probably hated her as much as he loved her, who sated his carnal desires with slave women whenever he so chose.

She winced and tried to put it all out of mind. Too many bad things swirled in her head this night.

"Better to be a witch," she whispered. Yet here she was, where she didn't belong, and being caught here could jeopardize all of that.

But she didn't move, didn't leave, for where was she to go? Far to the west before her, long from the slopes of Fireach Speuer, the huge moon, tinted bloody red, rode low to the horizon, the lines of moonlight streaming across Loch Beag's wind-stirred water, casting sparkles.

Aoleyn locked her gaze on that mesmerizing dance, trying to use the mystical night light to remove the images from her mind.

To no avail.

She saw Bahdlahn's mother, the warrior rutting atop her. The woman's eyes stared at her, helpless and hollow, as if her soul had long ago departed and only her body remained—and only remained for the sake of the boy.

That image had chased Aoleyn from the thick boughs of the slave encampment. Haunting her, those eyes had chased Aoleyn right past the tribe's proper encampment, running and scrambling, hands to the ground on the steep slope before her, up the side of the mountain. Up to the winter plateau, and to this grove just beyond.

And to this tree, to a place of her past, that she could hide from the present.

But she could not. She brought her gaze in closer, to the bank of the nearest lake, to the foothills of the mountain. Her gaze roved up the mountainside—far below her, she could see the low-burning fires of the Usgar camp.

The distance surprised her. She must have run and clawed up the mountainside for half the night! When first she had arrived here in the tree, she had looked back, expecting to see torches moving out from the Usgar camp, or perhaps the magical light of enchanted crystals, as Seonagh and others went out in search of her.

For a long while, she searched the darkness below, and for a long while, she wondered why they were not looking for her. Then the moon dipped low enough before her to demand her attention.

The full moon, hanging red in the sky. The red face of Iseabal.

The Blood Moon, the Fossa Moon.

The enormity of her journey had struck Aoleyn hard. She could not deny the unusual moon, wonderfully round and seeming flush with blood. The demon would be hunting!

Good fortune alone had kept her path separate from that of the demon beast.

Or had it?

She told herself that the creature wasn't real, reminded herself that the fossa was a fairy tale meant to scare the children of the tribe. That had been her opinion, at least.

But out here alone under the Blood Moon, that opinion so suddenly seemed rather thin to Aoleyn.

The thought unnerved her and she scanned all the area around her. Surely the fossa couldn't come here, so near the Crystal God, she whispered to herself, unconvincingly.

She scanned back down to the encampment, to the central bonfire that had blazed this night but now burned low. The fire, of course! The night was warm and they needed no fire.

But the moon was full, the Blood Moon, and so the fire would keep the beast at bay.

Aoleyn, in her foolish anger, had let that thought, had let all thoughts, slip past. She felt the eyes of Bahdlahn's mother chasing her from the pine grove and so she had to run. Nothing had mattered except that she escape that place, the uamhas boughs, and the camp of the horrible people who would keep such slaves.

And of course, there would be no one looking for her, for none but Aoleyn were foolish enough to be out of the camp under the light of the Blood Moon.

She clutched the tree tighter, her gaze locked on the distant, dying bonfire. This grove had always called to her, had always provided her comfort, a warmth in her chest near her heart. She had never told Seonagh or any of the other women of the Coven about that warmth, but when Seonagh talked of the magic of the tribe, it often started with descriptions of a woman's *center,* her soul, a line of life from the hair atop her head to the hairs of her pubis.

This line of life energy seemed stronger to Aoleyn when she was here, in this place in sight of Usgar. She needed to remember that now, for after looking into the eyes of Bahdlahn's mother, Aoleyn had come to sense a pit of darkness beside that line of life force, a place of despair and emptiness, a place of living death.

So Aoleyn had hoped that the warmth of the Crystal God would drive that emptiness away and had run here.

She thought to turn and glimpse the angled crystal obelisk—and wouldn't it be beautiful in the moonlight?—but she found that she could not.

She couldn't move her gaze.

It wasn't the dying bonfire that held her, but rather, the darkness beyond that one spot of light. The hairs on the back of her neck stood up and tingled.

She felt the weight of a predator's calculating gaze.

She couldn't move.

Beyond Loch Beag, the huge red moon touched the horizon. All would be dark soon until the predawn glow found its way around the black mountain.

And something dangerous was near, and Aoleyn probably wouldn't even see its face until she knew death.

"Look," she told herself breathlessly, trying to find her courage. She felt the chill as the night breeze tickled her sweat-covered skin.

Sweat?

She heard herself panting and thought it ridiculously, stupidly loud!

She thought herself a fool.

She thought herself a coward.

Nay, she could not abide thinking herself a coward!

She spun about suddenly toward the meadow encircled by the grove. She saw the physical manifestation of Usgar, quietly glowing in the red moonlight's reflections.

She lifted her eyes suddenly, reflexively, up the side of the mountain, to the higher spur beyond the uamhas caves, to the region where lay Craos'a'diad, the Mouth of God. The ridge's black silhouette stood out starkly to her, blocking the many stars beyond.

So clear that silhouette!

And so clear the black form that walked the high ridge. Low, it moved, crouched perhaps, and long, and even from this distance, Aoleyn could tell that it was longer than a man was tall.

Long and low, not quite feline and more like a weasel, Aoleyn thought.

A weasel, but huge.

The black head swiveled and a pair of eyes stared back at her.

Red eyes. Red, not green like those of a cat. Not yellow like those of the brown lizards Aoleyn used to chase about the mountain stones when she was a child.

Red eyes, staring down at her from that distant ridge. Too far away to see her, and yet they could see her, she knew.

She just knew. It was real. The fossa was real. And as horrible as they had said. Even so far away, the evil aura of the demon chilled her.

The creature moved slowly, still staring down at her, seeming to glide more than walk along the ridge.

Then it was gone!

Just gone, moving impossibly fast! And it took Aoleyn a few heartbeats to realize that the creature had gone over the ridge the other way, and not down into the darkness coming toward her.

And then came the roar, long and low, a rumbling vibration that climbed right up the tree in which Aoleyn perched and into her legs and through her body. A roar she felt as much as heard.

A roar that said, "I see you."

A roar like death itself, like the blackness in her belly beside her vibrant line of life.

A roar that stole the sparkle from her eyes and threatened to fill them with the same emptiness she had seen in the eyes of Bahdlahn's mother.

Aoleyn put her head against the tree. A tear rolled down her cheek and she had to clutch the pine tighter to stop a rumble of sobs from shaking her shoulder.

No. She would not cry.

She forced her thoughts back to that day years before, when first she had seen Bahdlahn's mother. She had been so excited then. The raiders had returned, with slaves! And a pregnant woman, the ultimate capture! A blessing from Usgar, surely!

Soon, though, that memory burned at her. She saw the woman borne into the camp; she saw the woman, in her bed, a man grunting atop her. She saw the anguish in the woman's eyes, not directed at the uninvited Aoleyn nor even at the man raping her, but at her son who entered the room, who saw what he should not have to see, because she, his mother, could not protect him.

And she, Aoleyn, was too feeble to help.

The pit in her chest grew. Bahdlahn's mother's face, her anguished eyes, would not leave Aoleyn's thoughts. And the pit grew, and it consumed her center, and the spiritual warmth of the sacred grove was no match for it. Her breath came out in short gasps; her anger rose.

The image of the demon on the ridge was there in her mind, a final darkness, death itself, and she knew that she could not escape.

But the beast had departed, she reminded herself, and the moon was nearly gone and so the hunting night of the fossa would end.

A low and feral growl escaped Aoleyn's lips. She would climb down the tree and run down the mountainside to the camp and wake Seonagh from her sleep and confront the older woman about how *wrong* all this was! She would tell Seonagh of the wrongness of the look in the eyes of Bahdlahn's mother, and oh, how could the Usgar put that look into the eyes of any woman? This practice was not godly, nay, it was evil! It could not stand! And Aoleyn would fight Seonagh if she needed to, or even the whole tribe, and she would win and . . .

And she was a sixteen-year-old girl.

She did not move. The moon set and the stars shone brighter, and a mystical glow shifting through the spectrum of colors caught her attention, down the mountainside and to the southwest. She didn't want to move, but she couldn't resist, and so she leaned forward in the tree, straining to see past a lower mountain spur, trying to see the source.

The Halo of Corona.

Daonnan to the Usgar tribe, eternity, wherein sat Corsaleug, the place of spiritual reward to those loyal to the true god.

Aoleyn had seen the glow of Daonnan before, but never like this, never before the actual source of the glow.

Was this a gift from Usgar to her to counter the dark pit in her soul that so haunted her? A reminder of better possibilities than the dark fates she had witnessed so clearly?

She stared long and hard at Daonnan and felt connected to it suddenly, as if this place, the sacred grove of Usgar, was truly amplifying the beauty of the heavenly display. She thought to climb down and cross around the western rim of the mountain to gain a better vantage, but held her place, transfixed.

For a brief moment, Aoleyn knew relief.

But high clouds drifted past and Daonnan diminished, and seemed so very far away. There was no hiding there, not now, and the red eyes and the dead eyes were there again, in her thoughts, staring at the emptiness within her, terrifying her, holding her.

She shifted back, hugging the sappy trunk, and there she remained until the predawn light ebbed about Fireach Speuer and the mountainside awoke around her.

Still she did not move, not even when morning came.

Innevah rested back in the dark in a rare moment of peace. She couldn't see anything, for the moon had long set and the boughs of her home made of nothing but pine branches and dirt had no other source of light, but she turned her head to the left, toward the interlocking branches of the two pines that separated her small shelter from that of her son.

The boy the deamhain called Thump.

Innevah was proud of him. He had heard her words through the years and convincingly played the role she had given him. He was Thump— he was "stupid" to any but those who looked most closely. That was the

only way her son could live past his change to young adulthood, Innevah knew. He couldn't become recognized as a threat to the deamhain or
they would torture and murder him most horribly.

But was it a fool's errand? Surely one day the deamhan Usgar would
realize the truth of Thump—Innevah had only delayed the inevitable.

The woman sobbed, thinking, not for the first time, that she should
have smothered her son when he was a baby.

Her own cowardice affronted her.

She sensed movement to her right and spun about.

"Innevah," came a soft whisper, and she knew the voice, and she
reached her arms out to invite an embrace that she sorely needed at that
dark moment.

"Anice," she whispered back, and she hugged the woman closely and
ran her hands about, feeling the two large bumps on Anice's head.

Anice was half Innevah's age, nearing twenty, and had watched her
brother sacrificed several years earlier. She wasn't from Fasach Crann,
but from Sellad Tulach, the northernmost of the lakeside villages,
perched in the nook of two mountains, with trails and houses running
up to the crest of a deep drop overlooking the black sands and stones of
Fasail Dubh'clach far below.

In their normal lives in their respective villages, Innevah and Anice
would not likely have been friends, let alone shared such a supportive
embrace. Rare were the interactions between the folk of their villages,
and usually they only occurred out on the lake, on boats battling over a
favored fishing spot.

Up here, though, in the clutches of Usgar, they had each other and
little more.

"Why are you so sad this night?" Anice asked.

At first Innevah thought it an odd question. When was she not sad?
When were any of them not miserable?

But Innevah couldn't deny the question or the reasoning behind it.
Yes, they were always sad, but rarely sobbing. Those who had survived the
Usgar for years, particularly the women, had long ago lost their tears to an
awful, hollow emptiness. This night was one of the rare times when the
suffering became too much for emptiness and emotional distance alone.

"My son saw . . ." Innevah whispered.

Anice's sigh told her that she didn't have to elaborate. Every uamhas woman knew exactly what there was to see.

"He is strong," the younger woman offered. "He will find a way through his pain."

"He is just a child," Innevah protested. "He should not have seen. I do not want him in such pain."

"Pain is all we can know," said Anice.

Innevah hugged her tighter.

There was no way to honestly disagree.

She should have smothered her baby those many years ago, she thought again, and not for the last time.

Aoleyn stirred from her sleep, the daylight beaming about her, the sun shining brightly above Fireach Speuer. It took her a moment to gather her thoughts, to realize that she was still in the pine, ten feet from the ground, and far up the mountain from her people.

Her back ached, and her eyes stung from the harsh light of morning so high up the mountain. But the worst was the ache in her chest, in her center.

With great effort, she managed to extract herself from the hardening sap that grabbed at her.

Haunted, she climbed down from the tree and headed back to the encampment. Many were about but none paid her any heed as she moved straight across toward Seonagh's tent.

She saw Bahdlahn and his mother among a group of uamhas clearing the ashes about the bonfire and gathering new kindling. There wouldn't be another Blood Moon this night, of course, but the fossa's hunt often provoked reactions among the other denizens of Fireach Speuer, the sidhe, or the great predators, or even a stampede of deer.

Aoleyn kept her gaze to the flap of her teacher's abode, not wanting to lock gazes with Bahdlahn, and certainly not with his mother.

One of the slave guards, whip in hand, offered her a smile and a nod, and she just moved faster, needing to be away.

These people didn't even realize that she had been out of the camp throughout the night, Aoleyn thought, and hoped.

But those hopes were dashed the moment she moved into Seonagh's tent, to find a glare of such intensity and anger that it took her breath away.

Aoleyn shied from the older woman, but only for a heartbeat, reminding herself of the look in the eyes of Bahdlahn's mother, reminding herself that this woman before her was complicit in that travesty.

She stood straight and matched Seonagh's stare.

Slowly, unblinking, without breaking eye contact for even an instant, Aoleyn crossed the tent to the washbasin. She turned away to wash away the dirt of the mountain, scooping lukewarm water from the basin with cupped hands.

Before she could bring the water to her face, she felt a hand grasp the collar of her tunic, yanking her backward and spinning her about. She nearly fell, but caught herself at the last instant, straightening to face her assailant just as Seonagh brought her hand around to issue a sharp backhand slap across Aoleyn's face.

Aoleyn yelped, as much in surprise as in pain.

"You are to sleep in your own cot," Seonagh said, her voice flat and emotionless. Aoleyn opened her mouth to respond, but Seonagh slapped her again.

"I . . ." the young woman stammered, and another smack snapped her head to the side.

"Were you with a man?"

Aoleyn stared at her blankly. "What? No," she answered. "No!"

Seonagh stared down at her, clearly disbelieving.

"Who was it?" the woman asked.

Aoleyn shook her head, her expression sour.

"Then where were you?" Seonagh demanded. "I will ask others."

"None will answer," said Aoleyn.

Seonagh's face contorted, her eyes going wide, and she stiffened as if she meant to slap Aoleyn yet again.

"I was not in the camp!" the young woman blurted.

"You stayed with the slaves?" Seonagh shot back, horrified. "In the grove?"

"No," Aoleyn started to say, but she bit it back, considering her options here. "Not with the slaves, but I was in the grove, yes."

Seonagh studied her carefully. "Are you lying to me, child?"

"No," Aoleyn said, and she straightened with some confidence, for it was not an untrue statement, even though it was obviously a deception. "I was in the grove."

Seonagh didn't respond, didn't blink, for a long while. "There are magical ways to learn . . ." she started to warn.

"Fetch the gray-flecked crystal, if you need," Aoleyn invited, for she knew that the Coven kept a certain crystal, thick with wedstones, that could be used to determine if someone was lying (though it was not overly reliable, Seonagh had taught her). Still, even if lies could be easily detected, clever Aoleyn figured she was safe enough, for in this case, "in the grove" wasn't an untrue statement, though surely Seonagh was thinking of one grove, the pines serving as the slave encampment, while Aoleyn had spent the night in another altogether!

"Why would you stay with them?" Seonagh asked suspiciously.

"I didn't," Aoleyn answered. "I mean, I was out and about. I just . . ."

"Out and about," Seonagh interrupted. "You were out of the camp. On a night of Iseabal's red face, you were out of the camp?"

Seonagh rubbed her chin, her eyes flaring, and Aoleyn braced for another slap. "How can one as promising as Aoleyn be so truly stupid?" Seonagh asked, and that stung more than a slap ever could. "Do you know what the fossa would do to you?"

"It is dangero—"

"Dangerous?" Seonagh mocked. She moved very close to Aoleyn's face, her eyes flaring with wild outrage.

The reaction shocked Aoleyn with its intensity, and its honesty! She knew the stories of the fossa, of course, but to see Seonagh so unhinged had her off-balance indeed.

"First it would chew through your ankles," she said. "So quickly. One bite." She snapped her fingers against her thumb before Aoleyn's face, startling the girl and drawing a gasp of surprise.

"How pretty would be Aoleyn's clever smile, I wonder, when you turned your head from the dirt to see your feet removed from your body? How confident your cry, I wonder, as the demon fossa dragged you away, and took you to its lair to eat you? To slowly eat you, and you would live for a very long time, though you wish it not!"

Aoleyn had nothing to reply, and so just stood there with her mouth hanging open, her black eyes rimmed with moisture, defeated.

"You never go beyond the edge of the camp without my permission. Do you understand?"

"Yes," the girl—and truly she felt like a little girl at that moment— answered deferentially.

Seonagh snarled anyway. "And when a task is assigned you, you are to do the task as given."

Aoleyn's expression changed in her surprise at the abrupt shift of the subject, and before she could stop herself, she shook her head—or started to, until Seonagh slapped her again, this time harder.

"I filled the baskets," she whispered in reply. "I did as you commanded, exactly as asked." Her voice wavered as she replied, for now she was simply overwhelmed, sobs welling inside of her.

"Exactly as commanded," Seonagh corrected her. "I need not ask anything of you. You were told to take an uamhas woman, and instead you took a child. A valuable child, at that. You knew better. You knew that you should be helped by an adult, by one of the lakewomen. But still you chose the child, simply so that you could defy me."

Aoleyn started to respond, but held her tongue. She focused instead on what Seonagh had just said: a valuable child? Aoleyn did not understand. The boy seemed so feeble, mentally weak. What could possibly be valuable about him?

She thought about asking Seonagh to explain, but reconsidered before her mouth began to move. She would ask Bahdlahn himself later on, but no, she would not ask this harsh woman. And particularly not now, when Seonagh was so clearly angry and when she was trembling with so many swirling emotions.

And Seonagh was rightfully angry, Aoleyn knew in her heart, and not just because Aoleyn hadn't returned the previous night. Despite her protestations, her choice of Bahdlahn had been intended to give offense. It was an act of defiance, as was her refusal to return to the camp the previous night.

Well enough, she figured. She wanted Seonagh to be angry. She wasn't quite sure of exactly where she had found this focus, but it certainly had something to do with that pit in her chest, that anger she had felt when she had looked into the eyes of Bahdlahn's mother. Aoleyn dropped her gaze to the floor, a gesture of submission, merely to placate Seonagh. But inwardly, she smiled.

Seonagh took her shoulder roughly and turned the girl toward the basin. "Now wash yourself, child," she said, her voice still edged in anger, but holding something else Aoleyn could not identify—concern, perhaps? "Then we can begin the day's lessons."

Aoleyn did as she was told. She washed, she ate, she sat quietly and obediently for her lessons with Seonagh.

Only occasionally did her thoughts drift away from the tasks at hand, her mind's eye again seeing the stares. The red eyes, the dead eyes.

So different, yet so alike, as if they were aiming for the dark place inside of her, but from different directions.

The stare of Bahdlahn's mother.

The stare of the demon fossa.

12

THE BELLS

It was the farthest east Talmadge had traveled in his life, so far that the mountains of the Barbican, which marked the western boundary of the Wilderlands, were behind him now. So far that he could ride to Ursal, the seat of power in the kingdom of Honce-the-Bear, in less than two weeks if he so chose.

But he wouldn't choose to do that. He was in the region known as the Wilderlands now, though it was far more settled than that to which he was accustomed. His discomfort grew with every hamlet he spotted, a fact that wasn't lost on his traveling companion.

"Sorry you followed me, eh?" Khotai Tsentsen asked when they set camp atop a bald hillock one night, the lights of a distant village shining in the southeast.

"I enjoy the company," Talmadge replied wryly. The statement was true enough. He had known Khotai for eight years now, since their meeting at Matinee, and it seemed like every passing year had them spending more and more time together, except for two years when their paths had not crossed. Talmadge did enjoy being around this woman, more than he ever expected. Her exotic looks, that strange cross between the pale Alpinadoran barbarians of the far north and ruddy-skinned To-gai-ru nomad of the high steppes, had not grown less attractive to the man. He had seen no one else quite like Khotai in all his life and all his travels.

Talmadge didn't think he'd ever get tired of hearing her tales of her years among the To-gai-ru, with their strange ways and culture, and every year, Khotai came back with new stories to perform—and perform, she did, as well as any bard.

"I think you just missed me last year, more than you'll e'er admit," Khotai teased, for indeed, the two had not met up at Matinee the previous year.

"Can you say any less for yourself? I came here instead of remaining at Matinee at your insistence, yes? And I've lost the last month of winter and the whole of spring, and I'll lose the rest of the season just getting back to Matinee!"

Khotai laughed at him. "If you're to ever shrink your world from Matinee to your mysterious lake in the mountains, you'll soon bore me," she said. "I don't like to be bored. Would that you might have joined me last year!"

Talmadge winced at the thought, torn now as he had been upon the invitation, for that invitation had been left open when he and Khotai had parted ways after Matinee in the summer of 843. Khotai had told him then that she meant to go to the east with the turn of the year, all the way to the Mirianic Ocean, to the great desert city of Jacintha, in search of her father.

As much as he had come to enjoy Khotai's company, the thought of entering a city of thousands and thousands of people terrified the man.

"I know. I know and I accept the truth of Talmadge," Khotai said, as if reading his thoughts, and she waved her hand at him.

"I am here, at least."

The woman nodded and smiled widely. "You've been invited to visit Redshanks!"

"You were, not I!"

"Mostly because he knew I could deliver you, and your pearls," Khotai said. "What woman or man roaming the wilds would refuse an in-vitation to dine at the house of Redshanks?"

"True enough," he admitted, and he nodded, thinking that almost all at Matinee would lift their flagons in toast simply to learn that the legendary Redshanks was still alive, for the man had not attended the gathering in more than five years.

"So no more of your complaining?"

Talmadge held up his hands in defeat.

Khotai tilted her bowl, draining the last of her stew, then tossed the bowl aside, burped with surprising volume (drawing a complimentary nod from Talmadge), and crawled about the small fire to cuddle up next to the man. She rested back in his arms, leaning back and forcing him back with her that they could look up at the millions of stars twin-kling this night.

"Tell me about the pirates," he bade her.

"No," she replied. "You tell me about strange-headed fisher folk at your mysterious lake and the demons of the mountain."

Talmadge snorted. "I have told you of them many times."

"Tell me again."

Talmadge knew where this was going. Several times over the years, Khotai had asked to travel along with him for his yearly journey to Loch Beag.

On more than one occasion, Talmadge had almost given in and taken her along, but always, right before he would say yes, he remem-bered the clo'dearche and the killing of Badger.

Though now he mostly only remembered the gruesome sounds, the vicious lizard chewing at the corpse of the hanging man, tearing flesh and crunching bone, sounds that had chased Talmadge across the lake waters, all the way to Car Seileach.

As uncomfortable as Talmadge was in coming to villages like the one of his childhood, he was even more unnerved by the thought of having someone, anyone, accompany him to Loch Beag ever again.

"Your father," he whispered. "You have not even finished your tale and you speak of places I will never see."

"Then go and see them!"

"Tell me."

Khotai sighed loudly and launched back into the story of her great adventure, crossing the desert of Behren to the great and exotic seaport of Jacintha.

Talmadge closed his eyes and let her words take him on that journey, and he fell asleep dreaming of water that showed no far bank, and of great sailing ships. He even heard the bells of one ship calling out, four notes repeating—*ding, dang, ding, dang*—in celebratory cadence.

But no, not ship bells. Church bells, like the ones of Talmadge's town, though he remembered them not in such exuberance, but in the low tonal peals of death.

The man's eyes popped open, to find that the stars were gone, replaced by the glow of predawn, to find that he was not dreaming dreams inspired by Khotai's tale.

The bells were really ringing, in this time and in this place—or at least, in the village not so far away.

Talmadge sat up, taking care, unsuccessfully, to not stir Khotai.

"What is it?" she asked before she had even opened her eyes.

Talmadge stood, hands on hips, staring at the distant structures. "I know not."

For all that he tried, he couldn't get the last time he had heard the toll of church bells out of his head.

Khotai was up beside him. "Well, let's go find out," she said, and started for the horses.

But Talmadge caught her by the arm and held her back, and when she turned, her expression grew curious.

"What is it?" she asked, but he didn't answer, and just continued to stare at the distant village.

"Talmadge?" she asked, confused.

But he had told her of his home town of Westhaven and the tragedy of the rosie plague, and the bells, tolling for his family, chasing him out of town.

"That is not a funeral peal," Khotai said emphatically, and she grabbed

Talmadge by the arm and forced him to look at her. "Those are bells of celebration."

Her stare more than her words broke the spell, and Talmadge blinked repeatedly, then, as she repeated her statement.

They packed up their camp, saddled the horses they had bought from a stable on the western edge of the Wilderlands, and walked down to Appleby-in-Wilderland, the village that served as home to the famed frontiersman Redshanks.

They found the town wide awake, with people dancing in the streets, and the markets already bustling. The name "Princess Jilseponie Ursal!" was shouted from balconies and rooftops.

"So that's it, then," Khotai remarked as they walked their horses along the cobblestone streets of Appleby-in-Wilderland, following directions townsfolk eagerly offered, toward the home of Redshanks. "Honce has itself a new heir."

Talmadge shrugged, hardly caring—and why should he? Even in his childhood, his family had never considered themselves part of this kingdom, and indeed, had generations before headed out to settle in an area where they need not worry of kings and lords and armies trampling peasants underfoot.

"Well, they seem to care," Khotai returned with a snicker.

"Do you have kings in To-gai?"

"Warlords," she replied. "We are nomads."

"Always at war?"

She shook her head. "War with the steppes and the vipers and the lions and the roaring winds, yes. War with each other, not so much."

"So what do the warlords do?" Talmadge asked.

"They lead the migrations," Khotai explained. "They determine the scouts and guide us in pursuit of the herds. And when we come upon another tribe, they speak for us, that we can determine the hunting grounds."

"And what do they exact in payment from their people, these *warlords?*"

Khotai looked at him as if she did not understand, and Talmadge smiled, for that was all the answer he needed.

"Your warlords are very different from the lords of Honce, I believe."

Khotai didn't pursue the reasoning. "Neither matter to us," she agreed.

They were at the porch of a log cabin, then, solidly built and larger than most of the other homes in Appleby-in-Wilderland. Before they had even dismounted, Redshanks opened the door and held his arms out wide and high in invitation.

"Bah, but you're late!" he said. "Every day before this, I been putting out extra plates and cooking a dozen eggs! I'm blaming you for this!" He rubbed his now-ample belly, jiggling the extra girth. "Couldn't be letting them go to waste, you know."

Khotai ran to give him a hug and he moved gingerly toward her. He looked good, Talmadge thought, though he noted a distinct stiffness and limp in the old hunter's step. He kept an eye on that as Redshanks led them into the house and the breakfast table, and understood then why the man hadn't been going to Matinee.

And sadly, why he likely would never do so again. It became obvious to Talmadge that Redshanks's days of wandering the wilderness were long behind him. He had kept his smile, and kept his spirits high, as he and Khotai began trading stories of the last few years, but the man had aged.

Talmadge offered to cook the breakfast as the two continued their storytelling. There was a great bond here between these two.

Soon he was only half listening, his thoughts turning to the unlikely journey that had brought him this far to the east, and uncomfortably close to the kingdom of Honce-the-Bear.

Suddenly something Khotai was saying caught his ear. "And you are now under the watchful eye of a new king yet again?"

"Not so new," Redshanks answered. "Been five years since King Aydrian made his departure at the end of an army of spears."

"He was killed?" Khotai asked.

"Exiled. Taken by Jilseponie far from the lands of men, so it's said."

"Jilseponie? The new princess?"

"Named after her, but not of her blood," Redshanks explained. "In her honor, and one she well earned, by all accounts. 'Tis a long tale."

Redshanks shrugged as if it didn't matter. "It would seem that the squabbling is over. One king or another, what does it matter? Their arguments are over their own power, and with little regard to what any of us might want. It's always been so."

"You came to live here, not I," Khotai pointedly reminded.

"I followed opportunity more suited to a breaking body," Redshanks said with a laugh.

"It is always about business for Redshanks."

"I have lived well!" he reminded.

Talmadge brought the food to the table then, and took his seat opposite the legendary frontiersman.

"I still do!" Redshanks added.

"Well enough?" Talmadge asked.

"More than that!" Redshanks answered through a mouthful of food.

"But you are not satisfied," said Talmadge. Khotai put her hand on his forearm to try to turn him from this course.

He did glance at her, but pressed on as he did. "If you were, you would not have asked us to visit."

"A favor for an old friend, perhaps," Redshanks said.

"Just that?" Talmadge asked doubtfully.

Khotai gasped a bit at that, but Redshanks took it as no insult, clearly, and laughed heartily.

"Well . . ." he admitted. "You ken me too well, I fear."

"But why?" Talmadge bluntly asked.

"Why?" he answered. "Opportunity!"

"You just said you were living well. You have all that you could need. Why chase more?"

Redshanks laughed again. "Ah, Talmadge, you beautiful peasant," he said. "Because it's there! Because it's exciting! Because when I stop chasing it, well, put me in the ground and throw dirt on me."

Talmadge just shrugged and shook his head.

"If you gave it a try, you'd come to see. I can show you the way, and might that you'd find a bit more smiles on that dour face o' yours if you followed that trail."

Talmadge leaned back in his seat and studied the man.

"You've the pearls?" Redshanks asked Khotai.

"Just a few."

"Bah!"

"Not a good year on the lake," Talmadge lied, for it had been better than he had let on to Khotai when she had told him of Redshanks's invitation. He had seen too much of the ways of the frontiersmen to let on about the wealth he carried so far to the east, down overgrown trails rife with highwaymen, where whispers moved faster than horses.

Redshanks sighed and leaned back. "Perhaps a year too soon, then," he said. "I still have many arrangements to make."

"What arrangements?" Talmadge asked. "What are you trying to do?"

"Right to the point, eh?" Redshanks replied with a grin. "I like that. You've seen me walk. I doubt I'll e'er cross the Masur Delaval again."

Talmadge looked to Khotai, not understanding.

"The river separating the more civilized lands," Redshanks explained. "Your pearls bring in a great price in the city of Palmaris on the eastern bank of the Delaval."

"And you want me to go there?"

"They're your pearls and my buyers," said Redshanks. "The fewer people I put in between those truths, the more for me and you."

"I have enough."

"There's never enough."

"Why?"

"Because more is life . . . excitement . . . enjoyment. You've this beautiful woman by your side! Oh, I know her charms and her skill. Would you not build a life of excitement and enrichment together?"

Talmadge understood at that moment that he and Redshanks would never agree on what those words, "excitement" and "enrichment," might mean. He said nothing, but let the man continue to explain the network he was setting up to funnel the goods more efficiently to this city of Palmaris and beyond.

Talmadge took note of Khotai, and saw her genuine interest. He could accommodate that interest, he believed, without having to journey to these places.

The three spoke into the afternoon, then went out and joined in a celebration for Princess Jilseponie.

Khotai and Talmadge stayed with Redshanks that night, but surprisingly, to both their host and Khotai, that single day was as long a delay as Talmadge would suffer.

Loch Beag, his yearly respite, was calling to him, and he had many hundreds of miles to cover to get there before snow covered the mountain trails.

Talmadge made a deal with Redshanks for the pearls he had brought, and even threw in a few for free in appreciation for the man's good intentions. He even agreed to return to Appleby-in-Wilderland in the next year or so to perhaps take Redshanks's plans further, though he made it clear that he would not be the courier.

"We'll see" was all Redshanks would say to that, and slyly, and with a look to Khotai.

Many times did Redshanks try to convince Talmadge to remain a bit longer, but the man would hear none of it, and he and Khotai were on the road back to the west soon after an early breakfast the next day.

The Barbican mountain range was far behind the couple when they came to a fork in the trail, one going northwest toward a distant river, the other southwest toward the Matinee. They were more than two weeks out from Appleby-in-Wilderland and had made fine time, although it was well into summer now and the Matinee remained a journey of more than a week—likely more, since the land was getting rougher, the going slower.

Khotai turned her horse down that southwestern trail, but Talmadge surprisingly dismounted and began pulling his packs from his mount.

"Too early to camp," she remarked.

"My road is north, to the river," Talmadge explained. "I've no reason to return to Matinee this season."

"You'll ride the river to your secret mountain lake?"

Talmadge smiled at her.

Khotai dismounted. "What will we do with the horses, then? Just set them free?"

171

Talmadge stopped grinning. "We are only a day's ride from the next stable. Sell mine and do what you will with the silver."

"You would leave me alone in the midst of the wilderness?"

Her feigned distress brought back Talmadge's chuckle. "Where you usually are, and with your usual company?"

"Take me to the lake," Khotai said earnestly, moving right before the man and staring at him hard with her dark eyes. "Have I not earned your trust?"

Talmadge leaned back from her and chewed his lip. The question was ridiculous, of course, for he had come to trust this wonderful woman implicitly.

But the request alone sent his thoughts cascading back to that awful day on the southwestern banks of Loch Beag. Even all these years later, the image of dead Badger settled heavily in his memories. It was the only time Talmadge had ever killed a man, and he hadn't much enjoyed the experience. So deep was his revulsion, and his shame, that he didn't even want to risk anyone ever learning the truth.

He shook his head.

Khotai started to argue, but she bit it back and simply stared hard at the man.

Talmadge started to turn away, but she grabbed him roughly. "I thought . . ." she said when their eyes met again. "I . . ."

She let him go and pushed him back a step, then stared at him a moment longer before shaking her head right back at him and spinning away.

She gathered up the horses and was away before Talmadge had even finished loading the small sled he meant to drag to the river. She rode away hard and kept up a great pace, and rode long after sunset, arriving at a small cluster of cabins, which included one of the stables scattered about the wilderness and Wilderlands trails, in time to get a fine dinner.

In the morning, she surprised herself by selling both horses and most of her goods right there in the hamlet, and when she departed, right after breakfast, she didn't continue to the southwest and Matinee, but straight north.

Khotai knew this land fairly well, and she could track a man as well as any.

She needed resolution with Talmadge. It was that simple. She loved the man, but needed more from him than a few months of most years at his side.

And if he proved not worthy of that love, she'd at least know his secret mountain lake and the tribes who traded pearls. Redshanks could certainly be counted upon to facilitate the trading route he had described, and if Talmadge didn't care enough to take the man up on his offer, she would.

13

INTENDED

In the month since the red glow of Iseabal, Aoleyn had noted a distinct shift in the attitude of Seonagh, one that had her continually off-balance in her duties and even a little fearful.

Aoleyn couldn't really put her finger on it, and eventually, she just shrugged and tried to let it go, glad that Seonagh wasn't heaping added duties upon her. And so this particular midsummer afternoon, she expected to be released from her lessons to wander the encampment when twilight descended, to find some scraps among the tables set out around the central bonfire, where the meal was being cooked by a group of women who were not in the Coven.

She finished her last chore, repairing a basket Seonagh had accidentally burned on one corner, and presented the item, then bowed and moved to leave the tent.

But Seonagh called her back.

"Not this day, child," she said. "Wash your face, and sit here." Aoleyn hardly heard the words, but the woman's tone struck her profoundly. The edge was softer than Aoleyn was used to hearing from Seonagh, or anyone else, for that matter. Had Seonagh garnered some more information about her indiscretion? Had she discovered that the refuge to which Aoleyn had referred wasn't the one harboring the slaves, but the sacred grove far up the mountain?

Aoleyn reminded herself not to infer too much here.

The young woman sucked in her breath. Where had she erred? She had crossed the winter plateau, barely aware of her surroundings, in her flight from the scene with Bahdlahn's mother. But the Usgar-forfach, the Elder, was up there, of course—he was always there! Had he seen her?

She tried to replay her journey through the winter camp. She hadn't seen any sign of the old man, or anyone else. She had even looked to his cottage, one of the few permanent structures up on the plateau. She glanced at Seonagh. The woman hadn't left at all this day. How would she have gotten any news?

The young woman frowned. The crystals, of course. The witches could see over great distances, could even free their spirits to wander the forest and mountainsides, so it was whispered. But Aoleyn shook her head and dismissed her suspicion, reminding herself that Seonagh hadn't even known she was out of the camp until she had volunteered the information. She glanced at the witch again, and tried to calm herself, and when that didn't work, she reminded herself that Seonagh was one of them, one of the Usgar, and they were all ugly and mean and cruel.

They kept slaves.

Aoleyn was still snarling when Seonagh lightly touched her shoulder, and as her head snapped around, the older woman motioned to a cushion of woven dried reeds, stuffed with fluffy white wool that the war party had brought back from their latest raids on the lake tribes. Aoleyn hesitated, looking about the room and then studying Seonagh's face, looking for some clue as to what was happening. She found no such hints, and a tickle of fear had her considering fleeing the tent and the encampment once more. She could outrun the older woman to escape into the rising dusk, and it might be worth the inevitable beating she'd take upon her return just to see the look on Seonagh's face after yet another act of defiance.

But Aoleyn dismissed that course almost immediately; she found that she was more curious than afraid. Seonagh was hinting at something different this night, and Aoleyn wanted to know what it might be. Perhaps she'd regret it—that seemed the most likely thing to her—but she shrugged and moved to take her seat.

Seonagh grabbed her by the shoulder, gently, and turned her about until Aoleyn's back was to the woman. Aoleyn did not resist as Seonagh began smoothing her thick black hair. The older woman's strong hands, which could be so rough and mean when they slapped Aoleyn, were firm and gentle now and, strangely, soothing. Aoleyn felt Seonagh's fingers moving through her hair, massaging her scalp, twisting and wrapping strands as if she were weaving a basket or a sleeping mat. The woman's hands moved deftly, swiftly, as if they had done this a thousand times and a thousand more. Aoleyn thought herself a fine basket-weaver, though she disliked the work quite thoroughly, but she realized now, feeling Seonagh working her hair into a perfect braid, how amateur her own movements truly were.

When Seonagh was finished—which was not very long at all—the woman stepped back and glanced to the side to regard Aoleyn's reflection in a polished silver mirror. She was smiling widely when she bade Aoleyn to do the same.

Aoleyn was feeling quite off-balance by then. She rose tentatively and moved to glance at her reflection, something she did not often do. She brought a hand up to her hair, to feel Seonagh's masterful work, but she was quite cautious, fearful of disturbing the braid. The hair from the right side of her head was pulled up and back, braided with the hair from the center, leaving her right temple and ear exposed; on her left, her hair hung wild and free, untied, protecting that side of her head.

Seonagh handed the girl a small doeskin bag. "When we reach the fire, empty the bag into it," she instructed.

Aoleyn squeezed the bag with her hand, finding it squishy and shifting, as if filled with a thousand tiny beads. Curious, she pulled back the top flap and peeked into the container, to find it full of seeds. "These are from the pinecones," she said aloud as she sorted it out.

"You thought that day's task mere busywork?" Seonagh chided. "Yes, those seeds, and more like them, are the fruits of your labor."

"But what are they for?"

"They are to be cast into the fire when we arrive."

Aoleyn stared at her, then at the seeds, then back at Seonagh.

By that point, Seonagh had her hand out toward the young woman, open palmed, holding a simple small flint knife that appeared quite old and quite well worn. "And you will also need this."

Aoleyn took it, hesitatingly. "Am I to throw this in the fire, too, then?" she asked earnestly, completely at a loss.

Seonagh's stern glare in response warned Aoleyn that Seonagh thought she was being mocked. The younger woman quickly painted a confused look on her own face, doubling down on that honest expression to show Seonagh that such was not the case. For Seonagh had put her off-balance again.

"Not into the fire. When he demands the blade, you're to hand it to him," Seonagh said matter-of-factly, and she turned toward the tent's exit.

"He?" Aoleyn asked, but of course Seonagh did not respond and simply strode purposefully from the tent. After a brief moment of doubt, Aoleyn tied the pouch of seeds onto her belt, tucked the knife in beside it, and skipped fast to follow, growing more curious with each step out of the tent.

She knew they were not going to the bonfire for a meal—they moved right through the camp and crossed the perimeter, the sentries offering not so much as a nod. Aoleyn's hungry stomach grumbled at the injustice, but she kept her thoughts to herself.

"Night will soon fall," Aoleyn said with some concern, for the moon was expected to be full this night, and she had heard the whispers that Iseabal might soon return in her red glory. Even without that daunting possibility, nights on Fireach Speuer were fraught with danger.

Seonagh didn't answer, other than to lift a crystal that shone like the stars, lighting the way out of the encampment and up the mountain trail.

The pair continued to climb, ascending the mountainside, the same path Aoleyn had walked the night of the Blood Moon. Was that the secret here, Aoleyn wondered, her thoughts spinning? Were they going to the sacred grove of Usgar? How did they know?

"We cannot get back . . ." Aoleyn said.

"Be quiet, girl," Seonagh replied. "There will be no Blood Moon this night."

"The seer spoke that it might be so."

"The seer spoke as the Usgar-righinn instructed," Seonagh interrupted. The older woman stopped and turned back, facing Aoleyn directly.

"It might be a Blood Moon," Aoleyn said sheepishly.

"Do you think we do not know these things?" Seonagh asked. "Do you think I would have brought you out here if the demon fossa was hunting?"

"We are halfway to the winter plateau."

"More than halfway," Seonagh corrected, and she turned and started up the mountainside at a brisk pace.

Before they arrived at the winter plateau, a fire came into view, high up on the ledge above and beyond the grove, higher than the uamhas caves, even.

Aoleyn paused and swallowed hard. The fire was up near where she had seen the demon fossa that terrible night. Was that a part of this journey? She felt then that she was surely to be punished.

It took Seonagh turning back many heartbeats later to even inform the girl that she was falling far behind.

"Come along," the woman ordered.

The hairs on Aoleyn's neck stood up as she recalled those red eyes of the hunting demon, the stare that had gone right through her, that had mocked her, that had promised her a horrible death. She wanted to say something to Seonagh, but the woman had turned away once more and was pushing far ahead.

For all of her courage, Aoleyn did not want to be out alone in the darkness.

When Seonagh reached the edge of the winter plateau and did not slow, it occurred to Aoleyn that perhaps they were heading to the sacred chasm, Craos'a'diad, the Mouth of God, a thought that excited her greatly. She had been there only once before, but she had been much younger and hardly remembered the place—and certainly she could not have then appreciated the importance of it.

She hustled to catch up to Seonagh, who was moving more slowly then, her eyes cast downward.

"Proper respect, girl," she whispered.

Aoleyn glanced up at her curiously, then glanced past her and understood, for from the open flap of the lone tent on the plateau, she noted a form, a man, staring out at her.

The Usgar-forfach.

Aoleyn cast her gaze to the ground and moved closer to Seonagh's side.

As with many of the Usgar, particularly the younger members of the tribe, the Usgar-forfach was more myth than reality. She hadn't seen him that night a month ago when she had passed very near to this place not once, but twice, but she hadn't looked very hard.

If her sacrilege was known, it was because the Usgar-forfach had seen her.

Aoleyn found it difficult to breathe.

Aoleyn grimaced and stopped.

Seonagh said nothing but quickly reached back and grabbed Aoleyn by the shoulder, and when Aoleyn shrugged away, Seonagh grabbed her by the braided hair and tugged her along.

"Do not tarry in sight of the Usgar-forfach when the tribe is in the encampment far below," Seonagh warned her quietly as they passed through and out the far side of the plateau.

To Aoleyn's surprise then, Seonagh did not veer toward the sacred grove, nor toward the uamhas caves and the path that led up to the Mouth of God. Instead, she led Aoleyn along a wilder route of broken stones and scrub bushes, making a direct line to the fire that burned high above. They were not climbing any path, though, and indeed were descending into a bowl, and the course took them to the base of a sheer cliff directly below the fire.

They weren't far from the winter camp, nor from the sacred grove, but in a place where Aoleyn had never been. Of course, the Usgar didn't wander much from the camp during the winter months, after all, for the snow always lay deep. And surely they didn't come to the cliffs, where the huge black-winged rocs perched.

That thought at first terrified Aoleyn, but then brought a bit of a smile to her face, despite her trepidation. She remembered the old crone who had raised her, the woman telling her often that the rocs would have little trouble in grabbing up a small girl with their mighty talons!

It was just a story to frighten her, Aoleyn had come to believe. Again, despite her reservations, despite her fears that her crime had been discovered and that she had been brought out here to be punished, she couldn't help but marvel at how different the world was beginning to seem to her, how more completely and wonderfully her heart and mind, now as a young woman, was beginning to weave together what had not so long ago seemed as discordant pieces and wild stories of a very big mountain.

Seonagh stood right before the cliff face, one hand in a fist, head bowed, eyes closed as if in deep concentration.

Aoleyn glanced around, but saw no path, nor cut stair. She wanted to ask if they had reached their destination, or how they might scale the cliff in the darkness. Before she could, though, Seonagh glanced at her and nodded to the stone before her, the woman's gaze directing Aoleyn to a cleverly cut hole in the stone.

A handhold, and inspecting it closely in the starlight of Seonagh's crystal, Aoleyn realized that there were many more, a ladder of handholds moving right up the rock face.

She put her hand on the lowest, but looked back to Seonagh, for this seemed a truly treacherous climb! Aoleyn could go up the tallest tree without reservation, and didn't shy from scrambling all about boulder tumbles. But this . . . this was an ascent straight up the side of a sheer rise, a cliff as tall as ten tall warriors standing one atop the other!

But Seonagh just nodded to her, imploring her to climb.

Aoleyn swallowed hard, brought her torso right against the stone, and started to pull herself up that she could reach the next hold with her other hand.

And suddenly she felt weightless, felt as though she could leap into the sky and never come down! She raised herself easily—so easily!—with her one hand, caught the next handhold and propelled herself higher, not even bothering to set her foot in the first handhold as she scaled higher. She felt as if she was floating up the rock face, and she gained speed with every pull. Again and again, hand over hand, she effortlessly ascended.

She glanced back down below at Seonagh, to see the woman, head bowed in concentration, one hand clenched tightly against her breast, pulling herself up the cliff methodically and carefully with her other hand.

Aoleyn understood that the magic was in that clenched fist, was coursing through Seonagh and being extended from Seonagh to her. The implications, the power, jolted the young woman. Aoleyn had felt the magic internally with the crystals she had touched, and again when she had gazed upon the crystal manifestation of Usgar. She knew, of course, that the blessed weapons could bring forth magical effects, like making the warriors lighter on their feet, offering a bit of flame to make a weapon strike more lethal, even to impart some minor healing to the fighters.

But this! This was something far more profound, something Aoleyn had never even dared to fantasize about.

This was all the whispers of the Coven's power revealed to be anything but exaggerations.

Aoleyn crested the cliff face, to see the fire and six people, two women and four men, visible in the light about it, including Mairen and another member of the Coven named Connebragh. Laoch Tay Aillig was there, and a couple of others with him, but they were back in the shadows and she couldn't recognize them from this side of the fire. The last man was Brayth. He sat before the fire, wearing no shirt, nothing at all from the waist up.

She focused too intently on the gathering, though, for as she came up over the ledge, Seonagh's levitating magic left her and she very nearly fell on her face, catching herself awkwardly to turn her tumble into a less-than-graceful stumble.

She had already felt very small, a girl again, when she recognized these powerful Usgar, and now the poor girl blushed fiercely and wanted to simply run away.

But she didn't. She righted herself and stood silently, if uncomfortably, and waited with as much composure as she could manage for Seonagh to come up behind her.

Even then, everyone continued to stare at poor Aoleyn, and those looks seemed to her to be growing more judgmental. She didn't understand until Seonagh nudged her, rather forcefully, toward the fire. When Aoleyn looked back in surprise, Seonagh led her gaze to the pouch on her belt.

The girl flushed red, even more uneasy, for she had forgotten all about the seeds. She quickly and roughly pulled the bag off her belt and fumbled with its drawstring, finally getting it open so she could spill its contents into the fire. She nearly dropped the bag into the fire as well, but managed to catch it just at her fingertips. "Sorry," she whispered, not to anyone in particular, and indeed, no one seemed to hear or care.

And a moment later, Aoleyn didn't care either, for as soon as the seeds hit the fire, they burst, casting off a pink haze, a sudden blast of heat and smoke that caught Aoleyn full in the face. She coughed and sputtered and stumbled backward to sit on the ground. She didn't actually mean to sit down, but suddenly the world had become very bendy, and standing was no longer an option. She felt as though she might throw up, but she held it down. Her eyes couldn't seem to come into focus. She saw the man who was sitting across from her reach out over the fire pit, holding something red, a slab of meat, which he dropped onto a stone in the center of the fire.

Aoleyn couldn't make sense of it, and felt utterly lost here, yet no one spoke.

After a moment, the man reached his hand across the fire, toward Aoleyn. She gazed at the arm, and then his bare chest, and saw something unexpected. Brayth's torso was intricately tattooed, delicate lines weaving all about. The light from the fire danced across his chest, mesmerizing Aoleyn. She thought them beautiful. She thought them profound. Brayth spoke, but she did not hear his words; whatever was said was not as important as those tattoos.

She felt a prod from behind, from Seonagh, and when she lazily looked up, the woman's scowl snapped her back to her senses.

The man spoke again, a single word: "*Corc*," the old word for a knife.

"Oh, yes," Aoleyn said, fumbling. Finally, she grabbed the flint knife from her belt and placed it upon Brayth's open palm.

Suddenly, his other arm came forward, directly across the fire, caring not at all about the wisps of flames that seemed to almost encircle his forearm, and he grasped Aoleyn by the wrist, and not gently. She tried to pull away, but the man was much stronger than she, and he easily yanked her in closer. He brought the knife up to the side of her forehead, and again she tried to shy away, tried to fall back from the sharp edge of the flint, but she could not.

Then, as suddenly as he'd lunged at her, he withdrew. She felt the slightest trickle of blood dripping down from her right temple, tracing the line of her high cheekbone, and all the way down to her chin. Reflexively, her tongue flicked out to taste her own blood, but she kept her eyes locked on the man. He took the knife and brought it to his own temple. Aoleyn saw the red stain on the blade as he moved it.

Her blood.

Then there was more redness, on his face, his own blood. On the flint blade, they mixed. He reached again into the fire, to the piece of meat cooking on the stone slab. In a series of practiced movements, the tattooed warrior stabbed the meat and lifted it to his free hand, held it aloft and adeptly cut it in half.

Brayth took up one half of the meat, and beckoned for Aoleyn to do likewise. Aoleyn hesitated—the fallen half of the meat was out in the center of the fire pit, surely she would burn herself trying to grab it!—but Seonagh prodded her from behind again, hard. Hesitantly, she reached out, expecting to feel the biting flames.

But she felt no heat. Her hand shimmered, a white glow surrounding it. Aoleyn paused for just a moment to consider this strange luminescence covering her arm. She took the meat between her fingers and brought it to her mouth. With the warrior holding her stare with his own, they each took a bite.

Seonagh said something Aoleyn did not quite hear, then stepped forward and tossed something into the fire—more of those seeds! A huge burst of purple smoke rose up into Aoleyn's face, and suddenly the world warped and bent again, even more so, and she could not hold her balance, and she was only slightly aware that she was lying down, and then not aware of anything.

"You must never!" Innevah scolded her son, trying to keep her voice down. The woman glanced all about, panicked, as if she expected a host of Usgar demons to crash into the tree-cave and drag Thump away to be tortured and murdered.

She rubbed her face, trying to find some measure of composure, as she looked back to her discovery: a broken branch as thick as two fingers and fully as long as her arm, with its end sharpened wickedly—even with a barb whittled in to prevent easy extraction.

She looked at her son, unable to form any more words in that moment of horror, and just shook her head. Then she grabbed him and pulled him in close for a desperate hug.

"I don't like what they do to you," he whispered.

Innevah pushed him back to arm's length.

Thump painted on a determined expression, full of hate, his young eyes promising death.

"They will do far worse if you strike at them," Innevah warned. "Do you understand me?"

The boy started to look away, but Innevah shook him hard. "Do you understand me?" she repeated emphatically.

"I won't," Thump replied.

"Promise me."

The boy nodded.

"You made this to stab a man, yes?" the woman asked, and she managed a smile. "Because of what you saw?"

Thump shook his head, but she didn't believe him. Not at first, at least, but then she recalled something else about that difficult night a month before.

"Was it for the young girl?" she asked, her expression one of horror.

Thump seemed genuinely confused at that question.

"The girl who took you out that day . . ." Innevah started to clarify, but Thump waved his hands frantically and shook his head.

"No, no!" he said. "No."

Innevah looked at him curiously. "Was she mean to you?"

The boy swallowed hard and shook his head, slowly at first, but then emphatically.

"Did you enjoy your day with her?" Innevah asked very seriously, enunciating each word to stress the importance of the question and of Thump's honesty here.

Several heartbeats passed before Thump answered, "She named me Bahdlahn."

Innevah's expression showed that she did not understand.

"Thump," the boy explained. "But hoofbeats. Running deer . . ."

"Yes, yes," Innevah said, catching on, for she knew the word. "But why would she give you that name when your name is known?"

The boy glanced down, and Innevah reached out and took him by the chin, forcing him to look her in the eye.

"They mock me," he said quietly.

"This girl mocked you?"

"No!"

Innevah began to catch on, and she sucked in her breath as she considered the humiliation her tactics had forced upon her son. Surely that was better than the alternative, particularly in the coming years, perhaps even months, when he came to manhood, when the Usgar would surely murder him. But still, the woman did not dismiss Thump's current pain; she understood that what was being demanded of her poor boy was beyond what anyone should have to endure. His entire life had been a carnival of horror and humiliation.

She pulled him close and hugged him again, in no small part because she didn't want him to see the tears pouring out of her eyes.

"She was nice to me," Thump whispered in her ear, and Innevah heaved a great sob.

But suddenly, she shoved him back once more as terror engulfed her.

"Did you talk to her?" she asked.

The boy shook his head, but unconvincingly.

"Did she hear you talk? Does she know the truth?" Innevah pressed.

Thump swallowed hard.

Innevah's first instinct was to slap him, to scream out in terror that her son had just signed a terrible death sentence. But she stopped short and fought for composure. She couldn't undo whatever had happened, and she really didn't want to put more trauma on the poor boy.

"No, you must never. Never!" she told him through gritted teeth. "You are stupid! Do you understand? They must never know!"

Thump stared at her blankly, and the pain of seeing that drove an emotional spear right into the poor, broken woman's heart. She reminded herself that this was for the good of her son and repeated slowly and clearly, "You are stupid."

14

ROUGH AND TUMBLE

He wasn't afraid to let the raft he had constructed continue its meandering way along the river at this particular point, even though night had fallen. Talmadge knew this area well, and knew that this late in the season, one that hadn't seen much rain, the river would hold no secret rapids.

So he glided along enjoying the stars, believing himself safer than he would have been with the raft secured along the banks. The wolves wouldn't come out onto the water, after all, and he'd hear a bear or a huge elk long before it got near to him.

His eyes slowly closed, his head drooped, lulled by the rhythmic flow and the trilling and croaking frogs. Of all the things he liked the most about the open and unsettled lands were the sounds of the night. They blended together and swirled around, like the leaves of a thick tree in a gentle breeze. Only rarely did these nighttime symphonies sound a note discordant—the last scream of prey caught, or the insane yipping of the thick-necked hyenas chattering before dinner over a fresh kill.

The frogs answered from bank to bank. The night birds cooed mellow crescendos to the river's soothing drone.

The shriek of a metal sword skipping off a stone . . .

Talmadge's eyes popped open. He tried to sort out that last noise, or was it a dreamed sound?

A shout sounded on the right-hand bank, then a grunt and a curse in a language Talmadge did not know. The man struggled to his feet and gathered his long pole, straining his eyes in the darkness.

He saw the light of a campfire, just back from the river to the right, the north, and heard a continuing, rising commotion.

A big part of him just wanted to float by. This wasn't his fight! But he heard a man cry out, "It got me!" in such desperate tones that Talmadge could not turn away. Into the river went his pole, and with the gentle current, it was no trouble for Talmadge to push the raft toward the riverbank.

He found a rocky eddy where it was easy to put in, and dropped the pole and leaped off the raft before it had even secured itself against the stones.

He stumbled in the muddy ground, but managed to pull his battle-axe from his back as he made his somewhat cautious way toward the fire and the apparent fight. He noted forms then, a couple of humans and smaller ones, ones that looked like older boys, perhaps.

"Goblins," he said, crashing through the brush. Before he had even cleared it, he came upon one of the ugly creatures brandishing a pair of hooked knives. The green-skinned humanoid leaped in surprise, swinging about, and launched a wild flurry of spinning arms and slashing blades that got nowhere close to Talmadge. The goblin's long ears, too, waggled wildly, its head gyrating, and Talmadge deduced that the whole of the motion was meant to present a wall of ferocity, was meant to intimidate and confuse.

But Talmadge had heard enough about goblins to recognize the ruse, and so he waded straight in. His overhead chop stopped the waggling and dancing as his axe buried into the monster's skull.

A yank brought the sharp sound of cracking bone as Talmadge charged past, into the firelight. He took a quick survey of the scene, noting a trio, two women and a man, forming a triangular defense against a bevy of darting and stabbing goblins.

A fourth frontiersman, a long and lean man, lay on the ground some distance to the side, squirming and slapping his arms about desperately. He bled from a number of wounds, and with more incoming as a group of several goblins rushed all about him, spitting and cursing and stabbing down at him with their spears, which really were no more than sharpened sticks.

"To us, friend!" one of the women called, spotting Talmadge, and he started that way. Only a step, though, for he realized that they would never get their formation to their friend in time—a point driven home as the end of a goblin's sharp stick was driven home, right into the eye of the poor soul lying on the ground.

How he howled!

And how Talmadge roared. He veered straight for the fallen man and through the small campfire. He kicked at it as he crashed through, sending embers and small burning logs flying at the goblins, and he followed the wall of sparks into their midst, sweeping across powerfully with his axe, sending them leaping back.

Back and forth, Talmadge whipped his weapon, shouting all the while, trying to buy some time for the fallen man's friends to join in. He glanced back at them briefly, to see their progress halted by a volley of thrown spears.

"Just take the hit," he mouthed under his breath, for none of those feeble weapons had any weight to them or any real power behind the throw.

Talmadge slid his hands as far apart as he could on his axe handle, and turned back just in time to see a spear thrust aimed for his gut. He swept his hands down and to the side, knocking the stab off target, then punched back with his left hand and the butt of his axe. He loosened his grip with that leading left hand, and when the punch fell just short, the goblin bit at him.

But Talmadge gave it a mouthful of axe handle instead, sliding the shaft through his loosened fingers.

The goblin's head snapped backward and it staggered back to trip over the fallen frontiersman.

From the left side came another goblin, but Talmadge just grasped the axe midhandle with his left, let go with his right, and swept it out to fend.

And from his left hip, he drew his short sword, a weapon that had been with him since the day he had walked out of his dying hometown. He roared and leaped forward, straddling the fallen man, stabbing and slashing and hopping about to keep the remaining four goblins at bay. The one on the ground tried to rise, but a thrust of the short sword laid it low, and Talmadge tugged his weapon back just in time, and fortunately at just the right angle, to knock a thrown spear aside.

The now-unarmed goblin cursed.

It should have fled.

Talmadge leaped at it. The goblin managed to sidestep the sword. The blade attack was a feint, though, coming in slightly to the left of the goblin and forcing it back to the right. Focusing on that thrust, the goblin managed to jump right under the head of the descending axe.

Talmadge whirled about and screamed at a goblin driving a spear into the man on the ground. Purely on reaction, he flung his axe, on target, but the weapon hadn't fully come around to dig in, and just bounced off the creature. That was enough to send it running, especially with Talmadge charging in fast behind.

The frontiersman paused only long enough to scoop up his fallen weapon—that was his plan, at least, but even as he bent for his axe, he felt an explosion of pain just behind his hip that sent him staggering forward and to one knee.

He glanced at the wound, to see a dagger sticking there, but he hadn't the time to go for it as a pair of goblins came in at him hard, spears thrusting.

He got stabbed in the forearm before he could sweep that arm and the axe aside, and traded hits the other way, a spear coming at his chest with his short sword catching a goblin in the throat, gashing it from ear to ear.

A finer weapon would have driven hard through Talmadge's thin leather jerkin and deep into his lung, and would have likely spelled the end of the man. Even as it was, the weapon stayed in place, embedded through the shirt and into Talmadge's flesh, painfully against his ribs.

He tried to slap at it to dislodge it, but was instead forced to bring his sword up before him to try to block another incoming missile. This time it was a stone, a heavy one, and it tipped off the metal blade and bounced off the side of Talmadge's head.

The world was spinning then, but the man knew that he could not simply lie down and huddle in pain. More goblins came in at him, or went past him, and only after many sweeps and stabs, hitting nothing at all, did Talmadge realize that they were in retreat and wanted no part of him, or of the other three humans, who had broken through the encircling ring.

"They should've stayed," Talmadge managed to say, dropping his axe and reaching tentatively for the spear sticking into his chest. He started to finish, "They could have won," but ran out of breath. He looked back to see that the trio were hovering over their prone friend, who was no longer moving and covered in blood, and paying Talmadge no heed.

Talmadge looked at the gash running the length of his forearm.

He felt like he would throw up.

He felt like he would faint.

He chose the latter, rolling down into the dirt, welcoming the darkness.

He wanted to open his eyes, but it took a long time for his body to agree. He could feel the heat of the fire before he actually saw the orange glow, then lolled his head to the side to see it more clearly.

He turned his head back, his gaze going up to the starlit sky. He was lying on his back. His chest ached, his hip was worse, and he had a throbbing headache.

Instinctively, Talmadge reached up for his temple, or tried to, but he found that his hands were caught beneath him. He struggled a bit, and realized that no, they weren't caught.

They were tied.

Had the goblins won?

"Hey, he's awake," he heard from the side, a human voice, a woman's voice, and no goblin.

A moment later, the woman leaned over him, looking down. "Ye wasn't hurt that bad," she said. "Are ye all about faintin', then?"

She laughed at him and moved aside.

The other woman was beside him then, kneeling and helping him to sit up.

The world spun for a moment with the movement, and it took Talmadge a while for his eyes to catch up to his senses. As they focused in, the first image he saw was that of a goblin, leering at him.

He tried to fall back, but the woman held him in place. He started to protest, but stopped short as he realized that the goblin wasn't alive, but was staked just to the side of the fire. Talmadge shook his head. He had only seen a few of these troublesome beasts over the years, all but a couple of times from afar, though he had encountered their sign—camps littered with half-eaten rodents and lizards. Every time he saw a goblin's face, Talmadge couldn't shake the ridiculous thought that someone had grabbed it by the nose and pulled hard, shrinking the thing's head into a tiny, wrinkled mess, and leaving the nose and ears absurdly long and crooked.

He preferred to see them dead.

Past the goblin, one of the people he saved was digging at the ground, with another form, long and tall, lying behind him.

Digging a grave, Talmadge realized, and he thought of the man on the ground, the goblins sticking him with their nasty spears.

"So, ye finally come back to us, eh?" asked the first woman.

"I got hit in the head," he mumbled.

"I should be hittin' ye in the head!" the woman retorted, with more than a little ire in her voice.

The man stopped his digging and came over then, hands on hips, a scowl on his dirty, bloody face. He spat on the ground.

"All ye had to do was keep him safe a bit longer," the woman said.

"He tried," the woman kneeling beside Talmadge started to say, but her voice thinned and disappeared under the withering gaze of her two companions.

"I killed a goblin," Talmadge said.

"Aye, ye did," the man agreed. "I'll give ye that."

"Why am I tied?"

"Because we're not knowin' who ye are," said the first woman, who seemed to Talmadge to be the leader. "Or we wasn't, at least," she added with a grin and she took a handful of pearls out of her pocket and began dropping them from hand to hand in full view of Talmadge.

"My name is Talmad—" he started to say.

"We know," the woman interrupted. "Know who ye are, and know what game ye got goin' for yerself all these years."

"Game?" Talmadge tried to make some sense of it all. He looked more closely at the apparent leader. She was fairly tall, and incredibly skinny, with long light-brown hair and a mouth full of crooked and snaggled teeth, more than one looking more green than white. Had he seen her before at Matinee, he wondered?

Probably, he decided, though he couldn't place her. Almost everyone out here not of the indigenous tribes attended Matinee.

The man beside her was short and barrel-chested, with a giant black beard and unkempt hair that hung below his shoulders—unremarkable among the frontiersmen, surely.

The woman at Talmadge's side was quite a bit younger than the other two, with her red hair cropped short. She had a nasty scar on the left side of her face, from ear to chin, but Talmadge thought her attractive, with a softness about her face, and gentle light eyes.

Yes, Talmadge had seen this one the previous year, but only from afar.

"So, Mister Talmadge," said the skinny one. "We saved yer life."

"I joined in your fight," Talmadge corrected.

The woman spat on the ground. "Bah, but we had it won. Only thing ye might've done was save Ricker, there, and ye failed at it, eh?"

"He was already down, being stabbed—"

"Shut up," the man bellowed. He came forward, moving past the staked goblin to tower right before the seated Talmadge.

"Ye shut up or I'll put me boot deep into yer craw, what."

Talmadge swallowed hard.

"Shut up except for what we're askin' ye," the skinny woman corrected, also moving over to stand beside the man. "Tweren't yer good fortune to come upon us, Mister Talmadge, and tweren't yer good choice to join in where ye wasn't asked."

Talmadge wanted to argue—the whole thing seemed so absurd!

But she rolled the pearls from one hand to the other in clear view then, and he began to better understand.

"So, we're thinkin' that it's time for Mister Talmadge to share his bounty," said the skinny one. "Ye're on yer way to that lake."

"No," he said.

The woman kneeling beside him whacked him across the side of the head with a thick stick, pitching him over to go facedown into the dirt. Before he could even straighten out, she grabbed him by the hair and the collar and tugged him back into a seated position.

With that handful of hair, she yanked his head around to look him square in the eye, and there was nothing soft about her appearance or demeanor now.

"Whene'er I hear ye lie, I'm to whack ye," she explained, holding up the stick, and seeming quite willing, even happy, to prove her point again.

"So ye're going to the lake," said the skinny woman, "and we're going with ye."

Talmadge wanted to scream at her. This wasn't the way they lived out here in the wilds. They didn't fight each other, murder each other, and especially not with someone who had come in to help them in a fight!

As tough as they were, the frontiersmen were not thieves!

Talmadge wanted to scream all of that, and yet he knew, obviously, that his protest would catch the wind and nothing more—and would probably earn him another crack on the head from the younger woman, as well!

So he sat there and shook his head, his expression dumbfounded, and full of disappointment.

"Now," said the man, "if ye take us to the lake and behave, we might let ye live, and even if we don't, we'll kill ye quick and easy."

Talmadge stared at him hard. He didn't need to ask what would happen if he didn't cooperate, but the man volunteered it anyway.

"And if ye're not behavin', we'll roast ye, bit by little bit, until ye do."

He reached into the remaining bits of campfire and brought forth a brand, and thrust the burning end in Talmadge's direction.

"Now what's yer choice, boy?" he asked, or tried to, for before he had quite finished, his words became a dissipating mess of undecipherable sounds, and he stared at Talmadge weirdly—too weirdly!—and so it took the seated man a few moments to even realize what had happened, to even realize that the brute had an arrow sticking into his face, through both cheeks!

His jaw crooked from the arrow, he garbled a few more sounds and went down to the ground, trying to summon the nerve to bring his trembling hand to the embedded bolt.

The woman beside Talmadge leaped up, drawing her sword. The skinny woman spun about to face the direction of the attack, falling into a crouch, sword in hand.

And in came the attacker in a full charge, shouting and waving a small whip in one hand, a hooked knife in the other. She dived and rolled and slid in between the two rogues on her back, whip cracking, and with legs up, feet kicking.

"Khotai!" Talmadge gasped, caught by surprise and by fear for the woman. Why was she on the ground? Had she tripped?

It took him a while to properly understand that this maneuver was by design, for Khotai fought prone from her back ferociously, spinning kicking, lifting up high with her legs and even lower back to drive away the two women.

She used the cracking whip as more of a diversion, but those legs were doing the damage—and more damage than Talmadge could imagine, with both rogue women bleeding from their thighs and pelvises and bellies!

For knife blades extended from Khotai's boots!

To the side, the man struggled to his feet, ready to join in despite the arrow still sticking through his face. Talmadge rolled over and to his knees, then struggled up as the man came across. With a growl of protest, Talmadge launched himself forward into the rogue, bulling him to the side and into the remaining campfire.

The man cried out and began frantically patting at his burning clothes, and rolling about, which jarred the arrow, which made him cry out all the louder.

Talmadge fell back down and curled, bringing his arms down below his bum and up along his tucking legs, trying to get his tied hands in front of him, at least. By the time he managed that and climbed back to his feet, the young red-haired woman was down on one knee, holding at a myriad of wounds and with one arm out toward Khotai in a gesture of surrender.

The other woman had backed out of reach, and so Khotai executed a graceful lift and twist, leaping up from the ground in a practiced twirl, landing on her feet before the woman and launching immediately into a high-flying circle kick.

The skinny woman ducked and came right in, but was straightened abruptly as Khotai came fully around, whip leading and whip snapping, right across the woman's neck. Dazed and stung, the skinny woman stumbled backward, but not fast enough as Khotai came in hard, her other hand holding the hooked knife, punching out, crushing the skinny woman's nose with the metal pommel.

The woman's head snapped back and she fell over to the ground and curled up, only semiconscious and groaning loudly.

Khotai spun back and rushed past the kneeling redhead, and over to Talmadge, who lifted his hands defensively and cried out, thinking that Khotai, in her battle frenzy, didn't even recognize him!

Down came her hooked knife, right between his extended arms, slicing the bonds.

Khotai motioned to one of the fallen swords. "Keep them caught!" she said and she leaped the fire and charged straight in at the man, spinning, whip cracking.

He straightened.

She dived forward and rolled onto her back, and as she did, Talmadge noted her hand going to her waist and grabbing at something set there.

He understood when she kicked the rogue inside his knee, the knife that extended from her boot cutting in hard and sending him down and squirming, this time to stay. As Khotai leaped up, Talmadge realized that the blade was retractable, like a cat's claws, with some kind of mechanism running inside Khotai's pant leg.

Khotai calmly walked back from the man, leaving him thrashing and howling on the ground. The skinny woman had stopped squirming then, and lay quite unconscious in the dirt, and the red-haired woman hadn't even attempted to stand up once more.

Khotai stopped short, though, and moved to the side, to the grave the man had been digging. She picked up a rock, a headstone, stared at it for a moment, then chuckled and moved to join Talmadge.

"Now what?" he asked.

"Not even a thank-you?"

"Thank you," he said. "Now what?"

Khotai shrugged. "We are justified in killing them."

"No."

Khotai stared at him and he made sure that there was no compromise revealed in his expression. He couldn't kill these three. He simply couldn't.

And Khotai smiled and seemed to understand. She looked around. "There is a gully not far from here. Long and deep. We lower them down the side and leave them. We will be long gone before they can make their way out."

"Leave them and then we go where?"

Khotai smiled.

Talmadge shook his head.

"Don't be stubborn," she said. "You owe me this at least. I just saved your life."

"They weren't going to kill me!" he insisted.

Khotai gave him a skeptical look, then tossed the headstone to the ground at his feet. It landed upright, giving the man a clear view of the inscription: "Talmij."

"They would have left you dead under the waters of your faraway lake," Khotai said, and Talmadge knew it to be true. "And would have explained any questions away by telling all that you were killed here by goblins."

The man shrugged.

"Good," said Khotai, clearly taking that as a surrender and a recognition that Talmadge would lead her to this faraway Loch Beag. "I will heat some water so we can clean up your wounds." She paused, then added, "And theirs."

"Why is this so important to you?" Talmadge asked as she started to walk to the fire.

Khotai turned to regard him, a wry grin on her face. "I am writing my story," she said. "We all are. I want my story to be wide."

Talmadge wasn't quite sure how to take that, but this wasn't the first time Khotai had spoken of adventures in that manner. When she was trying to convince him to go far to the east to meet with Redshanks, she had used similar words, saying that he needed to widen his tale.

The skinny woman groaned then and began to stir, so Talmadge let it go at that.

Early the next morning, the couple marched the three rogues to a ledge above a nearly vertical cliff. They set some ropes and forced the rogues down, one by one, and when the last had safely reached the bottom, they pulled up the ropes and tossed down some supplies, including the rogues' weapons.

"You are being more generous than most," Khotai said to Talmadge as he lowered that last bundle.

The man could only shrug and reply, "Goblins. I'll not leave them to be slaughtered."

"They meant to kill you."

Talmadge just shook his head to toss aside that unsettling thought. It was true enough, of course, and he would have been well within his rights, and none would have blamed him, if he had simply killed the three back in their camp.

But he couldn't do it—the mere thought of it horrified him. Maybe they deserved it, many would say so, but he simply couldn't.

He would write his story, as Khotai always said, but it would be one with as few dead at the hands of Talmadge as possible.

When he finished pulling up the rope, Talmadge turned to find Khotai sitting on a stone, chewing on a long blade of grass and staring at him with a sly little grin.

"What?" he asked.

"You've not the heart to kill them."

Again, he merely shrugged.

"You understand that's why I have fallen in love with you, yes?" Khotai said.

Talmadge almost pitched off the cliff. Had a breeze come up, he was certain he would have been blown into the gully.

Khotai laughed at him and spun off the rock, twirling gracefully to her feet on the other side, and started away to the west. "Come along," she said. "Maybe I'll even teach you how to fight."

Talmadge started to protest, but bit it back and let it go at that, and he was smiling too widely to even care.

Somehow and suddenly, his journey this season seemed much less daunting.

15

HIS

Aoleyn opened her sleepy eyes to discover, to her surprise, that she was back in her cot in Seonagh's tent. The light streamed in on her face through the open flap and she lifted her arm to cover her eyes.

The night had passed, at least.

Her stomach rumbled, reminding her that she'd barely eaten.

"Half-cooked meat," she muttered, trying to recall the events of that night, most of which were missing. She rose shakily to her feet.

Her head throbbed. She brought her hand to her temple, remembering—barely—the cut of the flint knife. There was no blood there, nor could she feel a scab. Had it been a dream, after all? She moved to the washbasin to check her reflection in its still, reflective surface.

Not a mark showed on her smooth skin.

She splashed some water on her face. "Was I dreaming?" she wondered aloud.

"Hardly," Seonagh said.

Aoleyn jumped at the sound and whirled about.

"It was not a dream," Seonagh calmly assured her when both steadied from Aoleyn's leaping response. "It was a ritual, one that all Usgar girls—young women—attend."

"What ritual?" Aoleyn asked, her voice thick with suspicion, and not a small amount of dread. "What did it mean? What was all the smoke for?"

The memories began flooding back to her, inciting more questions. The evening came again into perspective, but she could hardly make sense of what had happened. One moment stood out from the others, though, one mystery she needed to unravel.

"The markings on his chest, where did he get them?" she asked, remembering the mesmerizing play of the light across the dark inky lines.

Seonagh snorted but managed to stifle a louder and longer laugh—and only with great difficulty, Aoleyn noted. "He got the markings from us," she said. "Why, of course. They are called spatt'rings, or tattoos. Many men are so painted, with many designs."

Aoleyn's eyes lit up. "We women do it? Will I learn to do that? Will I be able to make such marks?"

Seonagh nodded and shrugged at the same time. "Perhaps," she said noncommittally. "It is one of the duties of the witches of the Coven. In time, if you are selected for that honor, you will learn that talent, yes. But it is a sacred and secret ritual, intimately tied to the magic wielded only by the Coven."

"You used magic last night," Aoleyn pointed out, rather harshly.

Seonagh seemed somewhat confused.

"You are not of the Coven," Aoleyn explained.

Danger flashed across Seonagh's eyes and Aoleyn retreated a step.

"Once a witch is ever a witch," she said as the moment passed. "I could not unlearn the beauty of Usgar. No one could. Once you have seen truth, child, you will never forget."

Aoleyn's black eyes flashed, too, but with hunger.

"If you are selected, you will understand." Seonagh said. "You will not learn the sacred rituals until you are inducted into the Coven properly, as a woman."

Aoleyn was nodding before Seonagh finished the thought. She could be patient. She pictured herself, a grown woman, covered in beautiful, mesmerizing tattoos, dancing in the firelight with the other women of the tribe . . .

"Wait," she said, a bit perplexed. "I've seen the women dance before, at the festivals and blessings. I've seen them barely dressed. I've seen you undressed! But no one has any of these markings?"

"Of course you haven't, child! Tattoos are for the men."

"But . . ." She could hardly find the words to express her disappointment. "They are so beautiful. If the Coven can make them, surely the witches could mark themselves?"

Seonagh's demeanor suddenly grew quite stern. "Aye," she said. "We could, but we will not. Tattoos are for the men, not for the women. They are a mark of status among the warriors of the tribe. They are earned, not given. Most in battle, or in the success of a hunt. You should be glad that your man at the fire last night had so many. It means he is an accomplished warrior, and well regarded."

"Brayth?" Aoleyn asked. "Who is he to me? Why should I—?"

"Your intended," Seonagh interrupted.

"Intended?" she asked, perplexed. "What does that mean?"

"It means once you're formally declared a woman, you will be his. His woman, his wife. And most of all, his problem, and no longer mine." Seonagh sounded gruff and angry, like Aoleyn had done something wrong, had gotten into trouble yet again.

"His wife? Who is he? Why should I want to be his wife?" Aoleyn asked.

Seonagh scoffed at her. "Want? What you want does not matter, foolish girl. The tribal leaders have decided that you shall belong to that man, and it shall be so."

"When?" she whispered.

"As soon as you are a woman."

Aoleyn stared at her, not hiding her confusion.

"Yes, I know you have bled," Seonagh said. "You are his now, and can be claimed by no others unless he dies. You will be wed to him as early as this coming winter solstice, though it's more likely that you'll have to wait some few years before assuming your duties to him, that you can be properly taught in the way of the crystals and Usgar—if you show that you are worthy of the training."

She said it like a threat, like her words were tying an inescapable noose around Aoleyn's neck. Seonagh already had all the power over her, and now she had just strengthened that position.

That pit in Aoleyn's chest returned, filling her with hurt and anger. Again, she could not pinpoint the precise reason—but it was something about the way Seonagh had said "his." She would be "his" woman, "his" wife, "his" property. Like the uamhas.

Like Bahdlahn's mother.

Aoleyn stumbled toward the exit. She mumbled something about being hungry, needing food. But in truth she doubted she could eat right then. She simply needed some air, to be somewhere else, away from Seonagh and all this disturbing talk.

She broke into a run as soon as she cleared the doorway. She didn't have a destination in mind; she merely wanted to be not here. But her feet carried her somewhere unexpected, and she didn't realize she was heading there until she arrived.

Outside the grove of thick pines that housed the slaves, Bahdlahn sat on the ground, playing with a stick.

"You will come with me," she commanded. Bahdlahn jumped up at the sudden sound of her voice, leaping about to look at her. He appeared wholly confused, but this time he didn't hesitate for long. He gazed at the ground as he walked, but he rushed to follow her without complaint.

Aoleyn led the boy a short way from the slave grove. She was feeling defiant, feeling like she had to strike back against the terrible reality that seemed to be closing in all around her. Seonagh's warning followed her, though, and so she certainly didn't want to get into too much trouble right now, so she decided against heading for the woods. Instead, she found a little nook on the cliff face, took a seat, and beckoned Bahdlahn to do the same. The boy obeyed without complaint.

"Your mother isn't from the mountain," she stated. Bahdlahn grunted, indicating that he understood.

"Is she from the lake towns?" Aoleyn pressed him. The boy grunted again, this time a noncommittal sound that seemed to Aoleyn to mean, *I don't know.*

Aoleyn nodded and answered her own question. "She is. She's from one of the lake towns. I know it. I remember the raid when the warriors took her and brought her here."

Bahdlahn averted his gaze, and Aoleyn got the distinct impression he was hiding something.

"That's why her head is . . . is so long," Aoleyn pressed.

Bahdlahn inhaled deeply, clearly disturbed.

"Has she told you anything about that place?" she asked.

The boy ignored her. She repeated her question, but he still did not respond and Aoleyn, who thought this terribly important, felt her frustration growing.

"No, you cannot pretend!" she said with a growl. "Listen to me! I know you understand my words, even if you pretend not to speak. You take commands. You know what the words mean. I know your mother speaks to you of the lake towns, so you know about them?"

Bahdlahn looked up. His eyes were wide, his face ashen. He seemed terrified. He did not grunt or nod, but Aoleyn knew she had sorted it out.

"Now, listen," she said, softening her voice, trying to sound non-threatening. "I don't care that you know about them. I don't care that you cannot speak, or choose to say nothing, or whatever it is that makes you grunt all the time. I'm not trying to trick you, or catch you doing something wrong or anything like that."

The boy looked doubtful, and seemed very small to Aoleyn in that moment. She reminded herself that he was really a child, not like her. He was nearing fourteen, but was much simpler than that, more like a boy of ten, it seemed to Aoleyn.

"Besides," she said, "if I wanted to get you in trouble, I could just tell the warriors whatever I wanted. Those fools would believe me over anything you might, or might not, say." Aoleyn was trying to make it light-hearted, a tease, but as she heard her own words, she realized that what she was saying here was clearly a threat, and one that no slave would take lightly.

Truly, the boy looked petrified. He started to rise, though his legs seemed as if they hadn't the strength to support him, but before he got up, as if he remembered that he had been commanded to sit, he let go and plopped back down, looking miserable and afraid.

Aoleyn glanced all around and patted her hands in the air. She moved very close to Bahdlahn, that he could look into her black eyes. "I'm not trying to get you into trouble," she said quietly. "Not at all. I just want to know some things." She kept her voice soft, and was surprised by how much she cared about making this pitiful little slave boy so uneasy. She thought back to that long-ago day when she had defended him against two boys of her own tribe. Bahdlahn seemed like he needed that same kind of protection right now.

"I'll ask questions, and you just nod yes or shake your head no, all right?"

The boy did not move a muscle. Aoleyn rolled her eyes at him. "That was a question, Bahdlahn," she said sarcastically.

The boy looked confused for a moment, then nodded, somewhat emphatically.

"Your mother," she said. "She came from one of the villages on the lake?"

Bahdlahn nodded.

"There are many villages there?"

The boy nodded again, glanced around, and held up all the fingers on one hand and two on the other. Aoleyn was surprised at how quickly Bahdlahn volunteered that information, and was surprised indeed that this supposedly feebleminded boy could even count to seven.

"Is it true that the lake is the end of the world? No one lives past it?" she asked. She already knew the answer—despite the tribe's legends, the mountain and the lake were not the only inhabited lands around. She was more curious whether Bahdlahn knew that than anything.

Bahdlahn nodded emphatically. He opened his mouth, as if to speak, but no words came forth. Aoleyn wasn't sure if he was considering what to say, or struggling to say anything at all. In either case, he closed his mouth again and kept nodding.

Aoleyn didn't believe him. There were people beyond the lake, and Bahdlahn knew it.

Aoleyn pondered where she wanted this conversation to go. She wanted—she needed—to know something, but she wasn't sure what to ask. Asking about the wider world would be useless; the child probably knew very little of the world beyond the mountain and the lake, and what he did know would be nothing more than stories his mother had whispered into his ear. The young woman had to remind herself that this boy who was not Usgar was even less worldly than she!

In her desperation, though, she had to believe that he knew something, but of course he had no way to communicate that little information without her directly asking, and she had no idea what to even ask!

But Aoleyn's troubles were closer to home, anyway. She felt that pit in her chest again, that painful lump of emptiness and rage.

"In the lake village, did your mother have a husband?" Aoleyn asked.

Bahdlahn looked at her curiously.

"Your father?" she asked.

Bahdlahn nodded again and grunted a little.

"Where is he? Still in the village?"

Bahdlahn cast his gaze down and shook his head, and Aoleyn got the message.

She had suspected as much. When Tay Aillig had become Usgar-laoch, the tribe had held a great celebration to recount his greatest victories. One of those spoken of was the raid that had captured the pregnant woman. In verse and in toast, the tribe had celebrated that victory. No Usgar warriors had been slain in that raid, but some of the lakemen had.

Aoleyn gave him a sympathetic look. Her own father was dead, as well. Perhaps from a raid battle, perhaps from a hunt, perhaps from the winter wind. No one would tell her about him or the circumstances. Her mother, too, was gone, soon after her birth, or perhaps during it. Again, none would recount the details to her.

Perhaps because of that, Aoleyn suddenly wanted to know more from Bahdlahn. "Your father," she asked. "Did he own your mother?"

Bahdlahn's face screwed up in apparent horror.

"Was your mother his to command?" Aoleyn pressed. "Was she his uamhas, his slave?"

The Usgar had an expression, "*nyonach'ard,*" which they used to mock someone who seemed truly dumbfounded by an insult or an accusation. Not until this moment, with the purely nonplussed expression on Bahdlahn's face, did Aoleyn begin to comprehend the depth of that remark.

Bahdlahn's jaw was still hanging open when he had recovered enough to shake his head even more emphatically, as if the entire notion was absurd, and revolting.

Aoleyn was aware of the disdain the warriors held for the men who lived by the lake. Was this, perhaps, one of the differences that drew such sneers?

"Your mother speaks to you about him," Aoleyn reasoned.

Bahdlahn didn't answer, but Aoleyn didn't need him to answer. He looked down at the ground.

"Fondly?"

Bahdlahn glanced up again, and Aoleyn caught the sparkle in his blue eyes, and she understood, for she recognized that look in her own eyes. Feeling the magic of Usgar had given her that inner sparkle. Aoleyn had felt the same as she saw in Bahdlahn now, the rush of a rapid heartbeat, the lightheadedness that followed. She had felt it that night in the tree near the great crystal protrusion in the sacred grove. She had felt it on the winter plateau. She knew how wonderful that feeling was.

Bahdlahn felt it when thinking of his father, and he could only know his father through the words of his mother.

The weight lifted from Aoleyn's chest, as if the dark pit beside her line of life energy was filling, buoying her. That was what she had needed to hear, some confirmation that her mounting revulsion as Seonagh had told her of the world she would soon know was not her perspective alone.

From the reaction of Bahdlahn, from that look in his eye, Aoleyn got the distinct feeling that things were very different in the lake villages below Fireach Speuer.

Aoleyn and Bahdlahn sat in their little nook for a long while, Aoleyn talking, Bahdlahn nodding or grunting or miming. It was nearly sunset when Aoleyn left Bahdlahn in the pine grove and returned to the encampment. Over the coming days, she would gather the boy and retreat to this sheltered spot whenever she could, for the pit in Aoleyn's chest always felt less substantial after those conversations with the little slave boy, who was not feebleminded, as he pretended and as the others believed.

From behind a rock not far away, Aghmor watched the young woman and the slave boy leave the sheltered nook. They weren't carrying anything, he noted, so why might they have been out here?

Had the child tried to escape, and this woman, Aoleyn by name, given chase and captured? Aghmor knew quite a bit about Aoleyn, and her spirited and headstrong reputation, to believe that a possibility.

He smiled as he watched her walking back toward the encampment, admiring the play of her muscles in her short and curvy figure. She wasn't the prettiest woman in the tribe, certainly was neither tall nor fair. Still, his best friend Brayth was a fortunate one, Aghmor thought, for the fire of Aoleyn was hard to deny.

Or perhaps Brayth would be monumentally unlucky, Aghmor considered, and his smile grew wider. He loved Brayth like a brother, even though Brayth had nearly killed him on that raid those years before.

Still, the young man couldn't help but grin at the trouble he pictured this young Aoleyn would give to his friend. Her spirit was the stuff of legend among the young warriors. It was said that the only time she cast her eyes down was to find a stone to throw into someone's face!

Brayth was in for a wild ride indeed.

Aghmor stopped nodding, and his smile disappeared a moment later when Aoleyn turned to say something to the young slave.

They were holding hands.

And the boy looked back at her and grinned and nodded.

16

CONFESSION

The deciduous trees swayed in a mesmerizing, multicolored dance, the autumn wind of late Parvespers blowing strong across Loch Beag. Borne by those gusts, small waves accompanied Talmadge's canoe to the lakeshore, beaching in the pebbly shallows right at water's edge.

Khotai hopped out and grabbed the front of the boat, dragging it up securely onto the land before Talmadge had even secured his paddle.

"Car Seileach?" the woman asked when he joined her on the beach.

"Another day's journey yet."

"We could get more hours this day. The sun has not touched the western rim."

Talmadge tried to verbally respond, but only sighed and shook his head. He had known that he would have to return to this ghost-filled spot from the moment he had agreed to let Khotai accompany him to Loch Beag.

"We go the rest of the way on foot, then?" Khotai asked.

"We'll be back on the waters at sunrise," Talmadge explained. "You'll meet the tribe before tomorrow's twilight."

Khotai shrugged curiously. "Why here, then? Why this place?"

Talmadge didn't answer.

"Is there something here?"

Talmadge nodded.

"Supplies? A safe haven for the night? Do you fear those three rogues are following us? I've seen no sign of them since we left them more than a month ago."

"This is the least safe place I know," he admitted, though he was thinking more of his emotions than his physical well-being.

"Then why?"

Talmadge looked back to the boat, then closed his eyes, trying to find the courage to continue. "You have to do this," he told himself under his breath.

"Talmadge?" she asked, her voice changing in timbre, becoming sympathetic, concerned even. "Talmadge, why have you stopped here?"

There was also a bit of trepidation in her voice, Talmadge realized, and he noted concern on her face, and that she had shifted one leg back defensively. Only then did he realize that he had reflexively put his hand on the hilt of his short sword.

He let go of the weapon immediately. "I've been here but once," he explained. "Since that time, I paddle farther out into the lake to loop about far from this place, though 'tis more dangerous out on the deeper stretches by far."

"When was that one time?"

"Thirteen years ago."

Khotai nodded and narrowed her eyes as if trying to do some calculations to sort this riddle.

Talmadge turned away, motioned for her to follow, and determinedly put one foot in front of the other, propelling him toward a nearby stand of trees, and one in particular.

He stopped before the thick branch, crossing horizontally some eight feet from the ground, and he licked his lips, trying to steady himself, when he discovered a rope still tied about a low and thick branch! Over the years, that thick cord had dug deeply into the wood, and seemed somehow a permanent fixture of this place now. It was knotted underneath, with a short and frayed length hanging down a foot or so.

Talmadge remembered tying that knot.

"Thirteen years ago," he heard Khotai say behind him. "Would that be the last time you brought one with you here? The year the man named . . ." Her face screwed up as she tried to remember.

Talmadge fought the words, but only for a moment, before blurting, "Seconk," he answered. "They called him Badger. I hung him up by the ankles right here, with that rope, so the lizards would eat him and not chase me back onto the lake waters."

There came no reply.

"I heard them eating him," he said, pushing as hard as he could. "I heard the flesh ripping and the crunching bones."

"And the screams?"

"He was already dead," Talmadge replied. He didn't turn about to face the woman, and could well imagine her standing behind him with her whip and dagger drawn, ready to stab him in the back.

"He died fighting the lizards?" she asked, and when he didn't immediately answer, she added, "No dishonor in using a dead man to shield a retreat. The dead are dead. We bury them when we can, but when we cannot—"

"I killed him!" Talmadge growled, spinning about.

Khotai jumped just a bit, startled, but relaxed quickly and made no move and showed no reaction. Nor was she holding her weapons, Talmadge noted.

"I put my sword, this sword, into his chest," he confessed. "Slid it right to the hilt. I smelled his blood and his last breath. I felt the warmth of that blood spilling over my hand."

"You do not sound as if you much enjoyed it."

"I hated it," he said through his gritted teeth, and truly Talmadge wanted to scream out then, or fall down crying. "You think I wanted to kill him?"

"Then why?"

"Because he tried to kill me. And before that, he would have let me die—he hoped I'd die so that he could take my share of the goods and trade them with the villagers of Car Seileach."

Khotai appeared confused—how could she not?

So Talmadge told her of the events of that long-ago day, of the giant clo'dearche lizards fleeing the water, of Badger's shove when he had gotten out of the canoe, and the man's run to the tree.

Of the taunting by Badger during Talmadge's fight with the giant lizard.

Then the prompting by Talmadge to get Badger to reveal the depths of his treachery as the pair headed for their craft.

"He stabbed for my back, but I was ready for it, and I knocked his blade aside and put my sword into the opening," Talmadge finished.

Khotai nodded, and seemed somewhat impressed.

"And you hung him here for the other lizards," she said, putting it all together. She smiled as she finished and moved to a spot just below and to the side of the rope, where she fell to her knees and began scraping at the dirt and brush. A moment later, Khotai held up her prize: a sizable portion of a human skull, upper jaw and teeth still intact.

Talmadge recoiled.

But Khotai was smiling knowingly.

"Is that the only time you've killed a man, then?" she asked.

He didn't answer, but his expression and the sheer level of discomfort here made it quite clear that this incident was indeed unique.

"He would have killed you?"

"Yes." Talmadge had to force the word from his throat.

Khotai nodded, her smile remaining. "In the time it took you to hang him up for the beasts, you could have gone to your boat and paddled far away," she reasoned.

"No, the lake monster was out there. It'd driven the lizards from the water, and schools of fish, too. I needed to stay on the land for a . . ." His voice trailed off as he came to realize how incredibly feeble his story sounded. He could have simply gone up the same tree Badger had climbed!

"Because you were mad at him for trying to kill you," Khotai said. "Outraged! Killing him wasn't enough for you. No, you had to insult his corpse, to let the lizards eat him as he had hoped they would do to you."

Talmadge had no answers.

"Admit it," she said, but quickly added, "to yourself. You'll feel all the better."

Talmadge stared at her curiously.

"Which bothers you more?" she asked.

He shrugged.

"Killing the fool or hanging him for the lizards?"

Talmadge swallowed hard. "All of it."

Khotai gave a little chuckle, one that showed both sympathy and amusement. "Now I'm getting why you demanded we let those three criminals go free back at the river," she said. "It'd have been smart to kill them, and we had every right. But Talmadge couldn't travel that dark road of killing again, could he, because the ghost of Badger's been chasing him for most of his life?"

He didn't deny a word of it, nor did he try to argue about his decision regarding the three people he had saved from that goblin attack.

"We all write the stories of our life," Talmadge said, echoing the philosophy Khotai had explained to him many times before. In Khotai's To-gai-ru world, the journey of one's life was considered a story unfolding, written by the subject with her actions. It was a way of looking at life that Talmadge considered both liberating and selfish, but the more the man had become familiar with Khotai and her ways, the more he had come to recognize the limited avenues of his life, and the more the philosophy had won him over.

"We do," Khotai answered. "Ours, each, is the tale of a life, one life, traveling roads and bouncing into others. But in the end, it is a solitary journey, a tale of one woman or one man."

"In my story it will be written that I killed a man," Talmadge said. "That is not a tale I wished to write."

"Few would wish to write that tale," Khotai replied. "Yet many do. Too many, especially out here."

"Has Khotai written such a tale?" he asked.

The woman didn't answer, other than to return a dubious stare, as if she couldn't even believe he would ask the question, or more pointedly, that he believed he had to ask the question!

"Many such tales?" Talmadge asked.

"My story is wide and thick" was all she'd say, and Talmadge understood her to mean thick with both lovers and enemies—dead enemies.

The roads of a life's story as defined by Khotai's way of looking at the world were usually more about people one bounced against than the physical roads one traveled.

"Well, now you know that mine is perhaps thicker than you had believed," Talmadge offered.

Khotai shrugged and returned a warm smile. "The fool tried to murder you and you were the stronger," she said in unvarnished tones. "His death is his own doing, and better that outcome than th'other. No matter your choice then, he'd have been eaten by the lizards whether you'd strung him or left him, or eaten by worms and beetles if you'd buried him, or by fish if you'd dragged him into the lake."

"Thank you," the man said, straight from his gut and before he could even consider his response.

"I cannot know what is in your heart," Khotai told him. "Not really. No one can know that of another. But we watch and hear and listen to each other and to common friends, and we make a guess. Long ago, I guessed that Talmadge was a good man, a man of honor. I'm not surprised that this journey with Badger, all of this, burdened you so, and for all these long years." She paused and dropped the skull and then swept her hand and gazed up toward the tree limb and the rope that had grown to be a part of it. "Your pain at telling me the tale only proves my guess."

The man felt better, felt as if a great weight had, at long last, been lifted from his shoulders. For most of his adult life, the incident here with Badger had haunted him—how he had wanted to take Khotai here before! To show her the way of the lake tribes and the sheer beauty of Loch Beag and the majesty of the Snowhaired Mountains, the Surgruag Monadh.

He looked down at the skull on the ground, then picked it up and held it aloft between himself and Khotai.

"Well, Mister Seconk, you entered my tale of your own accord," he said. "And you left my tale of your own actions."

He shrugged and tossed the skull, and motioned to the boat, for he had no more reason to be at this place.

More importantly, though, Talmadge had no more reason to avoid this place.

PART 3

WRITING THEIR STORIES

I am often amazed at how a simple difference in the way one looks at the world can transform one's actions so profoundly, as obviously as the turn of a prism can change the color of the world seen through it. What may seem a play on words can change the colors of the world around you.

Many of the tribes I have encountered name their members after the actions or duties or even a particular aspect of an individual. A hunter may be named Urcharsleagh because he can throw a spear with great accuracy, and so his talent becomes his moniker. Similarly, the tribes often name and number their gods in the real animals about them, or in storms they will have to know and learn in order to survive. There are gods of thunder and wind, and great deity beasts to represent the bears or hunting cats.

The simple association of language with action, of deifying the great natural events and animals, ties these peoples more closely with the world around them—every word becomes a reminder of responsibility or threat, and as such, they've turned their very language into an archive. Transferring information one might find in a library at a monastery in Honce.

It is brilliant in its simplicity, and a fair warning to those of us "more civilized" folk that too often overthink and unnecessarily complicate that which should be obvious. The answers to puzzles are, quite often, right there before us.

The obvious is sometimes the truth.

I am reminded of Marcalo De'Unnero, once my mentor, though more truthfully my tormentor. He led me down a myriad of tangled webs of justification, each walking me further from the simple truth of the immorality of my actions. So easy is it to justify selfishness and pride and all the deadly sins to one who would be so cooed.

De'Unnero viewed the world through a turned prism. He had so convinced himself of his elevated, godly duty to protect the ignorant peasants from the truth of their destiny that he could justify any action—murder, torture, war itself—under the guise of service to a higher purpose.

So many turn their prisms away from obvious morality, it seems, whether the thief in the streets of Palmaris, the murderer in the Wilderlands, the too-proud king, or the tyrant Father Abbot, so sure of the word of god that all must be sacrificed in service to that inaudible voice and invisible hand.

This is how we write our stories—and is that not our life journey? To write our personal stories?

A woman named Khotai told me that, though it is a simple way of look-ing at the journey of a life that should have been obvious to me, to us all. And yet it was not—not to me at the very least. Not until I encountered this exotic person, a rare combination of To-gai-ru and Alpinadoran her-itage, raised in the steppes of To-gai, yet wandering beyond the Wilderlands, the Wilderlands themselves, or even the avenues of Honce-the-Bear's great cities.

Khotai views her life as a tale to be created, to be written, by her every step and choice. She is an actor in her own play, as are we all. If she finds her play becoming dull, she will seek a new road, a new conflict, a new chal-lenge. Something, anything, to write a page that engages the protagonist, the prime actor, in this journey: herself.

She is not restless, but rather, engaged. She is not reckless, but neither timid. This is her story, her journey, her life . . . a wasted step is one less step to spend.

Thus has Khotai turned her prism, and thus does she turn her prism, never allowing for a static, dull, view.

It is a trick of semantics, perhaps, or a most simplistic reminder of a phil-osophical desire to die without regret of those roads untraveled or those mountains unclimbed. Either way, Khotai's way of viewing the world and her walk is a continual prod and an unceasing whisper that we, this part of our journey at least, are finite, with end.

So we all write our stories. Some end too soon, like the child who dies of plague before learning to even speak, or the mother who, upon finding a new and exciting road to travel, dies in childbirth before the first steps of that are even recorded.

Some stories are quite long, a century even (and many centuries for the Touel'alfar and Doc'alfar!), but walk a small circuit so often that the tracks are dug into the paths. The words repeat, repeat, repeat, and so the long story itself becomes nothing more than illusion.

You can repeat a sentence a hundred times, but it is still just one sentence.

To Khotai, this would be the same tale as written by one who died a child.

It is so simple, so obvious.

How I thank Khotai for showing it to me.

Aydrian Wyndon, "In My Travels"

17

AFFINITY

(The last day of the ninth month, Parvespers, God's Year 854)

Seonagh squared her shoulders, clenched her fists at her sides, and declared again, this time through gritted teeth, "Aoleyn is not ready." It was her third denial, and her most forceful retort, and she sucked in her breath as the powerful man towering over her scowled.

"It does not matter if she is ready or not," Tay Aillig said with a level of calmness that hinted of murder. "She is a woman, no longer a girl, and so she must now learn her place. And accept it."

He seemed as if he were about to continue—no surprise to Seonagh, for a long rant from the ever more forceful Tay Aillig was easily set into motion. This one was overly proud and surely did not like to be contradicted, and particularly not by a mere woman!

Indeed, she saw that flash in his eyes, a promise of a continuing spew of threats and anger, but an upraised hand just to the side stopped him short.

"Sit," said an old and shaky voice, but one that carried great weight among the Usgar, for it was that of Raibert, the tribe's Usgar-forfach, the appointed caretaker of the sacred winter plateau and the crystal caverns beneath Craos'a'diad. Raibert had earned his current position honestly, for he had been, as Tay Aillig was now, the Usgar-laoch in his youth. Then, as Tay Aillig hoped for himself, Raibert had become the Usgar-triath, the Chieftain, and his word had held as final arbiter on every issue for more than a decade before he had been bested in formal challenge by a giant of a man named Thorburn.

That had all occurred decades before, and Thorburn was now long dead, and so respected had Raibert been that whispers had lingered for years, even to this day, of reinstating him as Usgar-triath. For no other had the accomplishments and respect to assume such a title. But Raibert was in his ninth decade of life, too frail to take on such all-encompassing duties. While most of the tribe thought him half-mad, the rest of the tribe thought him entirely so.

Despite that, or because of it, the Usgar looked upon him with reverence. As if the crystalline god spoke through Raibert in every pronouncement. On those rare occasions when Raibert spoke, everyone listened. Even Tay Aillig. And if the old man's words sounded as gibberish, as was often the case, the Usgar looked past that and sought deeper meaning.

Raibert shakily rose to his feet. The light of the fire in the predawn cast eerie shadows on his face, accentuating the deep lines of age and the deeper scars left from a combative youth; his raids and hunts were still in the songs of Usgar skalds. He spoke slowly, heavily. "The witch speaks truly," he began. "This girl, Aoleyn, is not ready. But are women ever ready?" He gave a raspy laugh, permission for the other men to join in, and so they did, aiming their mocking tones squarely at Seonagh.

Raibert held up a gnarled hand for silence and stared hard at Seonagh. "This young Aoleyn has been properly claimed," he said, and laughed again, and there was something sinister there, Seonagh thought. "Some man's to ride her! Oh, if I were younger." And he wheezed and laughed some more.

Seonagh tried to hide her repulsion, but doubted she was being very successful in the attempt. Even Tay Aillig, who had never seemed overly interested in sex, appeared uncomfortable as Raibert began detailing some of his sexual adventures in great detail, laughing and wheezing. He went so long down his memories that Seonagh half expected him to drop his pants and begin stroking himself right there in front of them.

It wouldn't be the first time.

"She's bled," Tay Aillig said after Raibert had wrapped himself into some story of an encounter so deeply that he seemed to completely lose sight of the present. "Aoleyn is a woman, and she will be a wife or she will be a witch, or both. But not neither. She must learn what that means in the ways of Fireach Speuer."

Seonagh stared at him hard, not judging, but rather, trying to decipher. They didn't have to do this now, but if they didn't, then Brayth would be free to stake his claim to Aoleyn and consummate his marriage. If they did, and Aoleyn lived up to her promise, that moment would likely be put off, perhaps for a long while, as Mairen staked her own claim to the young woman. If Aoleyn proved to be the witch-in-waiting, the next in line for the Coven, Mairen would not allow her to become thick with child anytime soon.

It seemed to Seonagh that Tay Aillig preferred this second possibility.

"Might that I'll put the girl to her knees!" Raibert said unexpectedly, cackling with every word.

Seonagh felt her face screw up at the vulgarity of the old man.

Some of the fire of his youth yet remained, though, and before Seonagh could get out a word, Raibert snapped at her. "You do not decide things here, witch!" he said, pointing a crooked finger her way. "You have spoken your words and have been heard, which is more than you should expect! Now you must kneel to the decisions of the men, as Aoleyn would kneel before me if I so desired!"

Seonagh took a moment to compose herself. She thought of Hew, who had been her husband, who had so often spoken to her in such a manner, and usually with an accompanying punch.

She didn't much miss him.

She thought of Fionlagh, who would never say such things, and of her sister, Elara, and envied her fortune to have been chosen by such a man as that.

"I knelt to the demands of my husband, in accordance with the ways of Fireach Speuer," Seonagh dared to retort. "He is not here."

"He is dead," said one of the other venerable tribesmen, a man called Ahn'Namay. "Two dozen years. You should be dead as well, for as long, in fidelity and respect."

Seonagh stiffened, trying to not let the words shake her. Sometimes in Usgar culture, the wife would "accept" death when losing the man who had chosen her. Again, Seonagh thought of Elara, who hadn't chosen such a course, but who had broken with the fall of Fionlagh and so had been helped to the Corsaleug, the Jeweled Shore of Usgar heaven, by the other men, who so happily had thrown her into Craos'a'diad.

"And yet, here I stand!" she answered defiantly. Seonagh had been in the Coven when Hew had fallen from a ledge to his death while in pursuit of a deer, and so Seonagh had been beyond the wicked grip of angry men. "You, all of you, in your wisdom, tasked me with the teaching of this girl, like so many before her who have grown under my eye. And when those others neared womanhood, they were ready, I told you as much. But I tell you for the sake of all involved, including Brayth too, that this one is not ready."

"Then might be that you're losing your talent," Tay Aillig threatened. "Might that Seonagh's fading into her days as a crone. Might that being without a husband for so many the year has left Seonagh forgetful of the ways of Usgar."

Seonagh did not like where this rant was leading. "Oh, but I can control a girl," she said, but admitted, for Aoleyn's sake and not her own, "but not so much this girl."

"You admit failure?"

"No."

"Oh, but did you not just claim to be unable to tame her?" said Tay Aillig, letting the doubt hang in the air. "What use left for Seonagh, then?" he asked, and that wicked smile returned. "Might that you should be given to Craos'a'diad, after all, to serve again in your proper place as consort to Hew in Corsaleug. Aye, as you should have joined him a score of years ago."

Seonagh scoffed, but was dismayed to see the other elder tribesmen nodding, and of course, Raibert was giggling with dark amusement.

A long moment of uncomfortable silence dominated the small group then. Seonagh turned to Mairen for some support, but the Usgar-righinn wouldn't even look at her, wouldn't match her stare. Not there. Not then.

"I remember Hew!" Raibert exclaimed suddenly, as if just catching on to the conversation, surprising everyone. "Been dead a long time!" He looked at Seonagh and seemed perplexed, pausing as if his mind was trying to catch up with the stream of memories. "But you're still here, are you? Hmm. Might that it's time we seek another teacher for this unbroken filly, so that you might go to serve Hew."

Seonagh fought hard to maintain her composure, though surely her eyes widened at so blatant a threat. She understood, of course, that such violent talk was common among the men, particularly the older ones whose lust had long turned to impotent frustration. She knew that such talk often centered on her, especially when Tay Aillig was part of the conversation. Of late it seemed that the powerful man had come to profoundly hate her.

Fionlagh's failure and humiliation had happened on one of Tay Aillig's earliest raids, and the vicious warrior had been one of Fionlagh's harshest critics. Fionlagh's death at the claws and maw of the fossa hadn't sated his anger at the man, and Seonagh's subsequent attempts to rehabilitate Fionlagh's reputation, and to protect her sister Elara, certainly hadn't pleased Tay Aillig.

Seonagh had believed then, and still did believe, that the young warrior had lusted after Elara, who was much younger than Seonagh and only a few years older than him. In fact, as far as Seonagh knew, she was the only woman who had ever piqued Tay Aillig's interest.

She winced at recalling that suspicion now, given the man's obviously intense interest in the fate of Aoleyn, who possessed her mother's unusual beauty. Perhaps Tay Aillig was being driven by more than his hatred of her, Seonagh thought, and the implications of that scared her more than the thought of being cast into Craos'a'diad.

And now hearing the venerable Raibert laying bare the threat of violence against her staggered the woman, and reminded her just how precarious her—and by extension, Aoleyn's—situation truly was.

"No," she replied to Raibert, her voice as calm, strong, and steady as she could manage. "I have much teaching left in me."

"She's a woman!" Raibert snapped back at her. "We must learn her purpose. Are you a worthy inionnsaich or not?"

"I am," she flatly replied. His use of the old title for women whose entire lives had been devoted to teaching girls in the way of Usgar had touched Seonagh's pride and stung her sensibilities, harking back to a time when there were many more Usgar and women were much more valued than now.

"Then make young Aoleyn ready," the Usgar-forfach warned, seeming frighteningly cogent then. "This very season Aoleyn must walk the crystal caverns so that she is fully measured. We must know. The Usgar-righinn must know and choose. The girl must learn what it is to be a woman."

"She'll be married at next summer solstice," Ahn'Namay said, and sniggered. "Oh, but then she'll learn what it really means to be a woman."

The men all laughed.

Seonagh did not; she stared hard at Tay Aillig and got the feeling that he was laughing more because it was expected of him than because he thought it funny.

"She is willful," Seonagh warned them, aiming her words at the War Leader, who alone might be able to turn this decision the other way.

"So is Brayth," Tay Aillig replied coldly. "A fine warrior, strong and powerful."

The others nodded.

"Be warned, Seonagh. Brayth will teach the girl her place if you do not," said Tay Aillig.

Seonagh caught it then, clearly so: Tay Aillig didn't want Brayth on top of Aoleyn.

"And if you do not," said Raibert, "or if you cannot, then . . ."

He left the threat hanging there, but Seonagh mentally finished the thought for him: *if you cannot, then you will be cast into the Mouth of God.*

She bowed to the elders, cast a glance at a clearly mortified Mairen, and took three steps backward away from the fire, as was required of a woman leaving the presence of such men. Then she turned and strode off determinedly into the rising dawn, to find her student and prepare the willful young woman for the dangerous trials ahead.

Brayth intercepted Seonagh as she crossed the encampment. She and the fierce young man had rarely spoken a word to each other, so when she saw him approaching, she felt a mix of curiosity and of fear. The young warrior had developed quite a reputation among the witches of the Coven, none of it good. Few women in the tribe weren't married, and a warrior was not to betray the husband of a woman by cuckolding him—indeed, such an act was counted among the worst offenses of Usgar law.

From what Seonagh had heard from many of her friends, the fact that they had husbands hadn't stopped the overly amorous Brayth from making aggressive advances. Never had he been overt enough for the woman to get her husband involved, but enough to make the women whisper that it would not surprise them if something terrible eventually happened.

The slave women had been less fortunate. Brayth was well known to never shy about mounting them or beating them. Seonagh had little regard for the uamhas, of course, but even she had winced more than once at seeing the aftermath of Brayth's nocturnal visits: the bruises, the cuts, the fearful look in the eyes.

Seeing his approach now, seeing him at any time, made Seonagh glad of her advanced age. She had no husband whose honor would be assailed if Brayth attacked her; her protest would be but a whisper to the tribal leaders.

Still, the former witch was not without recourse.

She reached into a pouch on her belt, felt the tingling of her fingers as they ran over the cylindrical crystals in there, especially the one flecked with dark gray, the thunder stone. Seonagh was confident that she would need no husband, no man, none of the leaders even, to ward Brayth away if he attacked her. Nay, he'd get a jolt of lightning that would put him shivering on his back, and then he'd get more than that.

A lot more.

No doubt the tribe would admonish her, perhaps even cast her into the Mouth of God—some powerful voices among the men obviously wanted to do that anyway—but the smoldering corpse of an arrogant debaucher would remain quite dead.

And Aoleyn would be safe from him.

That thought caught Seonagh off guard, and had her looking askance as Brayth completed his approach, for it surprised her to admit to herself how much she actually cared for her niece. She wanted to protect Aoleyn, and she knew that the spirited lass wasn't ready for marriage to any man, and particularly not to this one.

Yes, if Brayth pressed her, she meant to kill him, and then it would be at least another year before the tribe selected a new husband to take Aoleyn.

The young warrior stood before her, his expression full of confidence, of bravado, but also with trepidation.

How often the mixture of those two emotions could be seen together, Seonagh thought, but only if one knew how to see them.

"Why do you smile, hag?" Brayth asked.

"Should I not smile upon seeing such a strong young lad?" she asked, counting on his ego to prevent him from seeing through the sarcasm, though she did put a bit of extra emphasis on "young." Not that the self-absorbed Brayth noticed.

The warrior shook his head. "I would ask something of you," he said.

Seonagh waited a long moment for the question, before recognizing that the man was waiting for her permission.

The woman crinkled her face, taken off guard at his unexpected politesse.

"Do tell," she said, trying to convey some measure of wisdom and experience in her tone, to remind the fierce young warrior that his deference was wise and had been earned. "If I've an answer, I'll give it."

"About my bride."

Again that long, pregnant pause, and Seonagh was unused to such respect from a man. "What about her?"

"There are some who say she spends a lot of time with the uamhas."
Again, Seonagh noted, a statement, not a question.

"She does."

"This troubles many."

Seonagh tried to keep the exasperation off her face. Was he meaning to actually ask her a question, she wondered, and so she asked one
of her own. "Does it trouble Brayth? Look about you. You live on a
mountain of gossip and unearned certitude. Everything troubles many."

Brayth grew suddenly animated, his face locking into a sneer. "If
Aoleyn lies with the slaves, she is impure and unfit to marry."

Seonagh stifled a laugh, but couldn't resist a bit of a snort, at least.
"She does not lie with the slaves!"

The young man stared hard at her, and she snorted again at the pre-
posterousness of his accusation.

"She doesn't even know fully what it is to be a woman, foolish
Brayth. Aoleyn has no desire, and would not sate it with any of the
uamhas, in any case. She is free of mind and full of curiousness, but she
is not an animal."

A wave of relief washed over the young warrior, visibly so. "Good,"
he snapped, nodding, and turned to walk away.

Among the Usgar, the women knew well to let a man have the last
word, and so Brayth's turn should have been the end of the discussion.
But Brayth had shown her deference, respect even, and Seonagh's curiosity got the best of her, and she couldn't resist.

"What does Brayth think of his intended bride?" she asked.

He turned back to her, clearly caught by surprise.

"You've barely met her," Seonagh pressed, "but seems you've heard
rumors of her ways. So, you've clearly been looking and listening, young
Brayth, so tell me, what thoughts have you of Aoleyn?"

Brayth seemed pensive, unsure even, and he didn't respond for many
heartbeats. He was out of sorts, Seonagh realized, particularly given
his reputation. Was she wrong about him? Were the rumors of his de-
bauchery and disrespect overblown?

"They say she is willful," Brayth finally answered. "Disobedient,
even."

In her reflexive desire to protect her niece, Seonagh considered lying to him. Before she began to respond, though, she decided that the truth might prove to be Aoleyn's best defense here, particularly if it unnerved this preening bull and made him a bit less sure of himself.

"Willful and disobedient?" she answered. "Aye, Aoleyn's both, and clever and quick when she wants to be."

"Wants? It's not a woman's place to want," Brayth replied, recovering a bit of his bravado—and indeed, Seonagh saw a cloud of danger flash across his undeniably handsome and angular face, reminding her of all the whispers.

Seonagh nodded and bowed.

"You've your job."

"I've taught Aoleyn as much on her place, but the lessons have not taken root of yet."

Brayth narrowed his dark eyes, and it occurred to Seonagh that her compliance might have given him too much confidence here. "Then teach her better," he said. "By your words or my hand, she'll know her place when she's my bride."

"She's not the first . . ." Seonagh started to argue, but the boy's wicked smile coming back at her forced her to change tactics. "Many the young woman have I taught," she replied, letting the tiniest bit of an edge creep into her voice. "I know my part."

"Yet, she has not learned," Brayth said.

"The child is immune to any lesson she does not wish to learn," Seonagh said with exaggerated exasperation, trying to inject a little levity.

Brayth didn't take it that way, though. "From you, perhaps. But hear me, old witch, if Aoleyn's not to learn macantas from you, she'll learn it from me."

Seonagh winced at the mere mention of the word. Macantas was the demand of complete submission from a woman, the tradition that forced from them meekness, the sacred and unbending word of the god Usgar that man should rule and woman should serve. The very core of Usgar law that would allow Tay Aillig to throw Seonagh into Craos'a'diad if he so chose.

Macantas, the tradition that had sent Seonagh's sister, Elara, flying to her death.

"I'll be glad to finish Aoleyn's lessons," Brayth ended, his dark eyes sparkling, his voice flat, inflection wholly passive.

He would matter-of-factly beat the spirit out of Aoleyn, and Seonagh understood then that Brayth would enjoy every moment of it.

A chill ran down Seonagh's spine, and she warmed it only by firming up her resolve to teach Aoleyn the truth of what it was to be Usgar, what it was to be an Usgar woman. She had to break the spirited lass or Brayth would destroy everything about Aoleyn that made her a daughter worthy of Elara.

Again, Seonagh was surprised to learn how much she cared.

When Brayth turned once more and started away, a shaken Seonagh did not stop him.

By the time Seonagh returned to her tent, Aoleyn had washed, dressed, eaten her breakfast, and completed her chores. Aoleyn was often energetic in the morning, but the level of this day's ambition surely surprised her teacher. Seonagh was more surprised, still, to find Aoleyn greeting her with a smile.

She met that smile with an openly skeptical look, but that didn't seem to diminish the mood of the beaming woman. Already, Aoleyn had heard the news, Seonagh realized. For years, the young woman had been begging for more training with the magic of Usgar, and she knew it was now coming.

"Whispers put you with the uamhas many times," Seonagh said with a rather nasty edge. "With the stupid one."

Aoleyn rocked back on her heels, her smile vanishing in a gasp, obviously taken aback by the bluntness of the accusation. It was true enough. Aoleyn always did her foraging near the slave quarters, and spent many hours in the company of Bahdlahn, who was nearing his fifteenth birthday and becoming quite the strong and tall young man. The slavers worked him hard, and his hard muscles showed it.

"Then it's true."

"My tasks take me near . . ." Aoleyn started to reply, but Seonagh wasn't listening.

"Why is that one even still alive?" she asked, more to herself than Aoleyn. "Were he Usgar, he'd be raiding and hunting this very year." She snorted derisively. "The whispers circle you, girl," she warned.

"From who?" Aoleyn asked, straightening her shoulders defiantly.

"The man who'll take you for his wife, for one," the older witch replied. Seonagh noted the sour look that crossed Aoleyn's face at the mention of Brayth, and that expression almost broke the older woman. She was glad of Aoleyn's obvious distrust of the man and even more obvious distaste of the whole arrangement, but she couldn't let anyone, particularly Aoleyn, know that she was glad of it. Especially not with mod-garadh, the trial of the crystal caverns, so near at hand!

Aoleyn shuffled from foot to foot nervously, and Seonagh thought her properly humbled.

"The man who will beat you until you bleed," the old witch added, but then heaved a sigh, letting it all go. "Sit," she said. "We've much to do."

Aoleyn stared at her for just a few moments longer, then moved for her chair. "Baskets or blankets?" the young woman asked, making no attempt to hide her sarcasm.

"No," Seonagh replied.

Slowly, Seonagh brought forth her hand and opened her fingers to reveal three small crystals sitting in her open palm. "Crystals. Today, the lesson is Usgar."

Aoleyn's black eyes sparkled and her beaming smile returned tenfold as she stared at the tantalizing items, reflecting a pinkish hue in one crystal, gray in another, and the clearest of the three, shining magnificently in a slanting morning sunbeam. The deep, inky darkness of several small flakes stood in stark contrast to the brilliance in that one, for it was thick with wedstones.

Seonagh knew she held Aoleyn rapt.

"You know these?" she asked, though of course she knew the answer. Still, she wanted to judge how fully Aoleyn understood the potential revealed before her in this moment. In truth, Aoleyn should not have known much, but Seonagh suspected differently. The girl was too ob-servant and clever—Aoleyn had studied carefully the ceremony when the weapons had been blessed, and had witnessed the levitational pow-ers of the malachite at the cliff, of course.

Aoleyn nodded eagerly, and the sparkle in her dark eyes gave it all away. "The children of the god," Aoleyn whispered reverently. "Magic."

"The source of magic?" Seonagh asked, and Aoleyn wagged her head eagerly in the affirmative.

"No!" Seonagh corrected, and that shocked Aoleyn out of her seem-ing trance, her eyes lifting to regard the surprising Seonagh.

"These are Usgar's instruments, but not the source of the song," Seonagh explained. "She who holds the crystal is the source. Here." She brought her hand to her chest, to her heart. Aoleyn did the same, touch-ing a hand to her center, but where Seonagh expected a look of intrigue and wonder, she saw instead the slightest cloud pass across Aoleyn's eyes.

The darkness passed, and Seonagh did not ask what it was about. Not now. Not with the trial looming.

"Hold still in body and mind," Seonagh said, knowing that the words would confuse the girl. That was the whole point, however, the very first and most important lesson of Usgar. Seonagh brought her full attention to the crystals in her hand, to the wedstone-flecked clear crys-tal. She let her center flow out from her, into the crystal, and through it. She focused her energy, and after a few moments, her spirit stepped out from her physical form.

The world looked different here, from outside her body. Everything in the room became washed out, gray, distant. No novice to this strange out-of-body experience, Seonagh was not disoriented, but when she looked at the girl sitting before her, the older witch was indeed startled.

While far-walking, as the Coven called it, creatures observed took on a glow, an aura, with humans shining most brightly. Everyone's aura appeared different, but slightly so, in a way Seonagh found difficult to put into words, much like describing the tiny variations in people's faces. She could explain the broad strokes of an aura, but that was never suf-ficient to properly paint the picture, for all the auras looked more simi-lar than different, and yet, to a trained eye, all were indeed distinct.

But Aoleyn's aura was something else entirely. The only word Seonagh could think of was "bright," but that hardly did the girl's glow justice. Aoleyn was veritably glowing, and not in a manner that bespoke simple magical potential, as one might see when peering in such a way at the Usgar-righinn, though surely a similar potential was apparent with this girl. Such an aura as that would show the fiery glow of a ruby, or the arc of lightning, or some other expression of magical might. However, with Aoleyn, Seonagh saw most of all the aura of the wedstone itself—but only for a moment, for then came a greater surprise, when Aoleyn's aura shimmered like gray clouds speeding beneath a brilliant rainbow. Green hues, like the flakes of the levitation stone—perhaps the most important crystal of all to people who ran the treacherous ways of Fireach Speuer—grounded that rainbow on both ends.

Seonagh was glad that she was out of her body, that the girl could not see a physical expression at that moment, for her physical face would not reflect her shock, or indeed her sudden admiration for this willful child, or the flash of sorrow and recognition that surely would have registered. For only once had Seonagh witnessed an aura somewhat resembling this, though not nearly as vivid and defined as Aoleyn's, and the memory threw her back to her first student, her much younger sibling, Elara.

The witch quickly forced herself past the swirl of emotions. The aura reading was important, of course, but it was not the primary task before Seonagh right now. She focused her thoughts and her spirit like a spear, and dived into the mind and soul of the glowing child.

A long while later, Seonagh's spirit fought her way out of Aoleyn's corporeal form and came back into her own body with a shocking return of her physical sensibilities. She took a quick inventory of her senses, wiggled her fingers and toes to ensure that she had returned to her corporeal form whole, then took a deep breath. For to possess the body of another was not without grave risk, and was rarely attempted by any of the Usgar witches, and never done so unless in urgent circumstances.

This was an urgent circumstance.

Seonagh looked down at Aoleyn, lying on the floor before her, thoroughly drained.

Seonagh, too, was exhausted, and it took all of her willpower not to fall down on the floor beside Aoleyn and let herself melt into a deep slumber.

She had expected some weariness, but nothing like this! Spiritually possessing another person was always trying, but if that person wasn't versed in the magic of Usgar, she couldn't typically put up much of a struggle, caught off guard by an experience so out of the ordinary that it could not be anticipated. But Aoleyn had battled mightily against the intrusion, and this young woman, this mere girl, had nearly won that struggle—at one point, Seonagh had feared that Aoleyn would fully expel Seonagh and spiritually exit as well to chase Seonagh back to her own body!

The witch thought back to her aura reading on Aoleyn, and how impressed she had been to find such strength and affinity to magic in the girl's glow, so much like her young sister, Elara.

She was doubly impressed now.

Aoleyn stirred before her, not as drained as Seonagh had believed, perhaps. The witch made a note to push aside her admiration and not let on to feeling here, thinking that Aoleyn was willful enough without having her pride prodded so.

Aoleyn groaned and went up on her elbows, shaking her head groggily and seeming lost, disoriented.

Seonagh understood, surely. Spiritual possession was the most disconcerting magic any Usgar witch would ever know, no matter how many times one performed it. Seonagh took a deep breath, sorting the words she would use to explain it all to Aoleyn, and why she felt she had to perpetrate such a violation. Those words fell away, though, when Aoleyn spun about suddenly into a sitting position facing Seonagh, the girl's black eyes sparkling and bright.

"Do it again!" a breathless Aoleyn implored her. "That was . . . that was amazing!"

Seonagh blinked repeatedly, unable to decipher and accept the reaction. "Did . . ." she started and stopped. "Did you understand what . . . ?"

"At first, you put the fear in me," Aoleyn interrupted. "I didn't understand, but after a heartbeat it came clear that you were teaching me!"

Seonagh cocked her head to the side, unsure. Indeed, the wedstone could be used to aid in teaching a novice witch the ways of the crystal magic, but that had not been Seonagh's intention with this possession of young Aoleyn. And such a dramatic lesson wouldn't be done at all unless and until Aoleyn had become a full member of the Coven. Seonagh had only taken the action this day to reveal to Aoleyn some measure of the dark side of magical power, to gird her against the spiritual assault she would certainly find when she ventured into the crystal caves.

"Yes, yes, of course," Seonagh lied in the hopes of extracting what Aoleyn might have learned during this unintentional lesson. "And was I successful, child?"

A beaming Aoleyn thrust out her hand. "Oh, aye!"

The witch hesitated, trying to gauge if it was really possible that this girl—no, this young woman—had actually pulled some valuable insight out of that possession exercise.

The mere thought of that possibility frightened Seonagh as much as it excited her.

She spent a long while just studying Aoleyn then, considering her options and the possible ramifications of anything she might do. Surely she would not give Aoleyn a crystal thick with wedstone! Would Aoleyn then possess her, perhaps even ejecting her from her own mortal coil? Using the magic of Usgar required both strength and discipline. Aoleyn had the first—Seonagh shuddered as she remembered yet again the brightness of Aoleyn's magical aura!

But the discipline . . .

Seonagh started to shake her head in denial, thinking it best to not give the young woman any crystals at all, but before Aoleyn's smile could even disappear, the witch reconsidered. She sorted the crystals in her pocket and found the one with the least destructive potential, one flecked bright green, the stone known as malachite.

"Show me what you have learned," she said, handing it to Aoleyn.

Aoleyn fumbled with it for a bit, to no effect.

"Not the crystal," Seonagh scolded, and pointed to her own heart. "Concentrate your thoughts on your own life energy, on the center of your being. Find that power and bring it forth through the . . ." She stopped, realizing that Aoleyn wasn't even pretending to listen and was instead purely focused on the crystal that she turned about in her hands.

Seonagh shook her head and sighed loudly. The girl lacked discipline, lacked even the basic manners to pretend she was listening.

But suddenly, Seonagh recognized even more profoundly that Aoleyn had power.

For everything in the room began to shake, trembling, a cup overturning by the water basin. It hit the ground and bounced, but did not go back down, but rather began to float.

The water basin, too, lifted off the ground!

The straw of the bed, and the bed—both beds!

Everything in the tent began to rise! Seonagh began to float!

The witch grabbed a tent pole to steady herself. "Aoleyn," she said with concern. "Child!" she added when there came no reaction.

The tent walls began to rise. The pole in Seonagh's hand trembled as if it would pull out of the ground.

"Aoleyn!" Seonagh yelled. "Child, stop!"

But, wearing an expression of pure ecstasy, Aoleyn did not react, did not even seem to hear her.

Seonagh heard a commotion outside. Under the rising tent side, she saw the running feet of a man, a large man, wearing heavy boots. The witch panicked—she could not let a man see this spectacle of an uninitiated child enacting such magic! She pushed off the pole and threw herself at Aoleyn, grabbing for the young woman's hand.

The tent flap flew open, but at just that instant, the levitation field dropped, everything, Seonagh included, tumbling to the floor.

Aoleyn opened her eyes wide, but Seonagh kept enough of her wits about her to grab harder at the crystal and tug it from Aoleyn's hand.

"What are you about, witch?" Tay Aillig demanded from the doorway.

Seonagh straightened herself and brushed some of the dirt away, trying to regain a measure of composure and dignity.

"I am showing the young woman what power looks like," Seonagh replied, trying hard to appear in control. She was wise enough to put a bit of deference in her tone, as well, though, not wanting to give Tay Aillig yet another reason to wish her harm. Out of the corner of her eye, she noted a curious look cross Aoleyn's face, as the young woman moved as if to speak.

She flashed Aoleyn a chilling glare, warning her to silence.

Somehow, surprisingly, the insolent Aoleyn got the message and shut her mouth.

"You are supposed to be preparing the girl," Tay Aillig scolded, "not destroying the encampment!"

"Destroying?" Seonagh mouthed silently, and Tay Aillig moved aside, but still held the tent flap aloft.

Seonagh's jaw dropped open. Several people outside stood staring at the tent in shock. Spears and tools lay strewn about the ground. And logs, some of them still burning, had been lifted and thrown from the central bonfire!

The larger pile of firewood across from Seonagh's tent lay scattered, and a shaken squirrel hopped frantically about the logs.

"Idiot witch!" Tay Aillig huffed. He added something about the foolish old crone as he spun about to leave, and ended with "you should be with your husband" as the tent flap fell closed behind him.

Seonagh found it hard to breathe, and she tried to suppress her gasps so that Aoleyn would not recognize the utter shock on her face.

For Seonagh had never seen such a thing.

She swallowed hard and looked down at Aoleyn, who was thankfully too wrapped up in her own thoughts to notice.

Perhaps I left the Coven too soon, Seonagh thought, but did not say. Indeed, she couldn't find any words to offer at that moment.

After a long pause, it was Aoleyn who broke the silence. "Another?" she asked. "May I try more magic?"

"No, child," Seonagh answered, and shuddered at the thought. "No.

Not now. I think you're quite ready for your trials. Now get some rest, for be sure that you'll be needing your energy in the very near future."

That brought a smile to Aoleyn's face and a renewed sparkle in her dark eyes, an expression that showed an understanding of, and clearly a hope for, some magical interaction at the hinted event.

Aye, Seonagh silently answered. But she knew that it certainly wasn't the magic that Aoleyn would hope to see.

18

INTO THE MOUTH OF GOD

The girl skipped so lightly that she seemed to be floating along behind her, Seonagh thought, though, thankfully, not literally; given Aoleyn's power to access the magic of Usgar, that was a disturbing possibility. It would take them several hours to go all the way around to the southeastern slopes of Fireach Speuer since they were using no magic to help them navigate the valleys and high bluffs. The witches of the Coven, several of them accompanying Seonagh and Aoleyn this night, knew the way well, though, and had timed their march so that they would arrive at the entrance to the crystal caverns at dusk.

As the sun fully set, Aoleyn alone would enter the caves.

Some tribal leaders had come along, as well, most particularly Tay Aillig, who continued to surprise Seonagh with his interest in the girl. He looked angry, more so than usual, and kept casting glances at both Seonagh and Aoleyn. He was hoping the girl would fail, Seonagh feared, not because of the possibly fatal consequences that would hold for Aoleyn, but because it would give Tay Aillig, at long last, the excuse he needed to be rid of Seonagh.

When the trial had been determined earlier in the summer, Seonagh was fearful of such an outcome, but that had diminished somewhat in the face of Aoleyn's power bared. The sheer magical strength of the young woman had certainly terrified the teacher, but it also made her a bit more comfortable that this neophyte would succeed at the coming test.

Just a bit, though; other promising young witches had fared ill.

She had said nothing to the other women of the Coven about that, however. On the day of Aoleyn's magical display, Seonagh had claimed credit for the massive levitation field to Mairen and the others, as she had to Tay Aillig. She could tell from their glances along this journey, though, that some of the witches had become highly suspicious of that claim. Even at the height of her power, Seonagh would have been hard-pressed to bring forth a field so large and potent, and several of her fellow witches certainly knew that.

She knew, too, that they often gossiped about this young woman, her niece, the daughter of Elara, wondering of her powers, but Seonagh decided to neither confirm nor deny their rumors. They would all soon enough realize Aoleyn's promise.

True to their plan, the group arrived at the cave entrance bathed in shadow, just as the lower edge of the sun reached the horizon around the mountain's bend. The air was chill and clear, and the moon would be full tonight, the sky full of stars, not covered by clouds. The conditions were perfect for the test, and Seonagh felt the tingling magic of the air.

Simply from looking at the girl, Seonagh could tell that Aoleyn felt it, too. Aoleyn bounced more than walked, and her hands kept running over the bare skin of her arms. The air was cold, of course, but Aoleyn was not trying to warm herself.

"Stand here," Seonagh commanded, directing Aoleyn to a spot just outside the cave entrance, beneath a massive crystalline structure full of wedstones.

"What should I—" Aoleyn started to ask, but Seonagh silenced her with a harsh *tsssk*. The four men stayed back, looking on keenly, while the witches advanced, surrounding Aoleyn, encircling her, and joining hands. At the invitation of the Usgar-righinn, Seonagh joined the ring, as well.

The last hints of daylight faded, and Seonagh and the witches closed their eyes, falling into the trance together, channeling their centers into the inviting crystal, together freeing their spirits and engaging in the far-walk.

Seonagh practically felt all her sisters gasp at once, as they gazed upon the glowing child. Seonagh herself was once again taken aback by the clarity and power of Aoleyn's aura, but she carefully hid her satisfaction. As the one most familiar with Aoleyn, she was the emotional center of this joint trance, and she guided the others with her willpower back to a calm state.

Together, as one, the women of the Coven assaulted Aoleyn's center. She was strong, but joined in cause, they were far stronger. They stripped Aoleyn's defenses and left her reeling. It took them a great effort, more than usual, but after a short while, their task was accomplished.

Seonagh opened her eyes, the far-walk dissipating. In the center of their ring, Aoleyn knelt, her face a visage of terror. Together, the women moved forward, and lifted the girl. They carried her into the entryway of the cavern, and dropped her unceremoniously on the ground. Then they stepped out and channeled more of their energy into the crystals, into the quartz itself that formed much of the crystalline threshold of this place. Together, they conjured an image, a wall, so that it appeared that they had sealed the cavern. Aoleyn would awaken some time later—Seonagh suspected it would be much sooner than usual—and she would find herself trapped within.

She would have to survive the night in the caves, her center stripped down by the Coven. It was no small task for an uninitiated woman, and many had failed before.

Some of those young women had died in these caves, mouths opened wide in a last unheard scream. Others had been pulled out of the darkness, but fully broken, never again whole. Some had become gibbering fools, others had resumed a more mundane Usgar life, but none who had failed a night in the haunted crystal caves had ever again gone near the magical power of Usgar.

Seonagh turned toward Tay Aillig and his fellows. "Are you satisfied?" she asked, feigning deference.

"I will be satisfied with your efforts when Aoleyn exits the cave in the morning," Tay Aillig answered.

"She will," Seonagh said, narrowing her eyes and hardening her visage, letting the man know that she was utterly certain of her prediction. Apparently Tay Aillig recognized that certainty, whether from the tone of her voice or from the look on her face she could not be certain. But she was feeling smug, and in this place, before the bared power of Usgar's magic, she was also feeling quite powerful and confident. Back at the encampment, Tay Aillig could punish her for even the perception of insolence, but here, so close to the source of her power, surrounded by the women of the Coven, Seonagh believed that she was the one in control.

And Tay Aillig knew it, too, and it surely did not sit well with him.

He scowled and turned away, stalking off to set up his bedroll. The women of the Coven would remain awake all night, maintaining the illusion of a sealed cave, but the men, who had no real purpose here other than to sate their own sense of self-importance, could sleep.

Seonagh rolled her eyes at the man, allowing a fantasy of putting him in the caves, where he would be driven mad, driven to his knees, and driven to his grave. Yes, she would like that.

With a guffaw, she turned back to her task.

Blackness.

The rattled young woman thought she had opened her eyes, but perhaps . . .

Just blackness.

Only gradually did Aoleyn come to understand that her eyes were open, and it took some time after that for her to even realize her own body again, that she was lying on the warm, very warm, stone. She was covered in sweat, her light clothing clinging to her damp skin. She felt very tiny, as if the entity of Aoleyn had been shrunken down to some miniscule amount and left to inhabit a gigantic body over which she had little control.

Slowly, she became aware of her heartbeat, and then the throbbing and buzzing in her head. Beside that heartbeat, her chest ached, and she became aware of her breathing—and that, in turn, made her consciously focus on her breathing so that she was soon gasping.

The tactile feelings gradually returned, as if her life force was flowing back out to her limbs, to her skin.

Aoleyn tried futilely to sort out the puzzle here—she had no memory of the recent past. So she reached back further, to the journey she had taken this night.

Or had it even been this night?

How could she know how much time had passed?

How could she know anything? Was she even alive? Was she still within her own body?

That last troubling thought led her to an inescapable memory, more a nightmare—except that it was true, she just knew. It was true!

They had invaded her. The spirits of the witches, of Seonagh too, had come into her. They had tugged at her consciousness, at her sensibilities, at her . . . self. They had made her small within her own frame, had pushed and pressed her, driving her deeper within herself.

She felt a profound pain in her chest, in her line of life and heart.

They had done this to her!

Aoleyn felt violated, horribly so. She wanted to scream, to lash out, to fight back, particularly against Seonagh. How could Seonagh have done this to her?

They had invaded her, and now left her here, wherever this was.

Panic welled in her. She forced one arm out to the side, feeling about, searching for grass, or dirt, a pebble, a stair, anything!

But there was just the hardness of a smooth stone floor, and it was warm, very warm.

She tried to sit up, but just rolled over onto her side. She reached out again, farther, and hit something sharp, like the edge of a waiting spear.

She recoiled instinctively, grabbing her wounded hand, and felt the wetness of blood, even feeling the gash itself, and it was a deep one.

It should have hurt more than it did, she believed, and then had that thought confirmed as the pain became sharper, more acute, and Aoleyn realized that it signaled a more complete return to her physical body, as if her spirit was finally expanding again with the corporeal coil.

She tried to sit up once more, and this time did so, shifting a bit to be closer to the sharp object she had struck.

She paused there and tried to collect her wits. She focused on the journey from the encampment, her last real memory, but her thoughts would not coalesce. All she could remember was that she had left the encampment with some others, with some witches and Seonagh, at least.

She shuddered as their spiritual intrusion came clear once more, but this time, she fought against her instinctive revulsion and tried to see the violation of her most core being in a different light, like when Seonagh had done it to her back in the tent.

Had the Coven been trying to teach her something?

She shook her head. The only lesson she could gather was one of inferiority, for they had spiritually pounded her down, had toyed with her.

Aoleyn swallowed hard and took a deep and cleansing breath. She reached out into the darkness again, this time more carefully. Her hand brushed the sharp point and she tapped her way past it, and along a widening shaft to a wall. She shifted and moved her fingers carefully. Yes, it was a wall—a wall covered with blades of some sort.

She looked the other way, then ahead, and up, and back.

Just blackness. Utter blackness.

Aoleyn wasn't particularly afraid of the dark. She loved being out in the night on Fireach Speuer, under the stars or even in the blackness of a cloudy, moonless night.

But this? This was different. This was a darkness so profound that it pressed in on her.

And then she realized that she was blind!

She recoiled again and let out a scream that sounded more like a broken gasp. In her movement, she climbed to her feet, and stumbled—pointedly not to the right and the blade-covered wall!

No, she went the other way, trying to move cautiously, but overbalancing and once again bumping her reaching hand into something sharp.

Another bladed wall!

What hell was this?

Aoleyn spun, and tumbled back to the hard floor. The heat pressed in around her. Why was it so hot?

She felt her sweat, all about her body, her light clothing grabbing at her.

She sobbed and felt the heat in her chest, along with the pain. Panic again welled up in her, like black wings rising from the floor to engulf her.

They had blinded her! They had taken her sight and thrown her into a pit of blades, into the maw of a monster, she thought, sharp teeth ready to clamp down upon her and tear her apart.

Young Aoleyn wept, expecting pain, expecting death.

Seonagh sat outside the cave with a pair of witches. Even though she was no longer of the thirteen, she was still *p'utharai*, still a member of that exclusive club of women who had learned to access the magical powers of Usgar.

All three of the women were spiritually joined through a crystal bar that each held with one hand. Thick with wedstones, this long crystal allowed the three to easily combine their focus and powers on two other crystals, one flecked with perfectly clear quartz, the other heavy with a singular stone, green and yellow, and resembling the eye of a cat. With the quartz crystal, the witches could cast their sight into the distance, and with the other, the cat's eye, they could see through the darkness.

So it was now, the trio looking in on Aoleyn as she began to fumble about the crystal cavern.

Seonagh winced when the young woman stabbed herself on the wall, and those outside heard the distant scream of pain and fear.

Aoleyn seemed lost and despondent, and in that moment, desperate to the point where Seonagh thought she might hurt herself so badly that she would end any chance she had to become a member of the Coven.

The older witch winced. Aoleyn's failure would be her failure, and her failure would likely facilitate the end of her life.

Her concern went beyond that, though; to her surprise she found that it extended to Aoleyn. The blood ties didn't really matter to Seonagh, and certainly she had taught many others before Aoleyn—and had enjoyed teaching most of those others much more than her dealings with this impertinent whelp.

But still, the promise of this one, of Elara's child, had excited Seonagh.

Aoleyn was more akin to her sister than in just her appearance. Elara had been a willful one, often acting beyond custom and without permission, as in the night she had tried to help Fionlagh, her husband, in his futile hunt for the demon fossa.

Perhaps that was why Seonagh had been so tough, and so judgmental, with Aoleyn.

She feared that the girl's willful nature would bring her only grief.

Maybe it was better for Aoleyn to fail here in the crystal cave. She might die, but she might also come to a mundane future. One where she would only need to worry about being Brayth's wife and the bearer of his children and not ever tapping into the potential danger of the magic crystals.

That might be the best outcome, Seonagh thought as she watched the poor girl stumble about in the blackness. There were far worse fates.

But in her heart . . .

Seonagh reached her left hand into the small pouch tied at her waist, feeling the crystals she kept within. She knew them so well that she could distinguish them by blind touch. She felt her personal wedstone. If she let go of the joining rod, she could walk free of her body and go to the girl, whisper to her spiritually, to encourage her, to guide her.

She brought her hand back out, holding nothing, and swallowed hard, reminding herself that she was joined with two other witches—women who had perhaps read her thoughts!

Seonagh let go of the distance sight for just a moment to regard the others and gauge their reactions.

That brought her some solace. These were good women, loyal to the Coven, loyal and respectful to the former witches. Just a few years previous, she had trained the younger, Connebragh, who was just a decade older than Aoleyn. The other woman, Sorcha, was much older, almost Seonagh's age, and they had danced about the crystal manifestation of Usgar side by side for many years.

What might these two do if she went to Aoleyn? Connebragh hoped Aoleyn would succeed, Seonagh was sure, but what of Sorcha? Might she see Aoleyn as a threat, or as a suitable replacement for her own place in the Coven's dance?

Seonagh mulled it over for just a few moments before realizing that she was far afield here, and in dangerous straits. These two women, like Seonagh, had survived the mod-garadh without any help—indeed, Seonagh had been in this same spot, holding this same crystal bar, when Connebragh had walked through the maw of Usgar. And in that time, Connebragh had been more distraught, more befuddled, more desperate than Aoleyn was now.

Why hadn't Seonagh felt any compulsion to fly free of her corporeal form to help Connebragh?

The old witch scolded herself silently and dismissed her reckless plan. She grasped the crystal bar more tightly and started to fall back into the trance.

But out of the corner of her eye she caught Tay Aillig, standing in the shadows of a rocky overhang, staring at her, smiling.

She felt naked under his gaze.

He could not know that which was in her heart, she told herself, but in meeting his stare, she did not know if she believed that.

Seonagh suddenly found it hard to breathe. He wanted Aoleyn to fail, she believed, so that he could demand Seonagh's death for the girl's tragic failure.

Hope flowed from Seonagh in that dark, dark moment.

She felt a hand on her own, and spun about to regard Connebragh.

The young woman offered a smile and a nod toward the common crystal bar—a reminder of Aoleyn, Seonagh understood. With her hand, Connebragh pressed Seonagh's hand tighter about the crystal bar, inviting her to look in on her newest student once more.

Tay Aillig stared at the three women huddled before the illusionary wall sealing the crystal cave. He quietly slipped his hand into the nondescript pouch sewn into his pants beneath his belt, the tiny compartment that held his secret.

He knew what they were doing. While other witches maintained the illusion, these three were watching over Aoleyn, trying to make sure she didn't die within the caves, as others had.

The warrior grinned wickedly. He knew he could interrupt their magical connection to the girl, whatever it might be. He could enact the power of the stone he found himself rolling between his fingers, send that antimagic energy out to the trio. Perhaps they would get around his powers in time, but the looks he anticipated seeing upon their faces, terror and confusion, made it almost worth the effort.

He caught the oldest of the trio, Seonagh, staring back at him, and narrowed his eyes.

She thought it was personal between them, Tay Aillig knew. She thought that he hated her because of the fool Fionlagh and her sister, Elara.

Perhaps that was part of it, but what Tay Aillig hated more was the mere existence of *p'utharai*.

Former witches.

They should not have access to the magic of Usgar any longer, Tay Aillig believed—and intended to make formal when he at last gained enough power.

The formal thirteen of the Coven were tightly bound by their rules, and kept busy with important tasks, but these others, like Seonagh . . .

They were impertinent women who had forgotten their place in the tribe. Even the other women, those who would never serve in the Coven, talked lightly about the former witches, laughing about them being "cheeky" or "brazen."

But no, Tay Aillig understood, they were simply unruly hags causing mischief and threatening the order that had sustained Usgar for generations.

If he knew for certain that interrupting the three now would cause more than a little grief, and would, in fact, lead to Seonagh's death, then it might well be worth the risk of revealing his unique stone!

But, no, the price was too high.

Because the *girl* in the cave intrigued Tay Aillig. With her curves and her black hair and dark eyes. Her small but strong frame that so completely resembled her mother's!

The powerful man had to take a steadying breath at the memory of Elara.

No, he didn't want Aoleyn to fail in this trial, even if it meant that he would pass on the chance to dispose of Seonagh.

If she failed, Aoleyn would never gain access to the Coven, and if she was not among the powerful witches of Usgar, then she would not ever be a suitable wife to Tay Aillig.

He knew.

He knew that it was Aoleyn, and not Seonagh, who had lifted the tent flaps, the logs, the weapons, the casks. Her affinity to Usgar was strong, her power almost frightening. When he finally arrived at the point of power where he could select his wife from any woman in the tribe, even ones already married if he so chose, this one, this Aoleyn, this daughter of strangely powerful Elara, would top that list.

But not if Aoleyn failed here and so was placed on a path of mundane servitude. Indeed, if Aoleyn was not bound for a place in the Coven, she would be given to Brayth as early as the next spring.

He thought of her; he pictured her in his mind. He remembered Elara and knew what Aoleyn would become.

Yes, he would have her one day.

One day soon.

"Listen to your breath," Aoleyn whispered. She silently counted to four as she breathed in, then forced herself to slow her exhale to the same four-count, consciously slowing her breathing, consciously focusing on her breathing.

She lay down flat on her back and pressed her legs against the stone. Then she started to call to her body, bit by bit. She flexed her toes widely, tightening the muscles in her legs, as well. Then she let go, fully, muscles relaxing, legs relaxing, feet dropping out.

She had to connect her mind to her body here, had to find her center and her calm.

She brought her fingertips to her thighs, feeling the flesh of her legs.

She sent her thoughts through her fingers, her light touch coaxing the legs to relax more deeply. She walked her hands up slowly, one to her belly, one to the plexus between her ribs. Then to the heart, the throat, the forehead, and from there, she pressed the heels of her hands into her eyes.

The darkness was no less complete when she brought her arms down beside her, and there she lay, feeling her body, counting her breath.

She heard Seonagh's voice in her head, demanding that she "find her center," and by that, she meant that place near Aoleyn's heart, the place where she found the music of Usgar and the magic of the crystals.

Hardly even aware of the movement, Aoleyn sat up. She crossed her legs and rested the backs of her hands on her knees.

She didn't fidget now. She didn't flick at her fingernails as she so often had when practicing these techniques with Seonagh.

That had been play, so Aoleyn had thought.

This was survival.

"One, two, three," she said under her breath, breathing in.

Become aware of your toes, she heard Seonagh's voice echoing from her memory. *Do not move them, simply become aware of them. You have toes.* Aoleyn had always laughed at that ridiculous statement—but only internally after taking a whipping for doing so aloud!

But of course she had toes! She had never before truly seen the purpose of such an exercise.

Right now, though, facing such dire consequences, Aoleyn found it oddly remarkable that she did, indeed, have toes, five of them on each of her feet.

"One, two, three," she said as she exhaled.

Become aware of your feet, Seonagh's voice said through her memories, and Aoleyn obeyed. *And of the ankles above them, and the lower leg above that.* Aoleyn consciously moved her thoughts up her legs, stopping to focus on each bit, finding herself marveling at her own body.

One, two, three, she mentally counted as she inhaled.

Slowly, with no rush or sense of urgency at all, Aoleyn let her consciousness move through her body, up to her knees, her thighs, her pelvis, her gut. All the while, she counted and she breathed, slowly, deliberately. She felt her muscles, relaxed but strong, keeping her stable in this sitting position; she felt her blood, coursing through her veins hotly. She felt herself, her body, her soul.

One, two, three. *Focus on the flow of your breath, moving easily past your heart, and become aware of your very center.*

Aoleyn's eyes snapped open. In her hypersensitive state of meditation, she felt the movement. She still couldn't see, though, and remained certain that she had been blinded by the spiritual assault of the witches.

Now, though, it didn't matter, for another sense had awakened, one that had tickled her previously, teased her from afar, just out of reach. But for the first time she was truly aware of it, deeply and completely aware of it.

She felt it vibrating, that hollow spot in her chest. And, frighteningly, she felt the world vibrating with it, as if she held some mystical connection to all about her.

No, not the world, she realized. The floor, and the walls, and the ceiling. This place, this cavern—yes, she only then remembered. She was in the caves beneath Craos'a'diad, the Mouth of God.

And it vibrated with energy, with life! It was disconcerting to the young woman, overwhelming, and thrilling, and surprising, and somehow entirely familiar.

Become aware of your very center. Aoleyn heard Seonagh as if she were seated right next to her stern teacher, listening to one of her many lessons. And this time, unlike so many others, Aoleyn paid attention.

She felt her center, and tried to align its vibration with the song of the crystals within the cavern—like the one that had stabbed her, she realized!

Aoleyn almost lost the moment, then, and had to force herself to calm again, to count her breaths, to hold tight to the place of her intimate focus, to bring forth the magic of the song that was all about her.

She reached out—not physically, but spiritually, and she felt something, touched something.

Something tangible, as much so as if she had grasped it with her hand.

And suddenly, Aoleyn realized that she was not blind, for there was light, all about her, from the walls and the ceiling, shining brilliantly from several diamond-flecked crystals, the bright glow sparkling off the myriad of other crystals jutting from the walls and the ceiling all about her.

A beautiful light, Aoleyn thought, full of color and warmth.

The light of Usgar bathing her.

Seonagh inadvertently let out a gasp of relief and nearly fell over when the diamonds flickered to life in the cavern.

Her concentration faltered, throwing her out of the ritual joining and the far-sight spell, and she came back to her corporeal senses, as did the other two women. All three appeared drained, and rightly so. The magical crystals flecked with quartz were typically used for simple glimpses, spying something for a few heartbeats at a time. Yet this trio had been holding their ritual for a long while—Seonagh was surprised to see that the moon had risen above the mountain now.

Seonagh looked to her companions, noting that Connebragh, who was young and doing well with the Coven and so would see no threat from the rise of Aoleyn, seemed quite pleased by the development within the cavern.

Sorcha, though, simply looked drained. Seonagh understood—it was quite possible that Aoleyn would wind up being Sorcha's replacement in a few short years, and while that would simply move Sorcha to a similar position as Seonagh, it was not Aoleyn's fault. No matter what, someone would be called to the Coven to replace Sorcha. Aoleyn was simply the future; Sorcha, like Seonagh, the past.

It was always the way, Seonagh thought, that the older members of the community harbored resentment for the beauty, the strength, the talent, of the younger members. It was not just among the Coven either.

Seonagh figured this a universal truth for men and for women. How could an aging warrior, his muscles growing weak, not harbor some envy, some resentment, for the young emerging hero?

"She has heard the song of Usgar," Seonagh said to the other two. "Go and get some rest."

"And you as well," Connebragh replied, her suspicion evident. Typically, the witches would rotate the responsibilities of this night; now that the girl was awake and active with the crystals, the three of them were expected to pass off their duties to the next watch.

"In due time," Seonagh answered, and she smiled, knowing that she had confirmed Connebragh's suspicions, and not caring. "I will keep watch a bit longer."

Connebragh just shrugged and nodded, then started to rise. Sorcha did not even bother to stand, but simply lay down where she had been sitting and passed out.

"No call to exhaust yourself," Connebragh warned. "Aoleyn has found her power and created the light—she will not need constant watching."

Seonagh nodded. She knew that she, too, had to rest, somewhat at least. She took up the long quartz-flecked crystal, but did not reach for its magic. Not yet. She hoped to glance in on Aoleyn every short while, for just a glimpse, just an assurance. She reminded herself repeatedly that Aoleyn didn't need her then.

A bit of commotion over by a campfire caught Seonagh's attention. She noted the tribal leaders, and more pointedly, Tay Aillig, staring back at her. Then striding forcefully toward her. He was only visible in silhouette, but his gait spoke of anger—of course, all of that one's mannerisms constantly spoke of anger, a deep-seated bitterness toward the world.

Behind Tay Aillig, at the campfire, one of the venerable tribesmen rose slowly to his feet. Usgar-forfach Raibert looked fearsome in the firelight, despite his advanced age, and Seonagh shuddered to remember the man in his youth. He had never been particularly violent toward her, nor toward any of the women as far as Seonagh could remember, and he had rarely spoken. But in battle, Raibert had been the most feared man in the tribe, something Seonagh had witnessed personally only once. A cold sweat beaded on her brow just thinking of that long-ago day.

"You look fearful, crone," Tay Aillig said as he approached.

Crone? Seonagh thought but did not say. She had thought another decade would pass before she began hearing that moniker. More amused than insulted, she smirked and replied, "Not of you, man."

Of course, Tay Aillig's scowl showed no sign of relenting.

"The girl is awake," Seonagh said matter-of-factly.

"And yet, you're frightened," Tay Aillig reasoned. "Aoleyn must be in some danger, then."

Seonagh's sudden, wide smile stole his confidence, for it was a sincere and toothy grin.

"I never doubted Aoleyn," she said. "I'd be telling you more, but you're just a man, and not to know what the girl does in the cave. Not to know of the cave at all, eh?"

For a heartbeat, she thought Tay Aillig might lash out at her, though in truth, she didn't even care.

"Take care your words," he said deliberately, and loomed over her, physically imposing. "Or you might lose your tongue."

Against that obvious threat, Seonagh's hand reflexively moved toward her pouch and her private stash of crystals, and her mind ran an inventory of them, considering which ones she might use in combination to knock this man away or even destroy him. Surely Tay Aillig had little comprehension of the true power of Usgar, or what destructive forces an angry witch might conjure!

But Seonagh wasn't radiating confidence. She was exhausted from her extended look into the cavern. And her nemesis was right beside her, close enough to strike—and a single strike from Tay Aillig would kill.

She would have to produce some powerful magic before that to even have a chance, and she honestly saw no way she could accomplish that.

But at that moment, Seonagh did not care. She had suffered Tay Aillig's barbs and jabs for years in the encampment, but she would not suffer it here, in this sacred place, the entrance to the cavern that was the source of her Coven's power. This was a woman's place, not a man's, not any man's, and certainly not Tay Aillig's.

She rose to her feet with surprising grace, matching Tay Aillig's stare, looking him directly in the eye, her neck craning up at the man. Tay Aillig was nearly a foot taller than she, and right now he used all of that height to loom over her. But Seonagh did not back down an inch.

They held that pose for a long moment, neither blinking, neither moving, neither speaking, until a voice interrupted them.

"What are you about, both of you?" Usgar-forfach Raibert demanded, and only then did Seonagh realize that their little encounter had drawn outside attention. Tay Aillig blinked and stepped back, and Seonagh slumped back as well.

"The girl is awake," Tay Aillig told Raibert.

"And for what purpose do you know this?" Raibert asked, his tone brusque.

Tay Aillig stammered, so clearly uncertain.

"This is woman's work," Raibert chastised the younger man.

Seonagh started to speak up. "He demanded—" she began.

But Raibert didn't acknowledge that she'd even begun to speak, he simply continued on, chastising Tay Aillig. "We have no place in this affair and we are demeaned for even speaking of it. We are here only to watch over these lesser creatures and to decide if the girl should be given to Brayth now, or if she is destined for the Coven. Do not interfere."

He did not even wait for Tay Aillig's response, he simply swung about and walked back toward his campfire. Tay Aillig turned to follow, but stopped, and glanced over at Seonagh.

He no longer wore his scowl. Now his face was stone, his eyes unblinking, his smile creasing his face as if he knew something she did not. The scowl, the outward expression of anger, had never scared Seonagh, had rarely even unsettled her.

But this was different. This look, unreadable, had Seonagh's thoughts spinning and her heart pumping. A chill ran down her spine.

Tay Aillig's walk back to the campfire was not the aggressive stride that had brought him storming up to Seonagh's face. But there was something else in it—not humility, surely! Seonagh thought she recognized a not-insignificant amount of quiet confidence and satisfaction there.

She shuddered again.

19

HARMONY AND DISCORD

It wouldn't stop, each shivering note grabbing at the core of life energy and flicking it, like a million tiny fires burning into every reach of the tormented fossa. The creature wailed and threw itself about the debris-filled pit, sending shards of bone flying all about.

The beast leaped straight up, thirty feet, to crack against the ceiling, and tumbled back down into the jumble of sharp-edged skeletons. And it didn't even try to land on its feet, demanding for pain, shrieking for it. Anything to silence the assault of maddening magic.

And the beast howled and wailed, full voice, trying to overwhelm the discordant twanging that plucked at its life energies and filled it with such agony.

But no matter the demon's volume, the mountain's magic sounded clearly. No matter the crashing and churning, the fires burned bright and hot, so agonizingly hot.

The fossa leaped face-first into the wall, crashing hard, chipping the stone with its teeth. It sprang as it bounced away, flying across the tight pit to slam hard into the opposite wall, then back again.

And again, relentlessly, furiously, insanely.

A normal creature would have been killed, bones shattered in the wild rampage, the long falls into spearlike bones. But such assaults couldn't hurt the fossa.

But that song, that noise, that defiant, incessant twanging of the magic of Fireach Speuer! That, the fossa could not suffer!

After another long fall back into the pit, the creature burrowed deep under the pile of bones, and kept digging furiously when it came to the stone floor, its rending claws sending stone dust flying all about. It dug wildly, paws rolling, face planted firmly against the stone—which it even bit.

The magic had never been like this before, not this intense, not this loud!

The awful mountain sang now with full volume, as if mocking the beast. As if it would obliterate the beast.

In that moment of agony, the fossa hoped it would do just that—better nothingness than this unending torment!

The fossa dug, trying desperately to use the simple exertion, the focus upon its fury and its unending scream, to minimize the taunting notes of Fireach Speuer.

Trying desperately, and futilely.

The winding ways of tunnels began to mesmerize the young woman. Every wall thick with crystals—huge ones, many larger than even the stone of Usgar in the glade beside the winter encampment. All were shining in various hues, some from the inside, their diamond flecks brought alive through Aoleyn's call to the magic, while others caught that light and twisted it through their angled sides and colored with the various flecks of gemstones and minerals within.

It was more than warm in here, it was hot, and Aoleyn was glad that she was wearing only a simple shift. And even still, she felt sweat on her brow.

And then there was the music. She could hear such beautiful music!

But not with her ears. No, its vibrations were within her, flowing brilliantly, blissfully, elevating her mood and her heart with the song of Usgar.

Aoleyn took in her immediate surroundings. Far behind her, down an unremarkable path almost bereft of crystalline formations, loomed a solid, unremarkable wall. She had the feeling—perhaps it was a memory—that the witches had brought her into this place from that direction. Had they sealed the entrance behind them as they left? She pondered that for a short while, trying to make sense of it all.

What was this place, after all, and why was she here?

They seemed to be ominous questions to her at first, but only for a moment. For she heard the song and decided that this was not a place to dread.

The ceiling above her arched high overhead—as high as five tall men standing on top of each other. To one side, where she had touched the crystals, the cavern ended abruptly, while in the other direction it extended beyond her vision, narrowing and vanishing in twists and turns, to a deeper darkness beyond the range of the magic she had managed to call forth.

The floor beneath her was smooth gray stone, but she realized as she looked at the paths before her that they did not remain as such. She would be crawling over and under crystals if she meant to go deeper into the cave.

Perhaps she should stay put, she asked herself, and wait for the witches to return?

But what if they didn't? What if this challenge was to see if she could find a way out and not simply starve to death on a warm stone floor? Aoleyn smiled as she grew confident of what certainly had to be the truth. She would not stay in place. Not with these brilliant and glorious crystals all about, singing to her soul. The song quieted and the light diminished, but only for a moment, until Aoleyn reached out and touched the diamond-filled crystal again and called upon it, now with purpose and all her heart.

The light returned, then grew tenfold, reaching farther out than previous, and with a brilliance to rival a cloudless summer day under the high sun. It wasn't just this crystal she was igniting, either, but diamond flecks all about her in a widening circle, as if she was lighting distant torches with her thoughts.

Yes, she heard their song and answered their refrain, creating a glorious harmony sweeter than anything she had ever before experienced.

She heard other songs, too, some familiar, like wedstone and malachite.

One cluster of nearby crystals caught her attention and she moved to them, lightly touching them to feel their vibrating magic. They appeared quartzlike, but more opaque, greenish-gray. They sang of her imagination, of things she wanted to see, of images she might create.

She didn't understand at first, but on impulse glanced back behind her to the wall, almost as if the song of this crystal had bade her to do so.

She saw the wall, then through the wall! Outside, to the glade beyond, where sat Seonagh and some others, where, farther back and higher on the slope, a campfire burned and the men of Usgar moved about in the nighttime shadows.

Aoleyn waved, or started to, for she recognized that they could not see her. Something was out of sorts here, for the brilliant light in the cave did not spill out, but was blocked by the wall—but the wall wasn't really a wall!

Or was it?

"No," Aoleyn whispered, one hand still touching the smoky quartz formation. The song was telling her that the wall was an illusion, but it was also an effective one. One that worked both ways, clearly.

She realized then that she could simply walk out of the cavern. Was that the test? Aoleyn smiled. No, if it were that simple, then she would pass . . . but only eventually.

The song of this enchanted cavern reverberating within her, subtle and sublime, wonderful in its harmony. Aoleyn felt as if her entire body was vibrating along with it, pulsing with divine energy. As she fell deeper into her focus on that song, she began to recognize the variations in the music. Like the subtle bass of the smoky quartz she now touched, or the higher soprano sound of the diamond-flecked crystal she had previously used.

She felt as if she were holding Seonagh's crystal bars, all of them, and dozens more. With an intensity many times greater than those thin, singular notes, she found herself in the midst of a chorus. A thousand voices lifted beside a thousand drums' rattles, a thousand bells and a thousand flutes.

She could play them.

She turned her attention back to the diamonds, separated that song from the others. To this point, she had only worked with its intensity, lifting its volume, but now the clever girl coaxed it to sing more softly instead.

The light in the cavern grew dimmer.

She softened it more and more, extinguished it altogether, and then went further, focusing her thoughts upon darkness, something more absolute than the pitch blackness into which she had awakened.

Aoleyn felt as if she had gone there, as if she had created something more than an absence of light, but rather, a tangible darkness. She moved her focus to the side, separating one diamond crystal from the others, and she coaxed that one singular crystal to sing.

The darkness remained complete.

Aoleyn let go of all her call to the stones except to that one crystal, keeping it constant, keeping it soft. Instantly, she was bathed in the glow of just that shard.

The girl put her hand to her mouth, trying to sort the possibilities here. Had she actually done more than halt the magical light? Had she reversed it to create a physical darkness?

The thought shook her. Could she walk under the sun and blacken the area about her in profound shadow?

The potential for layers and layers of magical subtlety assailed her, overwhelmed her, and then, very soon, captivated her.

She brightened the cavern once more and moved about, looking to the various crystals, listening for hints of their songs, for the many and varied magical enchantment waiting for her call.

Aoleyn pondered the possibilities for a long while. She even glanced back at the distant illusory wall and thought to go out and ask Seonagh, Mairen, and the other witches if her revelation was indeed the secret of the Coven. But no, she decided, there lay before her something more pressing, more important, more exciting to do instead.

She turned toward the yawning passageway, leading deeper into the tunnels under the mountain. She took a few deliberate strides, her thoughts reaching out as she did for the flecks of diamond farther down the passage, bringing her magical light with her.

Aoleyn smiled. It was time to explore.

It should have stopped by now, but the discordant twangs had only gotten worse, plucking at the fossa's core with every note!

It was behind the wall—it had to be, right there!—and so the fossa threw itself headlong into the wall, scrabbling, clawing, and biting, digging, determined to get through the stone. Dust and flecks flew all about.

But the music, that damnable music, moved, and the fossa scurried along desperately.

But no, it was on the other side of the pit then! The creature sprang away, colliding with its open maw, tearing away, shaving the stone with its swordlike tail—anything, anything, to get at the incessant noise!

Eventually, the demon fossa fell back to its pile of bones, defeated. It thrashed, sending shards flying, and bit some of those into pieces as they spun in the air.

No. This could not stand.

Up leaped the creature, to the slanting rocky crawl space atop the pit, and out it crawled, belly rubbing the stone. The pain increased when it crossed that narrow crawl space, coming into the wider tunnel. Out of the shelter of its pit, the magic of Fireach Speuer burned brighter, and more painfully.

The fossa pushed on anyway. It had to get to the source, to destroy the source—a human, of course, playing with the crystals.

Around the last bend, the fossa came in view of the cave exit, and beyond that, the mountain was not dark. For the moon was full, the sky clear. But it was not a red moon, no. The light of the Blood Moon muted the magic of the mountain and allowed the tormented creature to walk free. But this was a pale silver orb. One whose light magnified the agonizing song of the mountain.

The fossa growled and tried to press on, but was driven back, slowly pedaling backward, step by step, at first, fighting the pain and the pressure so that it barely inched along the narrow crawl space.

The moonlight won, the song won, and the fossa spun and leaped back into its death-filled pit, burrowing down to the bottom of a bone pile, then scrabbling at the stone, wanting to get through, wanting to find the source, to kill and devour the source.

Anything to end the ringing pain.

Somewhere in the midst of that futile, frenzied assault, the fossa paused to identify the voice of the song, the signature of the source.

Someday, it promised itself, playing the thought over and over as a litany against the twanging notes.

Someday it would eat the source, slowly, painfully, bit by tiny bit.

The magical light followed Aoleyn as she made her way deeper into the cave, the area behind her going dark, while the area in front brightened. It wasn't that the magical light was upon her form, but rather that the call she made to the diamond-flecked crystals continued along with her, and so thick were these particular crystals about the walls and floor and ceiling that to an unknowing outside observer, it would seem as if she was carrying some sort of magical lantern.

The hallway forked, and, in looking down each passageway, she saw that both of those forked, as well. The floor was no longer smooth and easy under her feet, so she had to clamber over giant crystals, or duck, even crawl, under others, and in going over the first one, the bare skin of her leg settling against it, she let out a little yelp of surprise from the sting and understood why it was so hot in this place. The crystals were alive with energy.

Too much so, she realized, for her lungs were beginning to burn with each breath.

Fearing she would need to turn back, Aoleyn reached once more into the magic around her and found a soothing crystal striated with lines of green and milky white off to the side wall of the chamber. She made her way to it, a small and curling crystal, and put her hand about it, calling upon its power.

She was bathed in a soft white glow. The heat diminished. She thought of Mairen climbing under a bonfire, creating a fireball around herself to rekindle the blaze, then stepping out unharmed.

Aoleyn let go of the crystal and stepped away, trying to maintain the protection. She felt herself tiring almost immediately, so she went back, grabbed it again, and simply on a guess, broke the small crystal off the wall. On she went, carrying the crystal, using its magic to minimize the growing heat.

She didn't spend a lot of time in trying to decide which passageways to take, but just plowed ahead, unafraid, and enchanted by the magic all around her, by the song of Usgar.

"A labyrinth," she whispered at one point, and she thought it curious that she had whispered the words instead of just speaking them, for there was no one around. Yet, she didn't want to speak loudly in here, she realized, out of respect, out of a sense of reverence the young woman had never before known in her life.

The sheer beauty and power of this place humbled her.

But it didn't deter her, and she pressed on, recalling one of Seonagh's— no, not Seonagh's, one of the old crone's fables about a child lost in a labyrinth within the mountain. To avoid becoming lost, he, thinking himself clever, always went left at every fork or intersection. As fine a way as any to navigate such a maze, she thought, and so she took a step down the left passage.

But then Aoleyn remembered the ending of that story. Perhaps it was some sound or smell or something just beneath the level of conscious recognition, but the wandering child got a bad feeling about one particular fork. So proud was he about his plan, though, that he stuck to it. In his blind pride he stumbled into the lair of the monster that had made the labyrinth its home, and was eaten. The moral of the story, the old crone had told Aoleyn, was that she should never fear simply becoming lost, because even if she thought she knew where she was going, she could still be vulnerable up on the wild ways of Fireach Speuer. Indeed, in the fable, the confidence the boy had gained from "solving" the labyrinth had tricked him into a false sense of security.

The moral Aoleyn had taken from the story was simpler: avoid monsters.

Aoleyn shrugged and took another step down the left-hand fork. It was a bit dimmer in here, as this passage had fewer diamonds. Something about the vibration of this passage was unsettling to her, somehow discordant.

The young woman stopped in her tracks. She had her answer. She would follow her instincts, like the boy in the story had not done. She would reach out with her affinity to the crystals, listen to their song, and follow whichever path resonated better within her center.

She wandered for a long time, through a myriad of turns and forks and intersections with more than two choices. She listened to the crystals at each turn, following the vibrations, confident that she could backtrack in the same manner—so confident, in fact, that she wasn't even noting her choices or marking the walls.

Aoleyn was strangely unafraid. This place felt safe to her, as if she had come home at long last, a place calling to her heart and her mind, inviting her to secrets beyond anything she could imagine.

She felt calm, protected by the magic, and she felt . . .

A breeze!

The young woman paused and spent a long time sorting that out. She licked her finger and held it aloft. Yes, a breeze. A slight one, to be sure, but a current of air, down one of the passages. Perhaps an exit? She followed the breeze, down a long, winding corridor, and when she rounded a bend she saw ahead a faint light that was not coming from the diamond crystals. To be sure, Aoleyn ended her call to the magic, letting the crystals grow completely dark.

But the light ahead remained . . . silvery?

Moonlight.

Figuring she had won the night, Aoleyn increased her pace, rolling over one crystal, then nearly falling and impaling herself on another as she tripped on a small crystal root low to the floor. As a precaution, she called the magical light, just a bit, once more, and proceeded. Her curiosity about the caverns was far from sated, but knowing that she had found the way out and could leave if necessary would be grand. She decided to locate the exit, then go exploring. Both the ways of the labyrinth and, more importantly, the properties of the many pretty-colored flecks she had seen within the multitude of crystals. She wanted to know everything about this place before she fell under the withering gaze of Seonagh. She wanted to know more about this place than Seonagh did, more than even the Usgar-righinn!

Aoleyn gasped at her prideful determination. This was a place of Usgar, clearly, and it occurred to her that she should not be competing with the greatest witch of the tribe in such a manner! Still, she wanted to impress Seonagh, impress them all, and pass their test. "I will even tell them of the old crone's fable," she decided, and smiled widely.

That smile was so easy to come by in this place of Usgar's song. She pressed on, hardly thinking, hardly looking past her next step, basking in the song.

But that song lessened soon after she had turned down this breezy passage, she soon realized. At first, she thought it her own focus dissipating, but no, that wasn't it. The energy here in this passage was different than the others. A chill coursed her bones and she shivered.

She told herself to stop and go back, but she found that she couldn't. Something tugged at her subconscious, pulling her ahead. A few strides later, the light diminished even more, so much so that it took Aoleyn a few moments to understand that the passage had emptied into a wide, yawning cavern.

Her trepidation grew. She sensed few diamond-flecked crystals in here, and they responded to her call with less vigor than the ones in previous passages, giving off an eerie light. Almost like there was a glowing darkness, tingeing the edges of the silvery moonlight.

Aoleyn looked up to see the moon high in the sky above—the ceiling of this deep cavern was the sky itself. The mountain wind moaned as it rushed about those high walls, and sounded to Aoleyn like a giant inhale.

"Craos'a'diad," she whispered. She couldn't be sure, but . . .

The cavern spread out wide all about her, but she moved to the center, drawn there inexorably. It wasn't just the moon, or the breadth of the cavern, but the shadowy darkness that drew her, and she quickly realized that the floor fell away before her; a huge, deep pit, with no visible bottom, filled most of the place. The eerie darkness emanated from it, fighting the edges of the moonlight. Not a physical darkness, Aoleyn thought, but something different, something more profound, something that made this place so different from the rest of the labyrinth, made it cold instead of warm, frightening instead of inviting.

If the rest of the place emanated life itself to Aoleyn, this place seemed quite the opposite.

Consciously, Aoleyn told herself to be away from that pit. She even found herself whispering "go back" repeatedly as she slid her foot forward.

Had she found the monster of this labyrinth?

Her freedom shone above her, high above, tantalizingly and unattainably. She wanted to be out of this place, but there was no place to climb; there were no walls near enough to the maw above for her to hope to get there, for the opening was right above this pit. The cavern's walls were far away in every direction, all ending at the high ceiling, none near that lone crack that was letting in the moonlight.

At last, she managed to pull away from the pit, if only just a few steps. The spell broken, Aoleyn considered her options. She didn't want to wander the hallways any longer, not even to get back to where she had started, and certainly not to explore anymore. There was a chill in her bones and she had seen enough.

"This is my test," she whispered, and the epiphany shined as brilliantly as the moment she had turned on the diamond-flecked crystals.

She thought of the night of the ritual with the tattooed man who would be her husband, and of how she and Seonagh had climbed the ledge to the fire.

The green-flecked crystals, the malachite.

Aoleyn closed her eyes and tried to sort out the songs of Usgar. She ended her call to the diamond and listened for the subtle vibrations of other notes.

She moved to the wall and felt the crystals, but it was difficult for her to sense their magic through the mind-numbing chill that had crept into her bones.

"Focus," she whispered, squeezing her eyes tighter. She imagined herself climbing the wall, using the crystals growing near the ceiling to pull herself along to the opening.

At last she felt the same magic as she had felt in Seonagh's tent, the same magic they had used to get up the cliff.

Sensing more than seeing, she reached for a slender crystal rod protruding from the wall. Gripping it tightly, she shoved down with all her strength, breaking it off. She yelped as she cut her hand in the process.

A deep wound. Aoleyn felt her blood pouring out, feeling light-headed and close to fainting. As she caught hold of another crystal to steady herself, she recognized its magic as that of a wedstone.

Hardly thinking, Aoleyn reached out to it and brought forth its power, its warmth driving back the chill of the cave and washing into her hand, sealing her wound.

Her relief lasted only until she heard the whispering hiss behind her.

A profound coldness pierced through her, shocking her with pain. She stumbled backward, away from the wall. Her eyes popped open wide, but she could still see very little.

The whispers grew around her, sinister and cold.

She saw a light, tiny and far. The moon, she thought, and she stumbled toward it.

She tried to call out to the diamond-flecked crystals again, but she couldn't find her focus at that moment.

A cold hand grabbed her and she screamed.

But no, not a hand, she realized.

Something icy brushed against her back.

Aoleyn spun about, to see a deeper blackness before her, a human shape, but unnaturally stretched and swirling, constantly in flux, blowing apart and coalescing at random. Aoleyn could just make out a face, her face?! As though she was looking into some dark mirror.

Or her face in death?

In desperation, she punched out at it, but her fist and the crystal she held passed through the non-thing. She felt coldness, that terrifying shiver, grasping at her chest.

And the shadow specter leered at her, and wanted to steal her warmth, to devour her with its cold. Or it was her own being, her shadow self, calling her to her grave.

Aoleyn cried out again and fell back. Her lungs burned with cold and she could not see. And the floor was gone and she was falling, into the pit, into the darkness, and she was dying, and there was no hope.

20

VIRGIN VISTA

Khotai slipped her hand into Talmadge's as he stood out by the lake-shore, staring up to the southeast, where the full, silvery moon hung over Fireach Speuer as if put there just to limn the mountain in brilliant silver light.

Talmadge glanced over at the woman and started to look back to the heavenly orb.

But he didn't, instead catching the reflection of the moon in Khotai's dark eyes, and suddenly she became to him more than a bystander, but an integral part of the beauty of this windy night beside the loch, with the village of Car Seileach behind them.

This was their third visit to Loch Beag together, though Talmadge hadn't yet dared take her beyond the village of Car Seileach. The tribe had welcomed Khotai more openly than Talmadge had thought possible. Talmadge assumed it was because her To-gai-ru upbringing had given her a greater affinity to their ways, a greater appreciation of the rhythms of the land, than any travelers from Honce-the-Bear the tribal folk may have encountered.

In a way, Khotai spoke their language even better than he.

Talmadge shook his head, admiring her beauty, almost lost in the sheer attraction he felt for her.

"What is it?" she asked, turning to return his stare.

"I feel foolish," he said.

Khotai arched her eyebrow, her expression doubting.

"The moon is beautiful," he said, looking back to the southeastern sky in a clear move to change the subject.

"Yes." Talmadge could feel her gaze still upon him.

"It is so bright you can even see the fish swimming in the lake," he exclaimed, pointing. "Look!"

But he knew that she wasn't about to be distracted, and he finally sighed.

"Why?" she prompted.

"I didn't want to bring you. Ever. Now that seems a foolish choice indeed."

"I told you that two years ago."

"I know."

"And you're just now sorting that out?"

"It is more than that. Much more."

"I have kept your bed warm, and you mine," she said and squeezed his hand.

"It is more than that as well," he answered without hesitation.

"Truly?" she replied, a sudden flash of indignation filling her voice and face, and causing Talmadge's eyes to widen as he realized that his statement could be construed as quite an insult to the woman's love-making techniques!

"No, I mean . . ." he stuttered and stammered.

Khotai laughed at him, warmly.

"Truly," Talmadge went on, trying to realign the conversation once more, suddenly realizing that it was important to him to express these feelings.

"I did save your life with those fools back on the river," she said. "It took that to get you to let me come along."

"Not even that," Talmadge answered somberly, "though I'll never forget your heroics, fear not. It's more. I have carried around the ghost of Badger for so many years, and now . . . now it is like the sun, or this beautiful moon, has chased the shadow away. And it is more than even that." He paused and sighed, amazed at all of the emotions suddenly flowing through him, demanding release—emotions and feelings he had never before recognized, but that now seemed as clear as the moon hanging over the mountain.

"I hide out here," he admitted. "I hide from the other frontiersmen with their bullying and raucous foolishness. I hide from the fighting and the disease." He looked her squarely in the eye and spoke to her nod. "I hide from my memories, from the pain."

"You walk the same road over and over because your own footprints comfort you," Khotai said. "You accept—"

"I accepted having nothing, being nothing. Having no one and being no one . . ." Talmadge said quietly.

"To avoid the pain." She moved closer and kissed him on the cheek. "Your life is a bard's tale, and better that story if your life is a tree with spreading branches. Write your own story, my dear Talmadge. Wander the ways of the world and of those feelings that burn and twist within you. Put your fears aside—should not the greatest fear of all be the fear that you will die without ever having lived?"

"So easy to say," he replied.

Khotai laughed at him and kissed him again, then whispered into his ear, "You took me to this place, did you not? And twice took me back."

When he didn't immediately respond, she pushed him out to arm's length and painted a pained expression on her face. "Do you regret that choice?"

Now it was Talmadge's turn to laugh, and with more than a little embarrassment.

"Of course not," he said to Khotai's knowing smirk, but before he had even finished the response, the woman was tugging him along toward the small hut the tribe had offered them. They left the flap open, for the door faced the lake and there were no huts between this one and the waters, and doing so let the silvery moonlight sparkle and splash in upon them in their lovemaking.

Talmadge thought this night a chapter of his story that he would never forget and ever relish.

Under that same moon, high up on the mountain, Seonagh stared at the crystal of far-sight with a look of complete frustration. She had privately looked in on Aoleyn, to glimpse the girl leaving the entryway and moving along the maze of the crystal cavern, lighting the diamond crystals with ease.

But Seonagh wanted more than a simple glimpse! She wanted to send her magical vision back in there now to follow the girl's progress. Could Aoleyn call up some of the other crystals as easily as she had ignited the magical light? Would she find Craos'a'diad and would she at last recognize it for what it was?

In the larger scheme of things, that didn't really matter, she supposed. Aoleyn had revealed her easy affinity with the magic of Usgar, and just the display Seonagh and the other two had witnessed would surely be enough to secure her a place in the Coven when came the next opening. No other woman of the tribe not already among the witches was re-motely close to this girl's inherent understanding of the crystals—and Seonagh even wondered how many in the Coven possessed such insights.

Mod-garadh had been held by the women of Usgar for generations—forever in the counting to the tribe's memories and oral histories. It was not without danger, for some women simply could not handle the unre-lenting blackness and the radiant magical energy of the cave. Some few panicked wholly, and would lie shivering on the floor throughout the night, feeling the effects of the cavern in an acute, unfocused way. They were usually broken and mad by morning, some never to recover.

For truly, mod-garadh was one of the two great dangers to young Usgar women, the other being childbirth.

All who went into the cavern felt that panic to some degree, Seonagh knew. She had, and so had Elara and Mairen, and just as had Aoleyn. The measure of the young women was more regarding how they recov-ered from that panic, and whether they could then go on to enact the magic that would show them the beauty of Usgar about them. For the majority of women who could regain their calmness, the night would be spent in meditation, feeling the vibrations of the cavern in the spot where they had been placed. Even these women would emerge the next day exhilarated and eager to continue the magical training—but alas, it would be minimal.

Rare were the girls like Aoleyn, ones who proved so naturally attuned to the crystals that they could produce light or other effects. Most of these women would still simply stay in the antechamber of the caverns and explore the magic of the various crystals. When Seonagh saw Aoleyn producing light and standing, she thought the girl might take this path, and she was happy.

But Aoleyn's affinity with the crystals was matched by the uncontrollable young woman's insatiable curiosity, and she had taken the rarest, and most dangerous, path of all, setting out to explore the ways of the labyrinthine cavern.

It was said that women choosing this path had been, without exception, the greatest singers of Usgar's song—if they survived.

But that was the problem, for most of those who went into the caverns on their own during the trial, so untrained and unprepared, never returned.

Seonagh winced, reminding herself that her own fate would be tied to Aoleyn's. If the girl did not return, Tay Aillig would likely get his way and return her to her husband.

She looked down at the crystal of far-sight once again, frustrated to the point where she wanted to throw it away. There was nothing to do now. Magic could not be sent deeper into the caverns from the outside, not through far-sight or far-walking or any other means the Coven had ever discovered. The vibrations of the multitude of crystals within simply prevented such outside intrusions.

Aoleyn was alone.

Seonagh, too exhausted to even walk back to the Coven's fire, collapsed upon the ground into a fitful sleep of terrible dreams.

The moon was still up, though low across Loch Beag, when Talmadge crawled to the threshold of his hut and peered out at it once more.

He loved it here. Perhaps what he had said earlier rang of truth: that he was hiding from his pain, but that didn't change the fact that he truly loved this place. The light was different here, both under the sun and the moon, and he found it comforting and pleasing.

He glanced back at Khotai, sleeping on the mat, and considered her words, her way of life. To her it was a storybook, and one to be made thick. Or as she told it, her life would be no pole, but a tree, spreading wide with hundreds of branches, hundreds of side roads to catch her fancy, and full of blossoms. She had known many men, and had probably killed many, too. She had traveled the world, to the Mirianic Ocean and now, as far out here in the wild as any To-gai-ru or Bearman of Honce had probably ever gone.

"Except for Redshanks," Talmadge whispered with a chuckle.

"What about him?" came Khotai's voice from right behind him, and she was against him before he could even turn to regard her, looking out at the full, silvery moon.

"Nothing," Talmadge answered. "I was just thinking that he has probably enjoyed this very sight from this very place."

"The book of his life is thick."

Talmadge smiled.

"Six other villages?" Khotai asked, and not for the first time in the two years since she had first known this place.

"Seven if you include the one on the mountain."

"You don't include that one."

"No."

"So, six?" she asked again. "You will be visiting six more before you turn back to the north and east."

The man shrugged.

"Are all the views as grand as from here?" Khotai asked, although Talmadge realized that she was asking much more than that. This time, though, the question sounded a bit different to him.

"The same," he replied, though he broke his response a bit short. "Mostly the same," he corrected.

"So if e'er I was to make that journey, I'd see little different than I'm seeing this night, looking out across the lake?"

"The mountain would loom behind you from Fasach Crann," Talmadge admitted. "A giant shadow upon you the whole of the morning. There is a different feel to that."

"But that's the place you like the most," said Khotai, and the man nodded. "Mostly the same things to see, though?" she asked.

Talmadge paused and considered his next words carefully. He didn't want to lie to Khotai, not ever, and there was one place out here where there was indeed much, much more to see. Sellad Tulach, all the way across the lake, directly opposite Car Seileach if one rowed directly to the east from this spot. Sellad Tulach overlooked the Desert of Black Stones, and most of the world, it seemed.

Talmadge realized and admitted that he wanted to share that view with Khotai.

He pointed straight out across the lake and said, "The world looks different from the other side of the lake, from Sellad Tulach."

"Mountain view?" Khotai asked, properly translating the name. "There are many ways in which the language of To-gai resembles the words spoken here," she explained. "It would not surprise me to find that the tribes here came from the steppes."

"Or maybe the other way around?"

Khotai thought it over for just a moment, then nodded.

"I want to see the world from that place, then," she decided. The way she spoke and the way she backed off from Talmadge and stiffened just a bit told him that she expected a roaring argument over that. Three times he had taken her to this place, Car Seileach, the safest of the lake villages, the one most open to outsiders—and the only easy approach to this region came down this side of the lake—but in their previous journeys, he had never wavered on his refusal to bring her to the other, less inviting and far more dangerous villages.

Indeed, Talmadge's first instinct was to shake his head, and his denial of her request was almost out of his mouth.

Almost.

But he looked at her, sitting back, chewing her lip, so hopeful, and he knew that he couldn't deny her.

"There are two other villages only a day's walk," he explained. "We will go to them together this time, and return to this place in no more than a week. If you hold in the good graces of those lakemen and the ones here, I'll take you across the lake and let you see the world from the high vista of Sellad Tulach."

"And if not?" she asked slyly.

"I'll bury your corpse," Talmadge replied immediately. "If the lakemen have not already eaten you."

Khotai's face went through a series of quite funny expressions then, as she tried to wind her way through his surprising statement. In the end, though, Talmadge's grin gave it away, and the woman went back to him to share his view of the full moon.

And to kiss him.

21

CURIOSITY AND COURAGE

She could see nothing. She knew she was in the dark pit—and indeed, even the light of the moon had disappeared when she had gone over the edge—but she could not feel the walls about her.

Just the wind, growing as she plummeted ever faster, whipping her shift about her, bending her face out of shape, threatening to rip the two crystals from her hand so much so that she clutched them tightly to her chest and slapped her other hand above them. And she felt, too, the cold, deepening, reaching into her bones, stealing her life.

She felt herself tumbling over backward, head down. Aoleyn tried to cry out, expecting to shatter her skull at any moment. Not that it would have mattered, she realized, and perhaps would be better if she landed that way, to end it quickly.

She reached her thoughts out, seeking some diamond-flecked crystals so that she could at least see. She sent her thoughts out all about, seeking the song of Usgar, seeking crystals on the walls, if there even were walls.

But she found nothing out there, and it wasn't until Aoleyn retrieved her sensibilities that she felt the first tug of Usgar, from one of the crystals she held.

She reached into it with all her strength, and heard the song deep within, far away, tiny. But she felt those green flakes and sang back to them. She felt their vibrations and she sent her own, from her heart, from her line of life.

She sang louder and forgot she was falling, so deeply did she fall into the glow and magic of Usgar. No longer did the notes seem tiny and far away. She could picture them now in her mind, coming closer, answering her call.

Together, they sang, Aoleyn and the magical crystal.

It took her many heartbeats to even realize that her fall had slowed, that the wind was but a breeze now, and she opened her eyes.

But saw nothing, for the blackness seemed deeper still.

She hung there for just a moment, disoriented. Was she upside down? Were her feet below her and near to a floor? How far had she fallen?

She thought she had made an error then, for she began to move again, and panicked as she feared it a fatal mistake as she once again began to gain speed.

Aoleyn threw her thoughts fully into the crystal, screamed for it to help her, to stop her descent.

But no, she was speeding once more.

Seonagh stirred and opened her eyes to greet the sunrise, a sunrise that had come earlier because they were on the back side of the mountain. After a moment of reorienting herself to her surroundings and trying to recall all about the previous evening, she was surprised to learn that she was no longer lying right before the entrance to the crystal cavern, but was, rather, back by the campfire.

Connebragh winked at her, clearly recognizing her confusion, and Seonagh nodded and understood. Connebragh and the others had carried her here. As anxious as she remained about Aoleyn's fate, Seonagh couldn't be mad at that choice, for how much more might her bones ache had she spent the night on the cold ground?

She pulled herself up to a seated position and regarded the sunrise. Her head immediately swiveled, back down to the cave entrance, where a pair of witches maintained the illusionary wall.

"Aoleyn has not emerged?" she asked.

Connebragh shook her head.

"She is back near the entrance, though," Seonagh prompted. "You have heard her stirring. We will find her when we open the cave."

"No," said a somber Connebragh, shaking her head. "We've had no sight or sound of the girl since she began wandering the caverns."

"The sun is above the horizon," Seonagh protested. "Why is the cave not opened?"

"Soon."

"It is past time!" Seonagh climbed to her feet.

"Seonagh," Connebragh said, leaping up and taking her by the arm—and looking to the side, thus drawing Seonagh's gaze to the men, particularly Tay Aillig and Raibert, who were all looking back at her sternly.

"Seonagh," Connebragh repeated more quietly. "It is not your choice to make." She motioned down to the side, where another pair of witches were looking up at her. Both had bowls of steaming stew before them, tubers and roots, and one had another in hand and was filling it, for Seonagh, obviously.

"The Usgar-righinn will tell us when," Connebragh added.

With a sigh and a glance to the cave entrance, Seonagh sat back down and accepted the bowl from the other woman. She ate slowly, not really hungry, her stomach churning as she worried over the fate of her student, her niece. Her protégé.

"When last did anyone peer into the cavern?" she asked.

"When the moon touched the western horizon, as is permitted," Connebragh reminded. "That was many hours ago. Take heart, for we're sure to find Aoleyn sitting where we left her."

Seonagh returned the woman's comforting smile. She wished she could share that optimism, too. She glanced at the rising sun a hundred times over the next short while. It seemed to move not at all. Time itself had stopped, it seemed.

She wanted to scream out! To run down and take up a crystal and call forth its power to look inside the cave, to find Aoleyn! A feeling that Aoleyn needed her, that they would find the girl lying broken on the floor, overwhelmed her. Had Aoleyn's mind been shattered by the magic? Seonagh thought of her sister, reduced to babbling incoherence after her encounter with the power of the fossa. Had the magic of the cavern done the same to Aoleyn? Or was Aoleyn already dead?

She had to know!

She dropped her bowl and stood up to pace about, tapping her finger nervously to her bottom lip. She glanced up the rise and noted Tay Aillig staring back at her, and smiling his awful smile. The truth of his thoughts seemed clear to her. Ever was that one taking pleasure in her discomfort.

She tried to compose herself, unsuccessfully.

She nearly jumped out of her shoes when Mairen at last shouted that it was time to open the cavern.

The first rays of dawn seeped about Aoleyn's eyelids and roused her. Groggily, she pulled herself up to her elbows, blinked the sleep out of her eyes, and looked all about.

She was on the ground, right beside Craos'a'diad. For a moment, that confused her, but then she smiled, remembering her fall, remembering her magical halt to the fall and then her second fall.

Except, she had come to understand when she saw again the moonlight, that second plummet was really her soaring upward! She had brought forth the power of the green-flecked crystal to reverse her fall, and it had carried her right up through the ceiling of the cavern, this very chasm the Usgar called the Mouth of God.

Aoleyn closed her eyes and basked in the warm memories of the overwhelming magical song that had flowed so fully through her, and in the realization that she had passed her test, certainly, that she had escaped.

Her smile of self-satisfaction disappeared almost immediately, though, and she hopped up to her knees and began reaching all about with her hands, searching for the two crystals!

There they were, right beside her, and she scooped them up and brought them lovingly to her breast, particularly the green-flecked one that had saved her life.

Aoleyn crept over and glanced into the maw of the chasm, and saw, far below, the deeper blackness of the pit. She didn't know how far she had fallen that previous night, or how much farther she had to fall before she found its bottom, but it was a long, long way—it occurred to her that it was possibly deeper than Fireach Speuer was tall!

One day she would know, she vowed. One day she would take this crystal, or one like it, along with a diamond-flecked crystal for magical light, and explore that pit.

The thought brought a chill, though, and the memory of a shadowy creature confronting her—a creature she thought was the specter of her own death.

There were secrets in the dark depths of that pit, Aoleyn knew. The one thing Aoleyn liked about secrets was uncovering them.

They all approached the cave entrance together, women and men, and no one spoke a word. The Usgar-righinn gave a nod to the women maintaining the enchantment, and she released her magical energies, allowing the illusion to fade and the cave's entrance to be revealed.

And within, the long corridor and an empty chamber.

No one was supposed to say a word until the Usgar-righinn gave permission, but Seonagh couldn't suppress a small wail.

"Well, let us return to our people," Mairen said with a heavy sigh, and she offered a quick prayer of "Usgar take her kindly."

Seonagh, though, moved for the cave.

"No!" Connebragh and several others admonished her.

Seonagh caught herself midstep and glanced sheepishly at the Usgar-righinn, finding Mairen's cold stare waiting for her. She apologized and the group began filtering away.

"Perhaps you will find the girl when you enter the cave from a different entrance," Tay Aillig whispered to Seonagh as he walked by her.

Seonagh wanted to lash out back at him, but she didn't, caught by surprise at the man's tone, for truly he seemed disappointed, angry even, that Aoleyn was not here awaiting them.

Too many emotions and fears grabbed at her then, and so she just began walking off behind the others.

"Where are you all going?" The voice, the girl's shout, came from high above.

As one, the group gasped and looked upward, to Aoleyn, sitting on a ledge up on the cliff face, her feet dangling, swinging back and forth carelessly.

She met Seonagh's eyes directly, and the two exchanged heartfelt smiles.

The group gasped again—all but Seonagh—when Aoleyn kicked off from the ledge.

Aoleyn floated gently to the ground, landing gracefully among them.

"Brayth will have to wait," Seonagh said bitingly to Tay Aillig.

The man just grinned an unsettling, conniving smirk, and Seonagh got the distinct impression that he was hardly upset by that notion.

22

MAGICAL JACKS

Over the next few weeks, Aoleyn used every spare moment to experiment with the two crystals she had taken from the caverns. Seonagh and the other witches had let her keep them, and even more amazing to the young woman, she wasn't being discouraged in her experimentation with the magic. It also seemed to her that she was being given more free time.

The song of Usgar contained within the crystals seemed fainter than it had been in the cave, though, more distant. She didn't need a teacher to explain that the vibrations of magic within the crystal-filled labyrinth had somehow made the song louder and more accessible to her—never had Aoleyn felt more attuned to the magic than in her time wandering the caverns beneath Craos'a'diad, not even when she was in the tree beside the great angled crystal manifestation of the god itself!

She wanted to go back to the cave. She had even asked Seonagh if it would be possible. The answer made it clear there was no such possibility, and offered no compromise. Aoleyn was not a stranger to mischief, but Seonagh had made it clear that any excursion she might take secretly to the caverns would ruin her entirely.

Aoleyn's teacher had even hinted that if she snuck away for such a journey, she'd be caught and then would indeed go into the cave. Thrown into Craos'a'diad itself, and never to come back out.

Aoleyn dearly wanted to get back to the caves and knew that Seonagh had seen the near-desperation on her face.

Every time she tried to use her green-flecked crystal, she wanted to get back there all the more, for the song was distant out here. Aoleyn had trouble aligning her inner energy with the hum of the magic, more so than she had experienced while alone in the labyrinth. There was simply too much noise. The day-to-day life of the Usgar drowned out the crystal's song.

She could still manage to levitate, but barely, and there was no way she would risk the type of controlled descent she had used to rejoin Seonagh and the others outside the cavern. She could still lift other objects off the ground, but only the tiniest of stones, and nothing like she had performed with Seonagh's crystal that day in the tent.

Aoleyn didn't understand it, and it bothered her. Was it her? Had she somehow damaged her magical abilities?

Or was it the crystal?

She purposely awakened early one morning to try to find out. It was still dark, and she heard Seonagh's rhythmic breathing. Delicately, Aoleyn rolled off her cot and onto her knees on the floor, and slowly, so slowly, she crept across the room.

Aoleyn couldn't really see it in the darkness, but had committed this room to memory. She made for Seonagh's robe, which was hung on a hook at the foot of her bed, fighting hard to contain her excitement, repeatedly reminding herself to go slow.

She shuffled a bit too much, and Seonagh stirred. Aoleyn held perfectly still for many heartbeats before beginning again.

Her relief at reaching the robe was short-lived. The pockets were empty.

Her eyes had adjusted to the darkness a bit by then, and she made out Seonagh's form in the cot. Seonagh's shift had a pocket.

Aoleyn got to the side of the cot, and there she froze, settling in, letting Seonagh get used to the presence and settle more deeply into sleep.

Slowly, Aoleyn moved her hand, low, near the woman's belly, but not touching. She knew where the pocket was located and was fairly certain that her hand was positioned right over it, but there she held in place again, gathering her courage, steadying her hand.

She reached for the pocket. She felt the crystals.

She felt Seonagh's hand clamp hard over her wrist!

The older woman sat up forcefully, throwing Aoleyn's hand aside, and Aoleyn fell back from the cot.

A light came up, just a little one, glowing from Seonagh's pocket.

"What're you about, girl?" the woman demanded, and her eyes, lit from below by the diamond-flecked crystal in Seonagh's shift, looked demonic. "You would do well to tell me at once," Seonagh pressed.

"I . . . I just wanted to borrow—"

"Borrow?" the woman growled angrily. "How dare . . ."

She started to come forward, as if to attack Aoleyn, but she stopped herself and stared at the young woman curiously.

"Why?" Seonagh asked, her voice calm once more.

"I just . . . just wanted one, and only for a moment."

"And you could not ask?"

"I could not wait!" Aoleyn exclaimed.

Seonagh stared at her for a long while. "Why?"

"Just the green-flecked one, like the one you let me keep."

Seonagh nodded, reminding her that she had not answered the question.

Aoleyn swallowed hard, not sure how to actually explain her fears, or questions.

"Go on. We've come too far now for you to be lying to me."

Aoleyn pulled out her own crystal. "I can't do much at all with this crystal," she said.

"You jumped from a cliff and floated down."

"Here, I mean," Aoleyn explained. "I felt so . . . so mighty with it that night in the cave and the next morning. But here, it is almost useless in my hands." She sniffled, and was surprised that she was so near to tears. "I think I have lost the magic."

Seonagh shook her head and put on a comforting smile. "No, girl, you have not lost your magic. The crystals function more powerfully near Craos'a'diad. It is almost as if the crystals within the cave reach out to them and add to their strength, and to the powers of the witch."

"But I'm not as strong as I was, even here," she cried.

"Go fetch the crystal that let you float down to us," Seonagh bade her.

Aoleyn retrieved it and was surprised to see Seonagh holding a crystal of her own when she returned to the cot.

"Reach inside your crystal," said Seonagh. "Attune yourself to its song. Hear Usgar in your heart and be as one with the music within the crystal."

Aoleyn did as she was told. She felt the magic whispering within the crystal and within herself, but it seemed distant once more, barely accessible. After a few frustrating moments, she opened her eyes. "What shall I do with it?"

Seonagh motioned with her hand. "Give it to me."

Aoleyn handed it over, somewhat reluctantly, for she feared that she would not get it back. She was surprised when Seonagh took it, and held out her own crystal in exchange.

"Do it again, with mine," she explained.

Aoleyn brought the crystal in against her breath and searched for the song—and found it waiting for her, thrumming powerfully! Her eyes opened in shock.

"Did I break the other one?"

"No, silly girl!" Seonagh said with a laugh.

"But . . ." Aoleyn shook her head, seeming at a loss. She looked down at the crystal she now held and felt certain that she could leap from the highest peak of Fireach Speuer and use it to float down gently. She was smiling, despite herself, when she looked back at Seonagh, her expression curious, expecting an answer.

But Seonagh held silent, and wore her teacher's face sternly.

Aoleyn lost her smile and focused again on the gem, her thoughts spinning. She glanced at the crystal Seonagh now held, then to this one, before looking up again, nearly gasping as she did.

"They are not all the same!" Aoleyn blurted.

"What do you mean?"

"The crystals—even the ones with the same colors in them," she said, talking so fast that her thoughts could hardly keep up. "They are different in . . ." She stuttered about, looking for the word.

"Power," Seonagh offered, and Aoleyn wagged her head excitedly. "The one you hold now is quite powerful, quite loud with the song of Usgar," Seonagh explained. "This one you have given me can only whisper."

"Unless I am near the crystal cave—Craos'a'diad!" Aoleyn said triumphantly.

She felt quite pleased, and more so because Seonagh looked quite pleased.

"Go to bed, young Aoleyn," she said. "I will forgive you for waking me . . . just this once."

Aoleyn wagged her head happily and spun about.

"Aoleyn!" Seonagh barked, and Aoleyn swung about to see Seonagh motioning with one hand and holding Aoleyn's weaker crystal with the other.

The girl sheepishly completed the exchange.

Her fears had been calmed. But Aoleyn got no further sleep that night, her thoughts chasing many tangents in an attempt to sort out these beauteous revelations.

The Usgar encampment bristled with excitement as the last raid of the season drew near. While the warriors were down by the lake hunting for supplies and slaves, the camp would move to the winter plateau. The thought made Aoleyn giddy. She believed that she would find much greater magical powers nearer to Craos'a'diad, and Seonagh had hinted that she would be given new crystals to study during the short days of winter.

She would not participate in the ritual that preceded the raid this season, but in that, too, Seonagh had teased her, hinting quietly that Aoleyn would possibly be included in the dance and the blessing of the weapons.

The thought both intrigued and terrified the young woman, reminding her keenly that she was a woman now and that her days were relatively carefree compared with the responsibilities that might soon be upon her. Suppose she blessed a weapon incorrectly—her blunder could cost a warrior his very life!

During those last days of the summer encampment, Aoleyn found herself with little to do. Aside from the basic cleaning and food gathering, Seonagh set out no other tasks, and even encouraged Aoleyn to go and experiment with her crystal, or to wander as her heart led her. So she did, meandering about, using her green-flecked crystal to scare away a squirrel by lifting the acorn it sought into the air, then catching the squirrel itself with the magic as it leaped high for a tree.

The creature floated up to the branches, and as soon as she was certain it had caught on to one, a giggling Aoleyn released the magic.

She spent many hours seeing how high she could leap with the help of the stone. She ran, she jumped, using the magic to elevate her higher and farther by turn.

For all the silly ways Aoleyn found to amuse herself, though, the days remained quite long—at least until she found another who was as unengaged as she: the slave boy Bahdlahn.

"Nothing to do?" she asked, coming up behind him as he sat. Bahdlahn turned and smiled at her, but motioned for her to be quiet, then turned his attention back to watch a tortoise that was trying, unsuccessfully, to clamber over a stone.

At first, Aoleyn was more intrigued by the boy than the tortoise. He had been worked hard in the last couple of years, a beast of burden for the tribe. His days were spent hauling buckets of water, carrying deer and other animals killed in the hunts, or simply moving stones. He never complained. All of it was having a profound effect on the young man's body. He was thin—they didn't feed him very much—but his sinewy muscles were hard and tight. His filthy shirt was torn, revealing his upper back, and that, too, rippled with lean muscle.

Aoleyn admired his form, nodding at his strength, and found herself wondering if, in a couple of years hence, there would be an uamhas man in the tribe.

She blinked and noted Bahdlahn's intensity as he watched that poor tortoise trying to climb over the rock.

Aoleyn grinned and clutched her crystal to her breast.

The tortoise began easily walking up the side of the stone, climbed right over it, and gently floated back to the ground on the other side, to continue on its way.

Bahdlahn nearly jumped to his feet, and when he looked back to Aoleyn, the astonishment painted on his face made her giggle.

"I did it," she said, to which the boy responded with a confused look.

Aoleyn showed him the green-flecked crystal, from which he immediately recoiled.

"Oh, don't be afraid!" she said. "It is mine. I control it. It won't hurt you." She had an idea. "Do you want to play a game?"

The boy hesitated for a long while, then only tentatively nodded.

"I didn't have to ask, you know," Aoleyn reminded. "I could have told you that we were going to play a game, and you would have to, wouldn't you?"

When he didn't respond, she told him to stand up.

Aoleyn reached inside the crystal with all her power, focusing on him. "Jump!" she commanded suddenly, and she threw her telekinetic power at him.

Bahdlahn did jump, reflexively, but even with Aoleyn's magic, the young man didn't get very high, nothing out of the ordinary.

Aoleyn snorted. How she wished she had Seonagh's crystal instead! She imagined Bahdlahn flying up into the air, his feet higher than a tall man's head. He'd cry out, surely, and she could float him back to the ground.

The thought had her giggling once more.

And she found another idea.

"Follow me," she instructed, and she went back toward the Usgar encampment, just a few dozen paces from the camp's southern edge, down in a rocky dell and out of sight of the encampment.

"Watch," she told Bahdlahn. She sat cross-legged on the ground and spotted a nearby pebble. With the crystal, she magically floated it off the ground.

Bahdlahn gave a stifled little cry of surprise and fear.

"Oh, don't be afraid," Aoleyn scolded.

The pebble rose to the sitting girl's eye level, and she brought a second one up, as well, to the other side of her, but both very near.

Aoleyn took a deep breath, then let the magic drop, and so let the stones drop. Fast as a striking snake, her free hand shot out and caught the stones, one, two. She opened her hand before Bahdlahn, revealing her victory.

"I've caught as many as six," she bragged. "How many do you think you can catch?"

He seemed not to understand.

"Sit," she told him, and when he did, she asked, "Which hand will you use?"

He still seemed not to understand.

"To catch the pebbles!" the girl explained, and in her exasperation, she almost called him Thump! "Which hand? You can only use one."

Bahdlahn looked at his hands, shrugged, and held up the left.

Aoleyn nodded and chewed her lower lip, clutching the crystal tight once more. "Wait for me to tell you when to catch them," she said.

On the ground before Bahdlahn, a pebble shook and lifted, then a second and a third joined it, the three floating up to the sitting boy's eye level.

"Ready?"

Bahdlahn nodded.

"Go!" Aoleyn said and released the magic.

The stones fell and Bahdlahn caught them, one, two . . . and almost three, the last pebble bouncing off the side of his hand and flying aside.

"Oh, nearly!" Aoleyn exclaimed. "Put them down and do it again."

He caught all three the next try.

And so they made a competition of it, and were soon laughing. Then they worked together—how many could they catch using all four hands, Aoleyn wondered?

She tucked the crystal under her chin, and to her delight, discovered that she could hear the song in that position, even without her fingers about the item. As she did that, Bahdlahn fetched a bunch of pebbles, laying them all about the ground before them.

Instead of focusing her magic on one at a time, Aoleyn concentrated on the area itself, and sure enough, more than a score of pebbles floated into the air.

Aoleyn found it hard to breathe from the excitement, amazed by her control of the magic. This was the best kind of practice, she decided then and there! She was finding out so much more about what she might do, and it was fun!

"Ready?" she asked.

Bahdlahn nodded eagerly and rubbed his fingers together.

"Go!"

Pebbles flew every which way, and in the end, Aoleyn opened her hand and said, "Five," dropping the pebbles to the ground. Bahdlahn put his down beside hers and Aoleyn started counting them. She had barely begun when the boy said, "Twelve."

Aoleyn finished her count and nodded her agreement before her eyes went wide and she gawked at Bahdlahn. He had produced the number before she had finished counting. He hadn't counted, she realized; he had added. He knew that he had seven, and she had mentioned her five, and this boy, this simpleton whose own mother proclaimed as "stupid" had added them together in the snap of fingers.

Aoleyn stared at him for a long while, and Bahdlahn looked away.

"We should do it again," she said. "Do you think we can get more?"

The boy looked back and nodded, his smile returning.

"I have nine!" Aoleyn announced after the next round, though she didn't put them down. She looked at Bahdlahn slyly. "How many did you catch?"

Bahdlahn opened his hands, revealing seven once more.

"Seven," Aoleyn said. "So how many did we catch?"

The boy licked his lips.

"More than last time?" she asked.

He nodded.

"You know how many," she said suspiciously, obviously so.

He swallowed hard.

"Say the number."

He started to shake his head slowly, but Aoleyn sharply demanded, "The number!"

"Sixtee—" The boy stopped short and glanced all around, as if looking at a way to run away.

Aoleyn was beginning to understand. She didn't openly accuse him, then, however, and decided to keep going to see if she could get him to lower his guard.

"Sixteen!" she proclaimed happily, smile beaming. "We caught more than the first time!" Putting a bit more excitement than was necessary into her words, hoping to help Bahdlahn to not be nervous.

"We'll catch more this time!" Aoleyn promised.

They didn't. In fact, they came close a couple of times, but sixteen remained the highest number as they continued their game, round after round, laughing and playing. At one point, Aoleyn lifted three different stones and began experimenting with the magic in a different way, letting one drop, then catching it with the telekinesis as she let a second one drop, then catching that as the third fell.

As she did that, Bahdlahn took up three small stones of his own and began juggling them, and it occurred to Aoleyn that they were both doing the same thing, she with the magic of Usgar, he with nimble hands.

They soon went back to their other game, but by then the daylight was fast waning and it grew harder to even see the pebbles, let alone catch them. Still they tried, stubbornly, to beat sixteen, but now they couldn't get close, and wound up slapping more pebbles than they caught.

It didn't matter though; the silliness seemed to only make the time more precious, the day more fun.

But then the moon peeked over the shoulder of Fireach Speuer, as if to spy on them.

A red moon, the Blood Moon.

The face of Iseabal.

Bahdlahn gulped. Aoleyn turned to him just as he was jumping to his feet, already moving away before he had fully stood up. Rising, she caught him by the arm, but he tugged against her.

"Run," he said.

"Why?" the young woman asked him, staring at him earnestly. She knew why, of course, but what could this simpleton slave possibly understand about Iseabal? "Lizbeth," Bahdlahn replied.

"Lizbeth?"

Bahdlahn pointed at the rising orb and enunciated more clearly. "Elizabeth!"

"The name of the moon? You call it Liza . . . Elizabeth?"

He nodded frantically and kept pulling her along, clearly desperate to be out of there and back to his mother in the pine grove.

"That's what your people call it?" Aoleyn pressed. She knew that she had to let him go—he had farther to run than she did, after all, but there was something else here, some level of insight or understanding that she had not witnessed with young Bahdlahn before. "Your mother taught you that?"

He nodded again.

"What else did she teach you about it, besides its name?" she asked.

He shrugged and held up his hands.

"Lots, huh?" Aoleyn asked in a teasing and jocular manner. "And you can keep more still in that funny head of yours?"

He shook his head—too emphatically, she thought.

"You don't have enough words?"

"No," he said, sounding more cogent and determined than she had ever heard. "No time."

Aoleyn couldn't really argue with that, as surprised as she was by his reaction. This was the first time she had been with Bahdlahn with the Blood Moon rising since that long-ago day when they had been out collecting pinecones for Seonagh. Though, on that occasion, he hadn't shown such fear.

She pulled him with her instead of letting him run, taking him to the edge of the Usgar encampment, where the bonfire was already ablaze, and sentries moving out to the camp's perimeter.

"We're safe here," she said, finding an out-of-the-way place. "Tell me."

Bahdlahn glanced all around, focusing mostly on the camp and not on the darkness beyond.

She shook him. "Tell me and I'll take you back to your mother."

The boy swallowed hard.

"I know you can talk," she warned. "Might that I'll tell the warriors."

His eyes went very wide and he trembled visibly, and Aoleyn immediately got the sense that he would spring upon her and throttle her! Only then did she realize how important this particular secret truly might be, for only then did the young woman understand it from the poor boy's point of view—and from his mother's point of view. She, Innevah, had done this to him, from his earliest days, and only now did Aoleyn understand why.

"I will never tell them," she said quietly. "I will never tell anyone . . . Thump. And I will never let them hurt you."

He seemed to calm.

"What do you know about Iseab . . . about Elizabeth? Please whisper to me. It is important."

Bahdlahn put his lips to her ear and began whispering something she couldn't decipher, and it took her a lot of words—more words than she had ever heard strung together by the boy, certainly!—to figure out that he wasn't speaking the common language of the tribes, but rather, something that sounded more primitive and guttural, short and stout and very different from the flowing language of the mountain tribe. He spoke in a low monotone, not unlike the chanting the Coven used often in their rituals.

"Is that the language of the lake tribes?" she asked. "Some secret way of talking?"

"Older," Bahdlahn answered.

"Older?"

"The Ancients," he explained. "Old lessons."

"What does it mean?"

Bahdlahn looked all around again, and Aoleyn realized that he was making sure that no other Usgar were around, reinforcing her new insight of how critical it was to him—indeed, his very life depended upon it!—that no one understood how well he could truly speak.

"Elizabeth bleeds and the Beast wakes," the boy said, his voice hushed. "The world bleeds with her."

Aoleyn didn't know how to respond, for too many things bounced about in her head. Bahdlahn had spoken in two different languages! And he had spoken in a clear and reasonable manner, in complete sentences. In that moment, he seemed in no way to resemble a simpleton who was once called Thump.

Also, the lakemen clearly understood the danger of the Blood Moon. Had they been visited by the fossa, as well?

And who were these ancients, or ancient lessons, or whatever it might be?

It was all too much for Aoleyn at that moment, so when Bahdlahn whispered, "Please, home," she could only nod and lead the way.

Aoleyn ignored the sentry's call for her to stay in the camp and ran to the south with Bahdlahn in tow, sprinting the short distance to the slave grove.

Bahdlahn led the way, moving in with certainty through the tangled branches.

Aoleyn heard the boy's mother gasp with obvious relief when he pressed deeper into the pines. She, too, had seen the Blood Moon.

Aoleyn pushed her way into that inner chamber, to see Bahdlahn's mother hugging him close, her arms wrapped tightly about him, kissing him all over his head.

Aoleyn felt something welling up inside her she did not expect and could hardly fathom: envy.

Innevah looked past her boy to see Aoleyn, her face a mask of utter relief. She nodded at the young woman, then motioned for her son to go into his chamber beside hers, two natural shelters separated by some intertwined branches.

"Greetings, Innevah," Aoleyn said at last, meekly.

The woman's gaze went to the floor. She answered in a quiet tone, "Greetings, mistress."

"Not mistress," Aoleyn said, moving into the room and bending to bring her eyes to Innevah's level. "Just Aoleyn."

"I know."

"Your son has told you much about me?"

The woman looked up, her face twitching with nervousness. She shook her head slowly. "He cannot speak."

"But you know of me," Aoleyn stated more than asked.

"There are not so many Usgar," Innevah answered. "An uamhas must know."

Aoleyn let her stare linger for a little bit, then glanced to the side, to the corridor where the boy had gone. She noted him in the other chamber, moving back and forth.

"My gratitude, mistress, for bringing Thump home."

Aoleyn snapped her head back to look the woman in the eye. "His name is Bahdlahn," she said through gritted teeth. She wasn't sure why Innevah's use of the demeaning name had so bothered her. Perhaps it was because she was jealous of the obvious relationship between Bahdlahn and Innevah. Aoleyn had never known her own mother, after all, and from what she knew of her people, even if she had, she would not get hugged and kissed like that anyway. Seonagh was the closest thing she had, and she had only ever known a slap across her face from her teacher.

Or maybe it was something else, she began to wonder. She thought back to the first time she had looked in on Innevah and her baby, those many years before. She still remembered it, and vividly. The moment had been burned into her mind forever when she had heard Innevah telling her child, her innocent baby, that he was stupid.

"We call him Thump," Innevah said, again looking at the floor.

"And I say Bahdlahn," Aoleyn snapped back. "So which will it be?"

"Bahdlahn, mistress," Innevah said. "You are mistress, I am uamhas. It is not my place to choose."

Aoleyn wasn't sure how to move this conversation along. Many things continued to bounce about her thoughts, most prominently her understanding now that Bahdlahn was nowhere near as simple and stupid as she had presumed, even when she had come to believe that he wasn't simple enough to hold the name of Thump.

What was happening here was much deeper than anything she had before imagined. She was pretty sure she knew the truth, but only Innevah could confirm.

But not then.

She was about to bid Innevah farewell and take her leave, when a cry went up from outside. "To the fire!" they cried. "To the camp! The sidhe rascals have come! A raid!"

23

THE WORLD BLEEDS

Their time on the mountain plateau was nearing its end. The north winds had begun to blow and Talmadge and Khotai had visited four of the villages now, including crossing the lake to Sellad Tulach, the easternmost village, nestled among the mountains that lined the eastern edge of the plateau. In their initial journey to get to Loch Beag, Talmadge and Khotai had to approach from the northeast, crossing all the way around the northern edge of the plateau to the easier climb beyond the northwestern edge of Loch Beag. That corner of the mountain plateau presented a long trail, but not a vertical climb.

Talmadge had not second-guessed his choice to allow Khotai into more of the villages this year, for in every one, she had been afforded great hospitality. Talmadge's own acceptance to these lands had come much more slowly than his exotic friend was experiencing. She understood these people more than Talmadge did, even though he had spent many months among them. The To-gai-ru ways were similar to the folk of the tribes, the affinity to the land around them, the understanding and efficiency of the language and the daily routines. Khotai had been a natural fit here around the waters of the loch.

As soon as he had become certain of these perceptions regarding Khotai, and confident that they would be common about the tribes, Talmadge had changed his normal trading route, had decided to save the best village for last.

He wondered if he and Khotai might one day make Fasach Crann their home. They were still young enough to have children. Was it possible that his future would take such a turn?

"I've not known more amazement," Khotai said from behind the man, who was gazing back to the south, toward Fasach Crann. He turned about to regard the woman as she stood at the crest of the path they had walked, facing away from him.

He knew what she was talking about. She was overlooking the desert, some two thousand feet below.

Fasail Dubh'clach, the Desert of Black Stones.

Although he had been to this place many times, Talmadge understood Khotai's awe at the spectacle so far beneath them. He remembered the first time he had glanced over this very ledge, and the first thought that had occurred to him regarding the unusual landscape. They were high up on a mountain plateau, beside a huge lake that was, by all reports, very, very deep—deeper even than the mountains were high, so the tribesmen said. That lake lay in a natural bowl. What would happen to that bone-dry desert below them if an earthquake cracked the mountain wall? If the natural dam holding back such an immense amount of water someday failed?

What a sight that would be! And not a very welcomed one to any who might live down there in the Desert of Black Stones.

He walked over to stand beside his beloved Khotai, and appreciated the view even more. The sun had just set, but the deep night had not yet arrived, and he could still clearly make out the large shapes down below.

The stars were just beginning to shine, and soon an amount beyond counting would fill the night sky, their light competing with the full moon.

He stepped behind Khotai and wrapped his arms about her. Perhaps they might spend the night out here, feeling so much a part of something so much larger. Larger than each of them, larger than them together.

Like the way he felt about his love for her.

The night deepened, the stars began to shine, and both Khotai and Talmadge drew in a sharp breath, gasping in awe and reverence. Out across the low desert before them and down to the south, they saw the floating hues low in the sky. It was a rare sight this far north, but Talmadge knew it to be the Halo.

Khotai reached up over her shoulder to run her fingers across Talmadge's face. What was there to say? What words could express the serenity, the beauty, of this heavenly view, with the dark desert spreading wide far below and the magical equatorial ring of Corona shimmering with color to shame the very stars above?

The harmonious sweep of the Halo's hues continued far in the distance, holding them silent. But a moment later, they both painted on curious expressions when that distant shimmer shifted from its multitude of hues to a monochrome red.

Khotai looked back over her shoulder at Talmadge, or started to, but stopped halfway, her eyes going wide, and leading his gaze.

The red moon began to climb over the eastern shoulder of Fireach Speuer.

"We should get to the village, and quickly," Talmadge said. Only then did he realize that they really were all alone out here, and looking back, he noted the large fires being constructed within Sellad Tulach.

"Why?" Khotai asked, obviously sensing his sudden change of mood. "I like the privacy. I like the view." She gently stroked his face. "I like the company."

Talmadge couldn't help but grin at that, but as tempted as he was, he knew better. "The full moon," he explained. "The villagers huddle when the moon shines red."

"Fables?"

Talmadge shook his head. "Might be, but fanciful tales believed in heart. In all the villages. When the full moon's red, all the tribes—

even the Usgar, I am told—huddle beside great fires that steal the red glow."

"Because there are monsters about?" Khotai asked lightly, and it was clear to Talmadge that she wasn't taking any such threats seriously.

He wasn't, either, when he considered just the matter of some village fables about some demonic monster, but that was only one concern.

"If we stay out through this night, our return will be met with doubting eyes," he explained. "They'll want to know why. They'll want to know how. They'll know we doubted their . . . fables and so do not value their wisdom."

Khotai nodded and moved past him, taking his hand and turning him as she moved back toward Sellad Tulach.

"I've no wish to insult them," she said. "They've already come to like me more than they like Talmadge, and if I am to take over your trading routes, I need to continue that."

That brought a laugh to Talmadge and he playfully swatted Khotai on the rump as he caught up to her.

"They only suffer you because they like me so much," he said.

"You tell yourself whatever you need to hold heart," she was quick to reply.

Talmadge pulled her close.

"You should've taken me to this place years ago," Khotai said. "But I understand your want of secrecy."

"Not that," he said, stopping his walk and holding her back. "I . . ." He stammered for some response but couldn't find one.

"I know," she said, helping him out. "Badger's ghost haunted you. But there's more than that—be truthful, my love! This place, Loch Beag and the mountains, the desert below and the stars above, is pure to you, unspoiled. You would keep it that way, and you feared that showing your secret would despoil it."

Again Talmadge stammered, and in the end, he just shrugged and offered, "I don't feel that way now."

"I know!" she said, and she kissed him. "And glad I am of it, because I am already in love with this place."

Talmadge answered with a smile, and a silent agreement that he should have brought Khotai here years ago.

He thought again of Fasach Crann, where he hoped to be within a week. If their visit there went as he now expected, perhaps they would reconsider their future treks to Loch Beag and their prewinter returns to the yearly Matinee.

Aoleyn shoved and pushed through the tangled pines, bursting into the open night air. The main encampment was only a few dozen strides away, but it felt like a great yawning gulf to the frightened young woman. She had heard of the rascals, of course, creatures more commonly known as the sidhe. They all had. But she had never seen one, and from what she had heard, she didn't want to see one now.

It took her only a few moments to sprint across to the encampment, but by the time she arrived, the entire tribe was rushing about, this way and that. She glanced all around, unsure, but settled her gaze on Seonagh, who stood by the blazing bonfire, along with the witches of the Coven. The warriors rushed up from every angle, all carrying their crystal-tipped spears, to thrust them into the flames.

It seemed similar to the ritual before the raids, Aoleyn thought, but abbreviated and with less somber ceremony, with the warriors retracting the weapons very quickly, never getting their hands near the flames, then running off, some to formations, a few select others with a single witch—their wives, Aoleyn realized—heading for their private tents.

Aoleyn didn't understand that particular path. Wasn't there an urgency here? Weren't the warriors mustering?

"To my side, girl!" Aoleyn heard, and her attention went back to Seonagh, who was motioning to her furiously. Aoleyn rushed over to join her teacher, a hundred questions bubbling about her lips.

"Stay," Seonagh instructed.

"What is happening?"

"Hush, no time. Stay by my side!"

For once, Aoleyn did as instructed, and even held silent as Seonagh went back to her task.

She grabbed one of the dancing witches and pulled her from the line, directing her to a warrior who had just freed his weapon from the bonfire. The two, witch and warrior, rushed together, then ran off for a tent—for their tent, Aoleyn realized, for she knew these two and understood them to be married.

A movement to the side of that tent caught her attention, and she glanced back to the flap of the other tent, where she had seen the other couple disappear. Now just the warrior emerged, spear in hand, eyes and expression fierce, ready for battle.

Aoleyn wanted to ask Seonagh about that, but a deep voice behind her called out to her. "Aoleyn! Wife!"

Aoleyn jumped at the sound, the hairs on the back of her neck standing up. She swung about to see Brayth coming toward her, spear in hand. She always found that one unsettling, but tonight more than ever. His movements, his gait, his eyes—oh, his eyes! More feral than human.

Aoleyn let out a yelp as he stabbed his weapon out right before her.

"Bless my spear, my woman," he commanded

"I am not . . ." she stammered. "I do not know . . ."

"She is not your woman yet," Seonagh told the man, drawing a scowl.

"We've shared the meal before the venerated," Brayth said. "She has been to the trial of the cave. I will have my spear blessed, and will take her to battle with me!"

Aoleyn started to speak, but Seonagh put her hand up in front of her to silence her.

"She would be of little help to you," Seonagh said. "She does not know."

"Then show her," came another voice, startling all three, and they turned as one to see Tay Aillig staring at them.

"I have earned her," Brayth demanded. "I will not go out unshielded."

Aoleyn started to speak again, but Seonagh shook her. The young woman looked up at her teacher, and gasped at the sight of Seonagh's face, drawn and ashen, and so clearly afraid.

"Now!" Tay Aillig yelled at them.

Out from under the bonfire came Mairen, the Usgar-righinn, untouched by the flames. Watching her, Aoleyn wanted to use her own milky crystal and climb under that same fire right then!

But of course, she could not. She watched Mairen go to Tay Aillig, and the two walk off toward Mairen's tent.

Seonagh grabbed the shaft of Brayth's spear and wrapped Aoleyn's hand over it, then guided the girl to thrust it into the flames.

Aoleyn didn't know what to do, but Seonagh had not let go.

Aoleyn felt a tingling sensation almost immediately, not unlike the vibrations she had known in the crystal cavern. The fire was magical, she understood, created by the great woman, and through its magic, and the guiding energy of Seonagh, Aoleyn felt the various powers locked within the crystalline tip of Brayth's spear. She felt her own magic drawn out of her, joining with Seonagh's and flowing into the weapon, and then she understood more clearly than she had ever imagined.

Now the ritual before the raids made sense to Aoleyn. Now she realized the advantage the Usgar held over those they battled. Because Seonagh had just empowered the weapon, Brayth could bring forth the magical effects held in the flecks within this spear, including levitation and the healing wedstone, and the lightning of another gray stone.

"Come, and quickly," Seonagh instructed, retracting the spear from the fires.

"Just her," said Brayth.

"She cannot. Not alone. Not at the beginning." Seonagh led them toward her tent.

"I will know her!" he said, his eyes boring into Aoleyn.

"You are not yet married."

"We shared the meal."

From Brayth's tone, insistent, demanding, full of lust, Aoleyn figured out what was happening here. She wanted to scream out at the ridiculousness of it! The encampment was apparently soon to be under attack and he wanted to mount her!

As soon as they passed into the tent, Brayth reached for her, grabbed her by the shoulder, and closed his hand tightly on her shirt, as if to tear her clothing away.

Aoleyn didn't doubt that he meant to do just that.

"Kneel," he commanded, but Seonagh grabbed him by the arm once more and interrupted.

"We are too late," she said. "There is no time, and it should not be like this for her first time. Not yet."

Brayth stared at the older woman, and simply smiled, a perfectly wicked smile.

Seonagh seemed to wilt and backed away.

Brayth spun Aoleyn about roughly, grabbed the back waist of her trousers and shoved her over. He didn't push her to her knees—she grabbed a nearby chair to steady herself—but tugged down her trousers.

And he stabbed her, from behind, and a sharp jolt of pain shot from her most private place as she felt her skin roughly tearing, her blood suddenly flowing. She tried to stifle a scream, only somewhat successfully.

Brayth grunted and slammed against her repeatedly, viciously. She glanced over at Seonagh, who had her hand up over her face and seemed near to tears, or perhaps was already crying.

Brayth growled like an animal and slammed his hand down on her back and she could feel him tensing up, every muscle.

She started to protest, but saw the look on Seonagh's face, the woman shaking her head to stop Aoleyn from speaking, and silently mouthing, "No, no!"

Brayth grabbed Aoleyn's thick black hair and yanked her head back, then growled and shook . . . and stopped.

He let go of Aoleyn and stepped back, and she hastily pulled up her pants, but didn't turn to face him.

"You are ugly, but you did well," he said.

"Go kill sidhe, warrior Brayth," Seonagh said in reassuring tones. "The hero's dinner will await your return."

Brayth suddenly spun Aoleyn about and locked stares with her, and all the girl could think of was how she might get some of Seonagh's crystals—the green-flecked one, so that she could lift this man into the sky and drop him on his head if he came for her ever again!

Coincidentally, Seonagh took out one of her crystals at that very moment, and she touched it to the tip of Brayth's spear and whispered some enchantment Aoleyn did not hear.

"Go, warrior," she said.

The man yelled with full volume, a great battle cry, then charged out of the tent, the conquering hero.

"No," Aoleyn said when he was gone.

"Shut up, child," Seonagh scolded.

"I will not!"

The words had barely left her mouth when Seonagh grabbed her roughly by the hair and yanked her so hard that she nearly tumbled to the floor.

"This is your place," Seonagh said.

"It hurt!" Indeed it had, though the physical discomfort was the least of it! And Aoleyn didn't even know where to begin with the pain in her heart and soul!

"It will hurt less next time," Seonagh promised, her tone softening.

"There will be no next time."

The coldness in her voice struck Aoleyn as profoundly as a slap. Seonagh actually backed away. Aoleyn didn't know that she could be possessed of such turmoil . . . such raw anger. She was afraid of what she might do if she admitted to herself what she truly wanted to do in that moment.

"Then they will murder you, slowly, and every man will have you before they do!" Seonagh promised. She sighed then and her tone became more sympathetic. "It is not that bad, child."

"I don't like him."

"But surely by now you've noticed urges?"

"For *him*? No! *Never!*"

"That is not your choice," Seonagh said, still with sympathy. "It is not that terrible. Pretend it is someone else behind you, or think of the magic of Usgar and dancing about the god-crystal under a wintry night sky. Oh, if you could only come to know the god-crystal, you will find pleasure, I promise. When next Brayth comes for you, take your mind away and let him be done and gone."

Aoleyn winced, the advice reminding her painfully of that haunted look she had seen so many times in the eyes of the uamhas women.

"It won't happen often," Seonagh said. "Not if you join the Coven, as I expect. Then you'll know the god-crystal more than you'll know any *man*. Usgar will be your partner, and only rarely will you be called upon to satisfy Brayth."

The whole conversation had Aoleyn's belly tightening with disgust. This most intimate decision wasn't hers to make? The voices in her head and heart shouted in denial!

"I won't," Aoleyn said, but her voice was a whisper now, and Seonagh didn't seem to hear, or if she did, didn't seem to care.

"What is happening?" Aoleyn pleaded.

"This is why the warriors fight to earn a witch," Seonagh explained. "Those who do not have such a partner will go out to fight the sidhe alone. And Iseabal's face is red this night, so the demon fossa may be about!"

"All the weapons were already blessed."

Seonagh nodded. "But for those betrothed to a witch, there is more. The blessings of the weapon are but a minor power compared to that which we might do when the battle is near to us."

"I'm not betrothed. I do not want . . ."

Seonagh slapped Aoleyn so hard that she was knocked to the ground before she even realized the movement.

"No more," the woman warned. "Tay Aillig demanded it. You saw him go with Mairen, the Usgar-righinn, whose word is the word of Usgar. Your arguments are ended." She presented a bundle of crystals, grasped in both her hands and holding them out to Aoleyn. "Count to ten, girl, then wrap your hands about the symphony of Usgar."

Seonagh closed her eyes and began to hum softly, to chant, to find the song of Usgar, Aoleyn knew. So curious was she in watching the older woman that she forgot to begin to count. So she just picked up at five, then stumbled about, then just grabbed the crystals as Seonagh had instructed.

As soon as her hands touched them, Aoleyn felt their pull, insistent and powerful. Seonagh held many crystals, and Aoleyn did not have time to sort through them—the only one she felt for certain was the gray-flecked wedstone crystal, into which Seonagh was currently pouring her energies.

Abruptly, shockingly so, Aoleyn found herself pulled outside of her body, her spirit free from corporeal constraints. Seonagh's spirit was there, too, she understood, and it felt to Aoleyn as if the woman's spirit had taken her own by the hand, and insistently, as if she feared the girl might simply float away, unmoored. This sensation was so unlike anything she'd ever felt. She could fly! She could see the world around her, but it did not look real; most everything appeared faded, as if she glimpsed it through a thick fog. But the living things in the room, Seonagh and Aoleyn's bodies, glowed comfortingly. Perhaps the most interesting, within their cupped hands she saw another light, white and beautiful, and startlingly bright. It came from one of the crystals, she knew, but not the wedstone. She would have to ask Seonagh about that after . . .

After what? What was the purpose of this, Aoleyn wondered?

She felt Seonagh tug at her hand. Unsure what else she could do, she allowed herself to be pulled along. Right through the side of the tent, they flew, up and out of the encampment, and soon Aoleyn saw the ghostlike shapes of the warriors filtering through the trees. She knew immediately where the Usgar warriors were heading: to some high ground they could better defend.

She and Seonagh hovered there for a few heartbeats—and strangely, she thought, she could still hear her heartbeat—then dived suddenly, and dizzyingly, directly toward a bright and living form below, directly at, and then into, Brayth!

The young warrior jerked at the sudden, unexpected, completely foreign feeling. He had been told what would happen, of course, but words could not describe . . . this.

This was violation! Suddenly, Brayth found that he was not alone in his own body, and his every sensibility rejected that thought.

He wrestled instinctively against the intrusion, for even though he rationally understood this beneficial joining, every instinct within Brayth screamed at him to make it stop. His resistance was futile, though, for Seonagh had done this many times before and the young warrior had no experience with such magic whatsoever. Within mere moments, he knew he was defeated. Brayth stopped struggling, and when he did, he heard a voice whispering in his ear.

No, not his ear. Whispering in his mind. But the voice he still recognized.

Brayth and Aoleyn are joined as one.

And with Seonagh, came another voice, Aoleyn's voice, and it seemed on the edge of desperation, as if the young woman was as unbalanced as Brayth.

You are the weapon of Aoleyn's magic, Seonagh imparted to Brayth. *Just Aoleyn. I have done my part.*

And she was gone, Brayth understood. Just like that. And Aoleyn felt Seonagh's departure, too, he knew, for he could sense her unease. Now Seonagh's words when they were heading to the tent made sense. Had it been Aoleyn alone coming out to join with him, the first time for both of them, he would have reflexively rejected her and she would not have been skilled enough to overcome that rejection.

"Do not fail me, young witch," he said aloud. "Or I will beat you bloody when the night is done."

He gulped when he finished, and realized that it was Aoleyn's spirit making his physical form do that, making him gulp! It was so strange! And so intimate, more so, perhaps than lovemaking!

Even as that thought crossed his mind, he felt Aoleyn recoil.

You don't need to speak aloud, Aoleyn prompted him, and though he couldn't hear the words, he felt their coldness.

"I know," he answered, again with voice. He took a deep breath and glanced around, silently imploring Aoleyn to help him.

He knew that she understood a moment later when his vision shifted, when suddenly he could see in the starlight and red glow of the rising moon almost as clearly as on a sunny day. He took up his spear and ran off to catch up to the battle group. She was using magic, using the crystal flecked with spots that resembled the eyes of a cat to grant him such powerful nocturnal sight.

He found Aghmor near the back of the marching warriors, moving along cautiously, and easily caught up to the man—his poor friend, who had no witch to protect him and bring him great glory this night.

"The night is mine!" Brayth boasted, and he silently implored Aoleyn to offer a display.

A moment later, his spear tip flared to life with flames, burning with magical power. Aghmor nodded and slipped a step behind Brayth.

They came to the tree-covered ridge. It was not a dense wood, for the thin air up here kept the trees spindly and short.

Tay Aillig ordered them and all the others about, setting the defensive line, and not with a moment to spare as the frenzied sidhe scrambled up all about them. Nearly as tall as a man, the long-eared, long-nosed, gray-skinned sidhe ran on muscled legs and fought with thick and powerful arms.

They carried crude weapons: wooden spears and stone clubs, and some with thick hand-wrappings, laden with flat stones or actual claws taken from a great brown bear or a hunting leopard, to rake an enemy.

Before Brayth was able to sort out a target, the screams had already begun, cries of pain and those horrible shrieks only heard in the last moments of a man's, or a sidhe's, life.

Along with the folk of Sellad Tulach, Talmadge and Khotai stared up at the great mountain that anchored the southeastern corner of Loch Beag. They could see the distant fires, here and there, and whenever the wind blew just right, they could hear some commotion.

"Their fables?" Khotai whispered to her lover.

Talmadge merely shrugged. He didn't know what was happening up there, but surely, something was, something exciting and likely dangerous.

"That tribe, the Usgar, they don't seem huddled," Khotai noted.

Talmadge looked all around at the folk of the tribe, most with their two-humped skulls bent back as they stared up at the mountain. Those faces he noted were filled with trepidation. Something was happening indeed, and it was obviously not a normal occurrence.

"Say no more," he whispered quietly to Khotai, letting his concern show thick in his voice.

The woman squeezed his hand tighter.

The comfort of that grasp overwhelmed Talmadge. Once more, he silently chided himself for not bringing this wonderful companion with him to this place he so dearly loved sooner.

Up above, a light flickered and disappeared.

The wind blew, and carried the unmistakable scream of a man who knew he was about to die.

"Monsters," Talmadge whispered under his breath, and he glanced around at the folk of the village and reminded himself that they survived because they knew. They knew this land and the dangers it concealed. Their traditions, however much they might seem rooted in superstition, kept these dangers in their thoughts and guided their actions because of those same fables he and Khotai had just mocked.

Talmadge reminded himself to never make light of those tales, any of those tales, even the ones for which he had never seen any evidence, ever again.

When the sidhe came rushing in, their lack of formation surprised Brayth. He had only battled one small sidhe band in his life—more of an ambush than a real battle—but all of the warriors of Usgar trained for the rare encounters with these wicked goblin creatures. One of the primary lessons for any Usgar warrior was that the sidhe, as dull and primitive as they might be, knew how to fight in formation and with devious tactics.

Thus, Brayth could hardly believe the first wave of sidhe charging up the ridge. Haphazard, with no discernable line, most continued looking back over their shoulders instead of confronting the Usgar warriors who stood to destroy them.

And destroy them the Usgar did! Down the goblins went, one after another, and within heartbeats, the warriors were fighting with each other over who could get the next kill.

Off to the far side, Brayth got none, and he was too surprised to even focus his complaints.

They did not come for us, he heard in his head, an astute observation from Aoleyn, he thought. *They are in flight!*

Brayth nodded, for as he watched the unfolding massacre with that thought in mind, it all made sense. He knew then that if he wanted to claim some glory this red-tinged night, he would have to actively find some sidhe to kill.

"Stay close to the others," he instructed Aghmor, who was immediately to his left.

"Where are you going?" Aghmor demanded.

"They are all about. I go to scout the flank," Brayth answered, and he ran away. His bounding steps took him farther and faster than he intended, each stride covering the ground that would normally take two! It was Aoleyn, he realized, channeling the levitational magic as he went.

So he moved lightly, silently, and with great speed. Just down to the left lay a second ridge, rocky and with a line of short pines atop it. Rounding the top of that line of trees, Brayth found his sidhe, a small group streaming through a bowl-shaped lea of deep grasses just to the side of the battle.

"Be with me," he whispered aloud, imploring Aoleyn.

In Brayth charged, spear presented. He shot the nearest sidhe down just as it turned, startled, to face him, a bolt of lightning sizzling from his spear tip and throwing the monster aside, where it tumbled to the ground and twitched uncontrollably.

On the Usgar warrior rushed, roaring his battle cry. He sent his spear slashing to the side, taking a sidhe's club with it, and lighting its scraggly hair with the flames dancing on his weapon's tip in the same movement. He brought the spear back fast, the monster trying to counter with its club.

The distraction caused by the creature's burning hair cost the sidhe dearly; its club came in almost half-heartedly against Brayth's side as he pressed in, as his spear tip burrowed into the monster's chest.

The weapon tip exploded into flame, and the ugly sidhe squealed and fell dead before Brayth had even extracted his deadly magical weapon. He ran right over the fallen monster, noting the boiling blood bubbling from the hole in its chest.

"Flames!" he growled at Aoleyn, nearing three more of the beasts, who formed a semicircle to entice him in.

And in Brayth went, sweeping his spear right to left, the flames roaring ahead of the weapon, igniting hair and filthy clothing, lighting the branches of the trees that framed the small lea.

Brayth stabbed and roared. Another sidhe fell, stuck through the chest. A second tried to run away, but plowed into a low-hanging bough that was fully engulfed, and so the creature, too, became fully engulfed in biting magical fire as it tumbled down.

The third staggered away, not badly hurt, not burning brightly, but clearly too terrified to confront this mighty Usgar death-dealer.

Brayth started after, but stopped abruptly as he caught the motion of a spinning weapon out of the corner of his eye. He cried out and threw himself to the side, but not fast enough, and the axe buried into his left shoulder, driving him backward.

Pull it out! he heard in his head. *Remove it! Quickly!*

He reached for the axe, still backpedaling—and a good thing, too: out through the trees came a line of sidhe, advancing in formation.

Brayth tried to keep his sensibilities against the spinning world. He tried to hold his spear in his left hand, his trembling right hand reaching for the embedded axe. He grasped it, grimacing in agony, thinking there was no way he could find the strength to tear it out of his shoulder.

Back! Back! Back! Aoleyn screamed in his mind, and then, as if to accentuate her point, Brayth floated off the ground and was hit with a gust of wind that sent him flying backward, all the way to the tree line back at the top of the rocky ridge.

And in the windy jerk that began the flight, Brayth's hand came forward, holding the bloody axe!

He looked to his shoulder as he skidded down, saw the blood pouring forth, felt the waves of agony and dizziness, and knew he would collapse onto the ground to be murdered by the advancing sidhe.

More than the sidhe had noticed Brayth's glorious exploits. From just northeast of the rocky ridge's tree line, back and higher up the mountainside, Tay Aillig watched the display of magic with his mouth hanging open.

He knew where Brayth was getting that power—power he could not match because the Usgar-righinn, as agreed, had broken her tie to him after magically assisting him with levitation so that he could quickly form the Usgar line. Mairen did not want to be intimately tied to Tay Aillig any more than he wanted that haggard old witch joining him in spirit or in body.

But now he watched Brayth, watched the pulse of fire light up sidhe and trees alike, watched him fly back to safety to recover, and from a wound that should have ended his fighting this night.

Aoleyn! It was Aoleyn, Elara's daughter, Brayth's wife. What glories this man would know with this kind of power joining with him! Glories to outshine Tay Aillig, even.

Tay Aillig clamped his mouth shut, teeth grinding, as he watched the scene in the lea beside the main battle.

Another was watching, too, though not with physical eyes, and from behind the scrambling sidhe, for it had been the cause of the goblins' flight this night. The Blood Moon had risen and so the fossa had come forth, and now the song, the interminable, horrid vibration of magic, twanged discordantly at its life energy, insulting it, paining it, demanding a response.

It wasn't as bad as that night a few weeks before, but the pulse of pain was strong, so strong.

And this time, the fossa was out under the red sky.

This night, the fossa could put an end to it.

———

Brayth slumped down, almost to one knee, but before he got there, a wave of healing washed through him. The bleeding stopped, the skin knitted, and the strength in his left arm returned almost immediately.

The young warrior straightened to face the line of sidhe coming toward him, marching in a coordinated and tactical manner.

"Be with me," he muttered to Aoleyn, and he was not afraid. He would win here, and would slay a dozen more of these monsters— he would claim more kills this night than the rest of the Usgar warriors combined!

Still, Brayth knew that even with Aoleyn's help, this was going to be difficult, and he fully expected he'd be feeling the bite of several more brutal wounds before the fight was ended. He could defeat a sidhe one-on-one, but he was woefully outnumbered here!

But then, down to the left, a sidhe squealed and disappeared into the tall grass. Catching it out of the corner of his eye, Brayth couldn't figure out what had happened. Was it a ruse? A maneuver for the monster to get into the deep grass to conceal its advance? Had a spear hit it?

As Brayth stood there, pondering, the next sidhe went flipping over backward and down into the grass, again screaming, and the third in line cried out and started to run before it, too, disappeared.

Aoleyn? Brayth asked in his thoughts.

She didn't answer directly, but he understood from her jumbled thoughts that she was as confused as he!

Another sidhe went down.

And Brayth caught the movement across a bare patch of ground, a weasel-like black form, but huge, flashing across the patch, into the grass on the other side; there, another sidhe was brought down, and another went flying.

And Brayth understood!

"The fossa!" he gasped, barely able to breathe.

And the grass began shaking as the creature, low to the ground, streaked for him, like a coming gale. He couldn't hope to dodge or flee!

But into the air went Brayth, high, and straight up, and then he felt a wind at his back, hurling him forward across the lea.

Up from the grass leaped the fossa, impossibly high, its red eyes burning with inner demonic flames, staring at him hatefully, its opened maw showing gleaming fangs and biting at his feet!

And just missing. The creature landed and sprang right back up, but Brayth was higher now, up in the air beyond its reach.

Aim your spear! he heard in his mind, and he lifted the weapon as if to throw.

No! Just point it! Aoleyn telepathically implored him, and he did, and a blast of lightning erupted from the tip, shooting down at the demon fossa.

The bolt thundered in, shaking the ground, burning the grasses, and when the light diminished enough for Brayth to see, he noted the fossa, seemingly unhurt, and leaping again for him, higher this time.

"Kill it!" he cried to Aoleyn, aiming the spear tip to follow the black creature's descent.

Another bolt shot forth and struck the creature in midair. But it did not throw the fossa aside, not at all. It seemed instead to simply shoot into the thing, or was absorbed by it. As the fossa set back down, its eyes burned the brighter!

Another burst of wind hit Brayth, launching him along toward the distant trees.

On the ground, the fossa pursued, red eyes locked upon its prey.

Tay Aillig could barely sort out what he was seeing in the small meadow before him. The sidhe fell, the sidhe fled, and Brayth flew into the air with the fossa snapping wildly at his feet!

It was all too unexpected and crazy.

A lesser man, or perhaps a wiser one, would have fled immediately, run back to the Usgar lines and ordered a fast retreat to the encampment, and the thought did cross Tay Aillig's mind.

But there the sensible notion bumped against the man's determination and his anger. He was watching before him, both literally and figuratively, the rise of young Brayth, who, with help from his betrothed, would surely eclipse his glory!

Tay Aillig could not allow that.

The young warrior flew toward the distant tree line, but reversed course and soared back toward the nearer rocky ridge, just down to the left from Tay Aillig. Coming, too, was the fossa, leaping now and then at the warrior, whose spear responded with strokes of ineffective lightning.

Closer they came, the demon focused full on the warrior, on Brayth, who was being held up by Aoleyn through their magical connection.

Tay Aillig was hardly aware of the movement as his hand went to his belt, and was barely conscious of the small and smooth gemstone rolling between his fingers. He felt the power of the sunstone then, and before he could talk himself out of it, before he could really consider the implications, he sent forth the stone's enchantment, a burst of antimagic.

Flying Brayth became falling Brayth, the man plummeting right into a pine tree, shattering a branch and probably some of his own bones, Tay Aillig thought, given the grunt and wail coming out of there.

What had he done?

For all of his power and brutality, Tay Aillig winced and turned away as the black form of the fossa leaped into the pine at the same point where Brayth had disappeared.

The tree shook, branches shattered, and out the bottom they both fell.

And out from under the tree came the fossa, the demon monster of Fireach Speuer, running up the slope with the broken man hanging from its jaws, much of Brayth dragging along on the ground beside the running monster.

Right for Tay Aillig, it came. He couldn't dodge, couldn't flee. How feeble his weapon seemed against the bared power of the demon! He wished then that he had forced Mairen to remain with him in spirit, but even that, he realized, would not be enough.

He braced as the fossa charged in, but he might as well have been trying to stop an avalanche. He was hurled aside by the impact, and rolled desperately, trying to come around and bring his spear into line, for whatever good it might do.

24

THE REALM OF INSUBSTANTIAL

Back in the Usgar camp, Aoleyn's corporeal form let out a whimper in surprise as her magic failed her, as she felt her malachite and moonstone connection so suddenly severed. She watched the descent through Brayth's eyes, and cried out again with the branches shattering all about her as the man tumbled through.

She felt Brayth's pain and tried to focus on the vibrations of the wedstone, to send him healing.

The young woman hesitated. She felt the barrier between her magic and Brayth. Perhaps she could have broken through that barrier, whatever it was, and given him a chance. But Aoleyn remembered what he had done to her, how he had taken her.

She hesitated.

She cried out again, gripped by terror as she saw the horrible demon leaping at her!

No, not at her, she realized, but at Brayth, out there, in the field.

The beast bit in with those murderous jaws.

Aoleyn started to call to the wedstone, thinking that she must heal the man at once. But then she simply screamed again, her thoughts spinning. She felt her life energy fluctuating, splintering; she knew that the fossa had bitten Brayth's flesh, yes, but somehow, some way, it was also biting at Aoleyn's very spirit, breaking her apart, sending shards of agony through the flow of energy that sustained her life and magic.

She felt her life force being drawn out of her.

She had an idea, a desperate idea; if she had paused to think about it, the absurdity would have given her pause.

Aoleyn shifted all of her focus to the vibrations of the wedstone.

She felt the fossa's power stutter, as if the demon was shivering, and Aoleyn knew hope.

But then there came a flash, an intrusion, as if something or someone else had leaped into the battle. And then . . . blackness. Sudden emptiness.

Aoleyn thought she was dead, thought that she had left the world behind, so suddenly, and was tumbling, anchorless. She could not find her bearings. She was high above the world, and yet she was not in the world. Everything was tinted red, like the moon, Iseabal's bloody face. And it was so distant!

And she was lost.

Was this death?

Brayth lay upon the stones unmoving, his body tangled, his guts exposed. Beside him, the demon fossa leaped all about, seeming confused.

More than that, it seemed hurt, truly hurt: its front shoulder where it had collided with Tay Aillig was smoking and bubbling!

It dropped its face to the ground, snuffling, head swiveling all about. Searching.

Tay Aillig watched the spectacle curiously. Was the creature blind? It had cut down the line of sidhe with devastating efficiency, had tracked the movements of Brayth up in the air unerringly and so completely that it had flown into the tree exactly behind the man.

But now it seemed confused, even nervous, and seemed as if it could not see Tay Aillig, with whom it had just collided. And it was hurt worse than he, much worse! The lightning hadn't slowed it or even stung it, but the collision with Tay Aillig—no, he realized, the collision with his magic—had clearly hurt the creature.

What did it mean? The man was too shaken to fully sort it out. He wanted to slide farther away, but feared making any noise. He didn't want to engage this monster. Not now. Not alone.

He clenched his fingers tighter and felt the magic of the small and round gemstone he held in his hand, the sunstone. He felt the tiny sharp flecks of amethyst that were embedded in the stone.

He glanced at it, then back to the fossa. He had been calling upon the magic when the creature had charged at him—no, not at him, but had charged in his direction.

Oblivious to him, perhaps?

He focused and pressed, trying to keep the antimagic in effect now, as though his life depended on it.

The fossa couldn't locate him.

Tay Aillig was not well versed in the ways of Usgar. He had come upon this curious gem quite unexpectedly years ago and had told none of the witches, nor anyone else, about it. He had learned long ago how to use it to interrupt the magic of the witches, if only briefly.

Now he had learned something else about the curious stone, it seemed, something that might save his life.

Up above him, the fossa clamped its jaws upon Brayth once more and began its run up the side of the mountain, the weight of the near-dead man not even slowing the powerful monster.

Down below, Tay Aillig dared to breathe again. On sudden instinct, he sent a burst of his magic at the fleeing demon.

It staggered! And stumbled!

Tay Aillig glanced down at the gemstone, his eyes sparkling.

She was lost, and floating in empty air, leaving the world, leaving life itself. She had no idea of where Brayth had gone, or if he was still alive.

She told herself that she didn't care.

She knew it to be a lie, though, for deep inside, she did care, and she wanted Brayth to be dead.

She remembered the murderous bite of the demon fossa, and expected that her desire would be granted. Guilt accompanied that notion, but Aoleyn found that the thought of the man's potentially horrible death did not trouble her as much as it would have earlier that same evening. And so, she let it go.

Instead, Aoleyn wondered if she was still alive.

All about her was dark, red and black, a world of silhouettes and shadows, with no sense of solidity or warmth, no sense of anything at all.

Silent, still, empty, dead.

But then, in the midst of the emptiness, there came a flash of color, green and bright. A flash of light that beckoned to her.

Aoleyn willed herself toward the tiny speck of light, flew faster and faster though she could hear no wind and feel no breeze or even any sensation of movement. She just saw the light, the only speck of brightness and warmth in the midst of the shadows.

It grew, now a beacon. It blinded her, but that did not deter her, no. She flew for it desperately, out of options, almost out of hope.

She passed through it, a sudden, lightninglike shock, and she shuddered, and felt the corporeal movement of her own body.

There she sat, groaning, whimpering, trying to sort out thoughts that would not straighten. She tried to remember her name, thought of Usgar, of the cave, and, to her surprise, of Bahdlahn.

Finally, she found some solidity, some sense of the life she had known. She felt and saw her hands trembling. A twitch kept knocking her head to the side, involuntarily. Her life force continued to crackle and jolt, and for a long while would not steady.

A mewling to the side caught her notice and grounded her. Surprised, confused, Aoleyn at last blinked open her eyes, to find herself sitting in Seonagh's tent.

Her crystals lay on the floor before her, and instinctively, she reached for them. But she stopped before her hand touched the pile, noticing that there beside her sat Seonagh. Aoleyn called to her.

The woman didn't seem to hear, didn't react at all to Aoleyn. But she, too, was shaking, and whimpering softly.

"Seonagh?" Aoleyn said curiously, reaching for her. She realized then that Seonagh was holding crystals of her own, and from the look on her face, the witch was deeply into them, was entranced in the song of Usgar.

Aoleyn pulled her hand back and thought again of her brief encounter with the fossa, and then realized the truth of her disengagement.

"Seonagh!" she cried. The woman had come to her in her joining with Brayth. The woman, her mentor, had thrown Aoleyn aside and out of the monster's magical grasp.

Seonagh didn't answer, but she did yelp a bit and her face scrunched, as if in pain.

She was still there, Aoleyn knew! Seonagh had rejoined Brayth and so now was doing battle with the fossa.

Aoleyn had to get to her, to help her. She reached for the symphony of crystals, unsure of how to even begin. She should start with the wedstone, she supposed, to escape her mortal coil.

Seonagh cried out, screamed in sudden agony and horror.

Aoleyn grabbed hard at the magical shards Seonagh grasped. She yanked the woman's hands apart and slapped the crystals from her hand, then pulled the former witch so that her face was very near, and began screaming for Seonagh to come back to her.

The older woman began to tremble and gasp. Her eyelids fluttered, but she did not open her eyes for any length of time, and in those brief moments when Aoleyn could see her orbs, they seemed unfocused, as if Seonagh was looking far, far away.

The older woman's lips moved, but no understandable sounds came forth.

Just grunts and gasps and empty breaths.

By the time a very shaken Tay Aillig stumbled back beyond the rocky ridge to rejoin his warriors, the original fight had all but ended. A handful of Usgar had been wounded, but only one seriously, and the ground about them was littered with the corpses of ten sidhe.

"Where is Brayth?" Aghmor asked, the moment he rejoined Tay Aillig at the right end of the line.

Tay Aillig shook his head, his expression grim, and that elicited a response the Usgar-laoch did not expect.

"What did you do?" Aghmor asked in a low voice.

Tay Aillig stared at him in disbelief, his eyes boring into the young man's until Aghmor had to look away. Tay Aillig let his gaze slip down then, to note that Aghmor's hands were clenched tightly upon his spear.

Not taking any chances, Tay Aillig dropped his own spear and stepped in closer, suddenly, then grabbed Aghmor's spear midshaft with his left hand and sent his right up under the man's jaw, grabbing hard.

Aghmor brought his own hand up to claw at Tay Aillig's wrist and tug as he tried to squirm away, but he could not break the mighty warrior's grasp.

Tay Aillig knew that he had the attention of the other tribesmen, all bristling nervously, but he didn't care. With frightening strength, he yanked Aghmor around and locked him in place, forcing the man to look up the mountainside.

Aghmor struggled futilely and grunted in protest against the painful clench, but then, all of a sudden, the man just stopped, and slumped, and his grunt became a gulp.

For up there across a clear expanse on a higher mountain spur, he noted the black form moving swiftly and low to the ground, dragging something.

Something he knew to be his friend.

Tay Aillig roughly shoved him back and retrieved his spear, then called to the others, "Form! Form! Sidhe to the right."

Indeed, the fight wasn't over, as the group that had been chased off by the fossa had now returned, with reinforcements.

"Bend the line!" Tay Aillig ordered, motioning for half a dozen warriors to come up above him on the mountain, forming a right angle to the main line, which he anchored. The rest of the sidhe came on then, once more, from their original direction.

Having had time to shake off the initial shock of the Usgar ambush, and no longer having to worry about the fossa, the sidhe moved against the tribesmen in force, a straight line of goblin Raiders with all flanks supported.

"Crouch! Hold!" Tay Aillig commanded. He did a quick count. He had more than thirty warriors still able to fight, against almost twice that number of sidhe, but they held the higher ground, except on this flank, where they were on even footing with their enemies.

He could have called for a retreat, but that would have sealed the doom of at least one of his warriors. He had already lost one.

No more.

The sidhe charge up the mountainside ended abruptly in a furious barrage of lightning and fire, as Usgar spear tips exploded against the front ranks.

"Hold this angle!" Tay Aillig told Aghmor, yanking him into position of the two wings of their line. "For your life and honor!"

Tay Aillig ran, straight up the mountainside, tapping each man on the back as he passed, telling them to hold fast. When he got to the last man, he reiterated that call, then to the surprise of them all, and to the ten sidhe coming in, the mighty warrior leaped out from the ranks, back toward the rocky ridgeline, to meet the charge alone.

He swept his spear across left to right, let go with his left hand as it flew out wide, until the shaft locked against his lower back, stopping the swing cold. A sudden twist sent the weapon sweeping back the other way, at belt level, and with such power that it slapped away the sidhe weapons and forced the monsters back.

Tay Aillig lifted his arm as the spear came around, sending it into a spin over his head, once and then again, and with each sweep, the man moved, up higher, down lower, changing his angle, shifting his hips, forcing the sidhe to react.

Tay Aillig let go of his spear in the sweep, catching it midshaft in his left hand, and turning back for a sudden thrust that put the tip into a sidhe's chest, releasing a burst of flames a heartbeat later.

Back across swept the spear, a mirror image of the first maneuver with Tay Aillig's left hand going out wide this time until the spear's shaft locked against his lower back, then sweeping left to right once more, and up over his head and around again.

Behind that second sweep came a sidhe, club swinging hard to smash Tay Aillig in the chest.

And he took it! He managed to keep his wits while shrugging off the explosion of pain, and turned back with sudden fury and force, pivoting around the creature and shoving it with all his strength to send it tumbling back toward his line of warriors.

They leaped upon the creature, Aghmor leading, all stabbing furiously and then retreating to their defensive positions once more.

Tay Aillig launched a ferocious dance, jumping and swinging, unconcerned about actually scoring any hits. He was baiting the enemies, nothing more.

He taunted and spat, and he kicked at the sidhe he had stabbed as it squirmed on the ground, garnering the attention of the sidhe and gradually moving back a step, then another.

"Aghmor!" he called, a warning.

Then he stopped, suddenly, and the sidhe leaped at him as one, spears and clubs leading.

But Tay Aillig called upon the green flecks in the weapon Mairen had blessed, and with a sudden twitch, leaped backward, the levitation strengthening his spring. He landed right before his line, the sidhe bearing in on him, and fell as he touched down.

"Throw!" Aghmor appropriately commanded, and his and a half-dozen other spears flew out into the faces of the charging sidhe. These were followed by seven warriors, each drawing knives, throwing punches, kicking, tackling, grabbing for fallen weapons—Usgar spear and sidhe club—anything to inflict pain.

Moments later, Tay Aillig was back among them, rushing between grappling Usgar, cracking one sidhe hard against the head with the butt of his spear as he passed.

Then out he slid, down low to one knee, and out he stabbed with all his might the other way, out and up, and he caught a sidhe in the belly and drove upward, rising to his feet with a roar, lifting the squealing and squirming creature up before him, then up above him.

With a heave, Tay Aillig sent the skewered sidhe flying away, back down the mountainside and back behind him, so that it crashed into its companions battling the Usgar line below.

Tay Aillig heard the cheers from his lower line, and the surprised screams of the sidhe, but he didn't let it divert his attention. He turned back the other way, sliding the butt of his spear shaft out as he went to parry aside a sidhe spear. He turned all the way under it as he lifted it, putting his back to the monster, and before it could take advantage of that, it got a face full of Tay Aillig's flying elbow, once and again.

Down it went and around came Tay Aillig, his spear spinning in his hands, twirling up high, changing its angle perfectly so that when he again faced the fallen sidhe, he could stab straight down, impaling it in the chest.

He ripped it right out again, though, and flung himself left and down low, sweeping the spear across to take the feet out from another charging sidhe.

Up he went to face yet another. A thrust drove it back, and on the retraction, Tay Aillig slid the shaft back again and stabbed it down several times, butt end first, into the face of the sidhe he had tripped, then as he reset his balance to meet the one he had driven back with the thrust, he stomped down upon the neck of that tripped and now-dazed enemy with bone-crunching force.

The sidhe before him skidded to a stop and fell back, wanting no part of this wild warrior. With the reprieve, Tay Aillig glanced left and right, all about, and took a quick measure.

This end of the line had routed the sidhe that had come over the rocky ridge. Aghmor and the other six were bloody, but still up for a fight, which was more than could be said for the remaining sidhe.

"Form!" Tay Aillig shouted. "Swing the door!"

The warriors disengaged and finished their kills, gathered their weapons quickly.

"Aghmor, hinge!" Tay Aillig demanded, and Aghmor scrambled back to his original position, at the right end of the main forward line. Tay Aillig centered the other seven as they charged around the pivoting

Aghmor, sweeping down to drive hard into the left flank of the main body of sidhe.

Tay Aillig scored only one more kill. Shortly after the swinging maneuver, the sidhe broke ranks and fled as their flank collapsed.

A younger Tay Aillig would have ordered pursuit and chased the sidhe halfway down the mountain to satiate his bloodlust, but he understood the precipitating events of this bloody night. The sidhe had not come to raid the Usgar camp. It was entirely an accident that they had come this way at all, and so, routed here, they would not return.

A dozen Usgar warriors needed tending, himself included; every breath he drew pained him greatly against the ribs the sidhe's club had cracked.

The Usgar didn't even bother to kill those sidhe lying wounded on the ground. They gathered up their wounded and formed a defensive retreat for camp.

Tay Aillig kept Aghmor with him at the back of that formation, the two watching for any signs of enemies.

And both of them glancing repeatedly up the mountainside, to where the demon fossa had gone, to where dead Brayth had been dragged.

Aghmor understood that he had lost his best friend.

Tay Aillig believed he had just gained a powerful wife.

25

WHEN THE RED MOON SET

How sweet tasted the man-flesh. How satisfying to drink the blood.

In the dark, in the bone-filled pit, the fossa feasted on the corpse of Brayth, but this was just the dessert of its meal this day.

For the fossa had feasted on that incessant song, had bitten the magic of the mountains and had devoured it.

The human had thrown lightning at the creature, but lightning couldn't hurt the fossa! No magical evocations could weaken this creature. Not in the red light of the Blood Moon!

No, the lightning had only made the fossa stronger, had only given it energy and sustenance. And the deeper bite the fossa had inflicted on the purveyor of that magic was not physical. The sorceress had come against the demon, in the realm of the spirit, and in that realm, the demon ate more hungrily, and each bite fed it more fully than man-flesh ever could.

The demon had reveled in the groans and screams of this man it now consumed. But the silent screams of the magic-user, singing her songs to her false god, rang sweeter still.

The fossa lifted its bloody face and looked up the pit, though of course, it could see little in the darkness. But in its mind, the demon saw past the dark stones, back to the open air it had known this night, under the calming red glow of the full moon. Yes, that sweet full moon, red and serene, breaking the maddening sound of magic that hummed continually in this mountain. How fine the freedom, how wonderful the ability to fight back against that vicious hum!

The fossa held the pose for just a moment, savoring the memory of the open air.

Then it plunged its toothy maw down hard on the body, bouncing it among the bones, chewing bones, crunching ribs and breaking through.

When it came back up from the corpse, Brayth's torn heart hung out the side of its mouth.

"They think it the sidhe," Talmadge told Khotai after the moon had set, the folk of Sellad Tulach back out and about, many simply too excited by the events of that night to find sleep.

"Sidhe?"

"Mountain goblins," he explained. "Vicious brutes, though, bigger than the ones we see back east, but, thankfully, just as rarely seen. The folk believe we may have witnessed a battle upon the mountainside, sidhe against Usgar."

"Will they send scouts?"

"No!" Talmadge replied suddenly, and more forcefully than he had intended. "No," he said again, more calmly. "The tribes of Loch Beag do not go up the mountain. Not ever. They see the Usgar as demons in human form."

"That seems foolish."

"You've never met an Usgar."

"Have you?"

"I've seen the aftermath of their raids and heard the laments of . . . encounters. That's enough to keep me near the lake."

Khotai took a moment to digest all of that. She looked up the dark mountain and let her gaze linger there, and didn't hide the intrigue on her face.

"This is a dangerous land," she said. "Monsters in the lake. Big lizards that like to eat the flesh of men. Demon-men on the mountain. Goblins. I wonder why anyone stays."

"This is their home. The only one they've ever known, and not without its charm," Talmadge answered.

"Charming enough to keep you coming here? Or profitable enough?"

Talmadge laughed. "Both."

"And enough for you to keep it Talmadge's secret?"

He looked at her curiously, and shook his head to show that he knew where this was heading, and it was a discussion they had already had.

But Khotai simply smiled back and sidled up to him, draping her arms about his neck. "Or was it just me?" she asked in a husky voice. "Were you afraid that I'd steal your secret? Your profits?"

"I care nothing for that."

"What does Talmadge care about?"

"You."

The exciting events of the night seemed far away then as more pressing needs rose between the lovers. Khotai backed up, holding him close every step, then disappeared under the flap of their tent, Talmadge right behind.

She put her finger against his pursed lips to hold him back for a moment. "Will you be taking me back to this place?" she asked, lying beside him.

"Do we even have to leave?"

The question hit Khotai by surprise. But she didn't say no. She didn't say another word, in fact, until the sun was long up the next morning.

The Blood Moon hung low in the western sky when the Usgar warriors limped back into their encampment, many bleeding. Tay Aillig grimaced with every breath, certain that he had cracked more than one rib, but when a witch came to him with the healing wedstone, he brushed her aside and kept walking right past the gathering, across the encampment.

"Usgar-laoch, where are you going?" Mairen asked, rushing to keep up with him.

"Brayth was killed and taken," he answered, never slowing—and indeed, increasing his pace, "by the demon fossa."

Mairen paused for a moment, digesting the information, then gasped and rushed to catch Tay Aillig, joining him just as he went under the flap of Seonagh's tent.

There sat Aoleyn, sobbing, cradling Seonagh in her arms. The older woman didn't move; were it not for the occasional whimpers coming from her, the two newcomers would have thought her dead.

Tay Aillig moved over and pulled her away from Aoleyn, who tried to resist only briefly. He rolled Seonagh onto her back and used his thumb to lift her eyelid.

Mairen was there by then, shaking her head.

"What is it?" Aoleyn begged.

"You tell us," the Usgar-righinn prompted. "What happened here, child?"

"Brayth," Aoleyn breathed. "He was fighting the sidhe, when . . . when it . . . when the creature came onto the field."

"The demon fossa," Tay Aillig confirmed.

"We tried to get away," Aoleyn recounted, her voice breaking with a sob every few words. "I flew him. I flew Brayth up into the air, above the demon. But he fell—I failed!"

"You did not fail, child," Mairen said.

"The fossa caught him," Aoleyn stammered. "The fossa . . . caught me! The demon reached through, right through Brayth, and found me, and caught me! And Seonagh came to me . . . I . . . it . . ." She shook her head, thoroughly flustered, unable to put the experience into words.

For a long while, Mairen prompted her gently, while Tay Aillig stood there, towering over Seonagh's still form, his eyes clearly judging Aoleyn.

She felt that burn, intimately.

"What did Seonagh do?" the Usgar-righinn said suddenly, her tone sharp, demanding a response.

"She pushed me out of the way," Aoleyn blurted. "She jumped . . .

her spirit pushed me away, she took my place with Brayth. To block the fossa."

Mairen held up her hand, bidding the girl to silence, for there was no more to say. Mairen and Tay Aillig had seen this before, after all, and now they knew the truth of Seonagh's malady.

Mairen nodded to Tay Aillig, who lifted the limp woman into his arms.

"Help her!" Aoleyn pleaded as Mairen and Tay Aillig went for the tent flap. Tay Aillig didn't respond, just kept walking, but Mairen turned back and stared at Aoleyn for a moment, a flash of sympathy crossing her eyes as she shook her head.

Aoleyn slumped back as they left, and alone and in the dark, she cried. For all the traumas of that horrible night—Brayth taking her forcefully, Brayth dying before her, facing the dark reality of the fossa—this last one, the loss of Seonagh, stung most profoundly.

All the rest of the night, Aoleyn cried, and felt more alone than she ever had in all her life, because she knew.

She knew.

Seonagh wasn't coming back to her.

26

THE BITE OF MONSTERS

"Ah, Brayth," Aghmor said, shaking his head and taking a deep breath to try to steady himself.

He sat on a large stone with Ralid, the great-grandson of Chieftain Raibert, just to the side of the high plateau, taking a break as the women and uamhas went about their work of setting up the winter camp.

"A good man and fine warrior, by all the tales," said Ralid, who was several years younger than Aghmor and had just seen his second battle in the fight with the sidhe.

"The tales are not enough," said Aghmor with a little laugh. "He almost killed me once."

"You fought him?"

Aghmor shook his head and recounted the story of his and Brayth's first raid, when he had taken a brutal fall and Brayth had stood over him, ready to plunge his spear through Aghmor's chest.

"Ah, but he was just being tested then by Tay Aillig," Ralid said with a chuckle, and he added slyly, "Too bad, that. I'd be a rung closer to becoming Usgar-laoch without the likes of Aghmor standing ahead of me!"

The two shared a laugh at that, and Aghmor nodded in praise of the joke—but stopped short when he glanced past his companion, over to the camp, to see a short and dark young woman going about her chores with energy and enthusiasm, her long black hair flipping about as she bent and rose and hustled a log or tent pole over to a desired spot.

She glanced back once and matched stares with the man, her black eyes flashing.

"Oh, but what he lost," Aghmor whispered, rising to get a better view of the woman.

Ralid glanced over his shoulder and stood up, noting the target of the man's words.

"Aoleyn," he said. "Full of the fire, is that one. She'd be a ride!"

"A ride I mean to take."

Ralid started and looked at Aghmor curiously. Brayth was barely cold in the ground, and the man was already ogling his wife!

Aghmor just shrugged at the look. "Why not?" he said. "She's years younger, so I'm the right age. She was betrothed to my dearest friend and now he's no more, so it's only fitting and proper that I serve in his stead."

"Serve?"

"It will be a sacrifice," Aghmor replied, barely able to keep a straight face. "But for Brayth, I'll suffer."

"You will suffer indeed," came a third voice, and both young warriors turned to witness the approach of Tay Aillig.

Aghmor sucked in his breath and leaned back defensively, and Ralid began hopping from foot to foot with obvious panic.

"She is powerful and possesses a great . . . allure," Tay Aillig said quietly, moving up to the two, and glancing back to watch Aoleyn going about her chores. He turned back to look Aghmor in the eye. "You'll not have her, young warrior," he said, though not in a threatening or commanding way.

Aghmor didn't quite know how to take the statement, or warning, if that's what it was. He was off-balance, sitting before this man, the most powerful and physically intimidating man among the Usgar.

"The witch Seonagh was broken by the fossa," Tay Aillig explained.

Aghmor and Ralid both nodded, for it was common knowledge about the camp, of course.

"Aoleyn, too, was touched by the demon," the Usgar-laoch continued. "We're not for knowing how bad, but there are no chances to be taken. She might yet be following the witch into Craos'a'diad. But even if not, there'll be no talk of her pledging to any until we know."

"How long?" Ralid asked before Aghmor could.

Tay Aillig shrugged.

Aghmor and Ralid exchanged glances.

"Back to work," Tay Aillig commanded, and the two brushed themselves off and scurried away.

Tay Aillig grinned, watching them go, thinking himself quite clever. The Usgar-righinn was fairly certain that Aoleyn had suffered no permanent consequences from her brief encounter with the spirit of the demon fossa—nearly as certain as she was that Seonagh would never come out of her stupor. And given that they were only waiting for the first full moon of Calember, the tenth month, to sacrifice Seonagh into Craos'a'diad, it seemed as if Mairen was pretty confident!

Tay Aillig's grin became an open snicker as he considered Aghmor, remembering the inept fool's first raid, when Aghmor had fallen and nearly killed himself long before any hint of battle had begun. No, that one would not have Aoleyn.

Tay Aillig was fifteen years Aoleyn's senior, already into his thirties. He had not yet taken a wife. But he knew.

That one was for him.

If she continued with the promise she had shown, that is. He had seen the magical display by Brayth against the sidhe. He had witnessed the unharnessed power of Aoleyn flowing through the man and through his enchanted weapon, throwing fire and lightning. He had watched Aoleyn's magic launch Brayth up into the air, above the battle, above the leaping fossa. With Aoleyn's magical prowess supporting him, Tay Aillig would have the tribe. All of it.

He was Usgar-laoch now, because Raibert was old and infirm. Soon enough, Raibert would be gone, and Tay Aillig would claim it all, would become Usgar-triath. Still young and strong, Tay Aillig would fill both roles, as Raibert had once done, and so there would be no need for any Usgar-laoch. It would all be his.

"They're whispering terrible things," Aoleyn said to the woman.

Seonagh lay on her cot, her eyes wide open but unfocused, darting to and fro. Aoleyn could only guess what she was seeing in her mind, but the girl was certain it had nothing to do with her actual surroundings. Every so often, indiscriminately, Seonagh would issue a gasp, or a soft mewling sound, and even those reactions seemed unrelated to anything going on about her in the tent.

"You must wake up," she whispered insistently into Seonagh's ear. "Seonagh, you can't leave me. I need you. They whisper of Craos'a'diad!"

Aoleyn sat back, studying the woman carefully, hoping her last re-mark would shock Seonagh back to her sensibilities. They were running out of time, she knew, and she was running out of options!

She rolled a small crystal over in her hand. She could hear the dis-tant magical song of the wedstone flakes within that pellucid cylinder, but she didn't connect to it. Not yet.

She wanted to call to it, to use it to send her spirit into Seonagh to help the woman fight her battle, but she hadn't yet managed to do that.

For Aoleyn was afraid.

She had felt the cold darkness of the fossa, an absence of life more profound than death. A simple, inescapable void, unwalled, endless, a trap formed of the shadowy stuff of despair.

"Seonagh, please," she whispered, and she took the woman's hand in her own, brought it to her lips, and kissed it. It had surprised Aoleyn how much she loved this woman. Seonagh had become a mother to her, she now understood. A stern mother, perhaps, but now Seonagh's love for her shone so clearly to Aoleyn. Seonagh had leaped in front of the fossa's darkness. She had pulled Aoleyn out of that place, leaving her-self behind to cover the retreat. And she had known—of course, she had known! No skilled witch could enter such a profound darkness and not understand the truth of the mortal danger.

Still, she had come for Aoleyn. Seonagh had come to save this girl, a sacrifice no less heroic than if she had leaped in the way of a spear flying for Aoleyn's heart.

And that spear had struck home, so it appeared.

Aoleyn took a deep breath, steadying herself, steeling herself. She looked down at the crystal in her hands, Seonagh's own wedstone, and rolled it about, letting its vibrations permeate her form and find her living core. The crystal sang to her and she silently sang back. Hearing the song, emulating the song, strengthening the song.

She felt her spirit unmooring from her corporeal form and felt the unwitting invitation of Seonagh. She thought only briefly of the first time she had experienced this, and reminded herself that she had to be strong here, to know her boundaries and to fight as if her very life depended on her victory.

She started out of her body.

"Child, no!" came a shout, and Aoleyn felt her form jostled hard, felt fingers grabbing and tearing at her hands, tugging the crystal—and because she was unmoored, she couldn't respond fast enough to hold on.

She cried out and staggered, nearly falling over as she tried to reorient herself to the shocking reversion.

She stuttered and stammered and looked to the side, just in time to catch a punch in her face, one that laid her low. From the floor, she looked up at two forms, women, Connebragh and the Usgar-righinn herself, Mairen!

"What are you doing, silly girl?" Mairen demanded, shaking and rubbing her fist.

"It is a wedstone," Connebragh said, holding up the crystal. "Our fool Aoleyn thought to enter the spirit of Seonagh and do battle."

"Idiot!" Mairen snapped at poor Aoleyn. "Seonagh is lost to darkness and if you wander into the black, you will never find your way back!"

"I have to try!" Aoleyn pleaded.

"You have to do as you are told, and nothing more," said the Usgar-righinn.

"We can't just let her die!" Aoleyn leaped up to her feet, ignoring the line of blood running from her nose, even though she was spitting red with every word.

And then she got hit again, not physically, but more profoundly, as a wave of stunning energy rolled forth from Connebragh, from the very wedstone crystal she had taken from Aoleyn. The girl's thoughts chased shadows down a hundred side paths, and nothing from her consciousness seemed remotely connected to any limb or muscle. Her eyelids flickered, her words came out as jumbled nonsense, and she staggered and tumbled again, overwhelmed.

She had barely hit the floor when Connebragh was atop her, sitting on her chest and pressing the wedstone crystal across her throat, cutting off her air. Aoleyn tried to fight back, but she noted the uncanny strength in Connebragh's arms, and understood the woman's muscles to be magically enhanced!

"I should kill you now and save us the lingering grief of your idiocy!" Connebragh said down at her. Aoleyn slapped futilely and felt as if her throat was crushing under the pressure. She saw Mairen looming over Connebragh's shoulder and the Usgar-righinn seemed in no hurry to stop the murder!

Aoleyn knew that she was about to die.

"Too cold," Talmadge said, shivering by the house entrance even though he was bathed in morning sunlight.

"Oh, that wind," Khotai agreed as she neared, when the first gust of the wind blowing straight across the lake tickled her naked body. She moved closer to Talmadge, who lifted his arm to let her under his blanket beside him.

"It is wonderful here," Khotai said.

"Because of the company, I hope."

The woman laughed and kissed him on the cheek. "All the company," she said. "I've not slept so quiet in many years. I feel as if I am among friends—friends who would protect me."

Talmadge nodded, understanding every word. This mountain plateau was a wild place, full of monsters and hungry carnivores, thick with sidhe and with a notable demon rumored to be roaming the great mountain. And yet, for all of that, he, too, felt safer here than at Matinee, or in the Wilderlands, and surely more than in the Kingdom of Honce-the-Bear. Because here he was among a simpler folk, an honest and honorable folk. None here would try to steal his pearls or other goods, or even cheat him in a deal.

For the tribes of Loch Beag, life was a simple pleasure. The work was hard, certainly, the challenges ever present . . . but maybe it was just that, the need to cooperate and work together, the need to depend upon your neighbor in order to survive, that so appealed to him and Khotai. The tribes of the lake did fight against each other, but those battles were strictly coded. Seldom did anyone ever get killed, few even hurt. Most of the time it was just a matter of fishing boats vying for a favored spot.

"If a boat flips out there, every other boat about, from any tribe, will sail and paddle hard to the rescue," Talmadge said aloud, letting his thoughts carry him to that truth for Khotai's benefit.

She looked at him curiously.

"Community," he explained. "Even in their arguing, they're knowing the order of things for the best of them all. The tribes are neighbors, not just folk living near each other."

"And might that letting men and women die's not in their hearts?" Khotai said.

Talmadge nodded emphatically. "Whene'er I think of those people I know from Matinee, I remind myself that there are people like this."

Khotai wasn't about to argue that point.

"All the tribes are like that?" Khotai asked, snuggling closer.

"Yes."

"Even the one on the mountain?"

Talmadge pushed her back to arm's length and stared at her as if she had slapped him. "Usgar? No!" he said emphatically, shaking his head for a long while.

"The villagers call them deamhain," Khotai said. "Are they really that awful?"

"When they raid the villages, they kill any man they encounter, and take the women they find up the mountain with them," Talmadge explained. "Sometimes they kill them or take them as slaves. Sometimes they let them go to return home. But all are raped. The Usgar warriors would spread their seed to the villages in the most violent of ways."

"So, among the people here, there are some with Usgar blood?"

Talmadge shrugged. "Likely not here. Sellad Tulach is rarely hunted by Usgar. It's too far afield, with no easy way to get here other than the lake, and the Usgar won't go out on Loch Beag. But in some of the villages, yes, there are folk with Usgar blood."

"And they are treated no differently than those without," Khotai stated more than asked, obviously confident in her reasoning, and smiling widely when Talmadge confirmed it with a nod.

"And us?" Khotai asked. "How would they treat us if we stayed?"

"Perhaps someday we'll know."

Khotai pouted.

"I thought you were anxious to get the pearls to Redshanks," Talmadge said.

The woman heaved a great, exaggerated sigh. "Someday," she echoed, pulling away and out from under the blanket.

She only got a few steps from Talmadge before glancing back over her shoulder. "Will you let me return with you again next year?"

Talmadge just grinned wickedly as his eyes roamed up and down Khotai, admiring the view.

The room darkened around her. She felt herself falling back into herself, as if the essence of her consciousness, her very life, was diminishing within her dying body.

Her throat ached no more; she was beyond that sensation, drifting away into a realm of the spirit.

Dying.

She heard Usgar calling to her, to take her to Corsaleug, and so she followed the sound, hoping she would be found worthy of the god's halls.

But no, she realized somewhere deep inside, some tiny flicker of recognition. No, this wasn't Usgar, not the god himself, at least, but it was one of the magical manifestations.

Wedstone.

The flecks in the crystal crushing her throat.

Aoleyn's eyes popped open wide, but she hardly looked at the crazed, magically empowered woman choking the life out of her. No, she continued to look inside, to hear the song, to reach out for the vibrations of those gray flecks within the pressing crystal.

She found the magic and she threw it, hard, with all her strength, into the mind and soul of Connebragh.

The woman staggered. The only press on her neck then was from the simple weight of the leaning, stunned witch.

Aoleyn rolled her shoulders, driving her hand across, grabbing the crystal and pulling it out wide, then yanking it from Connebragh's hands, and without that support, the stunned witch fell forward.

Both hands on the crystal now, Aoleyn swung back violently, cracking Connebragh across the face as she slumped.

That shook Connebragh from the mental stupor, and she sat up straight, then cried out and came back.

But now Aoleyn had the crystal before her like a knife, and she stabbed out, driving the dull end into the woman's face. She heard the crunch of Connebragh's nose, saw the almost immediate flood of blood gushing forth.

Aoleyn struck again. She squirmed and thrashed. She began pounding at Connebragh's head as if she held a hammer, doing little damage, but keeping the woman at bay, even forcing her to rise up a bit to get out of range and to get her own arms in close to try to catch the crystal.

Aoleyn curled, one leg in tight, drove her foot up into Connebragh's crotch, and pressed with all her strength.

The dazed witch fell aside and Aoleyn tucked and rolled over backward, coming to her feet, holding the bloody crystal out before her with one hand like a weapon, bringing her other hand to her aching, bruised throat.

"Enough!" declared Mairen, aiming her words as much at Connebragh, who had recovered by then and seemed ready to leap back in to pummel the poor girl.

The Usgar-righinn held her hand out toward Aoleyn, toward the crystal.

But Aoleyn wasn't handing it over just then. She reached into the magic again, this time aiming the effects at herself, at her injured throat.

She felt the magical vibrations wash through her, and they seemed to realign her own being to harmony, thus healing her. She tried to hurry, expecting Mairen to yank the crystal away, or even to strike her with some other magic to stop her, but no, the Usgar-righinn stood there, seeming patient, and let Aoleyn finish.

Then Mairen motioned with her fingers for the crystal, and Aoleyn wisely handed it over.

Aoleyn held her breath, unsure of what would happen next, and she was surprised to see Mairen and Connebragh exchange looks that seemed more complimentary to Aoleyn than threatening.

"We saved your life this night, child," Mairen said to Aoleyn. "Perhaps it was worth saving."

Aoleyn could only stare, dumbfounded.

"You will have no more time near Seonagh," Mairen explained. "Bid her farewell now, if you must. Tomorrow we travel th'Way, and you will come with us, Aoleyn. You will see this."

"See this?" Aoleyn asked, to no response.

The next morning, she came to understand. The path out of the winter encampment that traveled between the lines of slave caves, then up the mountain to the highest peak and plateau of Fireach Speuer, was known as th'Way among the witches of the Coven. It was a fairly difficult climb, even this early into the season.

Mairen led the procession, which included several warriors and all thirteen Coven witches. Four of those men bore a litter, upon which lay Seonagh. They took great care with her, more than any man had shown her in life.

Aoleyn noted that areas of this hike had been worked and smoothed, some even with steps cut in to help with passage. Still, there was ice now, and areas without any such crafted aids, and so it took the better part of the morning to make the hike. The climb culminated in a treeless lea of stone and dirt and brown grass, centered by a chasm Aoleyn knew, a chasm out of which she had magically floated: Craos'a'diad.

Aoleyn understood. She wanted to scream out in denial, to scold Mairen, to call her so many names, most especially "murderess!"

But Mairen and the others had anticipated this, obviously, for Tay Aillig and another powerful warrior flanked Aoleyn as soon as Seonagh's litter was placed down before the chasm. They loomed over her, ready to grab her, ready to . . .

To do what, Aoleyn wondered? To pummel her, perhaps. Or choke her with their hands. She didn't have a wedstone handy this time.

The witches began to sing and dance about the unconscious form of Seonagh. For a long while, they spun and they dipped in perfect harmony, a truly beautiful sight to behold.

When the dance ended, the twelve lesser witches joined hands and formed a semicircle around Seonagh, the witch on either end near to the chasm lip. Inside that line stood Mairen, chanting and holding a crystal up before her.

Aoleyn tried to get a better view between the forms of the witches, but she couldn't make out much of Mairen's actions. She did, however, see Seonagh float up from the litter, rising into the air. The witches sang more fervently, as if in some orgiastic frenzy so suddenly, and before them Mairen danced and held her crystal up over her head.

Then the dance stopped and the song went soft and somber. With a casual flick of her hand, Mairen pushed the weightless Seonagh, who floated out over the chasm.

"No!" Aoleyn cried, leaping forward, or trying to, until Tay Aillig caught her by the upper arm with his iron grip.

The cruel man was barely stifling his amusement when he ordered his companion to help. They hoisted Aoleyn off the ground, she kicking her feet futilely, and carried her over to the side enough so that she could see past the semicircle of witches, and to Seonagh, hanging limply, helplessly, over Craos'a'diad.

The music stopped.

The witches bowed as one.

Seonagh plummeted from sight.

"No," Aoleyn whispered, and she slumped, tears flooding from her black eyes. She would have fallen to the ground, wanted to throw herself into the pit, but Tay Aillig and his powerful companion held her tight and tried to keep her upright.

She could only cry, couldn't even find the voice for a proper protest, instead simply wailing and screaming an occasional denial.

No one reacted. No one cared.

The witches took up a song once more, a marching song, and Mairen began again the procession back down th'Way to the winter encampment.

Tay Aillig and the other warrior carried the sobbing, defeated Aoleyn all the way.

"Down the cove. Down the cove," Talmadge serenaded, using the cadence of the song to keep the rhythm of his paddling.

Sitting and leaning with her back against the higher prow of the canoe, Khotai had stopped singing, and was just letting the serenity of the place wash over her. The sun was rising behind Talmadge, before her, casting long reflections across this southwestern corner of Loch Beag, tickling the water, which responded with wisps of stream.

"And there I'll find my lady fair, who'll kick my ass and mess my hair!" the oarsman improvised, drawing a laugh.

"True enough, and don't you be forgetting it," Khotai warned. Her expression changed, though, and she pointed off to her right, toward the southern shore of the lake and a cove that flowed back to where it became thick with the morning fog, and then seemed to wrap around farther to the right and out of sight. But there, on the land it rounded, Khotai saw smoke.

"Carrachan Shoal," Talmadge explained. "Breakfast fires."

"Not the village you told me about?"

"No, that's Fasach Crann, and we've a long way yet to go. We'll not be there before twilight."

"And we'll not stop here for a bit of food and rest?"

Talmadge snorted. "The folk of Carrachan Shoal are the least friendly of the lake tribes. Or might I should say, the most suspicious. They'd not openly welcome me traveling with you. The three towns—this one, Fasach Crann, and the one beyond that—are the most careful of the seven about the lake, because they're deepest in the shadow of the mountain."

"And the shadow of the Usgar," Khotai reasoned.

"Aye."

"But you said that Fasach Crann was your favorite of all."

"It took them years of seeing my ugly face in these parts, and the word of the neighboring tribes, for them to trust me," Talmadge explained, and he shrugged then and gave a self-deprecating chuckle. "I don't know why I've grown so fond of them. It might be because I find their heads the least off-putting!"

"They've got the long skulls," said Khotai.

"Aye, just a single cone, and covered in hair for most. They don't look much different than women of the Wilderlands with long hair, who tie it up in great buns as they go about their chores." He gave another self-deprecating chuckle and shrug. "It's funny to admit it, but they probably accept me more because I'm feeling easier around them. More than once is the time I've seen a villager with two humps on his head, and with odd hair to make the bumps clearer, and I've gasped in surprise—even now, after all these years of coming here."

Khotai nodded and grinned. "It takes some time to get used to," she agreed.

"Have you?"

"What?"

"Gotten used to it?"

Khotai laughed loudly. "No!"

"You will, a bit."

"I still love it here." She rested back once more then and let her gaze drift off to the south, watching the lines of smoke from the Carrachan Shoal cooking fires drift lazily above the fog while Talmadge went back to his song. She let her arm sling over the side of the boat and lazily ran circles in the water with her finger—and that water felt warm to her, compared with the crisp air this day.

Warmer still a short while later when the wind shifted around to the north, blowing in across the lake, and before Khotai or even Talmadge realized it, the fog began to rise more thickly around them.

"Bloody hell," Talmadge remarked when the first cold mist blew across the canoe.

"A wintry shift?" Khotai asked.

Talmadge sighed. "Sure to slow us down, and we've a long way to go." He shifted his paddle over to his right, Khotai's left, and gave a sharp and deliberate pull, turning the canoe discernably.

"It's not that cold," Khotai told him. "We can go on. We've warmer clothes . . ." She reached for her pack.

But Talmadge was shaking his head. "You can'no be out on Loch Beag in a fog," he explained in very grim tones.

Khotai looked at him curiously.

But Talmadge just shook his head back at her, and pulled even harder on his paddle, turning the canoe for shore. When they came around fully, Talmadge sucked in his breath with clear concern, so Khotai glanced over her shoulder.

While Talmadge had kept them running straight to the west, the southern lakeshore had receded in this area, so they were actually quite farther out than they had been, and more, obviously, than Talmadge was comfortable with!

"Take up a paddle," he said deliberately and calmly. She pulled herself forward and rolled to her knees, reaching for the spare paddle. She had just grabbed it when the canoe rolled suddenly in an unexpected swell, stern to prow.

Khotai froze and looked up at Talmadge, who was also sitting perfectly still then, not moving his paddle, holding one hand up for her to remain silent and in place. The canoe drifted, turning sidelong to the shore as the swell rolled under it and flowed toward shore.

The lake quieted around them and Talmadge nodded slowly. As

Khotai eased her way around, the man dipped his paddle gently and pushed.

Khotai lowered her paddle on the other side of the canoe, thinking to do the same, but before it touched water, the fog cleared just enough for her to see a huge shadow passing right under the boat.

She sat up straight, suddenly, and snapped her head as she gulped.

He hadn't seen it, but he did see her, and his expression widened in shock, telling her that he understood.

Then Talmadge was up above her, lifted high as the back of the craft was pushed from below. He went flying right over her as the prow dipped and swamped, and before she even sorted it out, Khotai found herself in the water. She let go of the paddle and kicked furiously to gain the surface.

And there she heard the roar.

And there she saw the flotsam and jetsam that had been their canoe.

Then she heard Talmadge scream, and saw it then. The lake monster of Loch Beag. A massive, black serpentine neck, the neck of a dragon, she thought, lifting out of the water, through the fog and out of sight.

And then came the beast's head, sweeping down, with its terrible maw full of teeth as long as daggers.

Half-drowned, shivering with cold, bleeding badly from the rake of a huge claw across his hip that had peeled leather and cloth and skin with frightening ease, Talmadge pulled himself onto a muddy bank. His lungs ached from too much inhaled water, or from a hit he had taken. Possibly from a tail or a flipper, or a leg.

He could not know for sure. It had all happened so fast, the boat flipping stern over prow, him flying through the air to splash into the water. The splashing, the thrashing, Khotai's scream—aye, that awful sound rang in his ears still and had chased him all the way to shore.

Talmadge had never really seen their adversary, the monster, other than a wall of darkness that had fallen over him as he thrashed in the water.

But he knew. Of course, he knew.

It took him a long while to gain his footing and his bearings. He looked up and down the shore, then started off to the west, thinking he might gain Carrachan Shoal in a few hours, or, hopefully, that he might find Khotai.

Only a few dozen strides along, Talmadge came around a tumble of brush and a fallen tree that forced him back into the ankle-deep water at lake's edge. He struggled and leaned heavily on the branches and came around the tangle, but then stopped short, seeing a familiar boot.

"Khotai? Khotai!? Khotai!" Talmadge cried, pulling himself around and grabbing the fallen woman by the leg.

Only to realize that, no, this was not Khotai. This was just her leg, severed above the knee.

Talmadge fell down to the side, against the fallen tree, vomited, and sobbed.

He never made it to Carrachan Shoal that day. He went the other way, walking, crawling, until exhaustion overcame him. Then he clawed his way along the next day, and into the next night, half-crazed with grief, weak with hunger and pain.

He woke up in a bed in a warm hut in the village of Fasach Crann, where he was tended through the winter, by the gentle folk he had come to love.

But when the snows left the following spring, Talmadge left the plateau with them, left his friends who had saved him after that awful day, left this village of Fasach Crann that he so loved, vowing never to return.

PART 4

SECRETS

It is natural to fear that which we do not know, that with which we are not familiar. Nature, too, elicits comparisons from each of us on those who look different or act differently—by gender, color, shape of the eyes, religion, even culture. We often crinkle our noses in disgust when we encounter another culture's cuisine, like the snakes and bugs the To-gai-ru consider delicacies, or the bog petals the Touel'alfar wrap around slugs.

So, too, would a To-gai-ru traveler crinkle her nose at the thought of cooked squid, or would a Doc'alfar visitor cringe at the sight of a cow being slaughtered.

Perhaps that is why the dark elves of Tymwyvenne are more inclined— or were more inclined—to think nothing of throwing a human into their bogs to be resurrected as a zombie slave.

This is the power of unfamiliarity, the ease with which one can look at the discordant and foreign ways or appearance of another sentient person and thus internalize that person as something other, something different, something terrifying. This isn't just true among the actually different races, between the humans and the alfar, or the powries and the goblins, but among the various human tribes that populate Corona as well. There is little mingling or understanding between the men of Honce-the-Bear, the large and ferocious Alpinadorans, the brown-skinned Behrenese of the desert lands south of the Belt-and-Buckle, and the flat-faced and narrow-eyed warriors of the To-gai steppes. Four distinct tribes, four distinct cultures, four distinct ways of existing in the differing environs from which each hail.

These differences have oft wrought conflict.

Honce-the-Bear was not always a united kingdom despite the similarities of life and appearance and language across the breadth of the kingdom. Many wars have been fought upon her hilltops and through her low valleys pitting armies of folk who could be brothers, sisters, cousins. Similarly, the Alpinadoran tribes have done battle, village against village. But in the history of Corona, the greatest and most vicious and longest-lasting wars have involved a clash of civilizations, not brother against brother, unless one can consider all humans to be brethren.

As one should, I have now come to understand, though my own journey took me through dark valleys of brutal battle.

It is my own journey—without those dark valleys—that I wish every man and woman of Corona might walk.

For I learned to see the world through the almond-shaped eyes of Brynn Dharielle. I witnessed the harmony of movement, the sheer martial beauty of Pagonel of Behren. I have trained with the Touel'alfar, and in the rejoining of the elven races, have come to know the ways of the Doc'alfar. I am better for this knowledge. The world has become smaller and more familiar, and more comfortable around me because I speak out in unjudging curiosity instead of lashing out in fear of the mysterious other.

And this curiosity has commanded my road since my days in the tutelage of the great Touel'alfar leader, Dasslerond, the Lady of Andur'Blough Inninness. Instead of returning to the east, to Honce-the-Bear, where I might have begun training in the Abellican Church of Father Abbot Braumin Herde, who personally invited me, or of traveling south over the mountains to Behr, to the Walk of Clouds to train with the Jhesta tu, as Pagonel implored me, or even to To-gai, to learn of the people who gave to me the gift of Brynn Dharielle, I ventured west instead, to untamed lands filled more with goblins and giants and other such creatures, the children of the beasts of the demon dactyls, than with people.

After the war, the road west was least traveled. The road west, beyond the Wilderlands, promised wholly unfamiliar cultures, languages, and ways. Because of my training, martial and magical, because of my understanding, bitterly earned, because of my need to atone, this path, I believed, offered me best the chance to contribute to the wider knowledge of the world.

My choice, my journey, has not disappointed, for out here, in the lands where the names of King Midalis or Father Abbot Braumin Herde are not spoken or known, in the lands where there are no monks or yatols or Jhesta tu mystics, or Samhaists, even, I have found—as I expected—the loud echoes of those more familiar lands.

The tribes out here eat different foods, serve a god or gods of different names, use different magic and different rituals, even from each other, but all bent toward similar ends.

And that is the one truth I have come to hold most dear: for all of our differing methods and manners, we all—Bearman of Honce, barbarian of Alpinador, Chezhou-Lei of Behr, To-gai-ru, alfar, Touel and Doc—we all desire the same destination.

Accepting these differences while denying the value of violence was the chosen path of Aydrian Wyndon, my father, and, I have come to know through bitter experience, the only trail worth walking.

And so I now walk.

This is my vow.

Aydrian Wyndon, "In My Travels"

27

FREEDOM TO FLY

(The last day of the Spring, God's Year 857)

Aoleyn stood on the high rocky outcropping, the night wind in her face. Far below her, against the dark of the rugged mountain, she saw the low fires of the Usgar encampment, and far, far below that, specks of light marking the villages on the lakeshore.

The woman adjusted the ring she had fashioned, its band a soft white and splattered with blue. A green stone had been set upon it, tied with a gray filament Aoleyn had magically fashioned, and for which she was most proud. She had discovered a great secret here, she believed, one that had given her insight into the magic of Usgar beyond anything the Coven had ever known.

She believed, but she couldn't know.

She adjusted the ring, moving it so that the end of that gray filament, wedstone, stabbed into her finger.

A simple thought stopped the bleed before it had even really begun, and Aoleyn settled more intensely, hearing the wedstone and using it to connect to the other gems she had taken from shattered crystals to fashion into her ring.

She felt their powers, strongly, an intimate connection indeed.

Aoleyn took a deep breath and stepped off the cliff.

She plummeted, then slowed, then called to that blue band to alter the angle of her fall.

She was flying, soaring down the dark mountainside, gliding above the stones and the ravines and the trees. She clutched a crystal in her other hand, and called upon that one, too, the cat's-eye, her vision enhanced in the low starlight—and just in time, for she saw one black stony bluff rising before her!

Aoleyn called upon her ring and lifted her arms and swooped upward as easily as any bird, flying fast over that ridge, then dropping fast behind it, turning as she went in her descent to follow the line of trees now.

She roused a deer with her passing, the creature jumping from a bed of pine needles and springing away. She heard the hoot of an owl, and an answering call from the other side.

In the span of a hundred heartbeats, she was already approaching the Usgar summer camp!

She turned sharply to the east then, not wanting to be spotted by any sentries, and called upon the blue stone with all her strength. She felt like she was sliding down a snowy slope, and turned and veered gradually, as if sliding in her fall.

Exhilarated, but gasping for breath, she came upon some trees and, instead of flying over them, lightly touched down on their branches. She took a moment to catch her breath and set off once more, refusing to stop, running, nearly weightless from the green stone, springing from branch to branch, tree to tree, with graceful ease.

The music of the night surrounded her and the music of Usgar filled her, as she ran across the treetops, giggling.

Free.

She came to a final rest in one particularly large pine, grasping the trunk, high up from the ground, near the top. Had she not kept herself near weightless by maintaining the magic of the green stone, she was sure she would have bent the thing right over.

She stayed there feeling very self-satisfied with her own cleverness. By manipulating other stones she had taken from the crystals, Aoleyn had fashioned wedstones into wire, and piercing her skin with those magical threads had given her a closeness to Usgar she had never known before, outside of the cave. Even now, so far removed from that crystal cavern, the song hummed loudly inside of her—and the two gems on her ring sang to her much more clearly than those in the crystals she carried.

"Whoo," an owl said from nearby.

Aoleyn clutched the cat's-eye crystal more tightly and peered into the darkness, finally spotting the great bird sitting on a nearby tree. She fumbled with some other crystals, finding one that was thick with blue, but a different hue and texture from the moonstone band she wore.

She reached into that crystal, then out to the owl.

The bird tilted its head and ruffled its wings, clearly disturbed as Aoleyn spiritually prodded it. The woman felt a connection, almost like when she had been with Brayth on the battlefield. She seemed to understand the owl's sensibilities, could sense its trepidation, too.

A sound distracted her, like a deer running—except then she saw through the owl's eyes, that it was no deer, but a simple mouse.

But its footsteps sounded as though they were made by a raging bear!

Aoleyn's connection to the owl broke as the bird lifted away toward its prey, and it took the disoriented Aoleyn a few moments to realize that she had heard through the owl's ears, and her amazement had her leaning on that pine tree for a long while.

She had had no idea of the power of this blue-filled crystal, had never heard of such a thing. It seemed to her like a wedstone, but for animals. Her spirit had been inside the owl!

Aoleyn nodded, giddy at the possibilities that were opening up before her. What might the stones in this crystal allow her to do once she had made a wedstone connection with them, too?

Oh how she wished she could stay out here all the time. Exploring Fireach Speuer in ways she had never imagined, studying the power of Usgar more intimately than she had ever hoped.

But she could not, she reminded herself; she had another task she must finish before returning to camp. She called upon the blue band of her ring once more and leaped away, now flying up the mountainside, then running again, but easily and almost weightless, tree to stone to tree. Up, always up, and when she came to a sheer cliff, she leaped up and flew, and so within a very short while she was again near the summit of the great mountain, but now more to the east than before.

She moved carefully, for the winter plateau was nearby, and she had to take care not to let Elder Raibert see her!

She moved up past the uamhas caves, quiet now with the slaves all far below.

Almost all, at least, for she heard a tap-tapping higher up th'Way, up near the top and the open area that held Craos'a'diad.

Aoleyn set down and walked, soon coming in sight of a man, bent over and working at the stone with a hammer and chisel.

Yes, a man, she told herself pointedly as she looked upon Bahdlahn, nearing his eighteenth birthday. He was tall now, and broad, with his muscles growing thick and tight under endless hours of hard labor.

Only a year before, when Bahdlahn's adulthood could not be denied any longer, the Usgar were going to put him to death, as they did with all the male slaves, thinking them too great a threat. There had been a great argument, for some thought him too stupid to be trouble, to be anything but docile.

In the end, Mairen had saved the young man, but only because she had convinced the others to work him to death instead, up here, fashioning th'Way so that it would be easier to climb.

It was a good plan, and certainly working this trail would prove beneficial to the Usgar during their winters up here, but there was one thing they had not counted upon in their calculations.

"Why are you working so deep into the night?" asked Aoleyn. "You know that when you finish, they're going to throw you off the mountain."

She said it jokingly, despite the weight of the subject and the kernel of truth, except that they both knew it would be many years before Bahdlahn could finish such a monumental task. He was carving stairs into solid stone, building railings and filling small ravines.

"I wanted to finish this one step," he said proudly, turning about with a grin for his friend.

"I brought you some cooked fowl," Aoleyn told him, pulling off her pack and tossing it to the ground.

"A wonder that they do not see my belly and gut me," Bahdlahn replied.

Yes, he could speak, Aoleyn now knew, and there was nothing stupid about him. The woman thought back to that long-ago day when she had heard his mother, Innevah, telling him that he was stupid. She had thought Innevah was insulting him, had wanted to yell at her for being so cruel!

But no. She was saving him. The Usgar thought him dull and so unthreatening, and while he was perhaps the latter, it was not from stupidity. He just possessed a gentle nature that impressed Aoleyn beyond anything else. For all the pain Bahdlahn had suffered, for all the humiliation, his spirit was not broken. His soul remained full of joy and appreciation—appreciation simply for being alive.

Bahdlahn went at the bird with ravenous delight. "Have you seen my mother?" he asked between bites.

"She is well," Aoleyn replied. "I try to find some secret moments with her, to tell her about you. It keeps her alive, Bahdlahn, her love for you."

The young man smiled and nodded, and seemed on the verge of tears.

How different was he from the hardened Usgar warriors!

"Did you build the hidey-hole?" Aoleyn asked him, letting her concern show through clearly.

He chuckled.

"You must," she said in all seriousness. "The Usgar-righinn says that Iseabal might show her red face next month."

"I've started one," said Bahdlahn. "In the big cave, way in the back."

"Tight and blocked with stone," Aoleyn reminded.

He nodded, and seemed unconcerned—and why not, Aoleyn thought; he had never seen the fossa, or felt the coldness of its stare, like death itself. There were few large animals up here so high on Fireach Speuer, either. No wolves or bears. Perhaps a snow leopard now and again, but the cats, for all their power, shied from men. He believed he was safe.

Aoleyn, who had faced the demon fossa through the eyes of Brayth, knew better.

"Fashion it," she ordered him. "Make it tight and block it with stone. Quiet and deep, I beg."

Bahdlahn stopped smiling so teasingly and painted on a somber face as he nodded his assurance.

"I will try to get them to let me bring you back to the lower camp if Iseabal will visit," she said. "They don't want you dead."

"They thought I would already be dead."

Aoleyn couldn't disagree. The Usgar hadn't given him much in the way of supplies up here, and he had to go to the winter plateau every morning and announce himself to Raibert. He had nowhere to run, little to eat, and should have worked himself near to death by now, and would have, had not Aoleyn found a way to pay him these secret visits. If, on one of the occasional inspections, the Usgar warriors were not satisfied with the simple uamhas, they would throw him from the mountain.

Aoleyn had heard the whispers below. The Usgar were shocked at how well this strong young uamhas was performing, and how well he was surviving.

"Where?" Aoleyn asked, fishing out a different crystal.

"Just my hands tonight," said Bahdlahn, holding forth his hands, his fingers all bloodied and nicked from hammering all the day on the stones.

Aoleyn took them in her own and fell into the magic of the crystal, and was soon imparting magical warmth into the young man.

She was feeding him, she was healing him, and she was sharing his smiles when both needed them.

"Do not come to me on Lizabeth's Night," Bahdlahn said to her as they sat there, holding hands, his voice very serious. "Promise me."

Aoleyn sighed, but nodded. "Unless they let me fetch you before moonrise, and bring you to the safety of the camp."

He nodded his agreement, but they both knew she'd never convince the Usgar to do any such thing. They didn't care if the fossa ate this stupid uamhas, as they didn't care if he worked himself to death.

They simply didn't care.

Bahdlahn headed back to the slave caves soon after, and Aoleyn bid him farewell. She didn't dare follow, for that was too near to Elder Raibert. She wanted to go to Craos'a'diad, which was only up over that one last rise, but she knew that she had been out too long already.

She moved off th'Way, scrambling through some brush to come to a cliff face, then called upon her magical ring once more and leaped away, and flew, joyous and free, down the darkened side of Fireach Speuer.

Too soon after, she set down just outside the Usgar camp, and crept to the back of the tent that she had once shared with Seonagh, but now was hers alone. Glancing around, confident that she hadn't been seen, Aoleyn went in through a secret flap she had cut in the back of the tent.

A light came up as soon as she entered, the hood removed from a burning lantern. The man who had claimed her to become his bride, Tay Aillig, was in there waiting for her, sitting comfortably, staring at her with smug contentment.

Aoleyn sucked in her breath, expecting to be beaten. What was he doing in here? He had claimed her, but they hadn't been proclaimed in marriage yet and were not sharing this tent. Tay Aillig hadn't even touched her since making the claim.

Was that about to change?

Aoleyn grew even more uneasy. She had only one sexual encounter with a man, three years before when Brayth had raped her. Looking at Tay Aillig, the Usgar-laoch, the War Leader, so always on the edge of anger, she realized that she would much rather be beaten.

"Oh, but my surprise," he said.

"I had to relieve—"

"Shut up. You've been gone the whole of the night."

Aoleyn swallowed hard. She told herself that she was a woman now, not a girl, and reminded herself that she had power, magical power, and now carried the gemstones to use it if necessary.

"Have you made it your duty to spy on me, then?" she asked, stepping into the room with as much confidence as she could manage. She didn't want him to see her fear. She understood men like Tay Aillig all too well—they only grew emboldened and meaner when they knew that people were frightened of them.

"Aye," he answered simply, and that stopped Aoleyn in her tracks. She stood there, mouth hanging open, staring at him.

"I have claimed you as my wife. Any woman would be glad of that."

Aoleyn nodded, not about to argue. She understood the ways of Usgar, whether she liked them or not. It wasn't her place to question, and she couldn't deny that almost every woman in the tribe would be thrilled to have Tay Aillig, perhaps the most powerful man in the tribe, as a husband.

Nor could Aoleyn deny the many jealous looks that had come her way since the War Leader's surprising claim the previous summer, immediately after the proper mourning period for Brayth had ended. Aoleyn wasn't considered especially beautiful among the Usgar, and was actually the smallest woman in the tribe. Although there were many whispers that she was next in line to join the Coven, who knew what might happen in the months, years, decades even, between now and the next opening among the thirteen witches of Usgar?

"Where were you?"

"Out."

"In the camp? With another man?"

"No."

"With the uamhas?"

"No. Of course not."

"Then where?" He leaped up from his seat and stormed over to tower above her, leering down in open threat. "You will tell me."

"In the forest," she replied, trying to remain steady. "On the mountainside. I go out all the time—almost every night."

"Where?" he demanded.

"I would know every valley, every tree, every cave," she said, improvising. "When I was with Brayth in the battle, I . . . my spirit, nearly lost its way. Had I known better the area where he fought, perhaps . . ." She let her voice trail off and looked down at the floor, but took some secret comfort in seeing Tay Aillig's feet slide back a bit.

Aoleyn looked up quickly, locking his eyes. "I will not fail my man again," she said.

His face became a mask of confusion, intrigue, pride—all sorts of emotions, but none of them clearly negative. Aoleyn knew she had distracted him.

"To know the mountain is to know Usgar," she went on, now with confidence. "The god's song is not steady, but ebbs and flows in different places, like streams of magic. I will know those streams, better than any."

Tay Aillig didn't answer, didn't blink.

"Are any stronger than Tay Aillig?" Aoleyn asked him.

"No."

"And so none shall be stronger than his wife in the ways of magic. Anything less would not be acceptable."

He nodded and seemed to be digesting that, but his demeanor changed suddenly and he came forward, painfully grabbing Aoleyn by the chin and yanking her face in line with his steely gaze. "You are destined for the Coven, and soon to be my wife. Yet you take such chances?"

"No chances," she insisted.

"You could fall in a ravine!"

She brought her hand up, holding the cat's-eye crystal. "I see as well as in daylight."

"You threaten your place on the Coven!"

Aoleyn shook her head emphatically, as much as she could against his iron grip. "The Usgar-righinn has no edicts against wandering the mountain in the night!"

"None. Other than good sense."

"I am not afraid. It makes me stronger. Do you not wish that?"

He was trying to stay angry here, but Aoleyn knew that her appeal and promise of strength had walked around his fury. And the only lie she had told was that she had not been with an uamhas, but he never questioned the lie because no one could have gone that far up Fireach Speuer and returned before the night was half through.

The rest of her story had been true. She was going out in order to become stronger, for she had found secrets that not even the Coven, blinded by their old rituals and etiquette with the crystals, could hope to realize. She was indeed getting stronger.

But not for Tay Aillig's benefit.

"You take care on your paths, we wouldn't want you to come to harm," Tay Aillig warned with a toothy grin and a brief tightening of her wrist. "And know that if your foolishness costs you your place in the Coven, you will be shunned by all men. And I will not marry you, but will take you often for my pleasure, and your pain."

He let go of her chin and reversed his hand, using the back of his fingers to stroke her cheek . . . but so awkwardly, almost as if he had only heard that that was how lovers touched.

So clearly there was something out of sorts here, but Aoleyn couldn't quite place it. It was as if there was no desire in the man beyond his hunger for power. Even with the threat he had issued, Aoleyn understood clearly that it was only half true, that he wouldn't take her for his pleasure.

He would take her to punish her, to satisfy his anger, not any carnal desire.

She was quite relieved when he left, particularly when she realized that she was still wearing the ring she had fashioned of moonstone and malachite, and wound with wedstone threading.

If Mairen found out that Aoleyn had broken sacred crystals to get at the flakes within, it would cost Aoleyn more than a place among the Coven.

She intended to go back into the caverns beneath Craos'a'diad, perhaps the very next night, but not in the way that Mairen would send her there for her heresy.

28

WHEN YOU FEAR, CHARGE!

Talmadge crouched behind a tree, peering through a bush to watch the man standing in the stony shallows of the river. He appeared to be a few years younger than Talmadge, and not as tall, but he was clearly a Bearman, a man of Honce. And no one Talmadge wanted to fight with, the veteran frontiersman knew when the stranger stripped off his shirt. This one was a warrior, no doubt about it, with a torso thick with muscles but otherwise lean, and arms that looked as if they could break Talmadge in half. He moved with grace, too, and even when he reached back for something in his ample pack, his legs shifted subtly, perfectly, to keep him in balance, to keep him ready.

It wasn't just the man himself that had Talmadge holding back cautiously: a most remarkable bow leaned on the pack, and a long sword, as well, and though the blade was hidden in a sheath, the handle and pommel spoke of incredible workmanship.

The man splashed himself quickly and repeatedly, then brought his cupped hands up to douse his head with the cold mountain water, rising and shaking vigorously.

"Are you planning to lie there all day and just watch me?" he asked then, turning to glance in Talmadge's direction.

Talmadge reflexively ducked away, rolling onto his back to put himself fully behind the tree.

"As you wish," came the call, and Talmadge knew he had been seen.

"I've some fine food to share," the stranger offered.

After a few heartbeats, Talmadge dared peek around the other side of the tree. There stood the stranger, his shirt back on, holding a waterskin he had apparently just filled. Notably, he hadn't retrieved his weapons, and he seemed wholly unconcerned with Talmadge.

A moment later, he glanced back, locking stares, and waved, winked, and smiled.

"I will leave you to your river, friend," he called. "Though it seems big enough and deep enough. Surely, it's filled with enough fish for us both, yes?"

Talmadge felt rather silly then. He climbed to his feet and moved out around the tree, toward the stranger, who smiled widely.

"Who are you who comes out so far from the tamed lands?" Talmadge asked.

"No farther than you," the stranger replied.

"I've not seen you at Matinee."

"Likely not, as I don't even know what that is."

Talmadge stopped his approach. "So's my point," he answered. "All who are out here from the land of Honce know of Matinee."

The man looked down to regard himself and held out his hands in a shrug. "Not all, I expect."

"Then you are new here," said Talmadge.

"I've not been this far south in many years," he replied. "And never on this side of the mountains."

"Then I ask again. Who are you?"

"A . . ." The man paused, then gave a little snort.

"Is that a difficult question?"

The stranger chuckled. "No. It is just . . ." He sighed, gave a self-deprecating laugh, and straightened. "I am . . . Bryan Marrawee of Dundalis."

"Marrawee? A strange name."

"An alfar name," the man said with a laugh.

Talmadge rocked back on his heels a bit. Elves? This stranger claimed a name from the elves?

"Alfar?" he echoed.

"Aye. Touel'alfar."

Now it was Talmadge's turn to snort, to which the stranger merely shrugged.

"It is as good a name as any," he explained. "And so it is one I choose to wear."

"And not the name your father gave you?"

"I did not know my father. Not really."

"Your mother, then?"

The man who called himself Bryan Marrawee nodded.

"She gave you a name, and not an alfar name."

"Yes, and no."

"And?"

"It is not one I choose to wear."

"I insist," Talmadge said.

But the stranger simply laughed, then sighed, and began packing up his belongings.

"This is not a land for uninvited men who choose no proper introduction," Talmadge warned.

The man looked up from his pack. "Pray tell me, who out here was ever invited? And now you would lay claim to the place?"

"I did not say that."

"But you just built a wall of condition, yes? Tell you my name or . . . or what? Be banished? Do you intend to banish me?"

Talmadge licked his lips nervously. "I only wish to offer advice."

"Offer your own name instead," said Bryan.

"I am known as Talmadge."

The man nodded. "Greetings, then, Talmadge. My offer of food stands."

"Am I to trust a man who will not tell me his true name?"

"My true name is that which I choose to wear. And yes, you should trust me. I did not kill you where you lay by the tree, did I?"

Talmadge looked from the man, who was still twenty paces away, back to the tree, which was more than twenty paces back, then turned back with a doubtful expression to find Marrawee laughing and gathering up his things. He lifted his sword belt and began to strap it on.

"This would be a lot more pleasant if you simply trusted me," Bryan said.

"I am not in the habit of walking up to strangers with my hands empty and open."

"But I didn't kill you."

Again, Talmadge gave a doubting look—or started to, for Marrawee dived to the ground, into a roll, and came up so easily and in steady balance to one knee, now with his bow in hand, and with his quiver right beside his hip, in easy reach. And by the time Talmadge had even realized the movement, or the quiver, Marrawee had drawn and knocked an arrow, a curious trio of feathers at its top separating as the shaft bent.

The blood drained from Talmadge's face as that arrow shot off, sped right past him, so close that he could hear the hum of the fletching as it zipped by. Talmadge stumbled aside, then managed to get into a crouch that he might dive aside if necessary.

But Bryan had already set down the bow. Talmadge glanced back, and was strangely unsurprised to see the arrow sticking into the ground right where he had poked his head around the tree.

There was nothing to doubt, then.

"Are you coming along?" Bryan said, drawing Talmadge from his shock. "I am desperately hungry."

The crying grew louder, along with denials, then pleas for mercy.

Innevah tried to block it out, for she understood what was happening in a tree-cave farther along the uamhas grove.

"No, I will, I will!" she heard, and it was just gibberish now, the poor girl's voice breaking into shrieks of stinging pain.

"No, don't!"

And the scream, probably the last one, to be followed by a night of unending sobbing, Innevah knew. The woman leaned back against the trunk of the pine tree that centered her residence, and closed her eyes, trying not to relive the experience.

For she, too, had had such a visit from a witch, twice before over the years.

The poor girl down the grove had become thick with the child of a rapist, half-Usgar. Down at the lake villages, when a woman caught in a raid and then released was found to be pregnant, the villagers accepted the fate and welcomed the child.

But not here. Not with the Usgar. Any child with half-Usgar and half-lakeman blood was an abomination that could never be allowed to draw breath. And thus the pregnant woman would be visited by the Coven witch overseeing the uamhas, now a vicious, sharp-featured and thin-haired woman named Caia. Caia took great pleasure in her duties, especially when those duties elicited screams like those coming down the grove this awful night.

Innevah almost laughed as she considered that; such an attitude certainly didn't make Caia any worse than the others.

A noise behind her had the woman turning about. It was too dark for her to make out details, but she knew that the figure crawling toward her was Anice, the closest woman she could call a friend.

"They are monsters," Anice said as she crawled up beside Innevah and wrapped the woman in a hug.

Innevah just squeezed her tighter and said not a word, for what might she say?

It was amazing that Innevah hadn't been thrown from a cliff or into that awful chasm the Usgar thought the physical mouth of their demon god. She was not young and tender now, after all, and she knew of no other women who had been kept around to her age. When she had been brought here, a lifetime ago—eighteen years!—there had been a couple of uamhas women slightly older than she was now.

They were long dead.

Perhaps it was because of Bahdlahn, she mused. He was still alive, up on the mountain, working himself to death, no doubt. The vile Usgar probably used Innevah to keep Bahdlahn in line.

At that terrible moment, Innevah didn't think that a good thing.

Perhaps it would be better if Bahdlahn just ran off, even if he was killed in the attempt.

And yes, she would prefer death right then, she realized, when the heartbreaking sobs began from the poor young girl.

Those sobs cut straight to Innevah's heart.

Talmadge watched the stranger, Bryan Marrawee, closely throughout dinner and afterward, as the man stretched out on a flat stone to regard the stars above. Bryan hadn't asked many questions, nor had he offered many answers.

"So, you've never been west of the mountains," Talmadge said after a long while of silence, trying to start a conversation. This region, north-east of Matinee, where the rivers flowed cold and strong out of the mountains, had become Talmadge's favorite hunting ground over the last couple of years, since he had stopped going to the mountain plateau far in the west. He often went by the spot where Khotai had rescued him from the three thieves, past the grave of the fourth.

He could envision her so clearly, sliding in among them on her back, her legs working with devastating kicks.

A sad smile crossed the man's face before he focused again on this most curious, and dangerous, stranger. Bryan lay back on the stone, smoking a long-stemmed pipe, blowing rings and watching the stars. The man had drawn his sword earlier to trim a log they used as a bench seat for their dinner. What warrior would use his sword for such a task?

But Bryan hadn't cared at all, and he had no reason to, Talmadge came to understand, as that magnificent blade, gleaming and with not a speck of tarnish or a nick to be found, easily chopped the branches. Talmadge had no idea of what metal might be in that sword, but he knew that he'd never before seen its equal. Even Redshanks couldn't claim such a blade.

"Far to the north," Bryan answered. "West of them up there, in the lands known as the Barbican."

"But not here?"

"I told you that earlier."

"But now you're here, and how far south will you—"

"I just buried my mother," Bryan interrupted, cutting Talmadge short.

The frontiersman stuttered with that for a few moments, then said meekly, "I am sorry."

Bryan shrugged. "She wasn't that old, but I knew she'd die young. She went peacefully, and unafraid."

"I lost my whole family some twenty years or so ago," Talmadge said.

Bryan turned suddenly and sat up.

"She wasn't old, but oh, the life she lived!" he began, suddenly perking up. "Her name was known throughout Honce-the-Bear, and carried into Alpinador, and even Behren. Not one in ten thousand folk could have lived a life as rich as hers. So full!"

"Then that is a good thing."

"Aye, though I miss her every day."

"It is good that you were close. Your memories—"

"She saved my life," Bryan went on, staring down at his own feet dangling from the side of the stone. "Saved my soul, perhaps, though that one's needing more than just saving, I fear."

"So you've come here?"

He looked up curiously. "What? No. Well, yes, I suppose. I had to go somewhere, and this place seemed better than the other side of the mountains."

"You've been there, though? To Honce-the-Bear?"

Bryan Marrawee laughed then, suddenly and from his belly, and Talmadge rocked back.

"Aye," the other man said. "And if I had half the courage many believe, I'd go again, on bended knee. So might that I'm a coward, or might that I'm just not ready."

"It was a difficult time in Honce?"

Bryan laughed.

"You were an outlaw?"

The man laughed harder. "My new friend, Talmadge, if only you knew."

Talmadge rested back farther against the tree and tried to sort that out.

"And why are you here?" Bryan asked.

"I live here, all about these lands."

"Why?"

It was a simple question, or was it? As he considered his answer, it occurred to Talmadge that the roads of his life had narrowed considerably, bordered by ghosts. He didn't want to go back to the Wilderlands, or past them to Honce, but neither could he bring himself to go west any longer, to the place he had once loved.

A ghost had kept him from that mountain plateau before, and so now again, but this time, it was entirely different.

"A single word poses such a puzzle?" Bryan said, drawing Talmadge from his contemplations.

"What?"

"Why?"

Talmadge held up his hands in surrender. "It would seem that I am a bigger coward than you."

"Do tell."

"I should be going west now, down this very river, and to a place I would have one day called home, perhaps," Talmadge explained, speaking more to himself than to his companion. "But there I lost a woman I loved, taken by a monster . . ." His voice trailed away.

"To get the pearls?" Bryan asked, and Talmadge nodded—and then the man's eyes opened wide indeed!

Bryan Marrawee laughed at him and hopped down from the stone. "A friend told me," he said. "Of course, I know the tale of Talmadge. You are in the ballads, sir, called out in the songs of the bards."

"What bards?" Talmadge stuttered.

"In the Wilderlands."

"But you said you'd never been this far south in many years."

Bryan shrugged. "I've not."

"But your friend has?"

"It would seem so, and you know, those bards are not known to be secret-keepers. Quite the opposite, I am told."

Talmadge scowled at the sarcasm.

"But fear not, secret Talmadge, for they probably got most of your tale wrong." As he spoke, Bryan picked up his weapon belt and hitched it around his waist, then picked up that magnificent bow.

Talmadge shrank back. He was too far away to hope to get near the man in time to prevent a killing shot, and no, so suddenly once more, he had no idea of what this stranger intended.

"I'm to the river to fetch some water," Bryan explained, wearing a smirk that told Talmadge he had seen the man's uneasiness. "I've found a few rather large bears down there." He held up the bow. "You can come if you wish."

Talmadge, still flustered by the surprising revelation, didn't immediately answer, and then just shook his head.

"You are welcome to stay the night in my camp," Bryan told him. "We can cut you a pipe of your own."

He gathered up the waterskin and started away.

Talmadge sat there for a long while, not knowing what to do. Part of him wanted to run off into the night, to be as far away from this dangerous, and potentially mad, stranger as quickly as possible.

He slowly rose, thinking to do just that, when he noted Bryan's huge pack. He looked all around, then made for it, peering out beyond it to make sure that the man was nowhere about. He pulled open the ties and threw back the flap, fumbling about in the clothing and tightly wrapped foodstuffs.

And then Talmadge's jaw dropped open, as he brought forth a breastplate as he had never before imagined! The armor gleamed silver, edged in gold, and had a line of gemstones set across it. Talmadge, who had some experience with Abellican magic, had no doubt that those stones were enchanted.

"A knight," he whispered, for he could see no other explanation other than that this strange man was a nobleman of high rank, or had been. The sword and the bow were clues enough, of course, but this . . . this was magnificent. Even Talmadge, who had never seen a knight of Honce-the-Bear (but had heard of the famed Allhearts) understood that surely few in the world possessed such armor.

He reached into the pack beside the breastplate and brought forth a small bag. He pulled back the drawstring and gently dumped the contents into his hand.

Gemstones! Sparkling in the starlight. A beautiful mix, ruby and diamond, zircon and malachite. So many, all varied.

Hardly able to draw breath, Talmadge eased the stones back into the bag, taking supreme care not to spill any. He quickly repacked the large pack and secured the flap once more, then moved back to his place at the tree, now doubly confused as to what he might do.

So he did nothing. He just waited.

And waited.

He woke up with the sun in his eyes, rising over the mountains before him. He blinked away the sleepiness and tried to recall where he was, and why he was there.

He jumped to his feet, hopping all about.

Bryan Marrawee was gone, and all his gear gone with him.

"Bandits?" Talmadge whispered, terribly afraid, for if bandits had taken the likes of that man, what chance might Talmadge have against them?

But he calmed before the notion could take root, for there in the dirt by the fire pit, Bryan Marrawee had written him a note.

I go to greet my ghosts, my new friend Talmadge.
You should face your own.
When you fear, charge!

Talmadge stared at the words for a long while, then closed his eyes and pictured Loch Beag. An image flashed in his thoughts. A leg, severed above the knee.

He took a deep breath. He hadn't been back to the loch since departing there with the spring melt after Khotai's death. He had thought that he would never go there again, but now he just snorted self-deprecatingly, reminding himself that this wasn't the first time he had held such a belief.

He thought of Fasach Crann, and, strangely, of Redshanks. Khotai had wanted to trade the pearls with the man. She had pleaded with Talmadge constantly to reconsider. What a fine adventure they could have in collecting the pearls from the tribes, then traveling halfway around the known world to deliver them for Redshanks to his friends in the city on the river—Talmadge couldn't remember its name.

Talmadge took another deep breath and held perfectly silent, listening to the roll of the distant river.

Gradually, a smile came over him, a smile for Khotai and the thick book she had written. Not unlike Bryan Marrawee's mother, he supposed. And quite like Bryan himself, he was sure. That notion didn't shame him, but, strangely, urged him.

"For you, my love," Talmadge said and decided, as bold a choice as he had ever made.

He would write those pages Khotai had desired. For her.

He checked his gear and took up his hand axe, that he could cut some logs and build a raft.

Innevah and Anice both winced when the screams at last died away, only to be replaced by sounds of the poor young girl being beaten and chastised. With Caia screaming at her for being stupid.

"You dare to not drink the potions?" she roared, and slapped the young girl again.

"I did . . . I did," the uamhas sobbed, her words becoming muddled under a rain of blows. They didn't hear the young slave cry out anymore, though, as if she had no more tears to give.

"She did drink the brew," Anice whispered to Innevah. "I saw her take it and spoke with her long about it. 'You don't want to bear an Usgar child!' I told her. She knew the punishment."

Innevah nodded, having no trouble believing Anice's story. The uamhas were all taught the consequences of getting pregnant, and were given potions from the witches they were told prevented such unfortunate circumstances.

But those brews weren't always efficacious, Innevah knew from firsthand experience. Twice in her long years as a slave, she had become pregnant from an Usgar warrior, only to have her pregnancy so violently ended by the cold magic of an Usgar witch.

She feared the latest batch of brew was likely bad, Innevah knew, her hand going to her belly. She moved it away as soon as she was aware of the reflexive movement, not wanting Anice to worry.

"You should go to her," Innevah said when at last the beating and the berating died away.

Anice nodded and crawled out of the small tree-cave.

Innevah took a deep, steadying breath while watching her go. As soon as she was alone, she moved to the back of her little room and moved aside some branches to let some moonlight and starlight shine in on a particular spot.

She brushed aside the pine needles, revealing a thick, flat stone. She needed another deep breath, then lifted the front of the stone, revealing a deep hole Innevah had secretly dug. The moonlight brushed the side wall, mostly stone, and just touched the treasure Innevah had caught.

She watched it coil and slide, a white-furred mountain viper. It was a small one, about as long as Innevah's forearm and nearly as thick. Innevah had come upon it purely by accident a few days earlier, sunning itself on the rocky ledge behind the pine grove. She should have crushed it with a rock, for these aggressive vipers were quite deadly.

But she hadn't. For some reason, Innevah had chosen to catch the thing with a blanket, and had dumped it into her secret hole.

She hadn't understood why at the time, at least not consciously, but after hearing the screams of the poor girl down the way, Innevah knew what instincts had guided her actions. She simply couldn't take it any longer. The years had broken her; the Usgar had battered her. She knew she would soon be killed anyway, because she was into her forties now, and the Usgar warriors preferred the younger slaves for their "visits." In the end, that was the only reason any of the female uamhas were kept alive, and Innevah was outliving her usefulness.

Why give them the pleasure? Or the sacrifice to their demon god?

The woman slowly slipped one hand into the opening. One bite, she knew. It would only take one bite and she would probably be dead before morning, before the Usgar found her. Even if they came upon her before she succumbed, there was nothing the witches could do against the poison of a white-furred viper. Their magic would not defeat this poison.

She should have done this—thrown herself from a cliff, or something!—years ago, she scolded herself, inching her hand down a bit more. But no, she had stayed alive for a reason. She had even learned to better pleasure the Usgar warriors for a reason.

Because she had a son, and he was still alive—Aoleyn had assured her that Bahdlahn was well, and that Innevah would see him again when they broke the summer camp and returned to the winter plateau.

Innevah heard the snake hiss and yanked her hand back. She closed the stone and stepped away, bringing her hand to her mouth in a silent scream.

Bahdlahn was still alive!

She desperately wanted to see him again, one time.

She brushed the pine needles back over her secret cubby, silently chastising herself for even thinking of taking her own life, before she had the chance to say farewell to her beloved son.

Before she moved back to the tree trunk to fall asleep, though, she put her hand to her belly and remembered again the screams of the poor girl—and, in the quiet of the evening, she could hear the girl softly sobbing.

Innevah went to the tree, shaking her head determinedly. But she did glance back more than once, considering the bite of a serpent.

29

PIERCED

Aoleyn closed her eyes to protect them from flying shards, and brought the heavy stone down hard on the crystalline cylinder, shattering it into a million pieces.

"Heresy," she whispered, as if in warning to herself. She called upon the large diamond-flecked crystal near her and brightened the light as she sifted through the dust and shards to find the desired gemstone: a garnet, and a powerful one. The stones she was now collecting were all powerful, for Aoleyn could sense their relative strength by holding the crystals and concentrating on them. She could also use garnet; she had found that the stone allowed her to "see" magic. This one was much stronger than the one she had used to find it, so she was excited about what it would show her in these miraculous crystal caverns.

She wasn't about to waste her time with stones of trivial size if she could find larger, more powerful ones!

She put the garnet near the pile of nearly a dozen gems and minerals she had already collected. Most of her time in the crystal caverns had been spent identifying the various stones encased within the crystals. With each one she recognized as magical and different, Aoleyn sought out the specific properties, then searched until she found one of suitable power to be worthy of her "heresy."

For yes, that's what this was, she knew, and knew, too, that she'd get terribly punished, perhaps even killed, if discovered.

But this was too beautiful, and so it was a chance Aoleyn was willing to take.

She knew that she had to be discreet, but there were only so many places to hide the gemstones and she didn't want to simply bag them. No, she wanted them upon her body, a part of herself through the threading she had learned with the wedstones. Weirdly, Mairen had inadvertently shown Aoleyn a way to do this, instructing the young woman in another, typically mundane task. The tribe made jewelry with pretty, mundane stones, and gold coins, taken from the lakemen.

They were pretty, and it was not forbidden for the women of Usgar to wear jewelry fashioned of them. And that Mairen had shown her and Gavina, a rival of hers for entrance to the Coven who was at least twenty years Aoleyn's senior.

Using a milky-white crystal thick with serpentine, and one ruby-flecked, Mairen had enacted the same fire shield that allowed her to walk out of a bonfire unharmed, then had taken up a golden coin and used the ruby to create a blast of fire all about her, greatly softening the gold. While still using the serpentine shield, Mairen's hands had then worked fast to fashion the substance into a brooch, and had even set a gemstone in it for good measure.

Aoleyn had her answer, and thus, she had begun wearing jewelry just a few days previous, and had even shaped a ring in front of Gavina.

She had already melted that ring again, to remove the worthless gemstone, and down here, she had created one anew, setting it with a magical serpentine and ruby, and molding it around that wedstone wire with just enough sticking out inside the band so that she could puncture her finger and heal the wound around with wire, in effect, piercing the ring to her finger.

She would never need Mairen's scepter to create a bonfire, she thought as she felt the pinch of the wire when she had first put it on. Nay, she would be her own scepter! And more! With this new insight, with the gems and minerals instead of the bulky crystals, and with the wedstone binding them to her physical form, Aoleyn believed that she would become a being of pure magic, a woman truly worthy of Usgar!

What next, she wondered? She thought to go deeper into the caverns to see if she could identify some new types of magical stones, but she dismissed the notion quickly. She had gotten too late a start.

Besides, there was something else she had to do. Gavina had taken note of the other ring Aoleyn had fashioned, the moonstone and malachite ring that allowed her to fly about the mountainside, free of earthly bonds. She took up the ring now and broke it apart with the heavy rock, retrieving the malachite and the wedstone wire from the broken moonstone band. She had already found another moonstone, a pretty, blue-white ball. It was quite small, but very powerful, Aoleyn knew.

She had plans for this stone and the malachite, and she didn't have much time. She put the fine wedstone thread aside and took up a different one she had fashioned with great care. Not just a simple wire, this one itself was ornamental, wire wrapped over wire to form a cascading series of tiny diamond shapes. Four strands of these of varying lengths—the longest as long as Aoleyn's middle finger, the shortest half that length—flowed out from a circular gray wedstone hub, like the fronds of a willow tree.

Aoleyn took up her graphite bar and selected four gemstones: the diamond she had just retrieved, the smooth round malachite striped in varying green hues, the new moonstone, and a beautiful purple dolomite. One by one, she put the gemstones to the end of a strand, squeezing them into the diamond-shaped wire mount, then flipping the last link over to squeeze them into the previous diamond-shaped wire, securing them on all sides.

Not satisfied with that (and shuddering at the thought of losing the moonstone and malachite in the middle of a flight down the mountain), Aoleyn then protected herself with the serpentine in her ring, and created sparks of lightning about the setting with her graphite bar.

She giggled as each setting softened temporarily, just long enough for her to squeeze it tightly onto the gemstone.

When she was done, she laid the small earring out on the floor before her, admiring it, and also very afraid of what she would do next, for it was purely her idea and something she had never before heard of.

With trembling hands, she picked up the wedstone hub and fiddled with the two points of wire sticking out its flat side. The serpentine wouldn't help her with this part, and she knew it was going to hurt!

Aoleyn lifted up her shirt and hunched over, lining up the longer wire. She closed her eyes, bit down on her lip to stifle any scream, and pushed it through, piercing her belly button. She resisted calling upon the wedstone then, for she knew the worst was yet to come, as she brought the threaded wire against the other prong, twisted them together and pushed them both into her belly so that the wedstone hub was flat.

And she shot herself with the lightning, and a thousand fires erupted inside her!

Aoleyn nearly swooned from the pain, but managed to call upon the wedstone, filling herself with its healing wash—warm waves of magic knit together her skin, closing tight about the wire prongs, securing the belly ring. When the process was completed, it felt as if it was merely an extension of Aoleyn herself.

She stood up, admiring her work and focusing, concentrating deeply on the stones.

Yes, she could toughen herself with the dolomite, strengthen her body against blows and make herself immune to pain, poison, or disease. That dangling purple stone gave her health. She could fly and she could float, could create brilliant light or steal all of it away! She could create fireballs, and protect herself from their burn.

And, most important of all, she was wedded to the wedstone, so Aoleyn could heal any of her wounds. The young woman's giggle turned into sobs, so proud was she of what she had accomplished here in this cave, of how she had taken the song of Usgar and made it her own in so many varied and beautiful ways.

And she wasn't done yet.

Yes, she remembered this pain, like little shocks of fire tearing through her belly, burning and biting.

It hurt worse than poor Innevah remembered, far worse, but she figured that was mostly because Caia was administering the medicine—how this one took pleasure in hurting the uamhas! And likely, Innevah knew, because the warrior who had claimed her as a wife was here all the time, taking his pleasure with the slave women.

It was possible that this baby Caia was destroying was her husband's. Innevah couldn't be sure, and hardly cared.

It ended with a bloody rush, and Innevah nearly fainted, overcome by the dramatic shift in her entire being.

She lay back, panting, trying to find some measure of balance and calm.

Caia zapped her belly again with that nasty crystal, hard enough to burn skin, and when Innevah cried out, the Usgar woman slapped her hard across the face.

"Are you too stupid to drink the brew?" Caia demanded.

Innevah had heard it all before, when Caia had been issuing her brutal abortion to the poor young girl down the line. Innevah wanted to respond, to tell the idiot Usgar that no uamhas would become pregnant by choice here! That batch of the contraceptive brew had clearly been ineffective.

The middle-aged woman was too smart to bother, though. Such words would just get her slapped again, and probably shocked again for good measure. It didn't matter how or why it had happened, not to Caia, certainly.

So Innevah just rested back and closed her eyes, pretending to faint away.

Caia slapped her again.

"Look at you," the Usgar witch taunted. "Old and drawn, shriveled like a grape left on the vine." She spat into Innevah's face. "Why would any even want you, but it's less now, to be sure, and will grow to nothing. Or might it won't. Might that you'll find the gorge this winter, eh? It's past time for it, don't you think? We'll throw you in and let your stupid boy watch! Ha, if he's even up there. Word's that he died, that the fossa got him and ate him bits at a time, slowly, so he felt all the pain."

"Why would—" Innevah screamed, sitting up, or trying to, until a blast from Caia's gray graphite stole all of Innevah's muscle control, threw her back to the floor, and left her jolting and shaking, limbs flying wildly, out of her control.

Laughing, Caia and the Usgar guards departed.

When her sensibilities returned, poor Innevah managed to turn her head toward the back of her small pine cave, toward the buried stone lid.

She should have let the snake take her, she told herself more than once, more than a hundred times, until sleep mercifully overtook her.

Aoleyn exited the crystal caves from the same tunnel she had first been brought to in this place. She knew the area here fairly well now, so it was with complete confidence that she leaped away, drawing the power of the green and blue-white stones dangling from the chains of wedstone now secured to her stomach. Up she soared to the first ledge, where she set her foot again and leaped away, scaling the rocky mountain with practiced ease.

She soon crossed the level of the Usgar winter encampment and the circular grove of short pines that surrounded the god-crystal. Normally, she would circle far to the left now, down and around below the encampment and out of sight of Elder Raibert, that she could approach Bahdlahn at work on th'Way from the north side of the mountain. This night, Aoleyn felt particularly empowered, though, and close to Usgar. She had become the god's instrument!

She ran swiftly to the pines and bounded over them with one single leap, landing in the circular lea and stumbling forward from her momentum, nearly colliding with the god-crystal!

She could feel the heat pulsating from it—not uncomfortably hot, but soothingly warm. She had no idea of what she was doing here, but on impulse, she reached out and touched the giant crystal.

It was humming, full of Usgar's song, vibrating with swift notes. Aoleyn eyes widened—she had never felt anything quite like this!

She moved closer and touched it with her other hand, too, and felt the thrum of the god-crystal filling her entire being, warming her, exciting her.

She backed away some time later, her black eyes sparkling in crystalline reflection, her breath coming in gasps, and truly, she thought this the best night of her life.

But now she had to be careful, she reminded herself, for she was not far from Raibert, and would cross near to the southern end of that camp to get to th'Way.

She went out the southern end of the grove, putting the trees between her and the Elder. With a great leap and flight, she went to the wall she had scaled with Seonagh that long-ago day when she had been pledged to Brayth. Now buoyed by the magic of the green stone, Aoleyn scrambled spiderlike across the cliff facing, then up and over it farther along to the east, coming over a ridge in clear sight of Craos'a'diad. Past it, she descended th'Way carefully, smiling when she heard the tap-tap of Bahdlahn's hammer.

She found him fitting a stone.

"Wouldn't it be easier to work in the daylight?" she asked, startling him, for with the green gem, she walked without a whisper of sound.

Bahdlahn jumped back and raised his hammer defensively, but then smiled and lowered it when he recognized Aoleyn.

"It is cooler at night," he replied.

"But the wolves are out at night!"

"They won't come this high."

"How could you know that?" Aoleyn asked.

"Because there's nothing big up here worth eating!" he said.

Aoleyn found herself charmed by his reasoning, by his intelligence, by the simple clarity and cadence of his speech. There was nothing simple about Bahdlahn, but how brilliantly had he played the role of idiot, as his mother had commanded—and that, too, she knew, was a testament to his cunning.

"There's you!" Aoleyn countered, and Bahdlahn had to laugh at that, and such an infectious giggle it was that Aoleyn, too, was laughing.

"Shh!" she warned.

"Shh!" he warned back at her.

Aoleyn composed herself. They weren't far enough from Elder Raibert for such outbursts. "And a wolf would find you a fine meal," she said, and she pinched Bahdlahn's thick arm—and was shocked at how solid it was!

"Is that why you fatten me up?" Bahdlahn teased.

"You just said that the wolves don't come up here."

"Ah, but the bears do."

Aoleyn started to laugh, but bit it back when she realized that he wasn't joking.

"They do," Bahdlahn confirmed. "Big ones. I hear the little rock slides when they paw about. They come up to lick the moths off the stones."

"What?" Aoleyn couldn't tell if he was being serious or not.

"They do," he insisted. "I've seen them. The moths sleep on the warm stones, and the bears sit by, licking the stones clean." He pointed to the east, to a spot where the ground fell away from th'Way steeply, affording a wide view of Fireach Speuer's higher slopes. "I can see them from there, but they don't come very close."

He paused and looked at her slyly. "Of course, if you keep fattening me up . . ."

Aoleyn appreciated the levity. Taking the cue, she pulled her pack off her back and drew back the string, revealing a heaping portion of venison she had collected after dinner.

"A good bit, this night," she told him proudly.

Bahdlahn nodded, but a cloud passed over his face.

"What?" Aoleyn asked.

"Less food and an earlier greeting would please me more," he explained. "I would take any word you speak over any morsel of food."

Aoleyn stared at him, her heart breaking. How lonely he must be, of course. He was up here all day, every day, quite certainly exiled and alone.

"Why don't you run?" she asked suddenly.

"I run up and down th'Way often."

"I mean away. Why don't you run away? They wouldn't even know you were gone for . . ."

"The old man comes here every day."

"You'd still have the whole of the night to get away," Aoleyn said.

"They would torture my mother. They've promised me."

Aoleyn winced and fell back a step. Of course they had. Of course the Usgar had levied such weight onto Bahdlahn's shoulders before leaving him up here to do his miserable work—work that would have likely killed him already if she hadn't been bringing him food and healing his many cuts and wounds, some of which were already pus-filled by the time she put the wedstone to them.

Bahdlahn was wearing bonds of guilt and responsibility that were every bit as thick and taut as the ropes often used to bind the slaves in the camp.

Usgar did this. She was Usgar.

Suddenly, Aoleyn wanted to be far from that place.

"In the middle of the ninth month, Iseabal will show her bloody face," Tay Aillig told a trio of young warriors, Aghmor, Ralid, and his nephew, Egard. "So says the Usgar-righinn."

"We will raid the lakemen at the end without worry, then," Ralid reasoned, but Tay Aillig shook his head.

"At the beginning," Tay Aillig explained. "And secretly, without the blessing of the Coven."

That got the attention of the three! Tay Aillig had summoned them specifically, and to an out-of-the-way place, and so they had all been suspicious that something was afoot. This revelation, though, was far more extreme than any had considered. They had whispered among themselves that perhaps the Usgar-laoch meant to participate in this season's raiding, or that he would name Aghmor as the raid leader. But this was something beyond!

Tay Aillig saw the confusion on their faces, so he prompted Aghmor to ask the obvious question.

"The blessings upon the weapons grant us the power to destroy the villagers," the younger warrior pointed out. "What gain in ignoring that?"

"We'll not enter a village," Tay Aillig replied. "Usgar is thick with foodstuffs this season."

"Thin with uamhas," Egard remarked.

"Thick enough," Tay Aillig answered. "We go to the lake to take one lakeman, or woman, or child, it does not matter, and that slave will be brought to Fireach Speuer to await Iseabal's bloody face."

He had the three looking to each other in confusion, which made him smile all the wider.

"And with that slave, we will avenge Brayth," he said, and that brought confused stares that turned into horrified expressions as they each remembered how Brayth had died.

"The fossa?" Aghmor breathed, and swallowed hard.

"We will lure the demon out with the slave and then, we will kill it," Tay Aillig informed them.

They didn't seem very excited about the proposition.

"I know how to kill it," the Usgar-laoch asserted with confidence. "I could have killed it that day when it took Brayth."

"But you did not!" Aghmor said.

"Because I did not know the truth of the beast until we crashed together, and then it was too late to strike. But now I know." He considered reaching into his secret pouch to bring forth the amethyst-speckled sunstone, but decided against it. He had never shown that to any in the tribe. If the Coven ever found out the properties of that item, the result would not be good for him.

"You are afraid," Tay Aillig said against the wall of silence. "You doubt me."

"Never, War Leader!" all of them said immediately.

"Yes, you do," he countered. "And you are right to be fearful. But I am not, because I know. I will kill the demon fossa. I need only a lure to bring it out, and you three to corner the beast that I can finish it."

"Could we not just use one of the uamhas we have?" Ralid asked.

"The idiot boy, Thump," Egard added, and the others nodded.

"He works the stairs of th'Way in service to the Coven," Tay Aillig told them. "Usgar-forfach Raibert watches him. He will not do. I will send you three down to find a slave. You three alone. More glory is yours."

"And we will kill the fossa?" Aghmor asked.

"I will kill the fossa," Tay Aillig corrected. "But in that, too, you will gain glory and standing . . . if you survive."

The young warriors exchanged looks again, full of trepidation, but mixed with intrigue.

"When must we choose?" Ralid asked.

"You already have," said Tay Aillig. "The choice was made when I asked you out here, and the choice was agreed when you came to this gathering. Now you'll be silent, for it's our own secret, and any who're whispering will feel my wrath."

He reached behind a tree and produced a large sack, tossing it to the ground before the five. Its contents clanged and scraped and the top fell open, revealing a cache of weapons. Not the crystal-tipped Usgar spears, but metal weapons the raiders had taken from the villagers over the years.

"Pick and practice," Tay Aillig told them. "With these, you will catch my lure, and with these, you will help me kill the demon fossa."

He slowly brought his index finger up over his pursed lips, and left them with a not-subtle reminder. "And . . ."

30

THE OWL AND THE SNAKE

Aoleyn emerged from the crystal caverns to find a blustery and chilly wind, the first harbinger of an approaching autumn. When one gust hit her so hard that it moved her sideways a couple of steps, she had to wonder if she could safely fly this night. Would she glide down the mountain only to be blown into a rocky crag?

The young woman dismissed the thought, confident that the moonstone she had secured to her belly would allow her to get down safely.

Indeed, Aoleyn was full of confidence this night—so much so that she had considered exiting the caverns by daring the darkness of the pit once more to float up through Craos'a'diad. She had even started that way, ready to face the ghosts, or whatever they were.

She had changed her mind, though, for she had accomplished much, but had already spent too long out here, again.

Besides, she wanted to try out her new powers, and her new anklet! She had been quite busy, weaving a wedstone wire in and out of the skin of her left ankle, a double strand. On one were two small bars of the gray stone with which she could create lightning, along with a pretty blue stone she had not completely discerned. Even more confusing to her were the purplish chips of sapphire on that second strand. She knew the gem from the mundane jewelry the tribe had stolen from lakemen, but she couldn't quite discern its magical properties, although it seemed to have something to do with enhancing, or shaping, the energy of other stones.

Yes, the blue zircon and the sapphires would need much further investigation, Aoleyn decided, but not this night, for she had also crafted new earrings, and these she knew how to use, and more importantly, why to use them. The powerful garnet dangled on a wedstone chain from her right ear, but her left had a cuff of turquoise, and with a cat's-eye gemstone set upon it. She closed her eyes and tapped that ear now, using the touch to focus her energy.

She opened her eyes to a new world, it seemed, where the low starlight was no hindrance to her vision, other than to steal color. Fireach Speuer was all grays and shadows before her, but every rock, every blade of grass was distinct. She could see as well as the nocturnal hunting cats, could navigate by starlight as if it were high noon.

She spent a long while adjusting to this new vision, basking in the serene beauty of it, filled with awe and appreciation.

She had intended to go straight off to visit Bahdlahn, but it would have to wait. For Aoleyn wanted to fly with her new vision, wanted to feel the wind . . . and defeat it!

She moved to the edge of the nearest cliff and just let herself fall off, bringing forth the powers of the green and blue-white stones set to her belly. She was gliding then, riding the night winds as easily as a hawk, floating with magic instead of wings. Down she went, down and around the mountain until she came in sight of the fires of the Usgar encampment.

Burning low, she noted, reminding her that she had been in the cavern for a long while this night. It bothered her more than she had expected to realize that she wouldn't see Bahdlahn.

With a sigh, Aoleyn floated to a nearby pine, the tallest she could see, and settled easily upon a high branch, using just enough of the malachite's powers to keep the branch from bending. There, from that perch, she studied the nighttime world around her.

Movement on the ground to the side caught her attention and she smiled widely when a beautiful fox trotted out gracefully from some brush.

This would be her first "capture," she thought, and she brought her hand back to her left ear, to the turquoise cuff, and she focused upon that and upon the wedstone to free her spirit, and like an arrow, Aoleyn's sensibilities shot away, flying for the fox, flying into the fox!

And she could see the world through the fox's eyes, and hear the world through the fox's ears! And she wanted to hear the fox's call, so she compelled it to cry out.

Most of all, Aoleyn read the animal's thoughts, and felt as it felt. It knew she was there, or that something was inside of it, at least. But another urge called.

Aoleyn heard the scrabbling of a creature—she thought it a large creature, but no, it was just a mouse, some distance away, scrambling under some leaves.

The fox stood very still, ears turning, honing in, and then the fox jumped up high and came straight down.

Aoleyn tasted the blood of a mouse. The shock of the kill and suddenness of the attack had her fleeing back to her own form.

Up high in the tree, the young woman giggled at her own squeamishness, but oh, what a grand gift this was! To understand the animals, to commune with them, to see and hear and smell the world through the animals of Fireach Speuer!

She heard a hoot.

She went perfectly still, perfectly silent, scanning the trees with her enhanced cat's-eye vision. Finally, she spotted the source, a great horned owl, sitting on a branch not so far away.

From her nighttime soaring about the mountain, Aoleyn thought she understood the freedom of flying, but her movements seemed crude and clumsy indeed after she entered the sensibilities of that owl!

She could see many times better than her cat's-eye, many times better than the fox, even. The sounds of the mountain assailed her. Hoots and howls, rustling leaves, blowing grasses, the wind through the stones. Such a dizzying, beautiful cacophony! The sounds of the mountain night were more alive than any dull-sensed human could begin to imagine!

It took little urging for her to get the bird to take wing, and then Aoleyn knew true freedom. Gliding silently, the owl cut through the wind and maneuvered through the trees with such perfect ease, passing dizzyingly close to tree trunks and thick branches—through the owl's amazing ears, Aoleyn even heard herself gasp from way back on her pine perch!

She forgot all about Bahdlahn.

She willed the bird closer to the Usgar campfire as soon as it came within sight, curious to see the encampment through this creature's eyes. What secrets might she see?

She was charmed indeed when she first flew past the camp, for it did not disappoint. She heard Mairen snoring—and it sounded like thunder—though she was certain that if she had been walking by the Crystal Maven's tent in her own body, with her own ears, she wouldn't have heard it at all!

She heard giggling from another tent, but decided not to pursue it. She heard as the fire crackled, and then saw one of the warrior sentries peeing in the woods.

She felt naughty and godlike all at once!

The owl swooped over and around the large encampment, then off into the night, but before it left the Usgar behind, Aoleyn noted something else, something curious.

She saw a form, a woman, slipping away from one of the tents, rushing from shadow to shadow into the night and back toward the uamhas pine grove. It wasn't a warrior going to rape a slave, she knew, so she urged the owl to turn back. It wasn't an Usgar at all.

She caught only one more glimpse of the woman, but it was enough for her to know: it was Innevah, Bahdlahn's mother.

But why?

Thoughts of Innevah's strange movements in the Usgar camp had flown from Aoleyn's mind by the time she had released the owl from her magical grasp and returned fully to her own body, still perched easily upon the branch—although that branch was bending more now, as she had lost some concentration on the levitational magic.

Still, she didn't fall. She leaped away, and brought forth the magical powers of her own flight. How clumsy she felt, then, compared with the freedom afforded in the owl's form, and Aoleyn winced to think how slow and clumsy she'd be without the magical powers she had discovered!

It was too late to go to Bahdlahn, she knew, so she set down outside the camp, behind her tent, and quietly sneaked in. Her mind was so full of possibilities and thrills of that night that she feared she wouldn't sleep at all.

She was wrong: she was soon snoring, thoroughly exhausted from her overuse of magic. But she dreamed the most amazing dreams, of flying and dancing with the animals. She also dreamed of Bahdlahn— perfect, wonderfully wicked dreams!

She awoke with a start, surprised that it was light, and that, from the sounds around her, it had come some time ago! She wasn't sure why she had awakened so suddenly, until she heard a scream, a horrifying shriek that chilled her to the bone.

She rolled out of bed and was moving before she even had time to think about what could be wrong, scrambling to and through the tent flap.

Many were out and about, calling and rushing to and fro, but most were converging on the center of that camp, near the main bonfire pit, and Aoleyn's eyes widened when she noted the source of the screams.

The witch, Caia, staggered. She wore only her shift, which had been torn. Looking down at Caia's bare legs she noticed a white-furred serpent, hanging by one fang from her inner thigh, its length dragging on the ground behind her. The snake wriggled, coiling about, trying to pull free, for its fang was hooked and caught deep into the woman's flesh.

A warrior ran over and stomped upon the serpent, and Caia's forward motion tore it free of her leg at last, sending her stumbling and tumbling to the ground.

The serpent turned on the man, coiling to strike, but it was Aoleyn, amazingly and completely on instinct, who struck first, stomping her foot and calling upon the blue stone in her anklet.

A patch of ice appeared beneath the man and the snake, and when the snake struck, it slid and missed, and when the man tried to dodge, he slipped and fell backward, crashing into the scorched remains of the previous night's fire. Now other warriors converged, stabbing their spears to kill the serpent, while some women, including Connebragh of the Coven, ran to the fallen Caia, who was sobbing and shaking her head, spitting curses in denial.

Aoleyn immediately shrank back, not wanting to reveal that her jewelry, most of which remained hidden, was more than ornamental. What had she done? She wasn't even certain! Several of her gemstones had called to her at once, her mind a jumble of how to react.

The blue stone on her anklet could create ice.

Now she knew.

But she didn't want anyone else to!

She certainly didn't maintain the enchantment, and the warriors all moved about curiously, shrugging and shaking their heads. One called out for the witch responsible to come forth and be hailed as a hero, but when no one took credit, another claimed that the white-furred snake must have done it!

"A foul beast with freezing breath!" another agreed.

Aoleyn stayed far back and out of the debate. She kept her gaze locked on Caia, and it was not a pleasant sight. The woman went into violent convulsions and began spewing up white foamy spittle.

Connebragh prayed over her with a wedstone crystal, but seemed to be doing little good. Aoleyn thought she should go and help, for surely Caia's life was more important than her secret. But Mairen appeared and ran to Connebragh's side, and Aoleyn shrank back farther, melting back into her tent to dress for the day.

Only then did she remember the sight of Innevah running from a tent—from Caia's tent, she realized—when she had flown past in the body of the owl.

Mairen exited Caia's tent, exhausted from her long hours of working the wedstone to alleviate the poor woman's terrible suffering. Three of the twelve Coven sisters were in there now, to be replaced by three others in shifts that went all day and all night.

The sisters poured out their hearts and magic for poor Caia, whose eyes were rolled back, who shivered constantly while drooling white spittle without pause.

Mairen rubbed her face and made her way to her own tent.

They had to try.

She noticed Tay Aillig coming at her before she reached the tent flap, so she picked up her pace, not wanting to deal with the man, with anyone. But, unsurprisingly, Tay Aillig just pushed into the tent behind her.

"I am tired, Usgar-laoch," she told him, holding her arm up to keep him at bay.

He just pushed past her.

"Aoleyn will replace Caia as the thirteenth," he said as she started to tell him to leave.

Mairen's protest stuck in her throat with surprise that this man would say such a thing! Tay Aillig was Usgar-laoch, yes, and among the most powerful men in the tribe, but the Coven was not his concern!

"The thirteenth?" she gasped. "Caia still breathes!"

"You cannot save her. It was a white-furred viper. There is no magic to defeat that poison."

"She still breathes!"

"We've seen this before," Tay Aillig replied somberly, shaking his head.

"This is not your concern."

"It is. Aoleyn will be the thirteenth."

"That is not your choice!" Mairen told him, and she started past him, grabbing him by the arm to escort him out of her tent.

But the powerful man tugged back, spinning Mairen on her feet to face him. "Aoleyn," he said.

Mairen tried to pull free, but the man wouldn't let her go, and nothing short of a lightning bolt would break this one's iron grip. And now he was hurting her. She wriggled again, futilely.

"It is not wise for a man to hurt the Usgar-righinn," Mairen warned, regaining her composure and pointedly straightening.

She was surprised when Tay Aillig let her go. "Aoleyn," he said, but it was more a plea now.

"Caia—"

"Is soon dead!" he said sharply, jolting her with his intensity and reminding her that she couldn't get away from him unless he allowed her to!

And the look on his face!

There it was, Mairen realized, and of course, she had suspected as much from the first whispers of Tay Aillig's surprising choice in a wife. He wasn't in love with Aoleyn, but with the power the promising young witch could bring to him. Mairen had heard of Brayth's exploits in the battle, before the fossa had taken him. Even in that fight with the fossa, the man, or rather, Aoleyn working through him, had floated and thrown bolts of powerful lightning at the demon beast. Truly, Aoleyn had shown herself well in that battle, by all accounts of those in the field, and now Tay Aillig had come to believe that she would serve his ambitions well.

His ambitions. Despite the threatening circumstances, a smile began to creep onto Mairen's face.

"You would be Usgar-triath," she said. "That is your plan."

She knew she had hit on the truth as Tay Aillig backed away a step.

"Elder Raibert is not well. This you know," Mairen reasoned.

Tay Aillig didn't respond.

Mairen moved up very close to him. "I am the Crystal Maven," she reminded him. "Usgar-righinn. There is none more powerful than Mairen in the song of Usgar."

She backed away when Tay Aillig laughed at her.

"So you wish me to claim you as my wife instead of Aoleyn," Tay Aillig said, denying nothing.

"What you desire is power," Mairen replied, and she looked up at him coyly.

"You are fifteen winters my senior."

"And she is fifteen your junior."

"And still young and beautiful," Tay Aillig said viciously. "You should have begged me a decade ago, old hag."

Mairen's expression went stone cold. "They will stop you," she promised. "You are Usgar-laoch, but haven't the tartan to claim as Usgar-triath."

"Elder Raibert grows frail."

"Ahn'Namay will be named Usgar-forfach when Raibert is no more. There will be an Usgar-laoch and there will be an Usgar-forfach," Mairen said with confidence.

Tay Aillig backed up a step and began to laugh. "Unless I service Mairen as her husband," he said slyly.

"Usgar-triath, Usgar-righinn," she said. She was surprised that she had been so forward here. Her position was secure, after all, as the most powerful woman in the tribe, the unquestioned leader of the Coven. She had been married twice, both long ago, but had been alone for decades now. She didn't need the companionship of a man, certainly, and though she thought Tay Aillig quite handsome and found his strength and exploits extremely attractive, this wasn't about any of that.

No, she wanted to win, wanted the most desired man in all of Usgar to desire her.

She wanted to beat Aoleyn.

That last thought had caught the Crystal Maven off-balance; she had to work hard to keep the surprise off her face. Aoleyn was small and dark. For all the potential of the young woman—no, the girl, Mairen decided—she was not even of the Coven, and could only join that sisterhood with *her* blessing.

Lots of Usgar women had potential, but only one could be Usgar-righinn.

It made no sense to Mairen that she should care about this, about Tay Aillig and the girl he apparently found desirable, at all.

But she did.

"Aoleyn is the thirteenth, old woman," Tay Aillig said then, with angry finality. "If you do not do this, you will betray all that you hold dear of Usgar tradition, and you will betray me. That is not a wise choice, I assure you."

The coldness in his voice sent a shiver through Mairen's spine, but she held firm against the overt threat.

Tay Aillig snorted at her, turned, and left the tent.

As soon as he was gone, Mairen slumped and had to lean on a table to keep her feet. She was truly exhausted by her work with Caia, and now emotionally drained from this unexpected and troubling encounter. How dare the Usgar-laoch demand of her his choice for the sacred Coven!

How dare he even speak of the thirteenth while poor Caia drew breath!

31

HEADLONG

The rope was still there. It was part of the tree now, with the branch actually growing around it, almost, it seemed to Talmadge, as if the tree had come to accept the rope.

He thought that fitting. Certainly his feelings about this place had changed, more dramatically than he had understood until he had stepped off his canoe and confronted the place once more.

The ghost of Badger was long gone, exorcised from his thoughts, the weight vanished.

Now he stood before the tree and he thought of Khotai, the love of his life, the woman who had shown him that his life was a journey, as narrow or wide as he desired it to be.

He missed her terribly in that moment, but still a smile of acceptance creased his face.

The image of her severed leg flashed in his thoughts, but it was a fleeting thing, chased away by the many other sweet moments that had defined their years together. He wanted her back—desperately so—but he also appreciated that he had known her at all.

Talmadge sighed and dropped his pack to the ground. He would camp here this night and set off to the south in the late morning—never again would he be on Loch Beag when the morning fog hadn't fully cleared!

He would never again remain on the lake for long, nor would he go more than a few feet from the shore.

Car Seileach was a half-day's paddle, but it would likely take Talmadge three days to get there.

He looked at the tree; he thought of Khotai. He was in no hurry.

He knew that Mairen's reasoning was sound; the witch's insistence that he would not so easily ascend to a position of complete leadership haunted Tay Aillig through the days. On more than one occasion, he even fancied ways he might kill Ahn'Namay; the only thing stopping him from making the attempt was his knowledge that there were others besides that one man who could lay claim to the title of Usgar-forfach.

That title was the sticking point, not the man. The tribe was typically led by three people—Usgar-forfach, Usgar-righinn, and Usgar-laoch—not two. Usgar-triath was a rare title, saved for only the most exceptional men—men who were still young enough and strong enough to lead in times of battle, but also wise enough to serve as judge in all the mundane matters of the tribe. Even though Raibert had made the title of Usgar-forfach somewhat of a joke, for the man did not even accompany the tribe to the summer encampment and was, by all accounts, quite unstable, when he passed, there would be many voices calling for a replacement.

Tay Aillig needed to do something dramatic to change that.

His hand went reflexively to his waist, to the hidden sunstone and amethyst jewel. He considered his encounter with the fossa, when he had sent the beast flying. He was fairly certain that he had stung it badly, without even trying.

But he could not know. Could he really hope to kill the thing?

Tay Aillig took a deep breath and nodded, still not sure of that, but he was certain that in the previous encounter, the fossa had been wholly blind to him.

Perhaps he and the three he had chosen wouldn't win against the fossa, but still, Tay Aillig was convinced that he could hide from the fossa and get away.

Thus, it was worth the chance. For if he won, if he returned with the head of the dire fossa demon, none would dare speak against him in his ascent to Usgar-triath.

Not even Mairen.

The folk of Car Seileach greeted Talmadge with warm hugs and fine meals as if he hadn't missed a season. The last time they had seen him as a broken thing reeling from the loss of Khotai.

This night, under the late-summer stars, Talmadge finally told the tale of the attack on the lake. Gasps and mumbled prayers came back at him when he spoke of the monster—even though all on Loch Beag knew of the creature, very few had ever actually seen it.

"Khotai is the first eaten by Sgath since before you first arrived, Talmadge," Whisperer Bragha, the leader of Car Seileach, explained to him. "And you, Talmadge, are the only man I have ever known to escape an attack. The gods blessed your way."

"The gods blessed your way," all the others said with reverence.

Talmadge stared at the leader, the whisperer, of the village. Bragha was not a physically imposing woman, though she was tall. Her hair and eyes shone lightly, giving her a wispy appearance, almost as if she might float away on a breeze. But any who had dealt with her knew that this only made Bragha more impressive and formidable. She could put anyone, particularly a man, off-balance with a sidelong glance, and she often did so to her advantage. Her remark truly touched Talmadge. To have the leader suggest that he had been blessed by the gods was about the highest form of acceptance any outsider could ever hope for here around Loch Beag.

"Perhaps if I knew your gods better, I wouldn't be so afraid to be on the water," Talmadge replied with a self-deprecating chuckle. "It took me many days to cross Loch Beag."

"Blessed," Whisperer Bragha corrected. "Not bless. They pushed you to shore. A meal escaped is often a meal delayed and less often a meal avoided."

The chuckles around the fire clued Talmadge in to the woman's meaning. They said that he had been lucky, not necessarily that the luck would hold. They also reminded him that he was dealing with a whisperer who weighed every word very carefully.

"We are eager to take your wares," Bragha went on. "Your absence was hurtful. But we are short with pearls and you are thick with gold and silver."

Talmadge nodded, for it was true enough; he had stockpiled quite the haul of trinkets, rings, fine chains, and jewels over the last couple of years, mostly because without Loch Beag, he had few connections who wanted such items in exchange for his fish and furs. Apparently, he had done better in accumulating barter than this tribe had done in gathering payment!

"As always, Whisperer Bragha, Car Seileach is first to choose," he said respectfully.

"How far will Talmadge go this year? The winds speak of early winter and you have spoken of short paddles on the water."

"I hope to visit as far as Fasach Crann," he replied, and only when the name left his mouth did he realize just how badly he wanted to see that place again. "But I would keep my canoe here, if you agree, and walk."

That brought some surprised whispers around the fire.

"You will not find many days there, if you even get there," Whisperer Bragha warned. "Your walk is longer by many days."

Talmadge nodded his understanding. The southern expanse of Loch Beag was broken with swift rivers flowing down from the mountains, and long inlets and marshes, and in many areas along his way, he would have to swing far inland to circumvent the obstacles. Still, those same inlets, like the one he had passed with Khotai just beyond Carrachan Shoal, were the reason he had found his canoe so far from shore and so vulnerable to Sgath. He had no desire to try his luck with that again, no matter how inconvenient or inefficient a hike might be.

"And your path will bring you to Frith Fireach," Bragha warned, referring to the foothills of the great mountain.

Talmadge nodded, not surprised, but still determined to walk to Fasach Crann and the villages in between that coveted place and this one.

"And the Reaper Moon will wear red this year, so whisper the creatures," said Bragha.

Talmadge nodded, thinking he would do well to remember to have himself in a village for the three days of the fullest moon. He recalled his night with Khotai the last time he had seen such a moon, when they had witnessed some great commotion on the mountain.

Yes, there were demons on Fireach Speuer, Usgar deamhain, at least, if not some greater, more sinister force. Still, Talmadge would walk, to Fasach Crann and back. Whatever might lurk up there could not be worse than the creature the tribes called Sgath.

And so he walked out of Car Seileach a couple of days later, confident of his choice.

"You're lucky you haven't lost it!" Aoleyn said to Bahdlahn as she examined his hand and the blackened finger he had crushed under a stone the previous day. She immediately sighed and assumed a more sympathetic pose, realizing that part of her anger was coming from guilt, for not having come to visit the previous night.

She went to work immediately with the wedstone magic, imparting healing warmth to the ever-uncomplaining young man. She couldn't believe that she had found him working, and using that very broken hand. His tolerance for pain shocked her.

And reminded her, painfully, that the lives of the uamhas were ones of pure stoicism, else they would be murdered. Murdered by her tribe.

Aoleyn felt some atonement in healing Bahdlahn, though it was remedy to but a tiny bit of the pain the traditions of Usgar inflicted on these poor folk.

"You should be done for the night," Aoleyn said to him, and she sent another round of healing magic into his hand. "For two nights. You need to rest . . ."

She stopped when she saw Bahdlahn looking at her and shaking his head emphatically. No, not looking at her, she realized, but looking past her. The young woman ducked as she turned about, and a good thing she had, for coming up th'Way, not far down the trail and stairs, was Elder Raibert!

With a gasp, Aoleyn rolled aside and crawled under and behind a bush, settling in just as Raibert came around the last bend, and over the last step.

"What are you doing, slave?" the old man asked.

Bahdlahn held up his bruised, broken hand and gave a little whimper, and raised the tone of his voice, Aoleyn noted, as if to mimic her own. He was trying to cover for her.

Clever, Aoleyn thought, and behind the bush, she shook her head as she considered the young man's earlier name, Thump, and the derisive implications.

"Do you think that excuses you from work?" Raibert asked sharply, and he brought his arm up, small whip in hand.

It was all Aoleyn could manage to stay concealed behind the bush, for truly she wanted to leap out when Raibert cracked the whip on poor Bahdlahn's shoulder—a not uncommon occurrence, she had learned in her many visits to the young man. Even though she should not have been surprised, though, actually seeing the brutality brought tears welling to Aoleyn's black eyes, and a level of fury she didn't know she possessed. She wanted to leap out of the brush, igniting the power of the gray bars and launching Raibert away with a pair of sizzling lightning bolts!

But she didn't. For Bahdlahn's sake more than her own, the frightened young woman stayed hidden and quiet.

"Move along!" Raibert roared, and he whipped Bahdlahn across the back as the young man hustled back to his work. "You finish that step this night or I'll be taking all the skin from your back, idiot boy!"

He cracked the whip again and again, in the air over Bahdlahn's head. Aoleyn could barely see the old wretch from her angle, but enough to recognize the glee stamped upon his ugly face.

Again, she had to fight to contain herself. She thought she could easily dispatch the fool and drop him into a ravine, and who would be the wiser?

But then she was crouching again, and even lower, sucking in her breath in terror, when a voice called out from far down th'Way.

"Raibert! Usgar-forfach, I would speak with you!"

Aoleyn knew that voice all too well.

"Finish the step!" Raibert said one last time, and he cracked the whip in the air just above Bahdlahn's head and turned about to greet Tay Aillig.

Aoleyn flattened on the ground, desperate to make herself invisible. She tried to remind herself that she could get away, that she could ease back here and leap from a high cliff.

But where would she go? There was no way she could be seen up here in the midst of night and ever go back to the Usgar camp!

Tay Aillig began talking to Raibert, some questioning about how the old man could possibly stay alive up here year after year, but Aoleyn hardly noted the words, more concerned about whether their conversation would cover her retreat.

Aoleyn thought her chance had come. She began to silently call upon the green stone set to her belly to lessen her weight so she could silently recede, but then she heard Tay Aillig become more specific with Raibert, and with words she could not dismiss.

"Why has the fossa not taken you?" Tay Aillig asked.

Aoleyn's fear melted into curiosity.

"How can Raibert stay alone up here, year after year, and not be devoured by the demon that haunts Fireach Speuer?"

How, indeed, Aoleyn wondered, for she had seen the fossa up on a ledge not far from this place, and not far from Raibert's tent in the Usgar winter camp,

"Why would you speak of the fossa?"

"Iseabal will show her red face this season."

"I care not," Raibert answered sternly. "The demon fossa comes through this place, but dares not stay. Usgar's song hurts its mind, you know. Hurts its mind, I say, and drives it mad." Raibert gave a little wheezing laugh.

Aoleyn winced and brought her hand to her belly when he admitted, "Drives us all mad."

She remembered the crone, her first teacher, who had told her much the same thing. Aoleyn heard the words in her mind as clearly as the crone had told her: *One mustn't stay there too long, or sure you'll be driven mad.*

When she had used Raibert to argue that point, the crone had told her in no uncertain terms that this man, the Elder of Usgar, was quite mad.

Aoleyn felt the gemstones she had wedded to her body, heard their song in her heart. She would know them better, she quietly assured herself. They would not drive her mad.

"The demon fossa can'no resist the song of Usgar, yet can'no withstand the magic, not in body, but in mind," Raibert went on, and Aoleyn swallowed hard, for it was almost as if he was reading, and mocking, her thoughts.

She saw Raibert give a little shrug, against the widening grin of Tay Aillig—what was he about, Aoleyn wondered?

"Might that we're not so different, we Usgar men and the deamhan fossa, eh?" Raibert said. "Might that we're more bound to Iseabal than Usgar, who makes whores of our women."

"Perhaps you are," Tay Aillig replied, shocking Aoleyn. "Are you an old woman, then?"

Aoleyn couldn't tell if Raibert was taking the insult in stride, or if he was fighting back with a mocking taunt, when he replied, "Is that your play, Usgar-laoch?"

"When you are dead, I will be Usgar-triath," Tay Aillig declared.

Raibert laughed again. "You fancy your spatt'rings thick, young warrior?" he said dismissively, and he laughed, as if the whole thing was a joke, and a preposterous one at that. With a wave of his hand, Elder Raibert started down th'Way, back to the winter encampment.

"Oh, it will be," Aoleyn heard Tay Aillig promise, too quietly for the departing man to hear, "after Iseabal's Blood Moon."

Aoleyn's eyes went wide, for she knew at once what Tay Aillig meant, and what he had planned. It was so clear to her: Tay Aillig meant to kill the fossa, and use that unprecedented glory to claim the tribe as his own!

The young woman replayed Raibert's words and thought back to the fight between Brayth and the demon creature, of how her lightning—bolts that would have melted a man, she was sure, for she had felt the power flowing through her spirit and through Brayth's spear—had done nothing to the fossa.

Except to madden it even more!

How might Tay Aillig . . .

"Enjoy your time, idiot," the brute shouted at Bahdlahn, breaking Aoleyn's train of thought. "Perhaps Usgar-triath Tay Aillig will suffer you to live."

Tay Aillig's laugh had no mirth in it at all. It sounded purely wicked to Aoleyn, as was confirmed for her as Tay Aillig finished.

"Likely not."

32

THE CRYSTAL MAVEN'S PLAY

"It is secure," Aghmor assured Tay Aillig, referring to a shallow cavern down the rocky slope on the back side of the uamhas grove.

"You will stay with the prisoner until Iseabal shows her face," Tay Aillig instructed Aghmor. "And one of you with him always," he added to Ralid and Egard. "The other to me and back with word."

The three younger men nodded.

"We go for one thing now," Tay Aillig reminded. "And only one. A single prisoner, nothing more."

"There will be no raid on the lake this season?" Ralid asked.

Tay Aillig shrugged, because it didn't matter. The Blood Moon was expected in two weeks; if a major raid was to happen it would have to be after that. Few expected it, though, for the winds were already turning and there was talk of breaking the summer camp immediately following the Blood Moon for an early journey to the winter plateau.

The War Leader held out his hands, beckoning. "Give me your weapons, that I might have them blessed," he said.

"This was to be secret, you said," Aghmor replied, handing over his spear.

Tay Aillig nodded and smiled. "Our secret. We four and one other. Now go and prepare. We leave at the dawn."

He gathered the four spears, a pair of hand axes, and a pair of long daggers, and hustled quietly around the back of the encampment, coming to the tent of Aoleyn. With a glance to make sure he was not seen, he slipped into the tent through the young woman's cleverly hidden back flap, and waited.

"You cannot," Connebragh said, her face a mask of shock.

Mairen fixed her with an icy stare, reminding her that it was not wise to challenge the word of the Usgar-righinn.

"Elara's daughter is—" Connebragh started.

"The choice is mine, given to me by Usgar's whispers."

"Gavina?" another of the witches remarked, seeming as perplexed as Connebragh.

"A snaggletoothed dullard," Connebragh said.

Mairen slapped her across the face. Connebragh fell back, anger flashing in her gray eyes. But only for a moment, as she stared at the unrelenting Mairen. Her face flushed with shame, for such words were not appropriate—certainly not now! The thirteen of the Coven, no matter who they were, demanded respect, without question!

"I am . . . surprised, Usgar-righinn," Connebragh said, lowering her gaze to the floor and shaking her head. "Aoleyn's power in the crystal caves seemed—"

"It is about more than simple power," Mairen told her, told them all. "And I was surprised, too," she said softening her tone and putting a hand on Connebragh's shoulder. "But I'll not question Usgar's will."

"Gavina has affinity, and she understands her place. I am not sure that any of us could say the same of the brat Aoleyn."

"There will be another time," another of the witches remarked.

Mairen snapped her head around to freeze the witch with a glower.

"Not for that one," she said, with more emotion than she should have, she realized, for she did not want any of her witches to come to realize that this was personal, not the whisper of their god.

"I don't understand," Aoleyn said. She had returned to her tent after supper, hoping to be out on the mountain quickly, but only to find Tay Aillig waiting for her.

"You do not need to understand. You only need to do what I have told you to do."

Aoleyn looked at the handful of weapons the Usgar-laoch had placed before her. He had told her to bless them, to excite the magic within them to make them more powerful. But there was no raid or approaching battle, no signs of sidhe about, that Aoleyn had heard. And if it was for a hunt, the men would have used different weapons than these, crystal spear tips thick with different magic, like turquoise and malachite.

These were weapons of war.

"I can'no . . . I mean, I am not supposed . . ." she stammered, and she wasn't even sure of where to begin.

"You can and you will, because I told you to," came the simple answer.

Aoleyn swallowed hard, terribly afraid. Memories of her encounter with Brayth filled her head, of how the man had taken her, and her virginity, right there in front of Seonagh. He hadn't said a word, just had done his business and left.

Was Tay Aillig going to do the same now? She certainly didn't want any sexual intimacy with this man who claimed that he would be her husband, but if he demanded it and she refused, the result would be violent.

Aoleyn did a quick survey of the gemstones and reminded herself that she had become an instrument of Usgar, a living weapon.

"Be quick!" Tay Aillig demanded.

"We have no fire."

"You don't need a fire. That is for the entertainment of the onlookers and the pride of the witches."

Aoleyn looked at him curiously at that. Was it true? Probably, she thought, but how would he know that?

No matter. Aoleyn took up the weapons one by one and sent her thoughts into their respective crystals. She found the song and pulled it forth, amplifying it with her own energy until it reverberated within the crystal, a vibration that would last for days.

She felt other curious sensations, mostly from the sapphire strand about her ankle, hinting to alterations in the various songs she had heard, but she dismissed them, not willing to take any chances at all here. She would do exactly as Tay Aillig had demanded, as quickly as possible, and hope that he'd then go on his way and bother her no more.

Her hand trembled as she at last handed the eighth weapon back, for she feared that Tay Aillig would spin her about and bend her over.

But he simply nodded, gathered up the haul, and said, "You will tell no one." Then he slipped out the back flap of the tent.

Aoleyn exhaled. What was that about? Why had he come to her, in private, to awaken the power of weapons used only for raids when there was no raid?

She rested back and sat there for a long while in the dark, wondering; her thoughts turned to that newer sensation, the one from the sapphire chain. Of all the gemstones she had set upon her body, she wasn't sure about those small flecks of sapphire. They were strong with magic, but from everything she could tell, their effects would alter shape, power, or form to the other magic. Thus far, they hadn't revealed any of their own powers.

Perhaps she would learn better when she was entered into the Coven, she decided, and she began to collect her wits, and thought to collect some food, so that she could go and visit Bahdlahn and the caves. That had been her intention, at least, but the visit from Tay Aillig had unnerved her. She couldn't risk a journey this night. Perhaps he had actually noted her hiding in the brush on th'Way when he had come to speak with Raibert.

Perhaps Tay Aillig meant to surprise Aoleyn and Bahdlahn with the very weapons she had just enchanted, that he and his companions could kill them both.

It was all too much for the young woman, so she sat there, in the dark, and pondered.

———

As he approached the rendezvous, Tay Aillig spotted Ralid and Aghmor alone, and when he paused to consider that, the War Leader hung back, hidden in the shadows. Soon after, he noted the approach of the third man, coming down fast from the Usgar camp. He let Egard beat him to the others, then came in cautiously, eavesdropping.

"It's true!" he heard Egard say.

"Why?" Ralid replied.

"Because Brayth died?" a clearly shaken Aghmor asked. "The War Leader will not be pleased."

Tay Aillig crashed into their midst. "About what?" he demanded.

The three looked to one another nervously, but Aghmor spoke up before Tay Aillig could demand an answer once more.

"Mairen has chosen Gavina for the Coven."

It was all Tay Aillig could do to hold onto the bundle of weapons.

"How do you know this?" he demanded, but he couldn't keep the rage out of his voice.

"We heard two women talking about it, just over the rise," Aghmor explained.

"The whispers are throughout the camp. Mairen was in Gavina's tent telling her," added Egard. "Balgair told me," he added, referring to an older man, Gavina's husband. "He lamented that it could not have happened sooner, when he was still able to hunt and fight."

Tay Aillig huffed, but didn't respond. He sorted his own weapons and threw the other six to the ground at the feet of his three warriors.

"They are blessed," he told them. "You go, and do not fail me! A single prisoner, nothing more. I will find you at the cave on the dawn of the sixth day. If you don't have my captive, then better for you to die in the foothills."

He turned about and stormed away, gnashing his teeth with frustration. How could this have happened? How dare Mairen!

There was much he needed to learn, but what Tay Aillig did know was that this would not stand.

———

Aoleyn finally found her resolve and the confidence that Tay Aillig would not be back to her that night. She gathered up a heavy cloak and moved for the back flap. She stopped when the front flap opened instead, letting the light of a lantern flood into the room.

"Usgar-righinn?" she asked, recognizing Mairen and Connebragh entering her tent.

It occurred to her then that Tay Aillig's demands of her might have been at Mairen's request. Was blessing those weapons some sort of a test? The last test before she was asked to join the Coven?

"Sit," Mairen told her, waving absently at a pile of furs just inside the door.

The woman's tone gave Aoleyn pause, for it was not the voice she would expect from one who was about to offer her the greatest opportunity to which an Usgar woman could aspire. She shuffled over and plopped down on the rugs obediently, but neither Mairen nor Connebragh joined her there.

Connebragh, in fact, went instead for the cabinet where Aoleyn's magical crystals were kept, and without asking, the woman gathered them up.

"You'll not need these now," Mairen explained.

Aoleyn didn't ask outright, but wondered if perhaps she would be given new crystals, more powerful and diverse.

"Yes, Usgar-righinn," she replied.

"Gavina will join the Coven as the thirteenth witch," Mairen stated bluntly. "It will not be you, girl. You are not ready, and may never be. You must learn now the more mundane tasks of an Usgar woman, and do them well, so that some man might still claim you as his wife."

Aoleyn wanted to reply, but her lips would not move! Gavina? Gavina was nearly twenty years her senior and could barely evoke magic from the crystals! Aoleyn liked her well enough, for she was possessed of some sweetness, but she hardly heard the song of Usgar even when it sounded like a leopard's roar in Aoleyn's heart!

How could they pick her? What would Gavina bring to the Coven beyond Aoleyn?

Aoleyn had more power pierced to her body now than most, if not all, collections of crystals in the tribe! And she had found a truer method to use the song of Usgar!

How she wanted to show that to Mairen at that awful moment— and it was an awful moment, more so than Aoleyn would have ever believed! She had not realized how badly she wanted her place in the Coven until now, when it was likely forever denied!

She wanted to argue, to lash out with fist and magic, to deny Mairen by defeating Mairen then and there, but she found that she could not do any of that, do anything, other than sit there, dumbfounded, her expression blank, her jaw hanging open.

The two witches left, taking Aoleyn's crystals with them, and the lantern, leaving Aoleyn sitting in the dark.

She couldn't move, her mind reeling this way and that as she tried to decipher everything Mairen had just told her. Had she failed Tay Aillig's test, if that's what it was?

And if it wasn't that, what might the War Leader think of all this? He had announced his intentions to take Aoleyn as his wife and she knew it wasn't because he was particularly attracted to her. He wanted the power she had given to Brayth in the battle with the sidhe and the fossa.

But what now?

The young woman sucked in her breath, her eyes going wide, and mouthed, "Bahdlahn!" and truly, she was terrified then for her uamhas friend. She reminded herself that Tay Aillig meant to kill the fossa, and to use that feat to gain full control of Usgar, to become the Usgar-triath.

She heard again his last words to her dear friend up on th'Way.

In the Coven, had she been selected, she might have found a way to help Bahdlahn, to get Mairen to intervene and somehow protect him, but now, with this demotion . . .

Mairen's tone and demeanor had made it quite clear to Aoleyn that she would garner no favors from that one anytime soon. When Mairen had told her to learn the more mundane way of life for an Usgar woman, she was really telling Aoleyn that her life would now be that, mundane, and so of little interest to the Usgar-righinn.

"Bahdlahn," she whispered again, and she fought to sort her thoughts and find some solution. Perhaps she should go to him and use her gemstones to carry him away to freedom. But she was certain that would get Innevah killed.

Then again, hadn't Innevah murdered Caia? Hadn't Innevah secretly put the snake in Caia's bed? Perhaps she deserved . . .

Aoleyn dismissed that out of hand, refusing to go to that dark, dark place.

She didn't know what to do, or where to go, or how to plan.

And so, overwhelmed, she sat there in the dark, rocking back and forth, the rest of the night.

33

DEAMHAIN

Talmadge picked his way carefully along the narrow, muddy trail, looking for markers to keep him on the right line instead of falling into the bog. Behind him, the candlelight of Clach Boglach twinkled in the distance. The small village was built on a marsh of backwater that breathed up and down with the tides of Loch Beag, and sang all summer with the hum of insects and the trilling of frogs, including some that were nearly the size of a man, and could swallow a child whole. More than one person had been saved from that grim fate only because someone had noticed wriggling feet sticking out of a giant frog's mouth.

The entire town was built on stilts and a person on foot could only get there safely at low tide, and only along the narrow, muddy, hard-to-find trails that Talmadge now walked. The folk there were the most unusual of all around the lake. They rarely went out upon the open waters, for food was all around them—lizards and frogs and giant newts and fish by the school—and their boats were flat-bottomed to float high on the swampy bog. They wrapped their heads for only one hump, like with the next town in line, Fasach Crann, but the Boglach tribe bent those humps left or right, and often so steeply that a quick glance might make someone think a tribesman had two heads!

In all his years of coming to Loch Beag, Talmadge had only ventured to Clach Boglach twice before, both by canoe, and he would have skipped the place entirely this journey except that he had met up with one of the sentries of the town who had invited him in for a leg-of-frog roast, a delicacy that Talmadge had always wanted to enjoy.

Now, leaving, he was glad that he had taken the side road. The adventures, the newness of an old familiar lake, had him considering his life as a journey once more, a journey moving forward and widening, and not shrinking out of fear and remorse. He still thought of Khotai with every step, but it was okay.

He was honoring her by returning here, he had come to understand, for she would not have wanted him to shrink his journey out of grief.

He hadn't traded much at Clach Boglach, for they didn't have any of the pearls he preferred, and so he still had quite a bit of barter in his pack with one more stop ahead, his favorite place of all, Fasach Crann. The village wasn't far away as the crow flew, but Talmadge was no bird, and he'd have a long walk to go around the long inlet that bordered the swamp east of Clach Boglach. In other months, he might try to ford there, but the villagers had warned him that this was the last mating season for the giant frogs before they settled under the waters for their winter nap, and the rampage was in particular frenzy right now with the cold winds blowing so early.

The frogs, and the inlet where they congregated to mate, needed to be avoided.

Talmadge heard their songs even after he came out of the marsh, the trilling and croaking chasing him up into the foothills of Fireach Speuer. From this higher ground, he looked back to the candlelight of Clach Boglach, and then to the west, to the candles in the windows of Fasach Crann, so tantalizingly close!

"Midmorn," he estimated optimistically. His pace would have to be swift, but it would be mostly downhill.

He found a fat oak soon after, and climbed into its lower branches, not wanting to camp on the ground. Soon enough, though, the wind had driven him from the tree, its bite cold and wet, so that it got right into his bones.

With no choice, Talmadge collected some fallen branches, cleared a little area, dug a hole, deeper than he would normally to shield it from both the wind and a predator's eyes, and struck up a small campfire. He heated rocks and set them under his bedroll.

At every town along the way, he had been warned that winter would come early, and these folk knew the land and knew the winds. As he lay there, he considered that perhaps he should just turn back, and be quick off the plateau. Even though they were barely into the ninth month, snow was not unheard of this time of year, and if that happened, the passes on the northern end of the lake would be closed to him.

"They'll let me stay," he told himself, thinking of Fasach Crann, and thinking that wintering in the lake town might not be the worst thing that could happen to him.

As he lay there, the warm fire and stones seeming to melt him into his covers, the idea became even more alluring. He had heard so many tales of the games the folk played on the frozen Loch Beag.

"Khotai, my love," he said to the night wind, "a winter here will add a new road to the journey of my life."

"Usgar-laoch," the woman said, inhaling so profoundly in her shock that Tay Aillig figured she might just faint.

"Gavina," he greeted. "I am told that you will soon enter the Coven."

She smiled widely, showing her crooked teeth. The blanket hanging behind her as a divider in her small tent shifted then, and Tay Aillig narrowed his eyes, thinking it might be her husband, a man he knew to be more closely allied with Ahn'Namay than with his desires. He would have to take care here.

The blanket rippled and a breeze blew from around it, revealing the back flap of the tent somewhat askew.

"Where is your man?" Tay Aillig asked.

"Out gathering food and wood," Gavina answered, and she suddenly seemed a bit nervous. Indeed, Tay Aillig got the feeling that the mousy witch was afraid of him, perhaps assuming that he would take liberties with her.

He laughed out loud at the thought.

"He should be proud of you," he said.

Gavina nodded, appearing more wary now than she was before.

"Tell me, witch," he gently coaxed.

Poor Gavina, clearly uncomfortable, shifted from foot to foot and shook her head.

"He is angry because he can'no more hunt," Tay Aillig reasoned, "and no battles lay before him. It is too late for your ascent to matter."

She didn't reply, other than to look up at him, but the surprise in her eyes told him that his assessment was right on the mark.

"But it will matter, to you and to him," the Usgar-laoch assured the witch. "As long as you're not the least of the witches."

Gavina looked at him with puzzlement. "The newest," she said.

"That is not the same. It is your game to prove yourself worthy of a place nearer to Usgar-righinn Mairen. What might your man think when he, not Ahn'Namay, is whispered to step in line behind Raibert?"

Gavina's eyes widened, hopefully, it seemed.

"He will be pleased with you then, yes?" Tay Aillig remarked.

"How might—"

"I know how," he answered. "Because I know a secret, one that even Mairen has not discovered." He glanced around, even though they were in a tent, as if making sure that no one could hear.

"When you are near Craos'a'diad, does the song of Usgar ring louder?"

"Of course," she answered, for that was no secret.

"There is another place."

"The crystal caves," she said, for again, all the women knew that.

"Still another, one that is not known to Mairen or any others."

Gavina stared at him intently, but seemed less than convinced. "How would a man know?" she asked.

"Aoleyn knows. It, this place, is her secret," he lied. "Did it not surprise you that she, half your age, is so much more powerful than you with Usgar's gifts?"

Gavina bristled.

"Everyone knows that," Tay Aillig said. "You know that. Aoleyn would soon be a witch were it not for her hot spirit. There is no question of her affinity to the crystals, merely her judgment in using them."

"Her power is undeniable," Gavina admitted.

"Because she found the place, and she would go there before every lesson so that the song was ringing in her ears when Mairen, and you, worked beside her with the magic of Usgar."

The woman's eyes went very wide once more, and she gnashed her teeth, looking very much like someone who had just been cheated out of a wager.

"Do you know the four stones in the west where the blueberries grow thick?" Tay Aillig asked.

Gavina nodded.

"Farther west from there, just to the first ledge where the sunrise can be seen, there is a high cliff of sheer stone, where you look down upon the tops of tall pines," he told her, and again she nodded, for surely she had seen this place.

"Perhaps this cliff is the back wall of the crystal caves," he said. "But there, in that spot, you will find that the magic is as strong as Craos'a'diad. I give you this because I once admired your man, and watched his steps on his last raid, which was my first raid. It would please me for you to please him."

"I should go then and return full of power."

"Better," Tay Aillig said. "I give you this secret as your own. Take it and give it to Mairen. Take her to that place and let her see your power there. Bring a stone of floating, perhaps, and walk down the cliffside. Amaze her. Share the secret with her alone, and she will thank you, and she will elevate you."

Gavina swallowed hard, obviously overwhelmed. "Why do you give me this?" she demanded.

"Your man—"

"No," she said, shaking her head. "There is more."

"Connebragh," he admitted.

"The second witch?"

"Yes, Connebragh. I hate her. It would please me to see Mairen find a new favorite among her dancing witches. It would please me for that new favorite to be you."

"Why do you keep rubbing your face and looking about with nervous eyes?" Egard asked Aghmor.

"Aghmor has been on many raids," Ralid interjected, though the defense of his friend sounded weak to all three of the hunting Usgar, for Aghmor's reputation was not one of grand heroism and battle lust. All three here were more than a little surprised that Tay Aillig had chosen Aghmor to come along!

"The raid is not blessed," Aghmor replied.

"Tay Aillig brought us blessed weapons," Egard reminded.

"'Tis not the same. The witches are not here with us."

"They never are when we venture so far from home," Ralid replied.

"This is different," Aghmor said quietly.

"Aye," Egard agreed, his voice full of strength. "Are we men or are we boys? This is Tay Aillig's test for us, to prove ourselves worthy of his circle when Usgar is his. This hunt shows him to trust in us alone, when he destroys the fossa! This is the first step on our own path of glory. We need no women to protect us! Our journey alone is in service to Usgar, and so it is a journey blessed."

"We are too low on Fireach Speuer for so much talking," Ralid said. "Let us hunt."

The other two nodded at that, and Aghmor let it drop and tried to keep his concerns from his expression as the three crept along in the dark night—a dark night that was soon interrupted by the candles and campfires of the nearby lakemen villages, particularly Fasach Crann, but there was another light. A single, small fire, to the southwest of that village, in the foothills of the mountain.

Aghmor swallowed hard in noting those flames, such a clear reminder of a hunting party he had raided beside Tay Aillig in pursuit of two uamhas, mere children, who had run off. The image of that poor, ugly girl, gutted and strapped down for the carrion birds, flashed in his thoughts.

"We are blessed," Egard insisted, pointing out the singular fire.

Though he had never been inland in this particular area, Talmadge was no stranger to life in the wilds, and knew the universal sounds—or lack thereof—that signaled danger.

When the foothills grew quiet around him, the hairs on his neck tingled and he sensed that he was not alone.

He quickly propped his cloak with his bedroll and some sticks, and set his sword belt beside it, showing only the scabbard of his short sword and hiding the empty, longer sheath underneath.

Long sword in hand, he crept from the fire and hid in some sage behind the large oak, sinking down silently, keeping his breathing controlled, forcing a measure of calm. Still, he felt the blood pounding in his ears. Every now and then came the sound of a possible footfall, the crackle of a fallen leaf, but he couldn't discern the direction in the windy night.

He was too far from the lake for it to be a giant lizard, he thought, and hoped, for he never wanted to face one of the clo'dearche again!

Perhaps a lynx—he was too far down the mountain for the cloud leopards—or possibly a panther. In any case, a great cat would likely avoid him and his sword. He took some comfort in his belief that he could probably fend off some wolves or a pack of coyotes.

He hoped it wasn't a bear. Anything but a bear!

He burrowed a bit deeper into the sage, reminding himself to trust his years of hunting experience, his knowledge of how to disappear from sight. He could sneak up on a skittish deer back in the Wilderlands; surely he could hide from whatever approached!

Slowly, careful not to rustle the brush, Talmadge withdrew his crystalline lens from his small rucksack. He called upon the magic and peered into it, to scout up the mountainside and see if he could identify what had brought the animals about him into such a silent crouch.

The night was too dark. Every tree looked to him like a monster.

The needle-covered branches of the trees rustled in the wind. The sage brush quivered around him. Suddenly the silence seemed even more ominous.

He shrugged off his rucksack, placing it softly on the ground beside his hip. He pocketed the lens—if he had to run and abandon the sack, at least he would save his most useful tool. He could feel, could hear, the blood pumping in his body, his heartbeat thumping felt like a drum in his chest. Surely it was loud enough to be heard by whatever was hunting him.

He squinted and peered, scanning the areas where the foliage met the sky, looking for silhouettes. He watched every shadow, and felt the breeze keenly, to align his senses with the rustle and movement of the trees and grasses.

His instincts told him to flee, but he knew better. Whatever was coming, it would surely see him if he tried to run; besides, he didn't have anywhere he could go. Worse, he still did not know the direction of the predator's approach. Or what it was, for that matter; but given the myths and legends surrounding this mountain, he was not sure he even wanted to know.

Cat, wolf, bear, whatever the predator might be, if it saw him before he saw it, he would likely die.

He tried to keep his breathing steady, tried to calm his heart, but every shadow flitting through the trees made it pound in his chest until he felt like it might explode.

His sense of the time disappeared; everything was either moving too fast, too slowly, even not at all.

"Come on," Talmadge whispered under his breath. "Don't be a bear."

And he saw something, the glint of a crystalline spear tip, and he wished it was a bear.

The Usgar had come.

Ralid held up one finger and smiled wickedly when they came in sight of the small camp.

Aghmor shook his head, though. How could it be that someone was out here alone? Why would anyone be alone among the foothills of Fireach Speuer?

Across from Ralid, Egard motioned for the two to hold, flashed his open hand a few times, indicating a delay count, then melted off into the night.

So quietly, so balanced, Aghmor thought. The young warrior was the nephew of Tay Aillig, and had gotten all of the warrior traits of the Usgar-laoch, the calm and the courage, it seemed.

The two remaining Usgar glanced from the camp and to each other repeatedly. Aghmor could see the anxiousness in Ralid's eyes, noted the way the man was rolling his spear in his hands, flexing his forearm muscles with every turn, wincing even, now and then, from the intensity of his grip.

Apparently too engaged with his anticipation of battle, Ralid wasn't counting.

So Aghmor did, five fingers, five times, and he looked to Ralid and waved the man forward.

Into the camp leaped the young Usgar warrior, rushing across the low-burning fire and kicking the embers at the apparently sleeping form. Hardly slowing, Ralid crossed the fire and spun his spear in his hands, whacking the form with the back end of the shaft, right where the victim's head should have been.

Should have, but was not, and Ralid's follow-through yanked the cloak from the ground and from the branch stuffing, revealing the ruse.

The attacker barely gasped before Aghmor skidded to a stop and backpedaled fast into the forest cover.

Talmadge saw his chance, one warrior alone, staring dumbfoundedly at the propped bedroll. He had seen the second warrior, as well, but in retreat. He had to get this one down fast.

Before he leaped up, his heightened senses had his neck hairs dancing once more.

There was someone standing right behind him.

For a brief moment, Talmadge hoped that perhaps somehow his camouflage would hold, and this third Usgar would bypass him. He was a skilled frontiersman, after all, and had melted carefully into this brush.

But no, he realized. He had been seen.

"Best to die on my feet, then," he told himself and gathering his nerve, he started to leap and spin, a single move that would set him defensively, sword leading.

He got about halfway up, and halfway around, when a boot slammed him in the face, throwing him back to the ground. And as he fell, the Usgar spear swept in and gashed his forearm, launching his spear aside.

The warrior hovered over him, leering down at him, dangling his spear tip menacingly over Talmadge's face.

That should have been the end of it, the end of him, Talmadge thought, but once again, his thoughts turned to Khotai, beautiful Khotai, lovely Khotai, sweet Khotai . . . deadly Khotai.

He rolled back onto his shoulders, right foot coming forward to kick the spear; when the warrior came forward a step to keep control of his weapon, Talmadge's left foot shot straight up, the heel connecting with the man's crotch with such force that it lifted the young Usgar up onto his tiptoes.

Talmadge retracted and kicked out with both feet, cracking the man on the kneecaps, jolting him and straightening his legs painfully as the force drove him back.

Talmadge threw himself over, rising up high on his shoulders, planting his hands and pushing off, so that his back roll landed him right on his feet.

But the young Usgar was there, charging in, spear leveled for Talmadge's gut.

Khotai had taught Talmadge well, though, and he had enough balance to turn, throwing his right hip back, crossing his right arm in a backhand parry to drive the spear out wide.

Not quite wide enough, though, and Talmadge howled as the crystalline spear tip gashed him just above his right hip.

He kept his momentum and focus, though, growling back the pain.

He grabbed the Usgar behind the neck, pulling him forward, then threw himself backward to take the man to the ground with him, tucking his legs to launch the man right over him and into the oak tree.

It was a good plan, except that Talmadge hadn't even touched back to the ground before the enchanted Usgar spear crackled with lightning, and instead of falling straight back, he went flying out to the side, tumbling into a stand of thin birch.

"Dactyl's arse," Talmadge cursed under what little of his breath he had left after that shock and tumble.

His senses hadn't even returned to him, but his mind was screaming for him to get up, and so he was on his feet before he had even registered how much pain he was in. His side burned, his arm twitched uncontrollably, and he could see nothing out of his right eye.

He grabbed a branch with his left hand, and when the Usgar charged, he tore it off in desperation, swinging it before him like a sword.

In came the Usgar, but out went Talmadge, fighting with the fury of a man who had nothing left to lose. Back and forth went the branch, whacking at the darting spear, connecting then stabbing forward as Talmadge stubbornly pressed on.

He had the warrior backpedaling, hitting him about the chest and head. If he had had his sword, the fight would be over—but he didn't have his sword.

He had a branch, just a branch, a thin piece of unwieldy wood.

The Usgar warrior was good, and recovered quickly, stealing Talmadge's momentum, now parrying and waiting for a single opening to thrust his spear into Talmadge's gut.

And the Usgar warrior wasn't alone, a fact that Talmadge suddenly remembered when a flying spear drove into his thigh from his right, and remembered again as he turned to meet a third Usgar who had leaped upon him from the left, bearing him to the ground.

Talmadge tried to turn, to bite, to scratch, to kick, but the world went dark when the flat side of an axe head whacked him across the head.

He rolled and tried to cover as the Usgar fell over him, raining blows and kicks until Talmadge was beyond pain, beyond all sensibilities.

The woman seemed frustrated. She clutched her crystal tightly and scrunched her eyes, shivering with intensity, and frustration.

"Can you feel it?" she asked.

"I feel only the cold wind," Mairen replied, staring at Gavina curiously.

"No," the frustrated witch replied and sighed.

"What is it you wish me to feel?"

"The magic."

"I am Usgar-righinn. I always feel the magic of our god."

"More magic here, like at Craos'a'diad," Gavina stammered.

Now it was Mairen's turn to sigh. Gavina had brought her out to this windy ledge, far afield of the encampment, with a promise to show her some revelation, something special regarding the song of Usgar. While the Usgar-righinn could appreciate the excitement of the soon-to-be witch, she was still in a foul mood and would only humor Gavina for so long.

She didn't answer, other than to stare incredulously at the middle-aged woman.

"I brought you . . ." Gavina stuttered and shook her head. "I wanted to show you."

"Then show me something."

"The magic. I wanted to show you that the magic here was thick, like in the caves! I wanted to float down this cliff and back to you, to prove to you that you were wise in picking . . ."

"Then do it," came another voice, surprising them both, and Usgar-laoch Tay Aillig walked around the ledge from the other end, moving past a shocked and angry Mairen to stand between and behind the two women.

"Why are you here?" Mairen breathed, barely able to contain her rage.

"He told me of this place," Gavina said, and Mairen's eyes widened in shock.

"Do it!" Tay Aillig prompted Gavina. "Float down! You have the power. You belong! The Usgar-righinn chose right."

"There is no . . . I can'no," a defeated Gavina said.

Tay Aillig heaved a great sigh, dropped his gaze, and shook his head, shoulders slumping in clear disappointment. "Oh, Gavina," he lamented.

"What game do you play?" Mairen asked him, or started to, for halfway through her question, the War Leader stabbed his arm out against the shoulder of Gavina, launching her from the ledge.

"Do it!" he said as she screamed and tumbled, flailing with her crystal, actually trying to access the levitational magic within it.

Mairen slapped her hand over her mouth and looked over, watching Gavina flailing. She hit a jag lower down that bounced her away from the cliff face, somersaulting, her crystals flying from her hands.

She missed one of the pine trees below, but didn't miss the flat stone beside it, landing headfirst with a sickening splat.

Mairen gasped and spun away. "Murderer!" she cried.

Tay Aillig simply laughed at her. "Why would you stand against me?" he asked innocently.

"Stand against you?" Mairen echoed in disbelief, backing and clutching her own crystals, reaching already into the levitational magic within one in case the murderous Usgar-laoch wasn't finished.

"Stand against me!" Tay Aillig reiterated. "You knew my desire, but you chose . . . that!" He swept his hand out to the cliff to make his contempt for Gavina clearer still.

"Instead of your plaything?" Mairen said, gaining confidence now, for the crystals were humming in her hands, their powers ready and at her beckon.

"Plaything? That foolish and ugly little girl?"

"Ugly?" Mairen echoed skeptically. "What does Tay Aillig know about ugly?"

He started to respond, but stopped short and stared at Mairen curiously. She knew where his thoughts were going, where his memory was leading.

"Because I refused you?" he asked. "I was a boy."

"You had killed lakemen by then!" Mairen snapped back, allowing more anger through than she had intended. She was surprised by the level of her residual anger here over something that had happened more than two decades before. But there it was, and she couldn't deny it, and she couldn't deny the truth behind her decision to pick Gavina instead of Aoleyn!

"I was a boy, not yet through my eighteenth summer."

"And I was an old and ugly crone," Mairen spat.

Tay Aillig laughed at her. "You had seen thirty winters? More? Yes!"

"And now I am old and withered and invisible."

Tay Aillig started to heave yet another sigh, but it was a ruse: he came out of it like a striking white-furred viper, one hand slapping across, taking the crystals from Mairen's grasp and sending them bouncing about the ledge, the other hand clamping on Mairen's throat.

Before the Usgar-righinn even understood what was happening, the powerful man was holding her out over the ledge with just that one arm. She grabbed at his wrist and kicked her feet.

"Why?" he said to her, his voice surprisingly calm and steady, she thought, sympathetic and even wounded. "Why would you stand against me? Do you not see the future?"

"Because I am old and ugly," she said with a sneer, daring him to drop her.

But he didn't. He pulled her back and ran her across the ledge to put her back against the mountain wall, and he kissed her, hard and passionately, and grabbed at her and pulled her close. She fought him and scratched his face, but only for a moment until she was kissing him back.

She was kissing this man who had just thrown an innocent woman to her death, and she didn't care!

And he pulled up her skirt and he took her right there, standing against the mountain wall, and they cried out and they shuddered, and they melted down in each other's arms.

"You're not invisible to any," Tay Aillig said to her. "You are Usgar-righinn, the greatest woman of Usgar."

"Will you tell yourself that while you hump Aoleyn?" She couldn't keep the edge out of her voice.

Tay Aillig laughed at her again. "Aoleyn is a tool and nothing more. I have seen her in the spiritual joining with Brayth. That is her great power, and it is one I need to become Usgar-triath."

Mairen was chuckling and shaking her head as she reached up to touch the deep scratch she had inflicted upon the man's face.

"You will not be Usgar-triath for many years," she said. "It has already been decided."

But Tay Aillig's grin was a confident one.

"What do you know?" Mairen asked him, tilting back her head to better survey the man's expression and demeanor.

"Soon enough you will see, mighty Mairen. And together we will rule without question."

"While you bed Aoleyn?"

Tay Aillig chortled and yanked her close and kissed her, rolling atop her yet again.

34

RIDDLES UNDER A RED MOON

Aoleyn went about her mundane chores the next day, unconcerned with the duties at hand. Whatever she was doing—gathering wood or berries, hanging hides, beating the dirt out of furs—she made sure to keep in sight of Tay Aillig.

The Coven had passed the word that Iseabal would make her red-faced appearance that night, and Aoleyn knew from that conversation up on th'Way that Tay Aillig meant to go after the fossa, or do something, at least, quite dramatic.

After the man's last words to Bahdlahn, Aoleyn wasn't about to sit idly by.

She stood before a hanging fur rug, absently whacking it with a stick, watching Tay Aillig and his nephew Egard, with whom Aoleyn had had more than a few unpleasant encounters over the years. She noted that Egard was limping badly, and constantly, and gingerly adjusting his breeches.

Aoleyn was quite enjoying that, until a young girl ran up to her.

"The Usgar-righinn will see you," the child said.

Aoleyn looked at her skeptically. Then glanced back to Tay Aillig, then up at the sky. It was already midafternoon.

"Now," the girl insisted, and she ran off.

Aoleyn hesitated, watching the girl's movements, thinking perhaps that Tay Aillig, knowing he was being watched, had sent the child to get away from Aoleyn.

But no, she surmised, for the girl ran back the other way across the camp, passing very near to Mairen's tent, where she exchanged nods with another Coven member who stood outside.

Aoleyn moved across the compound, but slowly, taking her time, and watching Tay Aillig all the while. So distracted was she that she walked right past the flap of Mairen's tent, and moved right alongside it before she even realized her mistake.

She turned and started back, but stopped when she heard talking from within, Connebragh's voice.

"How can this be?" Connebragh demanded, and her tone in speaking to Mairen surprised Aoleyn.

"She tried to prove herself in a most unfortunate way," Mairen answered.

"Why?"

"You would have to ask her."

Connebragh snorted, with what Aoleyn believed to be disgust.

"Aoleyn, then?" Connebragh said, and when Aoleyn heard that, she was reminded that Mairen was not a particularly patient person. She hustled around the tent and pushed in through the flap, to find the two witches sitting on some piled rugs near the tent pole.

She bowed respectfully and said, "At your call, Usgar-righinn."

"Yes," said Mairen, and Aoleyn heard no joy in her voice. "Gather some crystals and leave. Practice hard. You will enter the Coven at the winter solstice."

Aoleyn blinked repeatedly. She couldn't believe what she had just heard. She found herself replaying the words again and again in her head.

"Usgar-righinn?" she asked, at a loss.

"Go!" Mairen demanded.

Aoleyn bobbed in a series of badly attempted bows, then spun about and ran for the bin of crystals Mairen kept beside the tent flap, almost making it before Mairen spoke again, with a resounding, "No!"

Aoleyn skidded to a stop and spun about.

"No, I have another task," Mairen said, rising. She walked toward Aoleyn, sorting her own crystals as she did. She held out one to the young woman, a green-flecked crystal Aoleyn knew very well.

"Take this and come with me," Mairen demanded.

The Usgar-righinn looked back at Connebragh as she finished, "I have something for you to retrieve.

Connebragh gave a little snort and seemed darkly amused, Aoleyn thought, and that didn't comfort the young woman as she scurried behind Mairen across the camp. She resisted the urge to ask Mairen where they might be going when, to her surprise, Mairen walked right out of the camp, and kept going at a swift pace, down the trail and winding through some scraggly trees. They moved opposite from the uamhas grove, and Aoleyn didn't know this area very well—on foot. She had flown over this region, both in her own body and in the owl, but things looked different from this perspective. She couldn't imagine where Mairen was leading her so late in the day.

They came out of the trees to a ridge, then climbed down a low slope to the blueberry patches—yes, Aoleyn knew this place. She took some comfort in that familiarity, but it was short-lived, for Mairen crossed right through and kept going still, then moved onto a ledge, just a few steps wide, with a sheer drop before them and a sheer cliff behind.

Finally, without warning, Mairen stopped short, and the distracted Aoleyn almost ran into her.

"You have stayed silent all the way," Mairen said, in a voice to convey that she was impressed, which of course made the whole thing just another insult aimed at Aoleyn.

"Yes, Usgar-righinn," she replied obediently, keeping her eyes staring at the ground.

"Oh, for the sake of red Iseabal, look at me, child!" an exasperated Mairen demanded, and Aoleyn did so, to see a stern expression indeed staring back at her. "Are you not even curious?"

"I am!" Aoleyn blurted.

Mairen pointed over the ledge. "Both of your answers lie below."

"Both?"

Mairen sighed impatiently.

"How I am the thirteenth when a thirteenth witch was already picked, and why you have brought me out here," Aoleyn reasoned fast.

"Perhaps you are not so stupid, then," Mairen replied. She pointed over the ledge again. "Look, and look closely."

Aoleyn hesitated.

"Idiot child, if I wished to kill you, you would already be dead, and more horrifically than a simple fall off a ledge!"

Aoleyn gathered her courage and peered over. Her hand instinctively went to her belly, to the malachite and moonstone, as she stared down at the tops of tall pines.

"To the right of the tallest tree," Mairen said.

Aoleyn squinted against the glare of the low sun, shining from across Loch Beag and nearly touching the mountains behind the lake's left-hand bank. She noted some sparkles about the ground, and a flat stone, glistening red, reminding her that the Blood Moon would soon rise.

She scanned more intently, and noted something in the tall grass beside the stone. At first she thought it a fallen branch, but then realized it was something else, something that answered both her questions.

"The red stone," she breathed.

"Red with the blood and brains of Gavina," Mairen explained without sympathy.

Aoleyn gasped and stepped back, turning on the Crystal Maven, who merely shrugged.

"You have my crystal of levitation," Mairen said. "It is pure, its song strong. Do you think you can scale down into the ravine with it?"

Aoleyn looked at the crystal and concentrated on it just long enough to hear its song. A little smile came to her as she realized that, as strong as this crystal might be, its notes sounded tinny and distant compared with the roar of the malachite stone set in her belly ring.

"Yes," she answered, and she was sure that she could, even with just Mairen's crystal.

"Then go," Mairen instructed. "Gavina fell with crystals. Retrieve them."

"And her?"

Mairen's face screwed up weirdly. "Yes, dear," she answered with dripping sarcasm. "I am sure that you will be quite strong enough to carry up a woman half again your weight."

Aoleyn held up her hands innocently.

Mairen cuffed her on the ear, a stinging slap. "Get the crystals, you idiot."

Aoleyn quickly turned about and stepped off the ledge, drawing a gasp from Mairen, who obviously had thought she would call upon the magic first to test it before plunging! For confident Aoleyn, though, so tied into the Usgar song through the wedstone piercing, it was no worry, and she was floating before she had ever really begun to fall.

She started to turn over, thinking to use her moonstone to swoop down instead of just a floating descent, but she wisely deferred, for Mairen, watching from above, didn't even know she had a moonstone.

She came down right beside the tall pine, across from the red-stained stone, and quickly moved around. She knew it was getting late and worried that Tay Aillig would be gone before she returned, but she stopped abruptly anyway when she came in sight of that stone.

Aoleyn had seen garish wounds, had seen injured warriors returning from a raid or a sidhe battle, had seen a man writhing in pain with his chest and belly torn wide by the swipe of a bear, but none of that could prepare her for the sight before her now. Gavina had hit headfirst, she understood, and the mess on the stone was more lumps of brain than simple blood.

It took her many heartbeats to steady herself and begin moving again, and even then, every step came with great tension, as she saw more and more of the truly broken woman. Gavina's right arm was behind her back in a manner in which an arm should not be able to bend. The shoulder had fully shattered and the upper arm was straight across to the other shoulder, the lower arm hooked limped over Gavina's left side.

The woman lay on her belly—Aoleyn could not have called it face-down, for she had no face, nor anything remaining that resembled a head. Her skull had exploded on impact, and just the stem of her back-bone and brain remained.

On a branch just above and beyond the dead woman, Aoleyn spot-ted a crow with an eyeball dangling from its beak.

"Find your strength," Aoleyn whispered, closing her eyes. "Bahdlahn," she then repeated many times, reminding herself of the possible conse-quences of Tay Aillig's plan, whatever that plan might be.

She took a deep breath, then moved stridently, searching about the stone to collect a couple of crystals. She glanced up at Mairen, and see-ing that the woman wasn't looking over at that time, she tugged her ear and activated her garnet, using it to guide her to any nearby magic.

One crystal had shattered fully, its flecks scattered about.

None seemed potent, so Aoleyn left them, not wanting to tip off the rest of the witches to the truth she had uncovered about Usgar's magic, that it was the stones, just the stones, and not the crystals, that sang. So when she found the last crystal, half broken and revealing its contents, that, too, she not only left, but threw far aside.

To the west, the sun began to set.

Aoleyn rushed to the cliff and glanced back one time to dead Gavina. Despite Mairen's slap, Aoleyn found that she hadn't the heart to leave the poor woman to the carrion birds.

She went over and grabbed Gavina by the back of her torn clothes, then called upon the green stone set in her belly ring and sent its magic out to the dead woman. With one hand, Aoleyn easily lifted her, and carried her back to the cliff. Then she called upon the green stone more forcefully, and upon the blue-white moonstone, as well, using both and her free hand to run her up the cliff.

As she neared the ledge, though, she found her power beginning to wane, and a level of exhaustion she had not anticipated beginning to seep throughout her body.

She gave one last push, both magically and with her hand, and managed to grab the ledge, then to heave Gavina over . . . almost.

She had to let go, and the dead woman fell once more, bouncing off the cliff in her tumbling descent and flying so far out that she crashed into the pine, disappearing into its boughs and not, to Aoleyn's notice, falling through.

Aoleyn gasped in horror, then grabbed the ledge with both hands, demanding one last push of magical energy to get her somewhat over, where Mairen grabbed her by the back of her shirt and helped tug her onto solid ground.

Huffing and puffing, when Aoleyn finally managed to turn over and regard the Usgar-righinn, she found Mairen chuckling derisively and shaking her head.

"Well, that should make it interesting for the warriors who will be sent to retrieve Gavina tomorrow," Mairen remarked. She turned to look Aoleyn in the eye. "You simply couldn't resist the chance to prove me wrong, now could you?" She snorted again, shook her head again, every sound, every movement tormenting Aoleyn for her failure.

She reached down and roughly helped Aoleyn to her feet, pointedly bringing the young woman in close so that their eyes were only a finger's breadth apart. "You know not your place. Your time in the Coven will be short, I fear," Mairen warned, "and will be the death of you."

She roughly took her own crystal and those Aoleyn had retrieved, then shoved Aoleyn ahead of her, back toward the camp.

Aoleyn led at a swift pace, for night was falling.

And the Blood Moon was rising.

It hurt.

It knew only that it hurt. It always hurt, and it always knew. Most of the time, it was a dull pain, throughout its body, claws to tail, like the background noise of a distant song. Sometimes, though, that song rang clearer, the notes of Usgar, and the pain responded, eliciting fury in the fossa, making it leap all about, throwing rotted flesh and bones, raking the walls of its filthy death pit.

All it needed was to make the pain stop!

It did not need food. It did not need water. It did not need anything, except that: to make the pain stop.

The fossa didn't sleep, but remembered sleep, and tried to sleep to forget its pain. But no, it could not, even when the song was far, far away.

The song vibrated through the stones of the den this night, lighting fires of agony on the tormented creature, like a thousand thousand stinging insects crawling on it, biting away. It leaped about in a frenzy to escape the pain, but of course the pain followed.

It let out a roar, loud and long and fearsome, and the sheer exertion dulled the pain for a moment. But just for a moment.

It raked at the walls of its den, its little stone cave. The stone was hard, but its claws dug in, such was its fury. New gouges creased in the stone, beside the cuts the demon creature had made the last time it hurt like this.

It did not remember the previous pain. It did not remember the previous day. It did not remember at all with regards to time, for time had no meaning to the eternal creature.

It only hurt.

It paced in a circle, angry and pained. It stopped to let out another roar, but when that did not reduce the pain, it returned to its pacing.

Outside, the sunlight had faded. The full moon rose, and scant light passed through the thick brush that covered the entrance to its den, but even that was vanishing, replaced with a dark umber. This night, the light was different, the fossa sensed from the blackness of its bone-filled pit.

This night, the moon was red.

Again the song of Usgar assailed the beast, and now it found familiarity. It had heard this song before. It recognized the speaker.

A speaker the fossa had vowed to kill.

And the moon was red.

A great leap launched the monster from the pit to the ledge, where it belly-crawled across the sloped stone, under the low roof, and into the tunnel that led to the entry cave.

The pain stung it, but the moon was red, and the demon was not driven back as it approached the open air.

Now it welcomed the pain, this pain, for the sharpness of it whetted its mind and its hunger.

Out into the night, it went, lit by the red face of Iseabal.

The fossa hunted.

Following tips offered by a woman working the central bonfire, Aoleyn found the cave below the uamhas tents. They had been here, Tay Aillig had been here, and recently. She found some clues: a drawing in the dirt, a spent torch, and, surprisingly, seven of the weapons she had blessed a few nights earlier, including all four of the long spears.

She found a sack, a rucksack unlike anything she had ever seen. It was not of Usgar make or design, its corners sealed with metal rivets.

Aoleyn tried to make sense of it all.

Did Tay Aillig have a prisoner?

Aoleyn knew she didn't have time to sit there and try to decipher it all. She exited and used her magic to scale the mountainside up to the top of the ridge behind the uamhas grove, and from there, she called upon her cat's-eye magic to give her night vision, and surveyed the land spreading wide below her.

Even in the nighttime, mountains seemed deceptive when looking down at them, the viewer's height disguising the sheer breadth and scope of the monstrous mound. Seeming not so far away, Aoleyn noted a small tree-filled expanse, a shadowy place showing a dusting of snow beneath, which made the trees stand out.

Aoleyn knew better, knew the tricks a mountain could play. She had crisscrossed these slopes many times, some on foot, but mostly in the air, and she understood the scope of the task before her, the many hidden ravines, the long, rolling terrain that appeared small and flatter from up high.

Even with her night sight and ability to soar down the mountain, finding Tay Aillig and the others, if they were even out there, would be near to impossible!

She had to try, though.

"Bahdlahn," she whispered, and she threw herself from the height and stretched out her arms, riding the wind.

"Iseabal," Aghmor breathed. The four warriors knew that it would be a Blood Moon this night, of course, but seeing the orb hanging over Fireach Speuer behind them took Aghmor's breath away.

Ralid's, too, although Egard gave a sinister snort and kicked the prisoner for good measure, and Tay Aillig merely smiled.

"That branch," Tay Aillig instructed, and Egard roughly dragged the brutalized Talmadge over to the spot, while Ralid readied a cord. They soon had the cord looped up high, and had one end fastened to the prisoner's wrists, which were bound tightly behind his back. On the other end of the cord, Egard pulled hard, yanking the man's arms up high behind him, drawing a gasp and cry of pain from Talmadge.

Egard pulled more, bringing the poor man right to his tiptoes and beyond, and with Ralid's help, they tied it off around the tree right there, keeping poor Talmadge hanging free as much as getting his toes to the ground. He kept moving his feet, desperately looking for some patch of higher ground that he could better set his feet, or even one foot, to take some of the pressure off his aching arms.

Tay Aillig came up before him, holding forth a crystal, one he had bade Connebragh to bless after Mairen had unexpectedly taken Aoleyn from the camp. He stuffed the crystal down the front of Talmadge's shirt, patting it to make sure the man wouldn't shake it free.

Not that it would matter, anyway, he believed. All the crystal had to do was attract the fossa. Whether it was on the prisoner or at his feet would matter not at all. Tay Aillig didn't even care if the demon creature killed the man.

"Should we start a fire?" Aghmor asked, trying to keep the fear out of his voice.

Tay Aillig shot him a glare that silenced him. He led his three hunters to a patch of brush in a tangle of birch. He set one man watching each direction, with him staring back at the strung-up prisoner. "We must see the demon first," he warned them.

Then he pulled forth his amethyst-crusted sunstone, and didn't wait to call upon its magic, hoping that it would effectively blind the fossa to him and those around him.

Or to him, at least. He had little hope that all three of his fellow hunters would return with him to the Usgar camp that night.

She kept hoping that Tay Aillig's band would light a fire. She stayed low to the ground in her glide, near the tops of the trees, but there was simply too much ground to cover! And with her silhouette against the starlit sky, Aoleyn rightly feared that Tay Aillig and his warriors would see her before she saw them.

She swooped down over one outcrop of stone and called upon her moonstone to lift her as she approached some trees, touching down lightly among the high boughs. There she held and tried to sort out her dilemma. Mairen's diversion had cost Aoleyn dearly, and likely, had cost Bahdlahn everything.

Not for the first time, Aoleyn thought she should go to Bahdlahn and flee with him. She could help him down the mountain, though not as easily as she had imagined, she realized, given her failure with the body of Gavina. She found flying and gliding fairly easy, but carrying Gavina had quickly exhausted her.

Still, if she couldn't find Tay Aillig, she knew that she might have to flee with Bahdlahn. Perhaps she could keep him far enough ahead of the pursuing hunters—hunters who would also be using the levitational powers of the green flecks to speed their way.

Aoleyn took a deep breath and tried to think clearly about the task at hand: finding Tay Aillig. He was after the fossa, and had spoken with Raibert, confirming what Aoleyn, too, had come to believe: that the creature heard the song of magic.

He hadn't gone to Craos'a'diad, she supposed, for he had left too late to make that climb this night, and with only the one magical spear tip.

Why had they taken that one item? Why just a dagger? Why hadn't they taken the other seven weapons?

It hit her, then, a sudden epiphany, one so obvious that she couldn't believe she had wasted so much time gliding and flying about the mountain relatively blindly.

She kept her cat's-eye earring engaged, but touched and called upon the other one as well, the one that allowed her to hear the song of Usgar.

Off she leaped, flying away and staying low, as much running and leaping almost weightlessly from tree to tree as staying aloft.

She watched with her eyes, but she listened through the garnet, and soon enough she heard the song of Usgar. She paused and considered the direction, determining that it was nowhere near the Usgar encampment.

"Tay Aillig," she whispered with some confidence, and off she went.

The demon fossa loped easily, crossing past the entrance to the caverns full with the symphony of Usgar. It turned and growled, but the pain was too acute and it could not stay. Down it went, past the region and back around toward the fire where the witches danced.

It heard the song from that distant camp, as always, and circled near, wanting nothing more than to go in and destroy them all!

But the demon creature knew better. So many singers of the magic altogether would find its weakness, it feared, and with so many warriors about, that could lead to its demise.

So it circled, listening, thinking that it might well go in anyway, quickly, for that one kill, to murder the human witch who had so tormented it with her magic that one night when the fossa could not come forth from its cave.

Wait. It did hear the song!

But not from the camp. Lower on the mountain, and around to the east, far away.

Off went the fossa, silent and swift toward the kill.

———

He didn't want to keep his wits about him, but he feared succumbing to the pain and weariness. Blood dripped from the gash on his head, obscuring his vision, and Talmadge was hardly aware of the approach of one of his brutish Usgar captors.

It was the big one, he realized when the figure stopped right before him, grabbing him by the hair, and roughly yanking his head up to look him in the eye.

To Talmadge, he seemed just a blurry blob.

"Still alive?" the warrior growled. "Good. It does not hunt the dead. The demon wishes to eat you while you are alive to feel the pain."

Talmadge had no answer.

To his surprise, the man wiped his sleeve across Talmadge's face, and while he was glad to be able to see again, even if only a little bit, the movement made his poor arms send fires of agony coursing through him.

The scene before him was bathed in a dull, reddish tint, and for a moment, Talmadge thought it to be the blood. But a shadow crept across the clearing, and the red light vanished, and he realized it was the moonlight.

Something he had learned in the villages came back to him then, about the monster, the demon fossa. He thought of standing beside Khotai in Sellad Tulach, watching the commotion on the mountain under a similar red moon. Yes, he took himself there, back to Khotai's soft embrace and passionate lovemaking.

"Fables," he whispered, to himself, for his tormentor didn't seem to care.

"It wants more than magic," the large warrior said. "Blood. It wants the taste of blood."

Talmadge shrugged. What did it matter? What did anything matter? "I am bleeding," he managed to say.

"Not enough," the Usgar said, yanking out the crystal knife from Talmadge's shirt and instead stabbing it hard into his side.

How he screamed!

The Usgar nodded, pleased. He twisted the knife a bit, eliciting more screams and setting it more firmly, then walked away casually.

—————

The song grew louder, though it was nothing major—certainly no witch casting magic, she understood. She thought of the dagger, blessed probably, and nodded, thinking that might be the answer, the source.

And she was getting closer, certainly. But then the song ended, abruptly, confusing Aoleyn. She slowed, but kept going in the same direction.

There, in a tangle of birch and brush, she spotted the three warriors of Tay Aillig's troupe. Just for a moment, though, for then a great darkness entered the birch, stealing her night vision, and even from this distance, she felt the magic of her levitation waver, just briefly.

Before she could begin to sort out the riddle, she heard again the song, from not far away, and so she moved that way, circling wide the birch, to see a man, the victim, hanging from a tree branch. The song of Usgar came from him, from the dagger embedded into his side! For a moment, her heart fell; this was no Usgar, but neither was his head misshapen.

But no, she peered closer, and it was not Bahdlahn.

She looked back to the birch tangle, but saw only the darkness of night, and darker silhouettes, of the Usgar men, it seemed.

Were they using a diamond to steal the light, as she had discovered?

She shook her head. When she had used the diamond, it had stolen all light, but she could make out the forms, just not with her cat's-eye magic.

It made no sense.

She used the garnet, and focused her thoughts on that tangle, and the strange sensation that came back to her sent a wave of nausea through her. A sensation she had never felt before, off-putting, unbalancing, and it seemed to her as if there was a song there, but . . . inverted? As though to perfectly complement and cancel the notes of her magic. An antisong, canceling the notes of Usgar's refrain.

Aoleyn shook her head. Was it the fossa? Was the demon among them?

Had Tay Aillig somehow allied with the beast? And if so, then what was all of this? What was he luring to battle him and his new demonic ally?

It didn't make sense.

None of it did.

In the clearing under the tree, the prisoner wailed in pain.

Aoleyn didn't know what to do. She couldn't let this stand. She flew out, away from the birch tangle, circling the prisoner in a widening perimeter, searching for the fossa, or for something, at least, to help her better understand.

Not so far away, she found a hunter, no doubt lured by the smell of fresh blood. But it was not the fossa.

Aoleyn took a deep breath, realizing the danger, but knowing that she was out of options.

She set down on a low branch, not so high above a giant brown bear. The enormous animal snuffled about some brush behind a fallen tree, seemingly unaware, but only for a moment. Suddenly it turned and stared straight at Aoleyn, sniffing still, trying to figure her out.

The bear showed no fear, and why should it? These great brown creatures had no rivals on Fireach Speuer, and even the Usgar hunters gave them a wide berth. More than a thousand pounds of power stared at Aoleyn now, barely ten strides away! She should have been terrified, she knew, keenly aware that the mighty animal could kill her with hardly an effort before she could bring any magic to her defense.

And yet, she was not afraid. She met its gaze, eye to eye, and felt the resonance of the turquoise in it. She said not a word, thought not a word, and yet somehow she was communicating with it.

The bear continued to sniff the air curiously. It rose up on its hind legs, head going up to perhaps thrice Aoleyn's height—even on the branch, the bear was not so far below her.

She continued to reach out through the turquoise cuff on her ear, trying to build some trust, some calm measure between them.

So far, so good.

But now came the test. Aoleyn thought of the poor man hanging at the tree. He needed her or he would surely die. Horribly.

She gathered up her energy, called upon the song of the turquoise more fully, and on the magic of the wedstone set to her belly button. She let her spirit fly free of her corporeal form, gathered up the magic of the turquoise with that spirit, and flew missilelike at the bear.

As soon as it realized the intrusion, the animal roared mightily in protest. It fell to all fours and swatted the fallen tree, tossing it aside like a hollow reed, and advanced upon the form of its tormentor.

How strange for Aoleyn to watch her own body through the bear's movements!

Strange and terrifying, for the bear was stalking her, and she could tell that it meant to destroy her. She couldn't reason with it, couldn't bring it back from its defensive anger.

So she didn't try. Instead, she attacked, mentally.

The hulking bear stopped and stood once more. It roared—because Aoleyn made it roar.

It turned because Aoleyn made it turn.

It headed for the tree and the hanging man.

35

POWER

It heard the song flowing through the trees, calling to it. It felt the wind on the song, and heard the song on the wind, and it felt the burning desire, to consume that wind, to consume that song.

It saw, clearly, for the first time in years, though it did not remember in years. It only saw the red-lit forest, the glowing patches of light and life, the animals tucked into their dens and hidden in their burrows. They feared it; it did not care for their fear. It did not care for their blood. Not now, not this night.

The fossa cared only for the song.

It slid through the forest, low and silent on padded feet, no more than a shadow under a bloodred moon.

Other melodies played, some louder, some softer, but this one, this moaning magic carried on the wind, called most loudly though very distantly, and so it ran.

And so the fossa hunted.

Aghmor swallowed hard when he heard the roar, so near and so full of strength.

"Fossa?" Ralid whispered, but Tay Aillig snapped his hand up into the air, demanding silence.

Another roar, deep and powerful.

Aghmor noted the War Leader shaking his head, seeming less than excited. Tay Aillig didn't think it was the fossa. Neither did Aghmor, and he surely hoped it was not.

The four warriors stood in a diamond formation in the birch tangle, with Tay Aillig in front, flanked by Ralid and Egard, and with Aghmor in back, opposite the roaring. He clutched his lakeman's sword, tightly, rolling his fingers about the leather-wrapped hilt. Despite his nearly paralyzing fears, he crept up closer to Tay Aillig, peering out from around the large man.

He saw the prisoner struggling still, trying to keep one toe or the other on the ground. The man snorted and spat, and dripped a stream of blood from his impaled side, and every twist or turn brought a groan as his arms remained above, almost wholly supporting him.

A rustle in the brush across the way caught Aghmor's attention, a sizable tree shaking suddenly with more than the force of the night breeze.

Aghmor heard his fellows suck in their breath when a form appeared, a huge silhouette, hulking and powerful.

"Fossa," Ralid breathed, and Aghmor shook his head, knowing it was not. He had seen the fossa, dragging his friend Brayth up the mountainside. It was nowhere near the size of this monster bear.

Tay Aillig kept his hand up in the air, emphatically grabbing at the air to demand silence.

Aghmor could hear the Usgar-laoch's breathing, short and agitated, as the bear meandered into the clear area near the hanging prisoner, sniffing the air loudly and finally settling its gaze upon the birch tangle, upon them.

Tay Aillig growled. "Drive the miserable beast away," he told his charges. "Scream and jump and drive it away."

Aghmor could hardly believe the agitation in the man's voice, but when he thought about it, it all made sense, of course. Tay Aillig had told them that he could kill the fossa, that he, and they, would become great heroes to all of Usgar.

"Drive it away!" Tay Aillig demanded, shoving Egard, and then Ralid, out of the tangle, and pulling Aghmor out as well, pushing the man out before him.

She felt the power rippling through the bear's limbs, through her limbs, with every stride. She came into the clearing and immediately looked to the birch tangle, and saw them, but more than that, she heard them, their every movement, every flutter of a leaf or crunch of a twig. And she smelled them even more clearly, four distinct scents!

Aoleyn's mind whirled at the amazing sensations. She thought of the owl's vision and hearing, and now this. She had no idea that a bear could smell so keenly. She had no idea that the nights of Fireach Speuer were filled with such vivid and distinct aromas.

It was that very thing, the smell of the poor prisoner's blood, that reminded her not to tarry. She started for the hanging man, but paused and took a moment to ensure that she had full control of this mighty animal. One instant where the bear took control, where the predator breathed in that rich scent of blood so near, and the man would likely be dead.

She rambled over, stood up tall, and with a single swipe of her powerful arm, raked the branch so deeply that she heard a profound crack within it. Her huge claws took the rope apart in two separate places, and immediately recognized her error. For the poor man tumbled, and the great bear wasn't nimble enough to safely catch him, and he groaned all the louder when he hit the ground, and jolted in pain, for he fell onto his side with the embedded knife banging against the ground.

Aoleyn wanted to help him, wanted to fly out of the bear and back to her own body and begin the healing immediately. She couldn't, of course, for the bear would probably kill the man, and now, she noted, Tay Aillig and his warriors had come out onto the clearing.

Aoleyn the bear reared on hind legs, towering above them. She hoped they would have the good sense to stay away!

But no, on they came, with weapons leveled. She couldn't believe it. She felt the strength of this form, and couldn't believe they would be so foolish!

Out ran the youngest to her left, Egard, and he hopped and shouted and clapped his hands together hard.

Aoleyn felt the bear's response, muted deep within by her overpowering possession. It felt a bit of alarm, perhaps, but more so, a sudden urge to run the puny man over.

Out came Ralid, circling the other way, to her right, and with Tay Aillig and the fourth, Aghmor, coming straight at her. All of them started shouting, waving arms, even whistling. They were trying to confuse the bear, perhaps to chase it away.

But Aoleyn wasn't confused, and she wasn't leaving.

She decided to make that very clear. Nearest her was Egard, so she reared onto the bear's hind legs and roared with all the power she could extract from this massive animal, a blast of fury that had Egard leaning back, then backpedaling fast.

With frightening speed, the bear turned the other way, fell to all fours, and galloped at Ralid, who was too near the prisoner for Aoleyn's liking. The young warrior fell back immediately, wisely, while Tay Aillig and the others began shouting, trying to distract the bear.

Aoleyn wouldn't be distracted. She charged at Ralid and had him in full retreat, closed on him as he neared some brush, and roared behind him, propelling him on his way as he dived over and through that tangle.

Aoleyn felt a sensation of true power when she spun the bear about then, to see the other three warriors skidding desperately to stop and reverse their direction!

Closest now was Aghmor, and Aoleyn knew all about Aghmor, the friend of Brayth. Never had that one been considered the bravest of warriors, and Aoleyn counted on that reputation now and burst toward him with frightening speed.

The man was in a dead run in a heartbeat, straightaway and with no apparent desire to stop anytime soon.

Tay Aillig, too, did not come in at the bear, though Aoleyn's action had put the animal sidelong to him and open to a strike. He didn't have a blessed Usgar spear, Aoleyn realized, and his present spear, stone-tipped, wouldn't likely kill a giant brown bear.

She turned on him and he hurled the weapon as she stood the bear up on hind legs once more.

The missile struck the animal's chest and started to penetrate, but Aoleyn brought a paw sweeping across to knock it aside before it could do any real harm.

Tay Aillig drew a sword, a metal one that seemed well crafted, but backed away, and held back Egard as he started coming forward.

Aoleyn dropped to all fours and measured her strides toward the duo, who backed equally as she approached.

She focused on Tay Aillig, and the Usgar-laoch tipped her off, for he did not know that this was much more than a bear, after all! For he was looking past her, with just a hint of a sly grin spreading on his face.

Aoleyn the bear whirled about even as the returning Ralid came rushing in from behind, leaping high, sword above his head for a devastating stab.

Purely on reflex, barely aware of the movement, Aoleyn swiped across a huge paw, intercepting the flying assault. She had only meant to block the attack, and surely not to hit Ralid with such force.

Such unbelievable power.

He was in the air still, sidelong and spinning, his weapon flying aside, and he hit the same tree holding the prisoner in an awkward, diagonal position, crashing in with his arm and left shoulder and right hip with sickening, bone-crushing force.

He hung there against the tree for just a moment, before rolling off to the ground, and only then did Aoleyn see the blood and the line of deep grooves the huge claws had inflicted across the man's chest.

He hadn't even fully settled to stillness on the ground at the base of the tree when Aoleyn knew that he was dead.

She was as angry as she was horrified, and she spun back to face the two Usgar warriors, both wearing expressions of sheer terror. She took no pleasure in seeing the awful Tay Aillig in such a state, not with the overwhelming smell of poor Ralid's blood so thick in her borrowed nostrils!

Up to her hind legs, she went, roaring and pacing forward deter-minedly. She didn't want to kill these two, but she wasn't going to let this play any longer.

Mercifully, she didn't have to, for both men turned and fled, and Aghmor, off in the distance still, was glad to join them.

Aoleyn the bear gave chase, running them off for many, many strides and let them get far ahead before releasing the bear, her spirit exiting its mind, relinquishing control.

She flew back effortlessly across the terrain, to the shining light she knew to be her own corporeal form, still sitting in the tree as she had left it. A dizzying sensation accompanied her back into that body, but she shook it away and jumped down from the tree, knowing the pris-oner needed her immediately, and hoping against hope that she could help Ralid, as well.

She ran into the clearing, saw the prisoner lying on the ground in a widening pool of blood, saw Ralid crumbled against the tree, unmoving, too still. She wanted to go to him.

But he was dead, Aoleyn knew, and this man before her was not.

She went to the prisoner and rolled him over, reaching into her wedstone. She sent the healing magic into him with full force, then again, then a third time as she eased the crystalline knife out of his side, sealing the wound even as her extraction opened it wide.

The man breathed deeply and seemed to settle, and Aoleyn scram-bled to the tree. Yes, Ralid was dead, she rationally knew, but she had to try. She jostled him and called upon her wedstone yet again.

But there was nothing to heal, no hint of a life force she could latch onto and expand.

The truth of it hit her, right in the face. Ralid was dead, and she had done it. She hadn't meant to kill him, not even to hurt him, her move-ment was simply intended to protect the bear from the man's sword.

She tried to tell herself that. He was dead, and Aoleyn had done it.

She had killed a man. She had killed an Usgar.

She couldn't take her eyes from the wound, three deep gouges cut-ting from shoulder to halfway across his chest—so deep that she could see between his ribs at one point, to his torn lung.

Tears welled in the young woman's eyes. She knew that she had to hurry. The bear could be coming back; stubborn Tay Aillig might be coming back! But she couldn't move. Not then. She couldn't even blink as the enormity of what she had done assailed her.

After Brayth had taken her that day in Seonagh's tent, Seonagh had told her that she had lost her innocence. That had, in fact, been one of the last things Seonagh had ever said.

But Aoleyn had never felt that way, not in the least. She had done as she had to do, and she had never done anything to hurt anyone else. She hadn't enjoyed the experience, certainly, had hated Brayth for doing that to her, and Seonagh for letting it happen, but the word "innocence" meant to her that she would have had to do something proactive; she would have had to initiate the action.

Now, though, staring at Ralid, Aoleyn knew the truth of it. Now, she had truly lost her innocence, and she could never retrieve it.

She had killed a person.

A groan from behind her shook her from her stupor, and once she glanced back at the prisoner, the spell of the sight of dead Ralid was broken.

Aoleyn ran to him and he shied as she moved to help him sit up.

Instead, Aoleyn cast another spell of healing upon him, and he straightened noticeably, and more of his wounds mended.

"Who are you?" she asked.

"Tal—" he said, but he sharply inhaled and leaned back, trying to get his bound hands in front of him. His eyes went wide.

Aoleyn glanced back to see the return of the bear.

"He won't hurt you," she promised, and with confidence, because she understood this animal, and it wanted nothing to do with her. It moved across the clearing, still some distance from Aoleyn and the man, and began snuffling at the bushes.

"Greetings, Tal," she said cheerily. "I am Aoleyn. Are you of the lake tribes?"

"Talmadge," he corrected. "And no. Who are you? And why are you here?"

"You should be glad that I am here," she said, moving to help him with his bindings. "And if you aren't from the lakemen, then why are you here?"

Before Talmadge could answer, there came a growl and a roar, and Aoleyn turned to see the bear, back to them, shoulders flexing as it swung furiously at something hidden behind its bulk.

"Deamhan Usgar!" Talmadge cried, kicking his feet, sliding away.

Aoleyn shook her head, knowing that could not be the case. The bear was struggling and swatting with all its strength—no man could stand before that power.

Up to its full height went the bear, and Aoleyn expected it to drop upon its foe. But it stayed up high instead and issued something that was not a roar, something that was more a shriek, sounding so strange coming from such a creature.

The bear shuddered and shook, and screamed—that was the only word Aoleyn could think of to describe the ghastly sounds coming from the animal.

It kept shaking, and Aoleyn blinked with shock as she noted a strange bulge in its back. She heard the man Talmadge struggle to his feet behind her, but she couldn't tear her eyes away from the spectacle.

A black head with shining red eyes tore through the bear's back, biting and wriggling, and the monster, the fossa burrowed through.

"By the gods," Talmadge gasped. "Run!"

"No," Aoleyn said before she could even consider the question. They could not run, she knew all too well, for she had seen this monster's charge before.

The demon fossa stared at the duo, stared particularly at her, Aoleyn thought, and she knew the murder in its fire eyes.

The bloody creature, catlike, weasel-like, slinked her way silently, on padded paws.

36

CIRCLE OF LIFE, CIRCLE OF TIME

Aoleyn had no time to think, so she grabbed at the most obvious offensive strike she could muster, and with a stamp of her foot, she called to the gray bars of her anklet, and following her fear, she threw all of her magical strength behind the stroke of lightning.

Blinding light filled the area, along with a reverberating thump of thunder that bounced Aoleyn and Talmadge right off the ground. The bolt flashed out instantly, slamming the fossa.

And the lightning stroke was gone, as quickly as it had arrived, yet the fossa remained, seeming unharmed, perhaps even stronger. The creature did not move, and it appeared to absorb the lightning. As though the fossa simply ate it.

Aoleyn had seen this before, on the battlefield with Brayth, and though this bolt, directly from her and not transmitted through her connection with Brayth, was much stronger, the effect had clearly been much the same.

Barely had the lightning dissipated when the fossa charged, but Aoleyn was not surprised and was already once more into the magic she had pierced upon her body. She changed tactics, going with the blue-white stone, a zircon, on her anklet, and she stamped her foot again, bravely holding her ground as the fossa roared in, as this creature, which could kill with a single bite or swipe of its claw or thrash of its swordlike tail, sped for her with murder burning in its red eyes.

Only at the last moment did Aoleyn fall aside, as the fossa hit her field of ice and went flying past in a wild tumble.

"To me!" she called to Talmadge and he scrambled to her side, and his eyes widened in obvious shock when he took her hand and became weightless, or nearly so! And as Aoleyn rushed him around the far side of the icy ground, again putting the magical field between them and the fossa, Talmadge found his entire body covered in a blue-white glow.

The fossa crashed into the birch tangle, its flailing tail taking down numerous small trees as it flip-flopped through. It came right back out, seeming unharmed and stalking in once again, now with more measured steps.

It paced toward the ice patch.

Aoleyn clutched Talmadge's hand more tightly, but kept her focus on her gems, on the ring she wore. She shifted it around with her other hand, feeling the pinch of the wedstone fastener, the conduit. She saw the hatefulness in the monster's eyes, and felt the monster's focus on her, only her. It knew her, she realized then. It recognized her, and probably from the fight with Brayth, she thought errantly, having no idea that the fossa had tracked her every burst of power from that night when she had first been in the crystal caverns. She swallowed hard, steeling herself against the sudden near-certainty that she was about to die.

The creature stopped just before the ice field, barely ten strides from the two, and began tamping down its hind legs, never blinking, never taking its hateful stare from the witch.

It could clear the ground to her in a single leap, Aoleyn knew.

"Jump," she whispered to Talmadge. "Straight up. Jump!"

And she loosed the fury of the ruby in her ring, and jumped up beside Talmadge, hand in hand, climbing with the power of the malachite, then calling upon the moonstone to propel them more.

The fossa jumped, too, a mighty, monstrous leap that sent it soaring right into the massive fireball.

Protected by the milky-white serpentine shield, Aoleyn and Talmadge flew out from the flames, above the leaping monster, and up into the tree, where they each grabbed onto a branch.

Below them, the fireball shrunk when it should have been expanding, and kept shrinking fast to nothingness, as if the fossa had simply sucked it inside of itself! Its scraggly fur shed wisps of smoke, little fires even igniting all about its body, as if coming from inside the monster, as if the demon fossa was itself an ember. But again, the monster seemed perfectly unharmed, even looked up and gave a low growl that sounded very much like a taunt to Aoleyn.

She looked down at the creature, standing in the midst of the fog of her burned-off ice field. She and the man named Talmadge weren't nearly high enough, and couldn't get high enough, she knew, certain that the fossa could run up this tree. She considered flying away, but she was sure from her earlier grapple with dead Gavina that she could not do that with Talmadge in tow. They'd never go fast enough or get high enough to evade the monster.

Aoleyn simply had no answers here. She had thrown everything, all the destructive power of Usgar, at the fossa, and it stood there unharmed—indeed, it only seemed to have gotten stronger.

And angrier.

They were both dead—or she was, at least.

"Run away," she told Talmadge. "It wants me. Run away."

"You can'no be serious!" Talmadge countered, and he ranted on about how he would not leave her.

But Aoleyn wasn't listening. She thought of her first encounter with the fossa, when Seonagh had saved her, but had been devoured. She couldn't fight the fossa then or now with fire and lightning and cold, but she could perhaps tie up the creature in a different kind of battle to allow this man, at least, to survive.

"Run away!" she growled at him, and she went to her wedstone and used it to flee her mortal coil—and on instinct, perhaps because this monster looked much like an animal, she brought forth the power of the turquoise, too.

Believing she had no chance, that she would be shattered mentally, at least, and likely devoured thereafter, the stubborn young woman went anyway, throwing her spirit into the fossa, which welcomed her into a yawning darkness.

Instantly, she was back in the anchorless void, staring into the coldness of death, the pit of a horrible infinity. She knew despair, and hopelessness, and cold. So cold!

She felt her life force itself being chewed and frayed, and it took all of her strength to stop it from shattering to shards of black nothingness. She didn't know how long she could hold out, though, and hoped it would be long enough for the prisoner to get away.

But then she understood that she could not, that the only reason the fossa hadn't already obliterated her was because it wanted to play with her.

And taunt her.

With images of Brayth's death, first of all—Aoleyn watched and felt Brayth die exactly as Brayth had seen it, and felt it, every horrifying chew and cut. Every fear, unimaginable terror, mind-shattering pain.

Brayth had soiled himself and pissed himself, she knew, and figured that she probably had, as well, back in her corporeal body.

Still she held on as Brayth expired, and so the evil creature taunted her some more, putting her into the midst of the terror of a deer it had killed, then the horror of slowly devouring another human, a lakewoman with two humps on her shaped head.

Aoleyn's soul quivered and nearly fell to pieces, the horrors too ugly to comprehend. She wanted to fight back, and so denied the creature and tried to take command of some part of the creature that it might rend itself.

But there was nothing, nothing to hold onto, nothing to torment, no way to exert her will. She was ungrounded, lost in blackness that had no discernable boundaries, and with no guiding beacon to be found. She was lost in the murderous pleasure of the fossa, in the final moments of horror of its endless stream of victims.

She heard the shriek of a sidhe as the fossa rushed past it, severing its feet to leave it helpless upon the ground, writhing in agony until the fossa circled back to eat.

And then it was not a footless sidhe about to be devoured, but a footless man, an Usgar, splayed on the ground, desperately trying to push past the pain and terror and ready his weapon. She felt his helplessness and fear, felt the internal turmoil as he tried desperately to remember that he was Usgar, a warrior, so that he might gather his courage and dignity in these last moments of his life.

She even heard his voice, his plaintive cry to "Elara!"

Aoleyn started with the surprise of recognition. Not with the word itself, but with the voice. She had no idea of how she knew that voice, but it resonated within her with a distant but clear familiarity. And somehow, this new tragic image unsettled her and threatened to destroy her more so than had the death of Brayth.

The fossa must have sensed that, she realized, for the bloody scene lingered this time and didn't flash forward to the next kill the demon wanted to display. Just there, where the pain was so intense on this young woman that would be its prey.

But Aoleyn, for all the agony, physical and emotional, didn't want the fossa to leave, didn't want to let go of this ugly scene unfolding before her. She felt the man's pain as if it were her own, both physically and in his soul. He had failed, but it wasn't his own death that was breaking him. He had failed his wife. He had failed his child.

Aoleyn didn't understand the significance of that, but in that moment, the man's pain, her pain, became too much to bear, and she tried to press on, to get the fossa to release this image.

But no, she stayed in this demon memory, lost in the hopelessness and despair.

And she saw herself, drawn and dying, being eaten by the fossa.

But no, she realized, with confusion swelling—was she not lost in the fossa's memories, or even in the horrifying immediacy of seeing her own certain doom? Was she seeing the future? Yes, this looked like her own last moments: the woman in her mind's eye looked like her, but an older her. Was she seeing her own doomed and damned future?

Surely she felt the agony as if it were her own, the last fleeting moments of clarity.

Don't fight the dark! she thought, but wait . . . *Embrace the light!*

Confusion cleared when Aoleyn recognized that these were not *her*

thoughts. Was this madness? The last vestiges of coherent consciousness, as with Seonagh?

Then she understood, and the epiphany came not with relief: this
was not her death, these were not her thoughts. This was not some vision
of her future.

These last moments of life and sanity were not hers at all.

It was a witch, connected to the doomed man as she had been to
Brayth. Or was it a ghost, an echo of that woman, taken and trapped
within the black pit of hatefulness of the demon fossa?

The doomed man with the voice she somehow knew . . . the dying
woman who looked so much like her . . .

And Aoleyn knew! But she was too late, alas! For she was falling then,
away from the world, away from sanity, and there was nothing to grab
onto.

The thunder rolled up the slopes of Fireach Speuer, shaking and shocking the three Usgar warriors who had been chased away by the giant
bear.

Glancing back for signs of continuing pursuit, Tay Aillig saw the
flash itself, and knew that it had not come from the sky, that it was not
a normal thundercloud from above.

"Usgar?" Egard asked, spinning about and seeing the confusion on
the War Leader's face.

"The fossa," Aghmor breathed.

But Tay Aillig shook his head. The fossa had never been known to
throw magic. The fossa didn't need magic!

"A witch," he decided. Had someone followed them from the camp?
Mairen came to mind, particularly given the power of that lightning
blast. Connebragh, perhaps. No . . .

For some reason that he couldn't comprehend, he became certain that
it was Aoleyn. The meddlesome young woman was often out of the
encampment, he knew. Had she stumbled upon his war party, only to
find herself face-to-face with a great brown bear?

He thought of running back down the hill, not out of any love for

Aoleyn, of course, but simply to protect the expected gains she could bring. But he couldn't fight that bear, not with the puny sword he now carried. If he had been wielding a blessed Usgar spear, perhaps . . .

He shook his head and turned about again, and led the other two off at a run, back up the mountainside, back to the Usgar encampment.

There came a moment of reprieve, something tangible to grab onto, only for an instant, and Aoleyn didn't know why, but in that moment of freedom, Aoleyn grabbed at the doomed witch's thoughts, embraced them, and somehow understood them, or thought she did.

Her fire and lightning and freezing cold had done nothing but deepen the murderous dark that was the fossa.

So Aoleyn embraced the light.

She grabbed the power of her wedstone and cast a wave of healing into the demon beast.

Its discomfort stabbed back at her, and she felt something else, some different reaction, a third entity wrapped within their spiritual combat. The young witch recognized something then, something about what this creature had been! The fossa was not one. It was two, bound as one in darkness, one demonic, one surely not!

She healed it again, and in the ensuing struggle, yanked her spirit free from the fossa's darkness and flew back to her waiting corporeal form, still in the tree, but now alone. For a brief moment, she thought and hoped that Talmadge had fled, but then she spotted him on the ground beside the demon creature, crawling away on his elbows, dragging torn legs behind him.

He had given her the moment of reprieve! He had leaped upon the monster when she and the fossa had been tangled in a spiritual battle.

Aoleyn couldn't think of that now, for both their sakes. She grabbed the wedstone on her belly, pressed it hard into her flesh, and threw another healing wave at the fossa. She slid off the branch and caught her fall only enough with the malachite so that she landed lightly on the ground right before the beast.

She was not afraid, for she understood now, and so was too filled with anger to be afraid.

The Usgar on the ground, the witch caught by the fossa in her spiritual embrace with its victim . . .

The demon fossa had killed her father and eaten the soul of her mother!

The turquoise called to her, as well—showing her that other animal, being trapped with the demon in this broken and monstrous coil—and she reached out again, now with both stones, throwing forth a wave of healing magic and twisting it as if she were tending a broken animal.

She was only a stride from the fossa! It could leap forth and bite her face off!

But no, it couldn't.

For now the battle was within it. Aoleyn was giving freedom to the creature caught within the fossa's demonic darkness.

The monster went into a horrifying spin, scrabbling, scratching, tearing at the ground, at anything near.

And mostly, at itself.

It spun and leaped and rolled, maddened beyond sensibility. Where Aoleyn's magic could not harm it, its own claws and teeth did, dragging bloody lines, skin hanging in torn flaps. It bolted all about, left and right, once right over poor Talmadge, who tried to cover up but got flattened and gouged. It rolled past Aoleyn, a ball of pure hatred, and she only barely got to the side in time.

It rolled and leaped and scrambled and darted farther away.

And that was the problem, Aoleyn suddenly understood, for proximity mattered, and as the monster moved farther from her, the demon within the monster regained more control; the darkness swallowed the light.

It charged across the clearing, but not approaching, went up one tree and leaped far away, landing in a ground-tearing fury. It looked briefly back at Aoleyn with most hateful eyes, then it ran into the brush, and the trees shivered with its passing.

Aoleyn ran off after it.

"What are you doing?" poor Talmadge cried.

She tried hard to ignore him. She had to get close, to reestablish the connection, to embrace the light within. But no, she couldn't begin to pace the monster, and it was running straight away, up the side of the mountain, tearing apart anything in its path.

Aoleyn looked back to the clearing, to the man who was bleeding once again, and then out to the west, where the Blood Moon was setting.

She looked back up the mountainside, to see a distant tree shudder, a black form leaping away, running into the dark night.

She couldn't hope to catch it.

It had never felt such a thing before. Such . . . discord. Cacophony. The music it had sought, twisted around and now less painful, but more profoundly devastating.

Devastating and beautiful, and calling to the other being, the one that did not feel the pain when the red moon was not above, when the music stabbed the tormented demon a million times in a million places.

This intended victim, this singer of the hated song, had twisted the mountain's notes to her own ends to use against the fossa.

It took a long while and a long ascent up the mountain before the fossa heard the music again, but there it was as it had been, stinging now unbearably, for the red moon was no more, the harmony of music and magic blowing on mountain winds. The song of the living that the fossa could not stand.

The demon fossa let out a long, low growl.

It stalked off again, retreating from the music, though now a part of the creature had reawakened and did not want to run from the song.

But the darkness held and the fossa slinked away for the safety of its pit of death, desperate to get out from under the stars and away from the musical wind of Fireach Speuer.

The Blood Moon had set. The night of the fossa had ended.

Aoleyn never took her eyes off the upward slopes of Fireach Speuer as she threw another wave of magical healing into poor Talmadge.

She had to go, and quickly, for every passing moment made it less likely that she could track the fossa. She had it hurt and knew its weakness and had to strike now.

For winter was fast coming, and she'd never find its lair, and another Blood Moon could be years away.

The outrage, the violation, within Aoleyn couldn't wait years.

Talmadge sat up beside her, praising her magical prowess. "Are you a monk?" he asked, a word she did not even begin to understand.

She ignored him anyway.

"You are free, go away," she said, not even looking at him. Any other time, and curious Aoleyn would have had a million questions for this man, this stranger who looked more like Usgar but was not Usgar than any of the lakemen from below.

But not now. She had seen her parents.

And she had met their murderer.

She was sure of it.

She pulled herself back up to her feet and started away, staggering under the weight of incredible exhaustion.

"Where are you going?" she heard the man Talmadge ask from behind. "You can'no!" he cried, and before Aoleyn had even crossed the clearing, he was beside her, holding her up.

"I am," she declared.

"You need rest."

The claim sounded obvious to Aoleyn, but she shook her head determinedly. "I can'no let it get away."

"It already did!"

"Its trail is clear."

Talmadge wanted to stop her, whoever she was. She had intervened and chased away his tormentors. She had come to him, so full of fire, so thick with blessed healing and divine lightning. He had some experience with the Abellican monks back in the Wilderlands west of Honce-the-Bear, and had seen magic—even used magic with his clairvoyance glass.

But looking at Aoleyn, the frontiersman didn't see Abellican monks. No, he saw Khotai, that same indomitable spirit, that same fearlessness that had sent Khotai spinning on her back into the midst of his three captors that long-ago day by the mountain river.

He winced at the memory, at how he had been thrown from Khotai by the monster of Loch Beag, how he couldn't get back to her.

How he hadn't even tried.

It wouldn't have mattered if he had tried, he knew, rationally. The one assault on the canoe by the overpowering lake monster had defeated any possible fight or rescue. Talmadge hadn't even been aware of his flight until he felt the ground beneath his feet in shallow waters. He hadn't meant to abandon Khotai.

But he had.

There it was, hanging before him, undeniable.

He knew then what he had to do.

"I am a tracker," he said, grabbing Aoleyn securely and turning her about to face him. "And I am strong now, from the gift of your magic."

He smiled wryly, then moved quickly, dropping and hoisting the woman up and over his shoulder.

"You rest," he told her and he started out of the clearing, following the obvious trail left by the maddened monster.

Before he had gone two steps, though, Aolcyn wriggled and rolled from his grasp, landing beside him. "Are you mad?" she demanded, slapping his hand away.

"You helped me, now I must help you."

"You're not going to carry me up the mountain!"

"You need rest . . . you can'no deny."

Aoleyn paused and took a deep and steadying breath. She couldn't deny her exhaustion, but it was different than she might have felt if she had spent a day hoisting heavy stones. This weariness was less physical and more profound, and she felt, more than anything else, as if she had to quiet her mind and not call upon the song of Usgar at all.

"This is my task," she said stubbornly, and she knew it was a stupid thing to say, but couldn't help herself.

"You are certain that you must pursue this creature?"

"Aye."

"Then this is the price of my debt. If you go, I go."

Aoleyn wanted to tell him that he had repaid his debt in full. He had leaped from the tree onto the fossa, breaking its spiritual hold on her soul, giving her the moment of freedom to fight back.

She wanted to tell him to go away, in any case, because, despite her determination, she believed she would die in this fight, and didn't want him to die beside her.

That's what she wanted to do, but she could not. She knew that she needed him for support, and not just physical support, and not just his tracking. She was terribly angry, but she was terribly afraid, and she realized that those fears were only going to grow stronger with every step up the mountain.

"I can walk," she said, and started off, Talmadge moving up beside her.

Soon after, she was leaning on him heavily with every step.

Long after that, she awakened with the first hints of dawn, to find herself across Talmadge's shoulders, the man still moving.

"Good morning," he said, easing her to the ground, and huffing with every twist, clearly weary.

Aoleyn faced him squarely, staring him in the eye.

He pointed a finger into his own chest, and introduced himself again, after the craziness of the previous night. "I am Talmadge."

She nodded. "Talmadge. From which village?"

He laughed. "From a village long ago and far away," he said. "I have no tribe."

She nodded. "No tribe is good."

"But you have a tribe. Aoleyn, yes? You are Usgar."

She nodded again. "I am called Aoleyn, yes, and yes."

"Well, Aoleyn of the Usgar, if you are so determined to face this monster, I will not stop you."

"You could not, if you tried."

"The trail is thinner, but we are near to its lair, I am sure," he said.

Aoleyn nodded. "Show me, then leave."

The man looked about and seemed to be wrestling with something, but at last he nodded.

"You are certain?"

"How many times will you ask?"

"Until you say no?" he answered with a grin, but Aoleyn didn't return the smile. She had rested, but the anger in her had not abated. The
demon fossa had killed her father and eaten her mother's soul, and she
had watched it, had felt it intimately.

Talmadge nodded at her. "Good enough, then," he agreed, and he
started along with Aoleyn right behind, soon, the northwestern side of
the mountain still dark with the morning shadow. Soon after, the two
crept to a ridgetop and stared down a small hollow to see an enormous
chunk of stone, the massive roof of a black cave at the bottom, hidden
behind a small stand of quaking aspens.

Aoleyn toed at the rocky ground before the cave. It had a vaguely
crystalline appearance, with edges too sharp and too clean for the
mountainside. Talmadge had noticed the strangeness of the cave entrance's appearance, too, Aoleyn noted, and had perked up upon seeing it.

"Your debt is paid," Aoleyn whispered.

"Not yet," he replied. "Not until I talk you out of this madness. You
can'no go in there."

Aoleyn surely understood his sentiment, for the stench of death
flowed out of that black opening, assaulting her senses and her courage.

"Be gone, Talmadge of no tribe, who will not even tell me of his
village."

"I have no village."

"You were born in the forest?"

Talmadge chuckled despite the grim mood and wretched scent. He
pointed out to the east, beyond the plateau, beyond the Surgruag
Monadh, beyond even the Desert of Black Stones.

"Far away," he said wistfully. "In a land called the Wilderlands—
though surely a land tame compared with this place—near a great kingdom called Honce-the-Bear."

"Honce-the-Bear?"

He nodded and smiled.

"There are villages there, in Honce-the-Bear?" Aoleyn asked.

"Many! Great villages and cities."

Aoleyn shook her head, not understanding what "cities" might be.

"Huge villages," Talmadge explained. "Full of houses and towers, and with a hundred people for every single lakeman, woman, or child all about Loch Beag—all of them! And the Usgar, too! All of them combined!"

His expression grew sly. "Turn from this place, Aoleyn of Usgar," he said. "Come with me to Fasach Crann, on the lake, and then beyond. Come with me to the east, beyond the black stones of Fasail Dubh'clach, and I will show you."

Aoleyn could not deny the curiosity he had aroused in her.

"Beyond the lake, beyond the mountains?" she asked.

"Aye."

"Farther than we can see from the top of Fireach Speuer?"

"Aye, much farther."

She shook her head. "There is nothing beyond the horizon."

He laughed again. "You're smarter than that," he said.

She nodded and this time smiled back at him, but they both knew that the distracting conversation, for all its delightful possibilities, was at its end.

"Go away, Talmadge."

"Aoleyn . . ."

"You can'no help me in there. You'd get me killed trying to save you."

Talmadge stuttered about for some recourse, but there was none to be found.

"Well, I'm heading down," he said in obvious surrender. "Sun's up, and I've a long walk ahead. Best to be off the mountain before night, or I might get hunted again. Even before night, if it's your Usgar friends come calling."

They are not my friends, Aoleyn thought but did not say.

Talmadge turned and walked away, leaving Aoleyn crouched at the top of the ridge, staring down at the cave that so fittingly looked like the gaping maw of a hungry demon.

37

THE FACE OF EVIL

An exhausted Tay Aillig, Egard, and Aghmor limped into the Usgar encampment just as the looming mountain before them began to limn with the light of dawn behind it. Their legs were scratched and bleeding, Egard had turned an ankle and leaned heavily on Aghmor for support. Aghmor's nose was certainly broken from running into a low limb in the dark. He had crashed to the ground and remained so still for so long that Tay Aillig was sure he had lost another warrior that terrible night.

But no, the trio had made it to safety, at least, which was more than could be said for Ralid.

Tay Aillig cared little for that, other than the consequences he might face for getting a man killed on a hunt of his calling, and without the sanction of the Coven or the blessing of Usgar-forfach Raibert. No raid or hunt was supposed to happen without two of the three—Usgar-forfach, Usgar-righinn, and Usgar-laoch—in agreement.

He'd just go to Raibert soon, he decided, before the tribe moved to the winter plateau, and remind the doddering old man that he had been given his agreement for the hunt.

Or maybe he'd go to Mairen.

The mere thought of confronting the Usgar-righinn had the man gnashing his teeth.

Behind him, Aghmor and Egard veered off, heading for their tents and some needed sleep, Tay Aillig knew. He didn't stop them, for both seemed near to collapse, and he certainly understood that feeling.

Standing on the edge of camp, most of the Usgar still asleep, Tay Aillig again tried to unwind the surprising events of the previous night.

His two surviving minions were despondent, of course, but he was too full of anger to feel that way. Anger at fate for putting a bear in that place at that time, a bear that came to his fossa lure, and in the last Blood Moon expected for a long while!

It had been the worst possible coincidence, a terrible turn of chance that had cost him his planned ascension to Usgar-triath. He should have the fossa's bloody head in his hands then, to walk into the camp in triumph.

The camp began to stir before him, women appearing to go out and begin the morning meal, men wandering out of their tents to go piss in the woods. None paid particular heed to Tay Aillig, and why should they?

Yes, that would be his greatest hope: that no one even knew that he and the three had gone out the previous night. Not much of a hope, though, for it did nothing to alleviate the ambitious man's disappointment.

His glory had been stolen away. Ancient Raibert wouldn't live much longer, probably not even until the next Blood Moon, the next chance for Tay Aillig to put his plan into motion. When Raibert died, Ahn'Namay would be named as Usgar-forfach, and that one likely had many years of life ahead of him.

Unless an unfortunate accident fell upon him.

Tay Aillig didn't like the idea of killing yet another Usgar, and particularly one so venerated, but he liked less the idea that he would be caught there, simply as Usgar-laoch—and even that formidable position would not hold for long as the younger men sought to take his place.

Shorter still might his reign be if the truth of Ralid's death became known.

He thought of the bear happening upon the lure, then fighting the

four men so determinedly. Food was plentiful this season, and that behavior seemed so unusual, even for an aggressive brown bear. Aghmor and
Egard had claimed it was maddened, surely crazed, and driven into them
by the fossa, like so many sidhe had been driven across the mountainside under the Blood Moon previous. But Tay Aillig considered, too,
the lightning he had seen behind him—a witch's lightning, to be sure.
The fossa might drive even a bear before it, of course, but Tay Aillig
suspected that such was not the case, not this time.

Standing there, the camp awakening around him, Tay Aillig became convinced that his plans had been foiled, not by fate, not by a mere
bear, not even by the fossa.

"Mairen?" he whispered to himself. Would he find her sleeping in
her tent?

He growled and he scowled and he stalked off to find out.

The stench and the overwhelming sensation of dread nearly stopped
Aoleyn as she approached the dark entryway, a black opening of about
waist height beneath the gigantic stone wall. She bent low and called
upon her diamond, relieved to see that the floor beyond was a bit lower,
so she wouldn't have to crawl through, at least.

She wanted to go in, but her legs would not answer her call.

She found herself breathing hard, in gasps, and then felt as if she
had to remember to breathe or she would not.

The gasps came faster. Aoleyn's eyes darted about, left and right. She
looked behind her, expecting to see the monster leaping upon her. She
looked into the cave again and imagined the ghosts of her mother and
father flitting about the shadows just outside the perimeter of her
magical light.

Were they waiting for her here? To welcome her to death?

When she sat down on the ground and slung her legs into the cave,
she truly suspected that she was climbing into the realm of death and
not the Jeweled Shore of Corsaleug—to the smoky underplane of Ifrinn,
where the fiends roamed and tormented deserving souls for eternity.

Aoleyn closed her eyes and steadied herself. She thought of the crystal caverns, where the song of Usgar rang supreme—those were not far from this place, she knew. This place, Fireach Speuer, her home.

This was not Ifrinn before her, she told herself. It only felt that way because of the creature within, because of the demon fossa. Magic was life, and life was magic, and around the fossa she had felt neither.

She hopped down to the cave floor, ducking so that she didn't crack her head on the low stone of the entryway. She called upon her diamond to shed brighter light, but held back. She feared to walk in the darkness, of course, but was she making herself an easier target?

She let the diamond magic expire, to see how bright the cave would be without it.

She ignited it immediately once more, having found herself in a blackness that was not natural! She glanced back at the entry, the exit, and saw the world beyond, waking with the morning light.

But it was muted and seemed so far removed, so far away.

Was this Ifrinn?

He had wanted to stay and ask the girl many, many questions, surely, but he had realized that he would not dissuade her, would not turn her from her course. Nor could Talmadge argue with her reasoning that he would be no help to her, indeed might prove a detriment, in the lair of that monstrous creature. He had leaped from the tree upon it, crashing with crushing weight. Had the beast even noticed? It had shrugged him aside and absently whacked him with that terrible swordlike tail, and the only reason Talmadge even had legs left was because he was falling before the blow, and so the tail didn't cut through.

Talmadge stopped in his tracks and glanced back up the mountainside. He worried that he was leaving this young woman, this child, to die. The thought of his severed legs had thrown his thoughts back to that awful moment on the banks of Loch Beag when he had found the leg of Khotai, his dear Khotai.

Perhaps he had left Khotai to die.

The breeze picked up, and Talmadge felt the invigorating, unseasonably cold wind on his face, and was reminded of that magical leap, nay that flight, up into the tree while holding Aoleyn's hand. He had never seen such a display of magical power! And the fireball! If the fossa hadn't—hadn't what? absorbed it? eaten it?—that expanding blast would have surely lit half the mountain on fire!

So perhaps this Aoleyn would win.

He laughed at the absurdity of it all, at his own helplessness, at his own smallness, and continued down the mountain, under the sunrise of the brilliant late-summer morning. The girl, the strange flying girl, had saved his life, beyond any doubt. Not simply from the Usgar hunters, but from the giant bear—in his decades on the frontier, Talmadge had never seen a bear behave so strangely! It was almost as if the great predator had come in to protect him from the Usgar. He stopped and pondered: had the girl done that, too?

The girl who had thrown lightning and fire, who had healed the deep wound of the crystalline knife? Who had shown up at exactly the right moment to save him and get him away from danger?

Talmadge ran his hand over the wound, flinching, pained by the slightest touch. The dagger had gone in so very deep, he understood, he knew. The strike had been mortal, surely, for even with the heroic healing, his side remained raw and red. He'd have a mighty scar to add to his collection when it fully healed.

Might an Abellican monk have performed this miracle? Would it have had to be an abbot, even the Father Abbot? Yet here he was, alive. For the first time since the fight, Talmadge truly appreciated how impossible that should have been.

"Thanks, girl," he said quietly, his whisper lost to the howling mountain winds.

He huddled up against that wind, crouched behind a boulder, unarmed and quite exhausted. A part of him wanted to take a nap, but he didn't dare. He needed to be off the mountain quickly, this very day, if possible, and back to the relative safety of Fasach Crann. The Usgar were still out there, after all, to say nothing of the demonic beast that had attacked him and the girl.

Talmadge glanced back up the mountainside. "The poor, doomed girl," he whispered.

An image of Khotai flashed in his thoughts, the last moment he had seen her before the canoe had upended, throwing them both into the water.

If Khotai had even hit the water—he couldn't be sure, for not a sound had he heard other than his own desperate splashing as he swam for all his life for the shore.

Fleeing, instead of trying to help her.

He was not going to do that again. He was too old to add to that burden.

Heaving a great sigh, Talmadge fished in his pocket to pull out the crystalline dagger. Such a tiny and inadequate weapon, it seemed!

"So be it," he said, and he turned about, fought away his exhaustion, and started back up Fireach Speuer.

This was death.

Not just the stench of death.

Not just the coldness of death.

No, this was a place of death itself.

Magic was life and life was magic, but here, Aoleyn wondered if there could exist either.

"It killed them," she reminded herself, thinking of her mother and father and all that she had lost. With that in mind, she bravely moved to the low corridor and crept in, and was soon crawling.

Her diamond light seemed to diminish in there, in this place that was not of magic.

She came through to an angled floor with a crawl space that seemed too tight for her to inch through. Every sensibility within the young woman told her to turn back, to run away, to be as far from this awful place as possible.

But she found herself flat on her belly under that too-low ceiling, inching forward with grim determination. For she could feel the coldness beyond.

The fossa was there, waiting for her.

The ceiling above her opened a bit, but she stayed low. The floor before her sloped downward, then disappeared into a dark hole, one that reminded Aoleyn of the pit she had encountered in the crystalline caverns, beneath the maw of Craos'a'diad. And like there, she could feel the ghosts in here, the lamenting spirits of the fossa's many victims.

Was her mother here?

She shook the thought out of her head. She couldn't be distracted, not for an instant. She had to be faster than the fossa!

It was there, just beyond her, in that pit, she knew, she could feel, she could hear.

She tapped her foot and brought a field of ice before her on the decline of the stone floor, and some surely falling into the pit beyond. She considered her options, on how she might fight the creature in these quarters, or how she might get out of this compromising position, and focused on the songs of the moonstone and the malachite.

She heard a roar, and the fossa leaped up before her to the stone, barely a stride away, its claws raking hard on the icy patch.

Aoleyn cried out and threw forth the power of the moonstone, a blast of wind that slammed the slipping monster and pitched it back over the edge.

And Aoleyn went right to her turquoise and wedstone, and sent her spirit flying behind it, diving down into the most horrible darkness she had ever known, toward the red eyes that peered up at her, and straight in to the beast.

Immediately, Aoleyn began again her healing.

The demon fossa howled, shrieked, caterwauled, and went into a murderous frenzy that flipped it all about the pit and sent bones flying all about.

Inside the creature's senses, seeing through the fossa's eyes, Aoleyn saw the ghosts swirling about, trapped and crying, the spirits of so many men and women, children even, and a thousand animal spirits as well. Somewhere there was her mother and her father, she knew, and she wanted to call to them, to free them!

All she could do was cast her healing, with all her strength, to burn away the demon side of their eternal tormentor.

She felt that seething hatred, too, the mind of the monster. Her second wave of assault didn't surprise it, as had her initial intrusion, and now it moved with purpose, scrambling to the back wall of the pit.

"No, no, no," Aoleyn heard her own mouth saying, up above, and she brought forth more magical healing, knowing that time was short.

The fossa leaped across the pit to the wall, caught on, and leaped back higher the other way.

"No!" Aoleyn cried, in her mind and body, for she couldn't defeat it in time, and she was not in her corporeal form to defend!

Her spirit flew free as the fossa sprang to the front wall again, up higher, murderous claws catching hold on the stone and launching it back higher on the back wall. Forward, it sprang again, but now over the lip, its momentum sliding it up the gradual incline, across the ice, one claw reaching forth to stab and hook Aoleyn's arm!

She just got back into her body, just recovered her senses, and she flew forward, caught by the demon, sliding across her own ice, and falling. Instinctively, purely on terror, the witch grabbed at the malachite to resist the fall, but only minimally succeeded, both Aoleyn and the demon crashing down hard into the pile of bones, more than one jagged bit stabbing into her.

She fled her body again—she had no choice—into the fossa, assaulting it with waves of Usgar's song, with the healing power of the wedstone.

She saw through its demonic eyes as it lunged for her form, tasted her own blood as the fossa chewed into her upper belly and lower rib, tearing her diaphragm, biting for her lungs and heart.

Aoleyn knew pain as never before, knew terror as never before, and so she ran and hid in the only place available.

In the song of the wedstone, in the magic of Usgar, and there she sent forth healing as never before, into the fossa, into herself, and she could feel the monster's agony, could smell its flesh burning.

But it was still biting, and her blood was pouring forth, and in this battle, the monster's fangs against her healing powers, she could not win.

She cried out for her mother.

But there was something else, something she felt from the other gemstone, the turquoise, something within the demon fossa.

Something that it had been, that hated the demon more than all else.

Aoleyn went there. Aoleyn healed, trying to keep her body alive, trying to burn away the demon.

The fossa chewed.

38

TALMADGE'S TEARS

Hands on hips, at a loss where to begin, Talmadge almost jumped out of his boots when a large and dark form came charging out of the cave, straight at him!

He cried out, he fell back, waving the crystalline dagger somewhat pathetically, and nearly tripped over his own feet and tumbled to the ground.

But the charging creature had less interest in fighting him than he had in fighting it, and it skidded to a fast stop and turned sideways to the man, stalking off and never taking its eyes from him.

Its feline eyes, for this was no monster, but a cloud leopard, graceful and beautiful. A ferocious predator, to be sure, but a shy one that did not seek out difficult fights.

Talmadge eyed it curiously, and began nodding his head at the big cat's profile as it loped away, low to the ground, long and sleek.

Like the monster from the previous night, though with a furry and plump tail and not some strange swordlike sheaf of bone.

When the cat was at last out of sight, Talmadge looked back to the black maw of the cave. It wasn't the leopard's lair, certainly, or the cat

would not have run off. But why was it in there? The monster had burrowed through a bear, so what might a leopard do against such power?

Or was this the monster? Talmadge had heard tales of creatures that
transformed in the dark of night, or under the glow of a full moon. Was
this legendary demon a were-creature, perhaps?

It was all too confusing, and interesting, but also quickly dismissed
as a musing for another day when the most pressing question weighed
in on Talmadge: what had happened to the young woman, to Aoleyn of
the Usgar?

"Oh, by Abelle's fat ass," Talmadge cursed, knowing that he had to
go in. "Aoleyn?" he called, as loudly as he dared, hoping against hope
that she was somewhere about out here.

He kept calling as he moved about, trying to construct a torch and
figure some way to light it. He gave up on that plan quickly, though,
with the mountain wind howling.

So he sighed and went to the opening, bent down, and peered in. He
noted a shallow cave, and would have thought it nothing more, except
he noted an opening in the back of it, a tunnel leading farther in.

He had to go there, for the only reason he could even note that passageway was because a light was coming from it, thin but consistent. The
light of a magical diamond, Talmadge knew. The young Usgar woman
was back there. He looked around for the leopard, but it was not to be
seen. Could she possibly still be alive?

He hopped into the cave and moved to the passageway, which had a
lower ceiling. He went in crouching, but gave up on that and crawled. He
went around a bend cautiously, the light growing at that corner, and
found that the passage opened up for a slanted floor, the uneven top of a
gigantic stone, with only a tiny clearance to the rough stone ceiling above.

The thought of crawling through such a space terrified Talmadge,
monster or no monster on the other end, but Aoleyn was back there—
or at least, her diamond light was back there.

"Aoleyn!" he called, for if there was a monster back there, it was
going to catch him whether he was silent or not. "Girl! Are you there?"

He paused and listened, but heard only the wind moaning through
the entry cavern behind him.

He lay on his stomach and squeezed under the ceiling and began inching through. He called to Aoleyn repeatedly, but heard no reply. All he knew was the diamond light, and a stench, growing stronger with every inch, and a sense of cold, deathly cold, that he had never known before.

But Talmadge kept going. He thought of Khotai, and decided that no, he wasn't going to leave this lovely young woman who had saved his life.

"Come on, monster," he growled under his breath, knife firmly in hand. The young woman was dead, he believed, and so there was no justice in the world, no beneficent god rewarding heroes and punishing demons. That thought chased him through the tight crawl space, burning at him, assaulting him. By the time he came to the wider area just beyond, a dark hole before him, he was too angry to be afraid. Now that terrible smell of death only made him want to fight, and now the sudden and empty cold . . .

"Cold?" he whispered in surprise.

Talmadge put his hand before him to test the stone ahead once more, but pulled it back immediately, for the stone there was much colder, was frozen and slick with ice, and actually hurt to touch!

"Aoleyn," he breathed, remembering her actions the previous night. He lifted his head as high as he could go, and noted the pit. The light was coming from in there, he could tell, casting a glow up the back wall.

That back wall held him transfixed for a long moment, staring at the gouges in the stone, claw marks as profound as a great cat might do to a stand of soft clay.

He searched about and pulled out the cord he had taken from the tree the night before, finding a jag where the ceiling met the floor where he could tie off one end. Wrapping the other end securely about his hand and arm, Talmadge inched forward, trying to see over the rim and whispering Aoleyn's name.

He came to the cold area but kept going, peering intently, and he finally came to where he was able to look over the ledge. There she was, sitting against the wall on a mound of bones.

Unmoving, the front of her clothing drenched in blood.

"Aoleyn!" he yelled. "Usgar girl!"

She didn't stir.

Talmadge lowered his head in despair. She was dead—she had to be. She was too still. There was too much blood. He thought he should go and retrieve the body, but he didn't even know how he might do that, for the cord wasn't long enough.

He said a prayer for Aoleyn, for this wonderful and strange young woman who had so bravely saved him, and he started back.

And he slipped on the ice and slid back the other way, over the lip of the pit. The cord tightened on his forearm painfully as he struggled, and he had nothing to grab onto, nowhere to put his foot even, for the side of the pit, too, was covered in magical ice. So he hung there and he flailed for a bit, grimacing against the pain, and thought himself stupid indeed, for if anyone came here in the future, they would find him hanging here, dead.

Finally, overcome with frustration, Talmadge brought up the crystal knife and cut the cord. He dropped the final ten feet to the bones, crunching and shifting beneath him.

"Idiot," he cursed himself, and he realized that he had to go and search the body to find the gemstone that she used to lift them the previous night and hope that he could bring forth enough magic to get him back up to the ledge. He moved over her tentatively, unsure, not wanting to desecrate her. He moved her shirt aside to inspect the mortal wound, a deep gash at the bottom of her rib cage—no, more than a gash, more like a burrow, and he thought of the bear the previous night.

"Oh, poor girl," he whispered.

He noticed the diamond, too, glowing brilliantly from a strand on an unusual belly ring she wore. Truly Talmadge had never seen anything like it, with its four strands each ended by a different gem, obviously magical—at least the diamond.

"Girl?" he asked repeatedly, moving very close, trying to make sure that she had expired before he took her gemstones, a task that seemed more difficult now, for that belly ring seemed quite secure and he might have to cut it off her.

He hugged her close, whispering comforting words to her, though he knew she could not hear. He said another prayer, though he had no god of his own and knew nothing about any Aoleyn might care for.

He slid his hand down to grab the gray hub of her jewelry, closing his fingers securely to see if he could somehow ease it out.

And there he found her, found Aoleyn, the thinnest strand of life!

"Girl? Girl?" he said, grabbing her face with his other hand and shaking it about, trying to stir her, to no avail.

She seemed quite dead, but he felt her life in his other hand, in that stone! No, he realized, not in the stone, but through the stone.

Talmadge was not practiced or trained in the use of gemstones. His only experience with magic came from the clairvoyance crystal in his pocket. He closed his eyes now, though, and he felt the magic in the gray stone on Aoleyn's belly, and he knew then that it was what the monks of Abelle called a soul stone, the stone they used in healing.

And this was the stone Aoleyn had used to heal him, twice.

"Please, please, please," Talmadge kept repeating, trying to focus all of his thoughts on that soul stone.

His whispers died away when he heard the song in the stone, and he went to it and embraced it, and tried to give it, somehow, to the poor woman.

But he could not. No matter how hard he tried, Talmadge did not know how to cast such a spell. He could hear the magic, could even call back to it and amplify the song, but no more, and he realized that he couldn't save Aoleyn, that the tiny flicker of life remaining within her was going to snuff out while he held her there in his arms, in that pit of death.

He began to cry.

He cried for Khotai. He cried for Aoleyn.

Tay Aillig was barely halfway to Mairen's tent when Connebragh intercepted him.

"Are you just returning?" the witch asked.

He stared at her hard, trying to intimidate her and back her away from those dangerous questions. Normally that would work on the malleable Connebragh, but this time, she held her ground, though her expression was hardly confrontational.

"Have you seen your wife?" Connebragh asked, and Tay Aillig surrendered his imposing stare for one of surprise.

"What about her?"

"I . . . I assumed that she would be with you."

He realized then that Connebragh hadn't been accusing him of anything with her first question, but that hardly seemed to matter at that moment, anyway. "She is not in her tent?" he asked.

"She is nowhere that I can find."

"And the Usgar-righinn?" the War Leader snapped. He thought back to the previous night in light of this new information.

"Seeking Aoleyn."

"Where is she?"

"I do not know! I just asked you . . ."

"Not Aoleyn!" Tay Aillig snapped. "Where is Mairen?"

Connebragh nodded at the Crystal Maven's tent. Tay Aillig waved her away and started for Mairen once more.

The commotion about the camp increased around him as he went. The Usgar were already on edge, with Gavina's death, the early onset of winter, and so, likely, the early climb to the winter plateau, and with the Blood Moon of the previous night, and so whispers of missing Aoleyn, and then of another disappearance, that of Ralid, began to echo about.

More than one glance fell on Tay Aillig, as well, and why not, since his wife and a man of about her age were both apparently absent from the camp!

Tay Aillig pondered the possibilities here. Perhaps rumors of a tryst between the two would be the best course of action. His own reputation would be sullied, of course, for being cuckolded by a man as mediocre as Ralid, but that might be better than having to admit that he led the missing man to his death in an unsanctioned hunt for the demon fossa.

All of that was bouncing around his thoughts when he pushed into Mairen's tent, to find her sitting with a couple of other witches.

"Be gone!" he ordered, and the two looked to Mairen, who was staring at Tay Aillig—at his uncompromising visage. She nodded and they scurried away.

"What have you done?" Mairen asked when they were alone.

"Nothing that concerns you."

"If it concerns Aoleyn, who seems to be missing—"

"Aoleyn is often missing," Tay Aillig interrupted.

"If it concerns her, it concerns me."

"If it concerns her, then that is of her doing, not mine. When did you last see her?"

Mairen look at him curiously, as if to ask what business that might be of his. Aoleyn was to enter the Coven, after all, and so Mairen's claim on the young woman would be stronger than any Tay Aillig might make!

"When did you last see her?" he asked again, slowly, enunciating each word clearly and powerfully.

"When we returned from Gavina's grave. Soon after sunset." She cocked her head, studying his expression. "What do you know?"

"Not enough," he replied.

"Are we to trust each other or not?"

"My plans last night were foiled," he admitted. "And Ralid is not missing. He lies dead far from here."

Mairen sighed and shook her head, but Tay Aillig added sharply, "Foiled by a witch, I believe."

"What do you mean?"

Now it was his turn to shake his head, and he added a little snarl for good measure. He told Mairen, then, with minimal detail, about the fight with the brown bear. "The beast ran us off," he finished, "and looking back from on high revealed to us the magic of a lightning stroke. The magic of a witch."

"The magic of Aoleyn?" Mairen asked, and Tay Aillig shrugged. "Aoleyn could not direct a bear," Mairen said.

"There are crystals with such magic?"

"For a bird, or a small newt. But not a—"

"Do not underestimate that one," Tay Aillig warned. "I saw her, fighting through Brayth on the field that day. You think me foolish for choosing her as my wife, but I saw her, her power bared."

"She is undeniably strong in the song of Usgar," Mairen admitted. "But what you claim is beyond."

"I make no claims. I ask questions. And I will find answers."

"To control a giant bear?" Mairen laughed. "Who would even think to try such a foolish thing?"

Tay Aillig fixed her with a stare to let her know in no uncertain terms that her mocking tone was not appreciated.

"What would you have me do?" Mairen asked more seriously. "If the idiot girl even returns alive, I mean. She has been announced for the Coven, but I can—"

"She will be in the Coven," Tay Aillig decided. "And we will watch her, both of us. And she will do as I need, as we need, or we will reveal her treachery and feed her to Craos'a'diad."

Mairen agreed with a nod.

Outside the tent, so did Connebragh, who had heard every word. She paused before entering, then went in in a rush to confirm to Mairen and the Usgar-laoch that yes, Aoleyn was indeed missing from the camp, and that another, warrior Ralid, was also gone.

Tay Aillig rushed back outside, moving quickly to the tent of Egard, his nephew, then to Aghmor, rousing his soldiers—there was no time for sleep.

"Gather others," he told them, "and go in search of Aoleyn."

"Aoleyn?" they asked together.

"She is not to be found."

"The lightning!" Egard gasped.

"Shut up," Tay Aillig was fast to reply. "There was no lightning." To Egard, he quietly added, "You lead a group down to Ralid, and there find signs of Aoleyn's passage, whether she was there or not."

The younger man seemed confused.

"Sneak into her tent and gather some of her things," Tay Aillig spelled it out.

"I will go with you," Aghmor said, but Tay Aillig held up his hand.

"You will go out alone," he instructed Aghmor. "To Elder Raibert. Tell him of the missing and ask him for his guidance. And check on the idiot uamhas who works th'Way."

"The one Aoleyn favors," said Egard, remembering that long-ago, painful, incident.

Tay Aillig shot him a threatening stare, even though he agreed with the sentiment. In his improvisation here, that's where his thoughts had led him—he could perhaps force Aoleyn's silence, if necessary, if it was her at the bear fight, and if she was even still alive and soon to return, by using the threat of murdering the uamhas boy against her.

The two young warriors stared at him with puzzled expressions.

"No one can know," he explained in a deadly serious tone, letting the weight of doom hang with every word.

Egard looked at him doubtfully, even shook his head a little bit. Tay Aillig understood, and perhaps it would be better to just tell the truth of the previous night, of how their grand plan to be rid of the fossa was ruined by bad happenstance with a giant bear.

Or better still to not find Ralid, and not plant evidence of Aoleyn having been there.

But no, he decided to stick with his instincts here. Mairen was with him, Raibert a doddering old fool. Unless these two foolishly revealed something, the only one who could possibly hurt him was Aoleyn.

But if he could so easily implicate and discredit her, and threaten her with the uamhas boy . . .

Better to set that battlefield, if it was to come, with all conditions against the young witch.

It took a long while for Talmadge to realize that he had done something terribly wrong here. He had mentally reached out to the magic in the gray soul stone, but not as he had intended, apparently, for he began to feel quite strange suddenly.

Detached from himself . . .

He knew that he should let go of the stone, but his hand wouldn't answer his call! So suddenly, his own body seemed no more a part of him than the dying Aoleyn's corporeal form!

Terror gripped him. He would die here, too, his spirit unbound, his mortal coil settling there, expiring.

And he was not alone!

But no, not the monster, not the demon, Talmadge suddenly realized, and he recognized the spirit, Aoleyn's spirit, and thought he was there, at the moment of her death, watching her soul separate from her body. He didn't know what to think or do, didn't know if he should feel blessed to witness such a moment of peaceful transfer, or horrified that he, too, would likely follow her spirit to the nether world, whatever that might mean!

Aoleyn, he said, not with his lips, but with his thoughts.

He couldn't see her spirit, exactly—it was more as if he could sense it, feel it—but he was sure that she heard.

Aoleyn, he thought again, and he flooded her with thoughts of sadness and regret, and the image of both of them there in the pit of death, his hand gently set upon her bare belly.

Aoleyn!

And then he could see her spirit, as if it were floating away, leaving her lifeless coil.

But no, he realized, the spirit wasn't Aoleyn, though the image seemed very much like the Usgar woman.

Who are you? he wondered.

The spirit didn't answer, but flew right down to him and engulfed him, and he felt it dissipate, as if to nothingness.

And a great sadness fell over him, one that broke his inadvertent magic spell of spirit-walking and sent him flying back to his body, where he closed his physical eyes and sobbed.

And then stopped, abruptly, and opened his eyes wide when he felt Aoleyn's hand over his own.

And felt, too, a sudden surge of magic, more glorious than Talmadge had ever before known.

EPILOGUE

She stood outside the cave, staring at the blackness, thinking of the spirits, the demon, the man she had killed, the man she had rescued. Thinking about life itself and what it meant, and what it meant when death arrived.

She had set the cloud leopard free of its demon possessor. She had set the spirits free of their demon captor.

And one of those spirits, a very special one, had helped her hear the song to guide her from the edge of oblivion.

"Elara," Aoleyn whispered, and she slapped her hand over her mouth and began to sob, overwhelmed beyond anything she had ever imagined. Elara, a name she hadn't known before, but would never forget.

She couldn't believe that she had gone into that pit of death.

She believed even less that the stranger, Talmadge, had gone in after her!

She wanted to dismiss the memory of her fight, that sickly, awful, excruciating feeling of the demonic creature burrowing into her belly, chewing her flesh as it devoured her life energy. Tearing at her gut to create a battle between the carnage and the healing, Aoleyn's magic holding back the monster like the lakeshore against the waves blown on a gale.

Aoleyn fell to her knees and threw her other arm across her belly, reflexively bending forward as she knelt to cover up her wound. She still couldn't comprehend the reality of that fight, the very edge of her bone-pile grave, or that she had somehow come through it.

Composing herself, she turned about and sprinted up the wall of the vale to the ridge where she and Talmadge had first seen the cave. She looked for him from up there, but he was already too far down the mountain, out of sight. He had offered to take her with him, down to the lake towns, and then across the lake and across the world, to this village he called Honce-the-Bear.

After yet another incident revealing the indecency of her people, and with her own curiosity for the wider world, Aoleyn had wanted to accept that offer more than a little.

But no, she could not. She was to be brought into the Coven, to learn more secrets of Usgar, to become powerful among her people.

She had defeated the demon fossa. Tay Aillig had meant to do that, and use the feat to gain control of the tribe. But now Aoleyn had done it.

What might she do with that heroic act? What changes might she bring? She had seen the truth of Usgar's magic more keenly than any others, she believed, but to what end?

What now would be her purpose?

It was too overwhelming for the woman, emotionally and physically exhausted, her heart wounded, her soul confused.

She wanted to go with Talmadge, she couldn't deny, but she could not. Not now.

What might happen to Bahdlahn if she walked away?

With a long, last glance at the terrible cave, Aoleyn started off around Fireach Speuer, not for the Usgar camp quite yet though. Instead, she called upon her gemstones, floated and flew, and ran from tree to high stone to tree again, up the mountain, toward the peak where the snow was soon to fall once more, and where remnants of the last dusting remained in the shadowed areas.

Talmadge moved with all speed down the side of the mountain, but despite his urgency—he knew that winter was coming fast, and knew, too, that so were the Usgar—he couldn't help but pause and glance back repeatedly, his thoughts flooding with images of that strange young woman who had saved him, and whom he had saved.

The moments in the pit, lost on the edge between life and death, had taken his breath away and still had him shaking his head in disbelief.

The road of his life's journey had nearly ended, but in that desperate moment, teetering on the edge, it had widened to lengths he had never before imagined. He knew that he would never view the moments of his life the same way.

For where before Talmadge had felt a sense of dread, and loss, now he felt a strange and glorious elation.

And freedom.

Freedom from the ghosts of his past as surely as the ghosts in that pit had found freedom. There was magic in the world, he knew now, in ways he had never even considered. And magic was life, and life was magic.

He pulled out the crystalline dagger and held it up, seeing the flakes within.

He understood more about the Usgar now, and he would tell the folk of Fasach Crann, and all the other towns. The Usgar were not demons, but mortal men.

The echo of some voices off a stony front to the side of Talmadge reminded him that he was not alone on this mountain. Aoleyn had assured him that the Usgar hunters would be out to retrieve the dead man, and likely in search of her, as well.

He veered the other way, into a deep hollow, disappearing into the trees, moving with all speed for all his life, carrying with him the dagger, his insights, and the memory of an exceptionally brave young woman.

She cried as much as she laughed, and did both more than she should have. She tried to hold fast to her determination, but the passing hours carried with them doubts and harsh reality.

And the memory of a young man named Ralid. A young man she had swatted with the paw of giant bear, tearing him, sending him spinning to crash catastrophically into the thick trunk of a tree. She could see him in her mind's eye, always there, crumbled and dead at the base of that tree.

Did she really expect to change them, or impress them, or gain some measure of respect among them? Them? The ferocious warriors and stubborn witches?

They would laugh at her and her tales of demons defeated!

Mairen would melt her when she discovered the blasphemy, that Aoleyn had shattered crystals in the caverns to extract the gemstones now pierced to her body!

The doubts chased Aoleyn every step.

The fears fluttered up around her like the black form of the fossa, like the flying splinters of shattered bones crushed in the demon's deadly maw.

On a high ledge, buffeted by cold winds, Aoleyn paused and grabbed at her belly, feeling the tenderness of a wound that should have ended her life. Even now, she couldn't believe any of it had been real.

Even though she felt the residual pain and profound soreness from the garish attack of the fossa, Aoleyn could hardly comprehend that the toothy maw had burrowed into her, as it had wormed right through the giant bear, leaving it dead in the clearing.

Madness. It was all madness. She stood up tall on the jag of stone, letting the wind buffet her. She didn't huddle under her clothes against the chill breeze—quite the opposite, she lifted her tattered shirt high, higher to reveal the reddened area of injury, then pulled it right over her head.

She spotted a patch of snow in the shadow of a great stone off to the side, and rushed to it, quickly removing her pants. She lay in the snow and rolled in it, wanting to feel the biting cold on every inch of her body. This was not the coldness of death, not that profound and frightening cold she had known in the lair, and in the heart, of the fossa. No, this was a sensation to affirm her life, to tickle her and nip at her and bring her sensibilities fully to this mortal coil that contained her spirit.

More than once, Aoleyn thought of soaring down the mountainside to find Talmadge, to run away to a new reality, far removed from the complications of Usgar, god and tribe.

Would she then be truly free?

But no, she could not, even doubting her grandiose plans. For one simple reason, Aoleyn could not leave: Bahdlahn needed her.

Tay Aillig's last words to Bahdlahn rang in her ears, that awful threat.

Aoleyn threw on her clothes and gathered up her courage and her magic, and leaped away, speeding across the mountainside. She landed and leaped, long and far, again and again, until at last she came to th'Way. She tried to paste a kind smile onto her face as she approached the young man, who was hard at his work, setting another stone step into its carved spot.

As she neared, Bahdlahn looked up and smiled wide, but only for a heartbeat before his jaw dropped and his expression became one of horror.

Aoleyn stopped with surprise, and returned his look with one of puzzlement—until she realized the truth of the image she was presenting, for the front of her clothing hung tattered and dark with dried blood, her blood!

"Aoleyn," the uamhas breathed, and he stumbled over the step he was setting in a weak-kneed effort to approach.

She ran down to him and wrapped him in a hug, whispering in his ear that she was okay. She even lifted her shirt for him to show him that the wound had healed. Still, it took him a long while to get his breathing back under control after the shock and the terror.

Aoleyn pulled him to the side and sat him down on a flat stone, then knelt beside him. "You must never tell," she instructed, and he shook his head, at a loss.

So she told him everything. She told him about the four warriors and the prisoner and that they were trying to lure the demon fossa.

"I became a bear!" she told him, and he gasped and leaned back to better study her. "I didn't become a bear, but I . . . possessed one. And

I chased them away to save the man, a man from across the lake and beyond the mountains."

She was rambling then, but she didn't slow, and told him of the poor bear dying to the fossa, and of all the rest, to the fossa's lair, to the edge of death.

When she finished, she took Bahdlahn's hands in her own. "Do you know what this means?" she asked.

He shook his head.

"It means that I am not afraid of them anymore," Aoleyn said, and she believed it. She cupped his face in her hands and moved very close to him and promised, "I'm not going to let them kill you."

Bahdlahn stared into her black eyes for a long while before finally nodding, and Aoleyn then wrapped him in a great hug.

She had no idea of how she might possibly fulfill that promise, but in that moment, it didn't matter.

She had fought the demon, had gone to the edge of death and even a bit beyond. Yet here she was, and here the fossa was not.

And Elara was at peace, and so it was with her.

Not so far away, crouched behind a stone, Aghmor heard every word and saw, his faced scrunched in disgust, every hug.

He didn't know what to think in that shocking moment. Part of him wanted to throw a spear into Aoleyn for killing Ralid!

Another part wanted to praise her for saving the poor prisoner.

The enormity of it all kept him in place, though, and silent. Not only was Aoleyn alive and out of the camp, but she was here, with this uamhas—this uamhas who was not stupid!

"You should go to my mother," he heard the uamhas say. "She will give you new clothes."

Aghmor grimaced, picturing the torture Tay Aillig would inflict on this slave, and probably on his mother, too.

And Aoleyn, that foolish and impertinent girl, the killer of Ralid, would be fed to Craos'a'diad, without doubt.

Aghmor scowled again as he imagined that horrible scene.

He slipped away soon after without confronting Aoleyn, and in the camp, he told Tay Aillig that he had delivered the message to Usgarforfach Raibert.

Nothing more.